MICHELLE REID

HOT-BLOODED
HUSBANDS

MILLS & BOON

Published in Great Britain 2013
Mills & Boon, an imprint of Harlequin (UK) Limited,
Eton House, 18-24 Paradise Road, Richmond, Surrey TW9 1SR

HOT-BLOODED HUSBANDS
© Harlequin Enterprises II B.V./S.à.r.l. 2013

The Sheikh's Chosen Wife © Michelle Reid 2002
Ethan's Temptress Bride © Michelle Reid 2002
The Arabian Love-Child © Michelle Reid 2002

ISBN: 978 0 263 90585 4

026-0513

Harlequin (UK) policy is to use papers that are natural, renewable and recyclable products and made from wood grown in sustainable forests. The logging and manufacturing processes conform to the legal environmental regulations of the country of origin.

Printed and bound
by CPI Group (UK) Ltd, Croydon, CR0 4YY

Michelle Reid grew up on the southern edges of Manchester, the youngest in a family of five lively children. Now she lives in the beautiful county of Cheshire, with her busy executive husband and two grown-up daughters. She loves reading, the ballet and playing tennis when she gets the chance. She hates cooking, cleaning and despises ironing! Sleep she can do without and produces some of her best written work during the early hours of the morning.

THE
MICHELLE REID
COLLECTION

February 2013

March 2013

April 2013

May 2013

June 2013

July 2013

THE SHEIKH'S CHOSEN WIFE

MICHELLE REID

CHAPTER ONE

DRESSED to go riding, in knee-length black leather boots, buff pants, a white shirt and a white *gutrah* held to his dark head by a plain black *agal*, Sheikh Hassan ben Khalifa Al-Qadim stepped into his private office and closed the door behind him. In his hand he held a newly delivered letter from England. On his desk lay three more. Walking across the room, he tossed the new letter onto the top of the other three then went to stand by the grilled window, fixing his eyes on a spot beyond the Al-Qadim Oasis, where reclaimed dry scrubland had been turned into miles of lush green fig groves.

Beyond the figs rose the sand-dunes. Majestic and proud, they claimed the horizon with a warning statement. Come any closer with your irrigation and expect retaliation, they said. One serious sandstorm, and years of hard labour could be turned back into arid wasteland.

A sigh eased itself from his body. Hassan knew all about the laws of the desert. He respected its power and its driving passion, its right to be master of its own destiny. And what he would really have liked to do at this very moment was to saddle up his horse, Zandor, then take off for those sand-dunes and allow them to dictate his future for him.

But he knew the idea was pure fantasy. For behind him lay four letters, all of which demanded he make those decisions for himself. And beyond the relative sanctuary of the four walls surrounding him lay a palace in waiting; his father, his half-brother, plus a thousand and one other people, all of whom believed they owned a piece of his so-called destiny.

So Zandor would have to stay in his stable. His beloved sand-dunes would have to wait a while to swallow him up. Making a half-turn, he stared grimly at the letters. Only one had been opened: the first one, which he had tossed aside with the contempt it had deserved. Since then he had left the others sealed on his desk and had tried very hard to ignore them.

But the time for burying his head in the sand was over.

A knock on the door diverted his attention. It would be his most trusted aide, Faysal. Hassan recognised the lightness of the knock. Sure enough the door opened and a short, fine-boned man wearing the traditional white and pale blue robes of their Arabian birthright appeared in its arched aperture, where he paused and bowed his head, waiting to be invited in or told to go.

'Come in, Faysal,' Hassan instructed a trifle impatiently. Sometimes Faysal's rigid adherence to so-called protocol set his teeth on edge.

With another deferential bow, Faysal moved to his master's bidding. Stepping into the room, he closed the door behind him then used some rarely utilised initiative by walking across the room to come to a halt several feet from the desk on the priceless carpet that covered, in part, the expanse of polished blue marble between the desk and the door.

Hassan found himself staring at the carpet. His wife had ordered it to be placed there, claiming the room's spartan appearance invited no one to cross its austere threshold. The fact that this was supposed to be the whole point had made absolutely no difference to Leona. She had simply carried on regardless, bringing many items into the room besides the carpet. Such as the pictures now adorning the walls and the beautiful ceramics and sculptures scattered around, all of which had been produced by gifted artists native to the small Gulf state of Rahman. Hassan had soon found he could no longer lift his eyes without having them settle on an example of local enterprise.

Yet it was towards the only western pieces Leona had brought into the room that his eyes now drifted. The low table and two overstuffed easy chairs had been placed by the other window, where she would insist on making him sit with her several times a day to enjoy the view while they drank tea and talked and touched occasionally as lovers do...

Dragging the *gutrah* from his head with almost angry fingers, Hassan tossed it aside then went to sit down in the chair behind his desk. 'Okay,' he said. 'What have you to tell me?'

'It is not good news, sir.' Faysal began with a warning. 'Sheikh Abdul is entertaining certain...factions at his summer palace. Our man on the inside confirms that the tone of their conversation warrants your most urgent attention.'

Hassan made no comment, but his expression hardened fractionally. 'And my wife?' he asked next.

'The Sheikha still resides in Spain, sir,' Faysal informed him, 'working with her father at the new resort of San Estéban, overseeing the furnishing of several villas about to be released for sale.'

Doing what she did best, Hassan thought grimly—and did not need to glance back at the two stuffed chairs to conjure up a vision of long silken hair the colour of a desert sunset, framing a porcelain smooth face with laughing green eyes and a smile that dared him to complain about her invasion of his private space. 'Trust me,' he could hear her say. 'It is my job to give great empty spaces a little soul and their own heartbeat.'

Well, the heartbeat had gone out of this room when she'd left it, and as for the soul...

Another sigh escaped him. 'How long do you think we have before they make their move?'

The slight tensing in Faysal's stance warned Hassan that he was not going to like what was coming. 'If you will forgive me for saying so, sir,' his aide apologised, 'with Mr Ethan Hayes also residing at her father's property, I would say that the matter has become most seriously urgent indeed.'

Since this was complete news to Hassan it took a moment for the full impact of this information to really sink in. Then he was suddenly on his feet and was swinging tensely away to glare at the sand-dunes again. Was she mad? he was thinking angrily. Did she have a death wish? Was she so indifferent to his feelings that she could behave like this?

Ethan Hayes. His teeth gritted together as an old familiar jealousy began mixing with his anger to form a much more volatile substance. He swung back to face Faysal. 'How long has Mr Hayes been in residence in San Estéban?'

Faysal made a nervous clearing of his throat. 'These seven days past,' he replied.

'And who else knows about this…? Sheikh Abdul?'

'It was discussed,' Faysal confirmed.

With a tight shifting of his long lean body, Hassan returned to his seat. 'Cancel all my appointments for the rest of the month,' he instructed, drawing his appointments diary towards him to begin scoring hard lines through the same busy pages. 'My yacht is berthed at Cadiz. Have it moved to San Estéban. Check that my plane is ready for an immediate take-off and ask Rafiq to come to me.'

The cold quality of the commands did nothing to dilute their grim purpose. 'If asked,' Faysal prompted, 'what reason do I give for your sudden decision to cancel your appointments?'

'I am about to indulge in a much needed holiday cruising the Mediterranean with my nice new toy,' Sheikh Hassan replied, and the bite in his tone made a complete mockery of the words spoken, for they both knew that the next few weeks promised to be no holiday. 'And Faysal…' Hassan stalled his aide as he was about to take his leave '…if anyone so much as whispers the word adultery in the same breath as my wife's name, they will not breathe again—you understand me?'

The other man went perfectly still, recognising the responsibility that was being laid squarely upon him. 'Yes, sir.' He bowed.

Hassan's grim nod was a dismissal. Left alone again, he leaned back in his chair and began frowning while he tried to decide how best to tackle this. His gaze fell on the small stack of letters. Reaching out with long fingers, he drew them towards him, picked out the only envelope with a broken seal and removed the single sheet of paper from inside. The content of the letter he ignored with the same dismissive contempt he had always applied to it. His interest lay only in the telephone number printed beneath the business logo. With an expression that said he resented having his hand forced like this, he took a brief glance at his watch, then was lifting up the telephone, fairly sure that his wife's lawyer would be in his London office at this time of the day.

The ensuing conversation was not a pleasant one, and the following conversation with his father-in-law even less so. He had just replaced the receiver and was frowning darkly over what Victor Frayne had said to him, when another knock sounded at the door. Hard eyes lanced towards it as the door swung open and Rafiq stepped into the room.

Though he was dressed in much the same clothes as Faysal was wearing, there the similarity between the two men ended. For where Faysal was short and thin and annoyingly effacing, Rafiq was a giant of a man who rarely kowtowed to anyone. Hassan warranted only a polite nod of the head, yet he knew Rafiq would willingly die for him if he was called upon to do so.

'Come in, shut the door, then tell me how you would feel about committing a minor piece of treason?' Hassan smoothly intoned.

Below the white *gutrah* a pair of dark eyes glinted. 'Sheikh Abdul?' Rafiq questioned hopefully.

'Unfortunately, no.' Hassan gave a half smile. 'I was in fact referring to my lovely wife, Leona...'

Dressed for the evening in a beaded slip-dress made of gold silk chiffon, Leona stepped into a pair of matching beaded mules then turned to look at herself in the mirror.

Her smooth russet hair had been caught up in a twist, and diamonds sparkled at her ears and throat. Overall, she supposed she looked okay, she decided, giving the thin straps at her shoulders a gentle tug so the dress settled comfortably over her slender frame. But the weight she had lost during the last year was most definitely showing, and she could have chosen a better colour to offset the unnatural paleness of her skin.

Too late to change, though, she thought with a dismissive shrug as she turned away from her reflection. Ethan was already waiting for her outside on the terrace. And, anyway, she wasn't out to impress anyone. She was merely playing stand-in for her father who had been delayed in London due to some urgent business with the family lawyer, which had left her and her father's business partner, Ethan, the only ones here to represent Hayes-Frayne at tonight's promotional dinner.

She grimaced as she caught up a matching black silk shawl and made for her bedroom door. In truth, she would rather not be going out at all tonight having only arrived back from San Estéban an hour ago. It had been a long day, and she had spent most of it melting in a Spanish heatwave because the air-conditioning system had not been working in the villa she had been attempting to make ready for viewing. So a long soak in a warm bath and an early night would have been her idea of heaven tonight, she thought wryly, as she went down the stairs to join Ethan.

He was half sitting on the terrace rail with a glass in his hand, watching the sun go down, but his head turned at her first step, and his mouth broke into an appreciative smile.

'Ravishing,' he murmured, sliding his lean frame upright.

'Thank you,' she replied. 'You don't look so bad yourself.'

His wry nod accepted the compliment and his grey eyes sparkled with lazy humour. Dressed in a black dinner suit and bow tie, he was a tall, dark, very attractive man with an easy smile and a famous eye for the ladies. Women adored him and he adored them but, thankfully, that mutual adoration had never raised its ugly head between the two of them.

Leona liked Ethan. She felt comfortable being with him. He was the Hayes in Hayes-Frayne, architects. Give

Ethan a blank piece of paper and he would create a fifty-storey skyscraper or a whole resort complete with sports clubs, shopping malls and, of course, holiday villas to die for, as with this new resort in San Estéban.

'Drink?' he suggested, already stepping towards the well stocked drinks trolley.

But Leona gave a shake of her head. 'Better not, if you want me to stay awake beyond ten o'clock,' she refused.

'That late? Next you'll be begging me to take you on to an all-night disco after the party.' He was mocking the fact that she was usually safely tucked up in bed by nine o'clock.

'Do you disco?' she asked him curiously.

'Not if I can help it,' he replied, discarding his own glass to come and take the shawl from her hand so he could drape it across her shoulders. 'The best I can offer in the name of dance is a soft shoe shuffle to something very slow, preferably in a darkened room, so that I don't damage my ego by revealing just how bad a shuffler I am.'

'You're such a liar.' Leona smiled. 'I've seen you dance a mean jive, once or twice.'

Ethan pulled a face at the reminder. 'Now you've really made me feel my age,' he complained. 'Next you'll be asking me what it was like to rock in the sixties.'

'You're not that old.' She was still smiling.

'Born in the mid-sixties,' he announced. 'To a free-loving mother who bopped with the best of them.'

'That makes you about the same age as Hass...'

And that was the point where everything died: the light banter, the laughter, the tail end of Hassan's name. Silence fell. Ethan's teasing grey eyes turned very sombre. He knew, of course, how painful this last year had been for her. No one mentioned Hassan's name in her presence, so to hear herself almost say it out loud caused tension to erupt between the both of them.

'It isn't too late to stop this craziness, you know,' Ethan murmured gently.

Her response was to drag in a deep breath and step right away from him. 'I don't want to stop it,' she quietly replied.

'Your heart does.'

'My heart is not making the decisions here.'

'Maybe you should let it.'

'Maybe you should mind your own business!'

Spinning on her slender heels Leona walked away from him to go and stand at the terrace rail, leaving Ethan behind wearing a rueful expression at the severity with which she had just slapped him down.

Out there at sea, the dying sun was throwing up slender fingers of fire into a spectacular vermilion sky. Down the hill below the villa, San Estéban was beginning to twinkle as it came into its own at the exit of the sun. And in between the town and the sun the ocean spread like satin with its brand-new purpose-built harbour already packed with smart sailing crafts of all shapes and sizes.

Up here on the hillside everything was so quiet and still even the cicadas had stopped calling. Leona wished that she could have some of that stillness, put her trembling emotions back where they belonged, under wraps, out of reach from pain and heartache.

Would these vulnerable feelings ever be that far out of reach? she then asked herself, and wasn't surprised to have a heavy sigh whisper from her. The beaded chiffon shawl slipped from her shoulders, prompting Ethan to come and gently lift it back in place again.

'Sorry,' he murmured. 'It wasn't my intention to upset you.'

I do it to myself, Leona thought bleakly. 'I just can't bear to talk about it,' she replied in what was a very rare glimpse at how badly she was hurting.

'Maybe you need to talk,' Ethan suggested.

But she just shook her head, as she consistently had done since she had arrived at her father's London house a year ago, looking emotionally shattered and announcing that her five-year marriage to Sheikh Hassan ben Khalifa Al-Qadim was over. Victor Frayne had tried every which way he could think of to find out what had happened. He'd even travelled out to Rahman to demand answers from Hassan, only to meet the same solid wall of silence he'd come up against with his daughter. The one thing Victor could say with any certainty was that Hassan was faring no better than Leona, though his dauntingly aloof son-in-law was more adept at hiding his emotions than Leona was. 'She sits here in London, he sits in Rahman. They don't talk to each other, never mind to anyone else! Yet you can feel the vibrations bouncing from one to the other across the thousands of miles separating them as if they are communicating by some unique telepathy that runs on pure pain! It's dreadful,' Victor had confided to Ethan. 'Something has to give some time.'

Eventually, it had done. Two months ago Leona had walked unannounced into the office of her family lawyer and had instructed him to begin divorce proceedings, on the grounds of irreconcilable differences. What had prompted her to pick that particular day in that particular month of a very long year no one understood, and Leona herself wasn't prepared to enlighten anyone. But there wasn't a person who knew her who didn't believe it was an action that had caused a trigger reaction, when a week later she had fallen foul of a virulent flu bug that had kept her housebound and bedridden for weeks afterwards.

But when she had recovered, at least she'd come back ready to face the world again. She had agreed to come here to San Estéban, for instance, and utilise her design skills on the completed villas.

She looked better for it too. Still too pale, maybe, but overall she'd begun to live a more normal day to day existence.

Ethan had no wish to send her back into hiding now she had come out of it, so he turned her to face him and pressed a light kiss to her brow. 'Come on,' he said briskly. 'Let's go and party!'

Finding her smile again, Leona nodded her agreement and

tried to appear as though she was looking forward to the evening. As they began to walk back across the terrace she felt a fine tingling at the back of her neck which instinctively warned her that someone was observing them.

The suspicion made her pause and turn to cast a frowning glance over their surroundings. She could see nothing untoward, but wasn't surprised by that. During the years she had lived in an Arab sheikhdom, married to a powerful and very wealthy man, she had grown used to being kept under constant, if very discreet, surveillance.

But that surveillance had been put in place for her own protection. This felt different—sinister. She even shivered.

'Something wrong?' Ethan questioned.

Leona shook her head and began walking again, but her frown stayed in place, because it wasn't the first time she'd experienced the sensation today. The same thing had happened as she'd left the resort site this afternoon, only she'd dismissed it then as her just being silly. She had always suspected that Hassan still kept an eye on her from a distance.

A car and driver had been hired for the evening, and both were waiting in the courtyard for them as they left the house. Having made sure she was comfortably settled, Ethan closed the side door and strode around the car to climb in beside her. As a man she had known for most of her adult life, Ethan was like a very fond cousin whose lean dark sophistication and reputed rakish life made her smile, rather than her heart flutter as other women would do in his company.

He'd never married. 'Never wanted to,' he'd told her once. 'Marriage diverts your energy away from your ambition, and I haven't met the woman for whom I'm prepared to let that happen.'

When she'd told Hassan what Ethan had said, she'd expected him to say something teasing like, May Allah help him when he does, for I know the feeling! But instead he'd looked quite sombre and had said nothing at all. At the time, she'd thought he'd been like that because he'd still been harbouring jealous suspicions about Ethan's feelings for her.

It had been a long time before she'd come to understand that the look had had nothing at all to do with Ethan.

'The Petronades yacht looks pretty impressive.' Ethan's smooth deep voice broke into her thoughts. 'I watched it sail into the harbour tonight while I was waiting for you on the terrace.'

Leandros Petronades was the main investor in San Estéban. He was hosting the party tonight for very exclusive guests whom he had seduced into taking a tour of the new resort, with an invitation to arrive in style on his yacht and enjoy its many luxurious facilities.

'At a guess, I would say it has to be the biggest in the harbour, considering its capacity to sleep so many people,' Leona smiled.

'Actually no, it wasn't,' Ethan replied with a frown. 'There's another yacht tied up that has to be twice the size.'

'The commercial kind?' Leona suggested, aware that the resort was fast becoming the fashionable place to visit.

'Not big enough.' Ethan shook his head. 'It's more likely to belong to one of Petronades' rich cronies. Another heavy investor in the resort, maybe.'

There were enough of them, Leona acknowledged. From being a sleepy little fishing port a few years ago, with the help of some really heavyweight investors San Estéban had grown into a large, custom-built holiday resort, which now sprawled in low-rise, Moorish elegance over the hills surrounding the bay.

So why Hassan's name slid back into her head Leona had no idea. Because Hassan didn't even own a yacht, nor had he ever invested in any of her father's projects, as far as she knew.

Irritated with herself, she turned her attention to what was happening outside the car. On the beach waterfront people strolled, enjoying the light breeze coming off the water.

It was a long time since she could remember strolling anywhere herself with such freedom. Marrying an Arab had brought with it certain restrictions on her freedom, which

were not all due to the necessity of conforming to expectations regarding women. Hassan occupied the august position
of being the eldest son and heir to the small but oil-rich Gulf
state of Rahman. As his wife, Leona had become a member
of Rahman's exclusive hierarchy, which in turn made everything she said or did someone else's property. So she'd
learned very quickly to temper her words, to think twice
before she went anywhere, especially alone. Strolling just for
the sake of just doing it would have been picked upon and
dissected for no other reason than interest's sake, so she had
learned not to do it.

This last year she hadn't gone out much because to be
seen out had drawn too much speculation as to why she was
in London and alone. In Rahman she was known as Sheikh
Hassan's pretty English Sheikha. In London she was known
as the woman who gave up every freedom to marry her
Arabian prince.

A curiosity in other words. Curiosities were blatantly
stared at, and she didn't want to offend Arab sensibilities by
having her failed marriage speculated upon in the British
press, so she'd lived a quiet life.

It was a thought that made Leona smile now, because her
life in Rahman had been far less quiet than it had become
once she'd returned to London.

The car had almost reached the end of the street where the
new harbour was situated. There were several large yachts
moored up—and Leandros Petronades' elegant white-hulled
boat was easy to recognise because it was lit up like a show-
boat for the party. Yet it was the yacht moored next to it that
caught her attention. It was huge, as Ethan had said—twice
the length and twice the height of its neighbour. It was also
shrouded in complete darkness. With its dark-painted hull, it
looked as if it was crouching there like a large sleek cat,
waiting to leap on its next victim.

The car turned and began driving along the top of the
harbour wall taking them towards a pair of wrought iron

gates, which cordoned off the area where the two yachts were tied.

Climbing out of the car, Leona stood looking round while she waited for Ethan to join her. It was even darker here than she had expected it to be, and she felt a distinct chill shiver down her spine when she realised they were going to have to pass the unlit boat to reach the other.

Ethan's hand found her arm. As they walked towards the gates, their car was already turning round to go back the way it had come. The guard manning the gates merely nodded his dark head and let them by without a murmur, then disappeared into the shadows.

'Conscientious chap,' Ethan said dryly.

Leona didn't answer. She was too busy having to fight a sudden attack of nerves that set butterflies fluttering inside her stomach. Okay, she tried to reason, so she hadn't put herself in the social arena much recently, therefore it was natural that she should suffer an attack of nerves tonight.

Yet some other part of her brain was trying to insist that her attack of nerves had nothing to do with the party. It was so dark and so quiet here that even their footsteps seemed to echo with a sinister ring.

Sinister? Picking up on the word, she questioned it impatiently. What was the matter with her? Why was everything sinister all of a sudden? It was a hot night—a beautiful night—she was twenty-nine years old, and about to do what most twenty-nine-year-olds did: party when they got the chance!

'Quite something, hmm?' Ethan remarked as they walked into the shadow of the larger yacht.

But Leona didn't want to look. Despite the tough talking-to she had just given herself, the yacht bothered her. The whole situation was beginning to worry her. She could feel her heart pumping unevenly against her breast, and just about every nerve-end she possessed was suddenly on full alert for no other reason than—

It was then that she heard it—nothing more than a whispering sound in the shadows, but it was enough to make her go perfectly still. So did Ethan. Almost at the same moment the darkness itself seemed to take on a life of its own by shifting and swaying before her eyes.

The tingling sensation on the back of her neck returned with a vengeance. 'Ethan,' she said jerkily. 'I don't think I like this.'

'No,' he answered tersely. 'Neither do I.'

That was the moment when they saw them, first one dark shape, then another, and another, emerging from the shadows until they turned themselves into Arabs wearing dark robes, with darkly sober expressions.

'Oh, dear God,' she breathed. 'What's happening?'

But she already knew the answer. It was a fear she'd had to live with from the day she'd married Hassan. She was British. She had married an Arab who was a very powerful man. The dual publicity her disappearance could generate was in itself worth its weight in gold to political fanatics wanting to make a point.

Something she should have remembered earlier, then the word 'sinister' would have made a lot more sense, she realised, as Ethan's arm pressed her hard up against him.

Further down the harbour wall the lights from the Petronades boat were swinging gently. Here, beneath the shadow of the other, the ring of men was steadily closing in. Her heart began to pound like a hammer drill. Ethan couldn't hold her any closer if he tried, and she could almost taste his tension. He, too, knew exactly what was going to happen.

'Keep calm,' he gritted down at her. 'When I give the word, lose your shoes and run.'

He was going to make a lunge for them and try to break the ring so she could have a small chance to escape. 'No,' she protested, and clutched tightly at his jacket sleeve. 'Don't do it. They might hurt you if you do!'

'Just go, Leona!' he ground back at her, then, with no more warning than that, he was pulling away, and almost in the same movement he threw himself at the two men closest to him.

It was then that all hell broke loose. While Leona stood there frozen in horror watching all three men topple to the ground in a huddle, the rest of the ring leapt into action. Fear for her life sent a surge of adrenaline rushing through her blood. Dry-mouthed, stark-eyed, she was just about to do as Ethan had told her and run, when she heard a hard voice rasp out a command in Arabic. In a state of raw panic she swung round in its direction, expecting someone to be almost upon her, only to find to her confusion that the ring of men had completely bypassed her, leaving her standing here alone with only one other man.

It was at that point that she truly stopped functioning—heart, lungs, her ability to hear what was happening to Ethan—all connections to her brain simply closed down to leave only her eyes in full, wretched focus.

Tall and dark, whip-cord lean, he possessed an aura about him that warned of great physical power lurking beneath the dark robes he was wearing. His skin was the colour of sun-ripened olives, his eyes as black as a midnight sky, and his mouth she saw was thin, straight and utterly unsmiling.

'Hassan.' She breathed his name into the darkness.

The curt bow he offered her came directly from an excess of noble arrogance built into his ancient genes. 'As you see,' Sheikh Hassan smoothly confirmed.

CHAPTER TWO

A BUBBLE of hysteria ballooned in her throat. 'But—why?' she choked in strangled confusion.

Hassan was not given the opportunity to answer before another fracas broke out somewhere behind her. Ethan ground her name out. It was followed by some thuds and scuffles. As she turned on a protesting gasp to go to him, someone else spoke with a grating urgency and Hassan caught her wrist, long brown fingers closing round fleshless skin and bone, to hold her firmly in place.

'Call them off!' she cried out shrilly.

'Be silent,' he returned in a voice like ice.

It shocked her, really shocked her, because never in their years together had he ever used that tone on her. Turning her head, she stared at him in pained astonishment, but Hassan wasn't even looking at her. His attention was fixed on a spot near the gates. With a snap of his fingers his men began scattering like bats on the wing, taking a frighteningly silent Ethan with them.

'Where are they going with him?' Leona demanded anxiously.

Hassan didn't answer. Another man came to stand directly behind her and, glancing up, she found herself gazing into yet another familiar face.

'Rafiq,' she murmured, but that was all she managed to say before Hassan was reclaiming her attention by snaking an arm around her waist and pulling her towards him. Her breasts made contact with solid muscle; her thighs suddenly burned like fire as they felt the unyielding power in his. Her eyes leapt up to clash with his eyes. It was like tumbling into oblivion. He looked so very angry, yet so very—

'Shh,' he cautioned. 'It is absolutely imperative that you do exactly as I say. For there is a car coming down the causeway and we cannot afford to have any witnesses.'

'Witnesses to what?' she asked in bewilderment.

There was a pause, a smile that was not quite a smile because it was too cold, too calculating, too—

'Your abduction,' he smoothly informed her.

Standing there in his arms, feeling trapped by a word that sounded totally alien falling from those lips she'd thought she knew so well, Leona released a constricted gasp then was totally silenced.

Car headlights suddenly swung in their direction. Rafiq moved and the next thing that she knew a shroud of black muslin was being thrown over her head. For a split second she couldn't believe what was actually happening! Then Hassan released his grasp so the muslin could unfurl right down to her ankles: she was being shrouded in an *abaya*.

Never had she *ever* been forced to wear such a garment! 'Oh, how could you?' she wrenched out, already trying to drag the *abaya* off again.

Strong arms firmly subdued her efforts. 'Now, you have two choices here, my darling.' Hassan's grim voice sounded close to her ear. 'You can either come quietly, of your own volition, or Rafiq and I will ensure that you do so—understand?'

Understand? Oh, yes, Leona thought painfully, she understood fully that she was being recovered like a lost piece of property! 'I'll never forgive you for this,' she breathed thickly.

His response was to wedge her between himself and Rafiq and then begin hustling her quickly forward. Feeling hot, trapped and blinded by the *abaya*, she had no idea where they were taking her.

Her frightened gasp brought Hassan's hand to cup her elbow. 'Be calm,' he said quietly. 'I am here.'

His reassurance was no assurance to Leona as he began urging her to walk ahead of him. The ground beneath her feet gave way to something much less substantial. Through the thin soles of her shoes she could feel a ridged metal surface, and received a cold sense of some dark space yawning beneath it.

'What is this?' she questioned shakily.

'The gangway to my yacht,' Hassan replied.

His yacht, she repeated, and thought of the huge dark vessel squatting in the darkness. 'New toy, Hassan?' she hit out deridingly.

'I knew you would be enchanted,' he returned. 'Watch your step!' he cautioned sharply when the open toe of her flimsy shoe caught on one of the metal ridges.

But she couldn't watch her step because the wretched *abaya* was in the way! So she tripped, tried to right herself, felt the slender heel of her shoe twist out from beneath her. Instinct made her put out a hand in a bid to save herself. But once again the *abaya* was in the way and, as she tried to grapple with it, the long loose veil of muslin tangled around her ankles and she lurched drunkenly forward. The sheer impetus of the lurch lost Hassan his guiding grip on her arm. As the sound of her own stifled cry mingled with the roughness of his, Leona knew she hadn't a hope of saving herself. In the few split seconds it all took to happen, she had a horrible vision of deep dark water between the boat and the harbour wall waiting to suck her down, with the wretched *abaya* acting as her burial shroud.

Then hard hands were gripping her waist and roughly righting her; next she was being scooped up and crushed hard against a familiar chest. She curled into that chest like a vulnerable child and began shaking all over while she listened to Hassan cursing and swearing beneath his breath as he carried her, and Rafiq answering with soothing tones from somewhere ahead.

Onto the yacht, across the deck, Leona could hear doors being flung wide as they approached. By the time Hassan decided that it was safe to set her down on her own feet again, reaction was beginning to set in.

Shock and fright changed to a blistering fury the moment her feet hit the floor. Breaking free, she spun away from him, then began dragging the *abaya* off over her head with angry, shaking fingers. Light replaced darkness, sweet cool air replaced suffocating heat. Tossing the garment to the floor, she swung round to face her two abductors with her green eyes flashing and the rest of her shimmering with an incandescent rage.

Both Hassan and Rafiq stood framed by a glossy wood doorway, studying her with differing expressions. Both wore long black tunics beneath dark blue cloaks cinched in at the waist with wide black sashes. Dark blue *gutrahs* framed their lean dark faces. One neatly bearded, the other clean-shaven and sleek. Both held themselves with an indolent arrogance that was a challenge as they waited to receive her first furious volley.

Her heart flipped over and tumbled to her stomach, her feeling of an impossible-to-fight admiration for these two people, only helping to infuriate her all the more. For who were they—*what* were they—that they believed they had the right to treat her like this?

She began to walk towards them. Her hair had escaped from its twist and was now tumbling like fire over her shoulders, and somewhere along the way she had lost her shawl and shoes. Without the help of her shoes, the two men towered over her, indomitable and proud, dark brown eyes offering no hint of apology.

Her gaze fixed itself somewhere between them, her hands closed into two tightly clenched fists at her side. The air actually stung with an electric charge of anticipation. 'I demand to see Ethan,' she stated very coldly.

It was clearly the last thing either was expecting her to say. Rafiq stiffened infinitesimally, Hassan looked as if she could not have insulted him more if she'd tried.

His eyes narrowed, his mouth grew thin, his handsome sleek features hardened into polished rock. Beneath the dark robes, Leona saw his wide chest expand and remain that way as, with a sharp flick of a hand, he sent Rafiq sweeping out of the room.

As the door closed them in, the sudden silence stifled almost as much as the *abaya* had done. Neither moved, neither spoke for the space of thirty long heart-throbbing seconds, while Hassan stared coldly down at her and she stared at some obscure point near his right shoulder.

Years of loving this one man, she was thinking painfully. Five years of living the dream in a marriage she had believed was so solid that nothing could ever tear it apart. Now she couldn't even bring herself to focus on his face properly in case the feelings she now kept deeply suppressed inside her came surging to the surface and spilled out on a wave of broken-hearted misery. For their marriage was over. They both knew it was over. He should not have done this to her. It hurt so badly that he could treat her this way that she didn't think she was ever going to forgive him for it.

Hassan broke the silence by releasing the breath he had been holding onto. 'In the interests of harmony, I suggest you restrain from mentioning Ethan Hayes in my presence,' he advised, then simply stepped right past her to walk across the room to a polished wood counter which ran the full length of one wall.

As she followed the long, lean, subtle movement of his body through desperately loving eyes, fresh fury leapt up to save her again. 'But who else would I ask about when I've just watched your men beat him up and drag him away?' she threw after him.

'They did not beat him up.' Flicking open a cupboard door, he revealed a fridge stocked with every conceivable form of liquid refreshment.

'They fell on him like a flock of hooligans!'

'They subdued his enthusiasm for a fight.'

'He was defending me!'

'That is my prerogative.'

Her choked laugh at that announcement dropped scorn all

over it. 'Sometimes your arrogance stuns even me!' she informed him scathingly.

The fridge door shut with a thud. 'And your foolish refusal to accept wise advice when it is offered to you stuns me!'

Twisting round, Hassan was suddenly revealing an anger that easily matched her own. His eyes were black, his expression harsh, his mouth snapped into a grim line. In his hand he held a bottle of mineral water which he slammed down on the cabinet top, then he began striding towards her, big and hard and threatening.

'I don't know what's the matter with you,' she burst out bewilderedly. 'Why am I under attack when I haven't done anything?'

'You dare to ask that, when this is the first time we have looked upon each other in a year—yet all you can think about is Ethan Hayes?'

'Ethan isn't your enemy,' she persisted stubbornly.

'No.' Thinly said. Then something happened within his eyes that set her heart shuddering. He came to a stop a bare foot away from her. 'But he is most definitely yours,' he said.

She didn't want him this close and took a step back. 'I don't know what you mean,' she denied.

He closed the gap again. 'A married woman openly living with a man who is not her husband carries a heavy penalty in Rahman.'

'Are you daring to suggest that Ethan and I *sleep* together?' Her eyes went wide with utter affront.

'Do you?'

The question was like a slap to the face. 'No we do not!'

'Prove it,' he challenged.

Surprise had her falling back another step. 'But you know Ethan and I don't have that kind of relationship,' she insisted.

'And, I repeat,' he said, 'prove it.'

Nerve-ends began to fray when she realised he was being serious. 'I can't,' she admitted, then went quite pale when she felt forced to add, 'But you know I wouldn't sleep with him, Hassan. You *know* it,' she emphasised with a painfully thickening tone which placed a different kind of darkness in his eyes.

It came from understanding and pity. And she hated him for that also! Hated and loved and hurt with a power that was worse than any other torture he could inflict.

'Then explain to me, please,' he persisted nonetheless, 'when you openly live beneath the same roof as he does, how I convince my people of this certainty you believe I have in your fidelity?'

'But Ethan and I haven't spent one night alone together in the villa,' she protested. 'My father has always been there with us until he was delayed in London today!'

'Quite.' Hassan nodded. 'Now you understand why you have been snatched from the brink of committing the ultimate sin in the eyes of our people. There,' he said with a dismissive flick of the hand. 'I am your saviour, as is my prerogative.'

With that, and having neatly tied the whole thing off to his own satisfaction, he turned and walked away— Leaving Leona to flounder in his smooth, slick logic and with no ready argument to offer.

'I don't believe you are real sometimes,' she sent shakily after him. 'Did it never occur to you that I didn't want *snatching from the brink*?'

Sarcasm abounding, Hassan merely pulled the *gutrah* from his head and tossed it aside, then returned to the bottle of water. 'It was time,' he said, swinging the fridge door open again. 'You have had long enough to sulk.'

'I wasn't sulking!'

'Whatever,' he dismissed with a shrug, then chose a bottle of white wine and closed the door. 'It was time to bring the impasse to an end.'

Impasse, Leona repeated. He believed their failed marriage was merely stuck in an *impasse*. 'I'm not coming back to you,' she declared, then turned away to pretend to take an interest in her surroundings, knowing that his grim silence was denying her the right to choose.

They were enclosed in what she could only presume was a private stateroom furnished in subtle shades of cream faced with richly polished rosewood. It was all so beautifully designed that it was almost impossible to see the many doors built into the walls except for the wood-framed doors they had entered through. And it was the huge deep-sprung divan taking pride of place against a silk-lined wall, that told her exactly what the room's function was.

Although the bed was not what truly captured her attention, but the pair of big easy chairs standing in front of a low table by a set of closed cream velvet curtains. As her heart gave a painful twist in recognition, she sent a hand drifting up to her eyes. Oh, Hassan, she thought despairingly, don't do this to me...

She had seen the chairs, Hassan noted, studying the way she was standing there looking like an exquisitely fragile, perfectly tooled art-deco sculpture in her slender gown of gold. And he didn't know whether to tell her so or simply weep at how utterly bereft she looked.

In the end he chose a third option and took a rare sip at the white wine spritzer he had just prepared for her. The forbidden alcohol content in the drink might be diluted but he felt it hit his stomach and almost instantly enter his bloodstream with an injection of much appreciated fire.

'You've lost weight,' he announced, and watched her chin come up, watched her wonderful hair slide down her slender back and her hand drop slowly to her side while she took a steadying breath before she could bring herself to turn and face him.

'I've been ill—with the flu,' she answered flatly.

'That was weeks ago,' he dismissed, uncaring that he was revealing to her just how close an eye he had been keeping on her from a distance. The fact that she showed no surprise told him that she had guessed as much anyway. 'After a virus such as influenza the weight recovery is usually swift.'

'And you would know, of course,' she drawled, mocking the fact that he had not suffered a day's illness in his entire life.

'I know *you*,' he countered, 'and your propensity for slipping into a decline when you are unhappy...'

'I was *ill*, not unhappy.'

'You missed me. I missed you. Why try to deny it?'

'May I have one of those?' Indicating towards the drink he held in his hand was her way of telling him she was going to ignore those kind of comments.

'It is yours,' he explained, and offered the glass out to her.

She looked at the glass, long dusky lashes flickering over her beautiful green eyes when she realised he was going to make her come and get the drink. Would she do it? he wondered curiously. Would she allow herself to come this close, when they both knew she would much rather turn and run?

But his beautiful wife had never been a coward. No matter how she might be feeling inside, he had never known her to run from a challenge. Even when she had left him last year she had done so with courage, not cowardice. And she did not let him down now as her silk stockinged feet began to tread the cream carpet until she was in reach of the glass.

'Thank you.' The wine spritzer was taken from him and lifted to her mouth. She sipped without knowing she had been offered the glass so she would place her lips where his lips had been.

Her pale throat moved as she swallowed; her lips came away from the glass wearing a seductively alluring wine glossed bloom. He watched her smother a sigh, watched her look anywhere but directly at him, was aware that she had not looked him in the face since removing the *abaya*, just as she had stopped looking at him weeks before she left Rahman. And he had to suppress his own sigh as he felt muscles tighten all over his body in his desire to reach out, draw her close and make her look at him!

But this was not the time to play the demanding husband. She would reject him as she had rejected him many times a year ago. What hurt him the most about remembering those bleak interludes was not his own angry frustration but the grim knowledge that it had been herself she had been denying.

'Was the Petronades yacht party an elaborate set-up?' she asked suddenly.

A brief smile stretched his mouth, and it was a very self-mocking smile because he had truly believed she was as concentrated on his close physical presence as he was on hers. But, no. As always, Leona's mind worked in ways that continually managed to surprise him.

'The party was genuine.' He answered the question. 'Your father's sudden inability to get here in time to attend it was not.'

At least his honesty almost earned him a direct glance of frowning puzzlement before she managed to divert it to his right ear. 'But you've just finished telling me that I was snatched because my father was—'

'I know,' he cut in, not needing to hear her explain what he already knew—which was that this whole thing had been very carefully set up and co-ordinated with her father's assistance. 'There are many reasons why you are standing here with me right now, my darling,' he murmured gently. 'Most of which can wait for another time to go into.'

The *my darling* sent her back a defensive step. The realisation that her own father had plotted against her darkened her lovely eyes. 'Tell me now,' she insisted.

But Hassan just shook his head. 'Now is for me,' he informed her softly. 'Now is my moment to bask in the fact that you are back where you belong.'

It was really a bit of bad timing that her feet should use that particular moment to tread on the discarded *abaya*, he supposed, watching as she looked down, saw, then grew angry all over again.

'By abduction?' Her chin came up, contempt shimmering along her finely shaped bones. 'By plots and counter-plots and by removing a woman's right to decide for herself?'

He grimaced at her very accurate description. 'We are by nature a romantic people,' he defended. 'We love drama and poetry and tragic tales of star-crossed lovers who lose each other and travel the caverns of hell in their quest to find their way back together again.'

He saw the tears. He had said too much. Reaching out, he caught the glass just before it slipped from her nerveless fingers. 'Our marriage is a tragedy,' she told him thickly.

'No,' he denied, putting the hapless glass aside. 'You merely insist on turning it into one.'

'Because I hate everything you stand for!'

'But you cannot make yourself hate the man,' he added, undisturbed by her denunciation.

Leona began to back away because there was something seriously threatening about the sudden glow she caught in his eyes. 'I left you, remember?'

'Then sent me letters at regular intervals to make sure I remembered you,' he drawled.

'Letters to tell you I want a divorce!' she cried.

'The content of the letters came second to their true purpose.' He smiled. 'One every two weeks over the last two months. I found them most comforting.'

'Gosh, you are so conceited it's a wonder you didn't marry yourself!'

'Such insults.' He sighed.

'Will you stop stalking me as if I am a hunted animal?' she cried.

'Stop backing away like one.'

'I do not want to stay married to you.' She stated it bluntly.

'And I am not prepared to let you go. There,' he said. 'We have reached another impasse. Which one of us is going to win the higher ground this time, do you think?'

Looking at him standing there, arrogant and proud yet so much her kind of man that he made her legs go weak, Leona knew exactly which one of them possessed the higher ground. Which was also why she had to keep him at arm's length at all costs. He could fell her in seconds, because he was right; she didn't hate him, she adored him. And that scared her so much that when his hand came up, long fingertips brushing gently across her trembling mouth, she almost fainted on the sensation that shot from her lips to toe tips.

She pulled right away. His eyebrow arched. It mocked and challenged as he responded by curling the hand around her nape.

'Stop it,' she said, and lifted up her hand to use it as a brace against his chest.

Beneath dark blue cotton she discovered a silk-smooth, hard-packed body pulsing with heat and an all-too-familiar masculine potency. Her mouth went dry; she tried to breathe and found that she couldn't. Helplessly she lifted her eyes up to meet with his.

'Seeing me now, hmm?' he softly taunted. 'Seeing this man with these eyes you like to drown in, and this nose you like to call dreadful but usually have trouble from stopping your fingers from stroking? And let us not forget this mouth you so like to feel crushed hotly against your own delightful mouth.'

'Don't you dare!' she protested, seeing what was coming and already beginning to shake all over at the terrifying prospect of him finding out what a weak-willed coward she was.

'Why not?' he countered, offering her one of his lazily sensual, knowing smiles that said he knew better than she did what she really wanted—and he began to lower his dark head.

'Tell me first.' Sheer desperation made her fly into impulsive speech. 'If I am here on this beautiful yacht that belongs to you—is there another yacht just like it out there somewhere where your second wife awaits her turn?'

In the sudden suffocating silence that fell between them Leona found herself holding her breath as she watched his face pale to a frightening stillness. For this was provocation of the worst kind to an Arab and her heart began pounding madly because she just didn't know how he was going to respond. Hassan possessed a shocking temper, though he had never unleashed it on her. But now, as she stood here with her fingers still pressed against his breastbone, she could feel the danger in him—could almost taste her own fear as she waited to see how he was going to respond.

What he did was to take a step back from her. Cold, aloof, he changed into the untouchable prince in the single blink of an ebony eyelash. 'Are you daring to imply that I could be guilty of treating my wives unequally?' he responded.

In the interim wave of silence that followed, Leona stared at him through eyes that had stopped seeing anything as his reply rocked the very axis she stood upon. She knew she had prompted it but she still had not expected it, and now she found she couldn't breathe, couldn't even move as fine cracks began to appear in her defences.

'You actually went and did it, and married again,' she whispered, then completely shattered. Emotionally, physically, she felt herself fragment into a thousand broken pieces beneath his stone-cold, cruel gaze.

Hassan didn't see it coming. He should have done, he knew that, but he had been too angry to see anything but his own affronted pride. So when she turned and ran he didn't expect it. By the time he had pulled his wits together enough to go after her Leona was already flying through the door on a flood of tears.

The tears blinded what was ahead of her, the *abaya* having prevented her from taking stock of her surroundings as they'd arrived. Hassan heard Rafiq call out a warning, reached the door as Leona's cry curdled the very air surrounding them and she began to fall.

What he had managed to prevent by the skin of his teeth only a half-hour before now replayed itself before his helpless eyes. Only it was not the dark waters of the Mediterranean she fell into but the sea of cream carpet that ran from room to room and down a wide flight of three shallow stairs that led down into the yacht's main foyer.

CHAPTER THREE

CURSING and swearing in seething silence, Hassan prowled three sides of the bed like a caged tiger while the yacht's Spanish medic checked her over.

'No bones broken, as far as I can tell,' the man said. 'No obvious blow to the head.'

'Then why is she unconscious?' he growled out furiously.

'Shock—winded,' the medic suggested, gently laying aside a frighteningly limp hand. 'It has only been a few minutes, sir.'

But a few minutes was a lifetime when you felt so guilty you wished it was yourself lying there, Hassan thought harshly.

'A cool compress would be a help—'

A cool compress. 'Rafiq.' The click of his fingers meant the job would be done.

The sharp sound made Leona flinch. On a single, lithe leap Hassan was suddenly stretched out across the bed and leaning over her. The medic drew back; Rafiq paused in his step.

'Open your eyes.' Hassan turned her face towards him with a decidedly unsteady hand.

Her eyes fluttered open to stare up at him blankly. 'What happened?' she mumbled.

'You fell down some stairs,' he gritted. 'Now tell me where you hurt.'

A frown began to pucker her smooth brow as she tried to remember.

'Concentrate,' he rasped, diverting her mind away from what had happened. 'Do you hurt anywhere?'

She closed her eyes again, and he watched her make a mental inventory of herself then give a small shake of her head. 'I think I'm okay.' She opened her eyes again, looked directly into his, saw his concern, his anguish, the burning fires of guilt—and then she remembered *why* she'd fallen.

Aching tears welled up again. From coldly plunging his imaginary knife into her breast, he now felt it enter his own. 'You really went and did it,' she whispered.

'No, I did not,' he denied. 'Get out,' he told their two witnesses.

The room emptied like water down a drain, leaving them alone again, confronting each other again. It was dangerous. He wanted to kiss her so badly he could hardly breathe. She was his. He was hers! They should not be in this warring situation!

'No—remain still!' he commanded when she attempted to move. 'Don't even breathe unless you have to do so! Why are females so *stupid*?' he bit out like a curse. 'You insult me with your suspicions. You goad me into a response, and when it is not the one you want to hear you slay me with your pain!'

'I didn't mean to fall down the stairs,' she pointed out.

'I wasn't talking about the fall!' he bit out, then glared down into her confused, hurt, vulnerable eyes for a split second longer. 'Oh, Allah give me strength,' he gritted, and gave in to himself and took her trembling mouth by storm.

If he had kissed her in any other way Leona would have fought him with her very last breath. But she liked the storm; she *needed* the storm so she could allow herself to be swept away. Plus he was trembling, and she liked that too. Liked to know that she still had the power to reduce the prince in him to this vulnerable mass of smashed emotion.

And she'd missed him. She'd missed feeling his length lying alongside her length, had missed the weight of his thighs pressing down on her own. She'd missed his kiss, hungry, urgent, insistent...wanting. Like a banquet after a year of long, hard fasting, she fed greedily on every deep, dark, sensual delight. Lips, teeth, tongue, taste. She reached for his chest, felt the strong beat of his heart as she glided her palms beneath the fabric of his top robe where only the thin cotton of his tunic came between them and tightly muscled, satin-smooth flesh. When she reached his shoulders her fingers curled themselves into tightly padded muscle then stayed there, inviting him to take what he liked.

He took her breasts, stroking and shaping before moving on to follow the slender curve of her body. Long fingers claimed her hips, then drew her against the force of his. Fire bloomed in her belly, for this was her man, the love of her life. She would never, ever, find herself another. What he touched belonged to him. What he desired he could have.

What he did was bring a cruelly abrupt end to it by rising in a single fluid movement to land on his feet beside the bed, leaving her to flounder on the hard rocks of rejection while he stood there with his back to her, fighting a savage battle with himself.

'Why?' she breathed in thick confusion.

'We are not animals,' he ground back. 'We have issues to deal with that must preclude the hungry coupling at which we already know we both excel.'

It served as a dash of water in her face; and he certainly possessed good aim, Leona noted as she came back to reality with a shivering gasp. 'What issues?' she challenged cynically. 'The issue of what we have left besides the excellent sex?'

He didn't answer. Instead he made one of her eyebrows arch as he snatched up her spritzer and grimly downed the lot. There was a man at war with himself as well as with her, Leona realised, knowing Hassan hardly ever touched alcohol, and only then when he was under real stress.

Sitting up, she was aware of a few aches and bruises as she gingerly slid her feet to the floor. 'I want to go home,' she announced.

'This is home,' he replied. 'For the next few weeks, anyway.'

Few weeks? Coming just as gingerly to her feet, Leona stared at his rigid back—which was just another sign that

Hassan was not functioning to his usual standards, because no Arab worthy of the race would deliberately set his back to anyone. It was an insult of the worst kind.

Though she had seen his back a lot during those few months before she'd eventually left him, Leona recalled with a familiar sinking feeling inside. Not because he had wished to insult her, she acknowledged, but because he had refused to face what they had both known was happening to their marriage. In the end, she had taken the initiative away from him.

'Where are my shoes?'

The surprisingly neutral question managed to bring him swinging round to glance at her feet. 'Rafiq has them.'

Dear Rafiq, Leona thought wryly, Hassan's ever-loyal partner in crime. Rafiq was an Al-Qadim. A man who had attended the same schools, the same universities, the same everything as Hassan had done. Equals in many ways, prince and lowly servant in others. It was a complicated relationship that wound around the status of birth and the ranks of power.

'Perhaps you would be kind enough to ask him to give them back to me.' Even she knew you didn't *command* Rafiq to do anything. He was a law unto himself—and Hassan. Rafiq was a maverick. A man of the desert, yet not born of the desert; fiercely proud, fiercely protective of his right to be master of his own decisions.

'For what purpose?'

Leona's chin came up, recognising the challenge in his tone. She offered him a cool, clear look. 'I am not staying here, Hassan,' she told him flatly. 'Even if I have to book into a hotel in San Estéban to protect your dignity, I am leaving this boat now, tonight.'

His expression grew curious, a slight smile touched his mouth. 'Strong swimmer, are you?' he questioned lazily.

It took a few moments for his taunt to truly sink in, then she was moving, darting across the room and winding her way between the two strategically placed chairs and the accompanying table to reach for the curtains. Beyond the glass, all she could see was inky darkness. Maybe she was on the seaward side of the boat, she told herself in an effort to calm the sudden sting of alarm that slid down her spine.

Hassan quickly disabused her of that frail hope. 'We left San Estéban minutes after we boarded.'

It was only then that she felt it: just the softest hint of a vibration beneath the soles of her feet that told of smooth and silently running engines. This truly was an abduction, she finally accepted, and turned slowly back round to face him.

'Why?' she breathed.

It was like a replay of what had already gone before, only this time it was serious—more serious than Leona had even begun to imagine. For she knew this man—knew he was not given to flights of impulse just for the hell of it. Everything he did had to have a reason, and was always preceded by meticulous planning which took time he would not waste, and effort he would not move unless he felt he absolutely had to do.

Hassan's small sigh conveyed that he too knew that this was where the prevarication ended. 'There are problems at home,' he informed her soberly. 'My father's health is failing.'

His father... Anger swiftly converted itself into anxious concern for her father-in-law. Sheikh Khalifa had been frail in health for as long as she had known him. Hassan doted on him and devoted most of his energy to relieving his father of the burdens of rule, making sure he had the best medical attention available and refusing to believe that one day his father would not be there. So, if Hassan was using words like 'failing', then the old man's health must indeed be grave.

'What happened?' She began to walk towards him. 'I thought the last treatment was—'

'Your interest is a little too late in coming,' Hassan cut in, and with a flick of a hand halted her steps. 'For I don't recall you showing any concern about what it would do to his health when you left a year ago.'

That wasn't fair, and Leona blinked as his words pricked a tender part of her. Sheikh Khalifa was a good man—a kind man. They had become strong, close friends while she had lived at the palace. 'He understood why I felt I needed to leave,' she responded painfully.

You think so? Hassan's cynical expression derided. 'Well, I did not,' he said out loud. 'But, since you decided it was the right thing for you to do, I now have a serious problem on my hands. For I am, in effect, deemed weak for allowing my wife to walk away from me, and my critics are making rumbling noises about the stability of the country if I do not display some leadership.'

'So you decided to show that leadership by abducting me, then dragging me back to Rahman?' Her thick laugh poured scorn over that suggestion, because they both knew taking her back home had to be the worst thing Hassan could possibly do to prove that particular point.

'You would prefer that I take this second wife who makes you flee in pain when the subject appears in front of you?'

'She is what you need, not me.' It almost choked her to say the words. But they were dealing with the truth here, painful though that truth may be. And the truth was that she was no longer the right wife for the heir to a sheikhdom.

'I have the wife I want,' he answered grimly.

'But not the wife you *need*, Hassan!' she countered wretchedly.

His eyes flicked up to clash with her eyes. 'Is that your way of telling me that you no longer love me?' he challenged.

Oh, dear God. Lifting a trembling hand up to cover her eyes, Leona gave a shake of her head in refusal to answer. Without warning Hassan was suddenly moving at speed down the length of the room.

'Answer me!' he insisted when he came to a stop in front of her.

Swallowing on a lump of tears, Leona turned her face away. 'Yes,' she whispered.

His sudden grip on her hand dragged it from her eyes. 'To my face,' he instructed, 'You will tell me this to my face!'

Her head whipped up, tear darkened eyes fixing painfully on burning black. 'Don't—' she pleaded.

But he was not going to give in. He was pale and he was hurt and he was furiously angry. 'I want to hear you state that you feel no love for me,' he persisted. 'I want you to tell that wicked lie to my face. And then I want to hear you beg forgiveness when I prove to you otherwise! Do you understand, Leona?'

'All right! So, I love you! Does that make it all okay?' she cried out. 'I love you but I will not stay married to you! I will *not* watch you ruin your life because of me!'

There—it was out. The bitter truth. On voicing it, she broke free and reeled away, hurting so much it was almost impossible to breathe. 'And your life?' he persisted relentlessly. 'What happens to it while you play the sacrificial lamb for mine?'

'I'll get by,' she said, trying to walk on legs that were shaking so badly she wasn't sure if she was going to fall down.

'You'll marry again?'

She shuddered and didn't reply.

'Take lovers in an attempt to supplant me?'

Harsh and cruel though he sounded, she could hear his anguish. 'I need no one,' she whispered.

'Then you mean to spend the rest of your life watching me produce progeny with this second wife I am to take?'

'Oh, dear heaven.' She swung around. 'What are you trying to do to me?' she choked out tormentedly.

'Make you see,' he gritted. 'Make you open your eyes and *see* what it is you are condemning us both to.'

'But I'm not condemning you to anything! I am giving you my blessing to do what you want with your life!'

If she'd offered to give him a whole harem he could not have been more infuriated. His face became a map of hard angles. 'Then I will take what I want!' It was a declaration of intent that propelled him across the space between them. Before Leona knew what was coming she was locked in his arms and being lifted until their eyes were level. Startled green irises locked with burning black passion. He gave her one small second to read their message before he was kissing her furiously. Shocked out of one kind of torment, she found herself flung into the middle of another—because once again she had no will to fight. She even released a protesting groan when her feet found solid ground again and he broke the urgent kiss.

Her lips felt hot, and pulsed with such a telling fullness that she had to lick them to try and cool them down. His breath left his body on a hiss that brought her eyes flickering dazedly up to his. Thick dark lashes rested over ebony eyes that were fixed on the moist pink tip of her tongue. A slither of excitement skittered right down the front of her. Her breasts grew tight, her abdomen warming at the prospect of what all of this meant.

Making love. Feeling him deep inside her. No excuses, no drawing back this time. She only had to look at Hassan to know this was it. He was about to stake his claim on what belonged to him.

'You will regret this later,' she warned unsteadily, because she knew how his passions and his conscience did not always walk in tandem—especially not where she was concerned.

'Are you denying me?' he threw back in a voice that said he was interested in the answer, but only out of curiosity.

Well, Leona asked herself, are you?

The answer was no, she was not denying him anything he wanted to take from her tonight. Tomorrow was another day, another war, another set of agonising conflicts. Reaching up, she touched a gentle finger to his mouth, drew its shape, softened the tension out of it, then sighed, went up on tiptoe and gently joined their mouths.

His hands found the slender frame of her hips and drew her against him; her hands lifted higher to link around his neck so her fingers could slide sensually into his silk dark hair. It was an embrace that sank them into a long deep loving. Her dress fell away, slithering down her body on a pleasurable whisper of silk against flesh. Beneath she wore a dark gold lace bra, matching high-leg briefs and lace-topped stockings. Hassan discovered all of this with the sensual stroke of long fingers. He knew each pleasure point, the quality of each little gasp she breathed into his mouth. When her bra fell away, she sighed and pressed herself against him; when his fingers slid beneath the briefs to cup her bottom she allowed him to ease her into closer contact. They knew each other, *loved* each other—cared so very deeply about each other. Fight they might do—often. They might have insurmountable problems. But nothing took away the love and caring. It was there, as much part of them as the life-giving oxygen they took into their lungs.

'You want me,' he declared.

'I've always wanted you,' she sadly replied.

'I am your other half.'

And I am your broken one, Leona thought, releasing an achingly melancholy sigh.

Maybe he knew what she was thinking, because his mouth took burning possession that gave no more room to think at all. It came as an unwelcome break when he lowered her down onto the bed then straightened, taking her briefs with him. Her love-flooded eyes watched his eyes roam over her. He was no longer being driven by his inner devils, she realised as she watched him removing his own clothing. Her compliance had neutralised the compelling need to stake his claim.

So she watched him follow her every movement as she made a sensual love-play out of removing her stockings from her long slender legs. His dark robe landed on the floor on top of her clothing; the tunic eventually went the same way. Beneath waited a desert-bronzed silk-smooth torso, with a muscled structure that set her green eyes glowing with pleasure and made her fingers itch to touch. Those muscles rippled and flexed as he reached down to grasp the only piece of clothing he had left to remove. The black shorts trailed away from a sexual force that set her feminine counterpart pulsing with anticipation.

He knew what was happening, smiled a half-smile, then came to lean over her, lowering his raven head to place a kiss there that was really a claim of ownership. She breathed out a shivering breath of pleasure and he was there to claim that also. Then she had all of him covering her. It was the sweetest feeling she had ever experienced. He was her Arabian lover. The man she had seen across a crowded room long years ago. And she had never seen another man clearly since.

He seduced her mouth, he seduced her body, he seduced her into seducing him. When it all became too much without deeper contact, he eased himself between her thighs and slowly joined them.

Her responsive groan made him pause. 'What?' he questioned anxiously.

'I've missed you so much.' She sighed the words out helplessly.

It was a catalyst that sent him toppling. He staked his claim on those few emotive words with every driving thrust. She died a little. It was strange how she did that, she found herself thinking as the pleasure began to run like liquid fire. They came as one, within the grip of hard, gasping shudders and afterwards lay still, locked together, as their bodies went through the pleasurable throes of settling back down again.

Then nothing moved, not their bodies nor even their quiet breathing. The silence came—pure, numbing, unbreakable silence.

Why?

Because it had all been so beautiful but also so very empty. And nothing was ever going to change that.

Hassan moved first, levering himself away to land on his feet by the bed. He didn't even spare her a glance as he walked away. Sensational naked, smooth and sleek, he touched a finger to the wall and a cleverly concealed door sprung open. As he stepped through it Leona caught a glimpse of white tiling and realised it was a bathroom. Then the door closed, shutting him in and her completely out.

Closing her eyes, she lifted an arm up to cover them, and pressed her lips together to stop them from trembling on the tears she was having to fight. For this was not a new situation she was dealing with here. It had happened before—often— and was just one of the many reasons why she had left him in the end. The pain had been too great to go on taking it time after time. His pain, her pain—she had never been able to distinguish where one ended and the other began. The only difference here tonight was that she'd somehow managed to let herself forget that, until this cold, solitary moment.

Hassan stood beneath the pulsing jet of the power shower and wanted to hit something so badly that he had to brace his hands against the tiles and lock every muscle to keep the murderous feeling in. His body was replete but his heart was grinding against his ribcage with a frustration that nothing could cure.

Silence. He hated that silence. He hated knowing he had nothing worth saying with which to fill it in. And he still had to go back in there and face it. Face the dragging sense of his own helplessness and—worse—he had to face hers.

His wife. His woman. The other half of him. Head lowered so the water sluiced onto his shoulders and down his back, he tried to predict what her next move was going to be, and came up with only one grim answer. She was not going to stay. He could bully her as much as he liked, but in the end she was still going to walk away from him unless he could come up with something important enough to make her stay.

Maybe he should have used more of his father's illness, he told himself. A man she loved, a man she'd used to spend hours of every day with, talking, playing board games or just quietly reading to him when he was too weak to enjoy anything else.

But his father had not been enough to make her want to

stay the last time. The old fool had given her his blessing, had missed her terribly, yet even on the day he'd gone to see him before he left the palace he had still maintained that Leona had had to do what she'd believed was right.

So who was in the wrong here? Him for wanting to spend his life with one particular woman, or Leona for wanting to do what was right?

He hated that phrase, *doing what was right*. It reeked of duty at the expense of everything: duty to his family, duty to his country, duty to produce the next Al-Qadim son and heir.

Well, I don't need a son. I don't need a second wife to produce one for me like some specially selected brood mare! I need a beautiful red-haired creature who makes my heart ache each time I look at her. I *don't* need to see that glazed look of emptiness she wears after we make love!

On a sigh he turned round, swapped braced hands for braced shoulders against the shower wall. The water hit his face and stopped him breathing. He didn't care if he never breathed again—until instinct took over from grim stubbornness and forced him to move again.

Coming out of the bathroom a few minutes later, he had to scan the room before he spotted her sitting curled up in one of the chairs. She had opened the curtains and was just sitting there staring out, with her wonderful hair gleaming hot against the pale damask upholstery. She had wrapped herself in a swathe of white and a glance at the tumbled bed told him she had dragged free the sheet of Egyptian cotton to wear.

His gaze dropped to the floor by the bed, where their clothes still lay in an intimate huddle that was a lot more honest than the two of them were with each other.

'Find out how Ethan is.'

The sound of her voice brought his attention back to her. She hadn't moved, had not turned to look at him, and the demand spoke volumes as to what was really being said. Barter and exchange. She had given him more of herself than she had intended to do; now she wanted something back by return.

Without a word he crossed to the internal telephone and found out what she wanted to know, ordered some food to be sent in to them, then strode across the room to sit down in the chair next to hers. 'He caught an accidental blow to the jaw which knocked him out for a minute or two, but he is fine now,' he assured her. 'And is dining with Rafiq as we speak.'

'So he wasn't part of this great plan of abduction you plotted with my father.' It wasn't a question, it was a sign of relief.

'I am devious and underhand on occasion but not quite that devious and underhand,' he countered dryly.

Her chin was resting on her bent knees, but she turned her head to look at him through dark, dark eyes. Her hair flowed across her white-swathed shoulders, and her soft mouth looked vulnerable enough to conquer in one smooth swoop. His body quickened, temptation clawing across flesh hidden beneath his short robe of sand-coloured silk.

'Convincing my own father to plot against me wasn't devious or underhand?' she questioned.

'He was relieved I was ready to break the deadlock,' he informed her. 'He wished me well, then offered me all the help he could give.'

Her lack of comment was one in itself. Her following sigh punctuated it. She was seeing betrayal from her own father, but it just was not true. 'You knew he worried about you,' he inserted huskily. 'Yet you didn't tell him why you left me, did you?'

The remark lost him contact with her eyes as she turned them frontward again, and the way she stared out into the inky blackness beyond the window closed up his throat, because he knew what she was really seeing as she looked out there.

'Coming to terms with being a failure is not something I wanted to share with anyone,' she murmured dully.

'You are not a failure,' he denied.

'I am infertile!' She flashed out the one word neither of them wanted to hear.

It launched Hassan to his feet on a surge of anger. 'You are not infertile!' he ground out harshly. 'That is not what the doctors said, and you know it is not!'

'Will you stop hiding from it?' she cried, scrambling to her feet to stand facing him, with her face as white as the sheet she clutched around her and her eyes as black as the darkness outside. 'I have one defunct ovary and the other one ovulates only when it feels like it!' She spelt it out for him.

'Which does not add up to infertility,' he countered forcefully.

'After all of these years of nothing, you can still bring yourself to say that?'

She was staring up at him as if he was deliberately trying to hurt her. And, because he had no answer to that final charge, he had to ask himself if that had been his subconscious intention. The last year had been hell to live through and the year preceding only marginally better. Married life had become a place in which they'd walked with the darkness of disappointment shadowing their past and future. In the end, Leona had not been able to take it any more so she'd left him. If she wanted to know what failure really felt like then she should have trodden in his shoes as he'd battled with his own failure to relieve this woman he loved of the heavy burden she was forced to carry.

'We will try other methods of conception,' he stated grimly.

If it was possible her face went even whiter. 'My eggs harvested like grains of wheat and your son conceived in a test tube? Your people would never forgive me for putting you through such an indignity, and those who keep the Al-Qadim family in power will view the whole process with deep suspicion.'

Her voice had begun to wobble. His own throat closed on

the need to swallow, because she was right, though he did not want her to be. For she was talking about the old ones, those tribal leaders of the desert who really maintained the balance of power in Rahman. They lived by the old ways and regarded anything remotely modern as necessary evil to be embraced only if all other sources had been exhausted. Hassan had taken a big risk when he'd married a western woman. The old ones had surprised him by deciding to see his decision to do so as a sign of strength. But that had been the only concession they had offered him with regard to his choice of wife. For why go to such extremes to father a son he could conceive as easily by taking a second wife?

Which was why this subject had always been so sensitive, and why Leona suddenly shook her head and said, 'Oh, why did you have to bring me back here?' Then she turned and walked quickly away from him, making unerringly for the bathroom he had so recently used for the same purpose—to be alone with her pain.

CHAPTER FOUR

Two hours, Leona noticed, as she removed her slender gold watch from her wrist with badly trembling fingers and laid it on the marble surface along with the diamonds from her ears and throat. Two hours together and already they were tearing each other to pieces.

On a sigh she swivelled round to sink down onto the toilet seat and stare dully at her surroundings. White. Everything was white. White-tiled walls and floor, white ceramics—even the sheet she had discarded lay in a soft white heap on the floor. The room needed a bit of colour to add some—

She stopped herself right there, closing her eyes on the knowledge that she had slipped into professional mode and knowing she had done it to escape from what she should really be thinking about.

This situation, this mad, foolish, heart-flaying situation, which was also so bitter-sweet and special. She didn't know whether to laugh at Hassan's outrageous method of bringing them together, or sob at the unnecessary agony he was causing the both of them.

In the end she did both, released a laugh that turned into a sob and buried the sound in her hands. Each look, each touch, was an act of love that bound them together. Each word, each thought, was an act of pain that tore them apart at the seams.

Then she remembered his face when he had made the ultimate sacrifice. Chin up, face carved, mouth so flat it was hardly a mouth any more. When the man had had to turn himself into a prince before he could utter the words, 'We will try other methods of conception,' she had known they had nothing left to fight for.

48

What was she supposed to have done? Made the reciprocal sacrifice to their love and offered to remain his first wife while he took a second? She just could not do it, could not live with the agony of knowing that when he wasn't in her bed he would be lying in another. The very idea was enough to set her insides curling up in pained dismay while her covered eyes caught nightmare visions of him trying to be fair, trying to pretend it wasn't really happening, that he wasn't over the moon when the new wife conceived his first child. How long after that before his love began to shift from her to this other woman with whom he could relax—enjoy her without feeling pain every time he looked at her?

'No,' she whispered. 'Stop it.' She began to shiver. It just wasn't even an option, so she must stop thinking about it! He knew that—he *knew it*! It was why he had taunted her with the suggestion earlier. He had been angry and had gone for the jugular and had enjoyed watching her die in front of him! It had always been like this: exploding flashes of anger and frustration, followed by wild leaps into sensual forgetfulness, followed by the low-of-low moments when neither could even look at the other because the empty truth was always still waiting there for them to re-emerge.

Empty.

On a groan she stood up, and groaned again as tiny muscles all over her body protested at being forced into movement. The fall, the lovemaking, or just the sheer stress of it all? she wondered, then wearily supposed it was a combination of all three.

So why do it? Why put them both back into a situation they had played so many times before it was wretched? Or was that it? she then thought on a sudden chill that shot down her backbone. Had he needed to play out the scene this one last time before he could finally accept that their marriage was over?

Sick. She felt sick. On trembling legs she headed quickly for the shower cubicle and switched the jet on so water sluiced over her body. Duty. It was all down to duty. His duty to produce an heir, her duty to let him. With any other man the love would be enough; those *other methods of conception* would be made bearable by the strength of that love. But she'd fallen in love with a prince not a man. And the prince had fallen in love with a barren woman.

Barren. How ugly that word was. How cold and bitter and horribly cheap. For there was nothing barren about the way she was feeling, nor did those feelings come cheap. They cost her a part of herself each time she experienced them. Like now, as they ate away at her insides until it was all she could do to slide down into a pathetic huddle in the corner of the shower cubicle and wait for it all to recede.

Where was she? What was she doing in there? She had been shut inside the bathroom for half an hour, and with a glance at his watch, Hassan continued to pace the floor on the vow that if she didn't come out in two minutes he was going in there after her.

None of this—*none* of it—was going the way he had planned it. How had he managed to trick himself into diluting just how deep their emotions ran, how painful the whole thing was going to be? He hit his brow with the palm of his hand, then uttered a few choice curses at his arrogant belief that all he'd needed to do was hook her up and haul her back in for the rest to fall into place around them.

All he'd wanted to do was make sure she was safe, back here where she belonged, no matter what the problems. So instead he'd scared the life out of her, almost lost her to the depths of the ocean, fought like the devil over issues that were so old they did not need raking over! He'd even lied to score points, had watched her run in a flood of tears, watched her fly through the air down a set of stairs he now wished had never been put there. Shocked, winded and dazed by the whole crazy situation, he had then committed his worst sin and had ravished her. Now she had locked herself away behind a bathroom door because she could not deal with him daring to make an offer they both knew was not, and never had been, a real option!

What was left? Did he unsheath his ceremonial scabbard and offer to finish them both off like two tragic lovers?

Oh, may Allah forgive him, he prayed as his blood ran cold and he leapt towards the bathroom door. She wouldn't. She was made of stronger stuff, he told himself as he lifted a clenched fist to bang on the door just as it came open.

She was wearing only a towel and her hair was wet, slicked to her beautiful head like a ruby satin veil. Momentarily shocked by the unexpected face-to-face confrontation, they both just stared at each other. Then he bit out, 'Are you all right?'

'Of course,' she replied. 'Why shouldn't I be?'

He had no answer to offer that did not sound insane, so he took another way out and reached for her, pulled her into his arms and kissed her—hard. By the time he let her up for air again she was breathless.

'Hassan—'

'No,' he interrupted. 'We have talked enough for one night.'

Turning away, he went over to the bed to retrieve the pearl-white silk robe he had laid out ready for her. During her absence the room had been returned to its natural neatness, at his instruction, and a table had been laid for dinner in the centre, with the food waiting for them on a heated trolley standing beside it.

He saw her eyes taking all of this in as he walked back to where she was standing. She also noticed that the lights had been turned down and candles had been lit on the table. She was no fool; she knew he had set the scene with a second seduction in mind and he didn't bother to deny it.

'Here,' he said, and opened the robe up between his hands, inviting her to slip into it.

There was a pause where she kept her eyes hidden beneath the sweep of her dusky lashes. She was trying to decide how to deal with this and he waited in silence, more than willing to let the decision be hers after having spent the previous few minutes listing every other wrong move he had made until now.

'Just for tonight,' she said, and lifted those lashes to show him the firmness of that decision. 'Tomorrow you take me back to San Estéban.'

His mouth flexed as the urge to say, Never, throbbed on the end of his tongue. 'Tomorrow we—talk about it,' he offered as his only compromise, though he knew it was no compromise at all and wondered if she knew it too.

He suspected she did, suspected she knew he had not gone to all of this trouble just to snatch a single night with her. But those wonderful lashes fluttered down again. Her soft mouth, still pulsing from his kiss, closed over words she decided not to say, and with only a nod of her head she lost the towel, stepped forward and turned to allow him to help feed her arms into the kimono-type sleeves of the robe.

It was a concession he knew he did not deserve. A concession he wanted to repay with a kiss of another kind, where bodies met and senses took over. Instead, he turned her to face him, smoothed his fingers down the robe's silken border from slender shoulders to narrow waist, then reached for the belt and tied it for her.

His gentle ministrations brought a reluctant smile to her lips. 'The calm before the storm,' she likened dryly.

'Better this than what I really want to do,' he very ruefully replied.

'You mean this?' she asked, and lifted her eyes to his to let him see what was running through her head, then reached up and kissed him, before drawing away again with a very mocking smile.

As she turned to walk towards the food trolley she managed to trail her fingers over that part of him that was already so hard it was almost an embarrassment. The little vixen. He released a soft laugh. She might appear subdued on the surface, but underneath she still possessed enough spirit to play the tease.

They ate poached salmon on a bed of spinach, and beef stroganoff laden with cream. Hassan kept her glass filled with the crisp dry white wine she liked, while he drank sparkling water. As the wine helped mellow her mood some more, Leona managed to completely convince herself that all she wanted was this one wonderful night and she was prepared to live on it for ever. By the time the meal was finished and he suggested a walk on the deck, she was happy to go with him.

Outside the air was warm and as silken as the darkness that surrounded them. Both in bare feet, dressed only in their robes, they strolled along the deck and could have been the only two people on board it was so quiet and deserted.

'Rafiq is entertaining Ethan—up there,' Hassan explained when she asked where everyone else was. Following his gaze, Leona could see lights were burning in the windows of the deck above.

'Should we be joining them?'

'I don't think they would appreciate the interruption,' he drawled. 'They have a poker game planned with several members of the crew, and our presence would dampen their—enthusiasm.'

Which was really him saying he didn't want to share her with anyone. 'You have an answer for everything, don't you?' she murmured.

'I try.' He smiled.

It was a slaying smile that sent the heat of anticipation burning between the cradle of her hip-bones, forcing her to look away so he wouldn't see just how susceptible she was even to his smile. Going to lean against the yacht's rail, she looked down to watch the white horses chase along the dark blue hull of the boat. They were moving at speed, slicing through the water on slick silent power that made her wonder how far they were away from San Estéban by now.

She didn't ask, though, because it was the kind of question that could start a war. 'This is one very impressive toy, even for an oil-rich sheikh,' she remarked.

'One hundred and ninety feet in length,' he announced, and came to lean beside her with his back against the rail. 'Twenty-nine feet across the beam.' His arm slid around her waist and twisted her to stand in front of him so she could follow his hand as he pointed. 'The top deck belongs mainly to the control room, where my very efficient captain keeps a smoothly running ship,' he said. 'The next down belongs to the sun deck and main reception salons designed to suitably luxurious standards for entertaining purposes. We stand upon what is known as the shade deck, it being cast mostly in the shade of the deck above,' he continued, so smoothly that she laughed because she knew he was really mocking the whole sumptuous thing. 'One half is reserved for our own personal use, with our private staterooms, my private offices etcetera,' he explained, 'while the other half is split equally between outer sun deck, outer shade deck, plus some less formal living space.'

'Gosh, you're so lucky to be this rich.' She sighed.

'And I haven't yet finished this glorious tour,' he replied. 'For below our feet lies the cabin deck, complete with six private suites easily fit for the occupation of kings. Then there is the engine room and crew's quarters below that. We can also offer a plunge pool, gymnasium and an assortment of nautical toys to make our weary lot a happier one.'

'Does it have a name, this sheikh's floating palace?' she enquired laughingly.

'Mmm. *Sexy Lady*,' he growled, and lowered his head so he could bury his teeth in the side of her neck where it met her shoulder.

'You're joking!' she accused, turning round in his arms to stare at him.

'Okay.' He shrugged. 'I am joking.'

'Then what is she called?' she demanded, as her heart skipped a beat then stopped altogether because he looked so wonderful standing here with his lean dark features relaxed and smiling naturally for the first time. She loved him quite desperately—how could she not? He was her—

The laughter suddenly died on her lips, his expression telling her something she didn't want to believe. 'No,' she breathed in denial. He couldn't have done—he *wouldn't*...

'Why not?' he challenged softly.

'Not in this case!' she snapped at him, not knowing quite what it was that was upsetting her. But upset she was; her eyes felt too hot, her chest too tight, and she had a horrible feeling she was about to weep all over his big hard beautiful chest!

'It is traditional to name a boat after your most cherished loved-one,' he pointed out. 'And why am I defending myself when I could not have paid you a better compliment than this?'

'Because...' she began shakily.

'You don't like it,' he finished for her.

'No!' she confirmed, then almost instantly changed her mind and said. 'Yes, I like it! But you shouldn't have! Y-you—'

His mouth crushed the rest of her protest into absolute oblivion, which was where it belonged anyway, because she didn't know what she was saying, only that a warm sweet wave of love was crashing over her and it was so dangerously seductive that—

She fell into it. She just let the wave close over her head and let him drown her in the heat of his passion, the power of his arms and the hunger of his kiss.

'Bed?' he suggested against her clinging mouth.

'Yes,' she agreed, then fed her fingers into his hair and her tongue between his ready lips. A groan broke low in his throat; it was husky and gorgeous; she tasted it greedily. A hand that knew her so very well curved over her thighs, slid up beneath her wrap, then cupped her bottom so he could bring her into closer contact with his desire. It was all very hot and very hungry. With a flick of a few scraps of silk they could be making love right here against the yacht's rail and in front of however many unseen eyes that happened to be glancing this way.

Hassan must have been thinking similarly because he suddenly put her from him. 'Bed,' he repeated, two dark streaks of colour accentuating his cheekbones and the fevered glitter in his eyes. 'Can you walk, or do I carry you?'

'I can run,' she informed him candidly, and grabbed hold of his hand, then turned to stride off on long slender legs with his husky laugh following as she pulled him behind her.

Back in their stateroom, now magically cleared of all evidence that they had eaten, they parted at the end of the bed, one stepping to one side of it, one to the other. Eyes locking in a needle-sharp, sensual love game, they disrobed together, climbed into the bed together and came together.

Hot, slow and deep, they made love into the night and didn't have to worry about empty spaces in between because one loving simply merged into another until—finally—they slept in each other's arms, legs entwined and faces so close on the pillows that the sleep was almost a long kiss in itself.

Leona came awake to find the place beside her in the bed empty and felt disappointment tug at her insides. For a while she just lay there, watching the sunlight seeping in through the window slowly creep towards her across the room, and tried not to let her mind open up to what it was bringing with it.

After a night built on fantasy had to come reality, not warm, like the sun, but cold, like the shadow she could already feel descending upon her even as she tried to hold it back for a little while longer.

A sound caught her attention. Moving her head just a little, she watched Hassan walk out of the bathroom wearing only a towel, his sun-brown skin fashioned to look almost like skillfully tanned leather. For such a dark man he was surprisingly free of body hair, which meant she could watch unhindered each beautifully toned muscle as he strode across to one of the concealed doors in the wall and sprung it open at a touch to reveal a wardrobe to provide for the man who had everything. A drawer was opened and he selected a pair of white cotton undershorts, dropped the towel to give her a glimpse of lean tight buttocks before he pulled the shorts on. A pair of stone-washed outer shorts followed. Zipped and buttoned, they rested low on a waist that did not know the meaning of spare flesh to spoil his sleek appearance. A casual shirt came next, made of such fine white Indian cotton she could still see the outline of his body through it.

'I can feel you watching me,' he remarked without turning.

'I like to look at you,' Leona replied. And she did; rightly or wrongly in their present situation, he was a man to watch whatever he was doing, even fastening buttons as he was doing now.

Shirt cuffs left open, he turned to walk towards the bed. The closer he came the faster her heart decided to beat. 'I like to look at you, too,' he murmured, bracing his hands on either side of head so he could lean down and kiss her.

He smelt clean and fresh and his face wore the smooth sheen of a wet razor shave. Her lips clung to his, because she was still pretending, and her arms reached up so she could clasp them round the back of his neck. 'Come back to bed with me,' she invited.

'So that you can ravish me? No way,' he refused. 'As the wise ones will tell you, my darling, too much of a good thing is bad for you.'

He kissed her again to soften the refusal, and his mouth was smiling as he straightened away, but as his hands reached up to gently remove her hands she saw the toughening happening behind his eyes. Hassan had already made contact with reality, she realised.

With that he turned away and strode back to the wall to spring open another set of doors which revealed clothes for the woman who wanted for nothing—except her man. And already she felt as if he had moved right out of her reach.

'Get up and get dressed,' he instructed as he walked towards the door. 'Breakfast will be served on the sun deck in fifteen minutes.'

As she watched him reach for the door handle the shadow

of reality sank that bit deeper into her skin. 'Nothing has changed, Hassan,' she told him quietly. 'When I leave this room I won't be coming back to it again.'

He paused, but he did not turn to glance back at her. 'Everything has changed,' he countered grimly. 'You are back where you belong. This room is only part of that.' Then he was gone, giving her no chance to argue.

Leona returned to watching the sun inch its way across the cream carpet for a while. Then, on a sigh, she slid out of the bed and went to get herself ready to face the next round of argument.

In another room not that far away Hassan was facing up to a different opponent. Ethan Hayes was standing there in the clothes he had arrived in minus the bow tie, and he was angry. In truth Hassan didn't blame him. He was wearing a bruise on his jaw that would appal Leona if she saw it, and he had a thick head through being encouraged to imbibe too much alcohol the night before.

'What made you pull such a crazy stunt?' he was demanding.

Since Hassan had been asking himself the same thing, he now found himself short of an adequate answer. 'I apologise for my men,' he said. 'Their…enthusiasm for the task got the better of them, I am afraid.'

'You can say that again.' Ethan touched his bruised jaw. 'I was out for the count for ten minutes! The next thing I know I am stuck on a yacht I don't want to be on, and Leona is nowhere to be seen!'

'She's worried about you, too, if that is any consolation.'

'No, it damn well isn't,' Ethan said toughly. 'What the hell was wrong with making contact by conventional methods? You scared the life out of her, not to mention the life out of me.'

'I know, and I apologise again.' Not being a man born to be conciliatory, being forced to be so now was beginning to grate, and his next cool remark reflected that. 'Let it be said that you will be generously compensated for the... disruption.'

Ethan Hayes stiffened in violent offence. 'I don't want compensation,' he snapped. 'I want to see for myself that Leona is okay!'

'Are you daring to imply that I could harm my wife?'

'I don't know, do I?' Ethan returned in a tone deliberately aimed to provoke. 'Overenthusiasm can be infectious.'

Neither man liked the other, though it was very rare that either came out from behind their polite masks to reveal it. But, as the sparks began to fly between the two of them, this meeting was at risk of being one of those times. Leona might prefer to believe that Ethan Hayes was not in love with her. But, as a man very intimate with the symptoms, Hassan knew otherwise. The passion with which he spoke her name, the burn that appeared in his eyes, and the inherent desire to protect her from harm all made Ethan Hayes' feelings plain. And, as far as Hassan was concerned, the handsome Englishman's only saving grace was the deep sense of honour that made him respect the wedding ring Leona wore.

But knowing this did not mean that Hassan could dismiss the other man's ability to turn her towards him if he really set his mind to it. He had the build and the looks to turn any woman's head.

Was he really afraid of that happening? he then asked himself, and was disturbed to realise that, yes, he was afraid. Always had been, always would be, he admitted, as he fought to maintain his polite mask because, at this juncture, he needed Ethan Hayes' cooperation if he was going to get him off this boat before Leona could reach him.

So, on a sigh which announced his withdrawal from the threatening confrontation, he said grimly, 'Time is of the essence,' and went on to explain to the other man just enough of the truth to grab his concern.

'A plot to get rid of her?' Ethan was shocked and Hassan could not blame him for being so.

'A plot to use her as a lever to make me concede to certain

issues they desire from me,' he amended. 'I am still holding onto the belief that they did not want to turn this into an international incident by harming her in any way.'

'Just snatching her could do it,' Ethan pointed out.

'Only if it became public property,' Hassan responded. 'They would be betting on Victor and myself holding our silence out of fear for Leona's safety.'

'Does she know?' Ethan asked.

'Not yet,' Hassan confessed. 'And not at all if I can possibly get away with it.'

'So why does she think she's here?'

'Why do you think?' Hassan countered, and gained some enjoyment out of watching Ethan stiffen as he absorbed the full masculine depth of his meaning. 'As long as she remains under my protection no one can touch her.'

Ethan's response took him by surprise because he dared to laugh. 'You've no chance, Hassan,' he waged. 'Leona will fight you to the edge and back before she will just sit down and do what you want her to do simply because you've decided that is how it must be.'

'Which is why I need your support in this,' Hassan replied. 'I need you to leave this boat before she can have an opportunity to use your departure as an excuse to jump ship with you.'

He got it. In the end, and after a bit more wrangling, he watched Ethan Hayes turn to the door on a reluctant agreement to go. And, oddly, Hassan admired him for trusting him enough to do this, bearing in mind the year that had gone before.

'Don't hurt her again.' Almost as if he could read his thoughts, Ethan issued that gruff warning right on cue.

'My wife's well-being is and always has been of paramount importance to me,' Hassan responded in a decidedly cooler tone.

Ethan turned, looked him directly in the eye, and for once the truth was placed in the open. 'You hurt her a year ago. A man gets only one chance at doing that.'

The kid gloves came off. Hassan's eyes began to glint. 'Take a small piece of advice,' he urged, 'and do not presume to understand a marital relationship until you have tried it for yourself.'

'I know a broken-hearted woman when I see one,' Ethan persisted.

'And has she been any less broken-hearted in the year we have been apart?'

Game, set and match, Hassan recognised, as the other man conceded that final point to him, and with just a nod of his head Ethan went out of the door and into the capable hands of the waiting Rafiq.

At about the same time that Rafiq was escorting Ethan to the waiting launch presently tied up against the side of the yacht, Leona was slipping her arms into the sleeves of a white linen jacket that matched the white linen trousers she had chosen to wear. Beneath the jacket she wore a pale green sun top, and she had contained her hair in a simple pony-tail tied up with a green silk scarf. As she turned towards the door she decided that if she managed to ignore the throbbing ache happening inside her then she was as ready as she ever could be for the battle she knew was to come with Hassan.

Stepping out of the stateroom, the first person she saw was a bearded man dressed in a long white tunic and the usual white *gutrah* on his head.

'Faysal!' Her surprise was clear, her smile warm. Faysal responded by pressing his palms together and dipping into the kind of low bow that irritated Hassan but didn't bother Leona at all simply because she ignored it. 'I didn't know you were here on the boat. Are you well?' she enquired as she walked towards him.

'I am very well, my lady,' he confirmed, but beneath the beard she had a suspicion he was blushing uncomfortably at the informal intimacy she was showing him.

'And your wife?' she asked gently.

'Oh, she is very well,' he confirmed with a distinct softening in his formal tone. 'The—er—problem she suffered has gone completely. We are most grateful to you for taking the trouble to ensure she was treated by the best people.'

'I didn't do anything but point her in the right direction, Faysal.' Leona smiled. 'I am only grateful that she felt she could confide in me.'

'You saved her life.'

'Many people saved her life.' Daring his affront, she crossed the invisible line Arab males drew between themselves and females and reached out to press her hands against the backs of his hands. 'But you and I were good conspirators, hmm, Faysal?'

'Indisputably, my lady.' His mouth almost cracked into a smile but he was too stressed at having her hands on his, and in the end she relented and moved away.

'If you would come this way...' he bowed '...I am to escort you to my lord Hassan.'

Ah, my lord Hassan, Leona thought, and felt her lighter mood drop again as Faysal indicated that she precede him down the steps she had taken a tumble on the night before. On the other side of the foyer was a staircase which Leona presumed led up to the deck above.

With Faysal tracking two steps behind her, she made her way up and into the sunlight flooding the upper deck, where she paused to take a look around. The sky was a pure, uninterrupted blue and the sea the colour of turquoise. The sun was already hot on her face and she had to shade her eyes against the way it was reflecting so brightly off the white paintwork of the boat.

'You managed to make Faysal blush, I see,' a deep voice drawled lazily.

Turning about, she found that Faysal had already melted away, as was his habit, and that Hassan was sitting at a table laid for breakfast beneath the shade of a huge white canvas awning, studying her through slightly mocking eyes. Her heart tried to leap in her breast but she refused to let it.

'There is a real human being hiding behind all of that strict protocol, if you would only look and see him.'

'The protocol is not my invention. It took generations of family tradition to make Faysal the man he is today.'

'He worships you like a god.'

'And you as his angel of mercy.'

'At least he felt I was approachable enough that he could bring his concerns to me.'

'After I had gently suggested it was what he should do.'

'Oh,' she said; she hadn't realised that.

'Come out of the sun before you burn.'

It was hot, and he was right, but Leona felt safer keeping her distance. She had things to say, and she began with the one subject guaranteed to alter his mellow mood into something else entirely. 'I was hoping that Ethan would be here with you,' she said. 'Since he isn't, I think I will go and look for him.'

Like a sign from Allah that today was not going to be a good day, at that moment the launch powered up and slipped its ties to the yacht.

Attention distracted, Leona glanced over the side, then went perfectly still.

Hassan knew what she was seeing even before he got up to go and join her. Sure enough, there was Ethan standing on the back of the launch. As the small boat began to pick up speed he glanced up, saw them and waved a farewell.

'Wave back, my darling,' he urged smoothly. 'The man will appreciate the assurance that all is well.'

'You rat,' she whispered.

'Of the desert,' he dryly replied, then compounded his sins by bringing an arm to rest across her stiff shoulders and lifting his other to wave.

Leona waved also, he admired her for that because it showed that, despite how angry she was feeling, she was—as always—keeping true to her unfailing loyalty to him.

In the eyes of other people, anyway. He extended that statement as the two of them stood watching Ethan and his passage away from them decrease in size, until the launch was nothing more than an occasional glint amongst many on the ocean. By then Leona was staring beyond the glint, checking the horizon for a glimpse of land that was not there. She was also gripping the rail in front of them with fingers like talons and wishing they were around his throat, he was sure.

'Try to think of it this way,' he suggested. 'I have saved us the trouble of yet another argument.'

CHAPTER FIVE

'WE HAVE to put into port some time,' Leona said coldly. She twisted out from beneath his resting arm then began walking stiffly towards the stairs, so very angry with him that she was quite prepared to lock herself in the stateroom until they did exactly that.

Behind the rigid set of her spine, she heard Hassan release a heavy sigh. 'Come back here,' he instructed. 'I was joking. I know we need to talk.'

But this was no joke, and they both knew it. He was just a ruthless, self-motivated monster, and as far as she was concerned, she had nothing left to— Her thoughts stopped dead. So did her feet when she found her way blocked by a giant of a man with a neat beard and the hawklike features of a desert warrior.

'Well, just look what we have here,' she drawled at this newly arrived target for her anger. 'If it isn't my lord sheikh's fellow conspirator in crime.'

Rafiq had opened his mouth to offer her a greeting, but her tone made him change his mind and instead he dipped into the kind of bow that would have even impressed Faysal, but only managed to sharpen Leona's tongue.

'Don't you dare efface yourself to me when we both know you don't respect me at all,' she sliced at him.

'You are mistaken,' he replied. 'I respect you most deeply.'

'Even while you throw an *abaya* over my head?'

'The *abaya* was an unfortunate necessity,' he explained, 'For you sparkled so brilliantly that you placed us in risk of discovery from the car headlights. Though please accept my apologies if my actions offended you.'

He thought he could mollify her with an apology? 'Do you know what you need, Rafiq Al-Qadim?' she responded. 'You need someone to find you a wife—a real harridan who will make your life such a misery that you won't have time to meddle in mine!'

'You are angry, and rightly so,' he conceded, but his eyes had begun to glint at the very idea of anyone meddling with his life. 'My remorse for the incident with the *abaya* is all yours. Please be assured that if you had toppled into the ocean I would have arrived there ahead of you.'

'But not before me, I think,' another voice intruded. It was very satisfying to hear the impatience in Hassan's tone. He was not a man who liked to be upstaged in any way, which was what Leona had allowed Rafiq to do. 'Leona, come out of the sun,' he instructed. 'Allowing yourself to burn because you are angry is the fool's choice.'

Leona didn't move but Rafiq did. In two strides he was standing right beside her and quite effectively blocking her off from the sun with his impressive shadow.

Which only helped to irritate Hassan all the more. 'Your reason for being up here had better be a good one, Rafiq,' he said grimly.

'Most assuredly,' the other man replied. 'Sheikh Abdul begs an urgent word with you.'

Hassan's smile was thin. 'Worried, is he?'

'Protecting his back,' Rafiq assessed.

'Sheikh Abdul can wait until I have eaten my breakfast.' Levering himself away from the yacht's rail, he walked back to the breakfast table. 'Leona, if you are not over here by the time Rafiq leaves you will not like the consequences.'

'Threats now?' she threw at him.

'Tell the sheikh I will speak to him later,' he said, ignoring her remark to speak to Rafiq.

Rafiq hesitated, stuck between two loyalties and clearly unsure which one to heed. He preferred to stay by Leona's side until she decided to leave the sun, but he also needed to deliver Hassan's message; so a silence dropped and tension rose. Hassan picked up the coffee pot and poured himself a cup while he waited. He was testing the faith of a man who had only ever given him his absolute loyalty, and that surprised and dismayed Leona because, tough and cold though she knew Hassan could be on occasion, she had never known him to challenge Rafiq in this way.

In the end she took the pressure off by stepping beneath the shade of the awning. Rafiq bowed and left. Hassan sent her a brief smile. 'Thank you,' he said.

'You didn't have to challenge him like that,' she admonished. 'It was an unfair use of your authority.'

'Perhaps,' he conceded. 'But it served its purpose.'

'The purpose of reminding him of his station in life?'

'No, the purpose of making you remember yours.' He threw her a hard glance. 'We both wield power in our way, Leona. You have just demonstrated your own by giving Rafiq the freedom to leave with his pride intact.'

He was right, though she didn't like being forced to realise it.

'You can be so cruel sometimes.' She released the words on a sigh. To her surprise Hassan countered it with a laugh.

'You call me cruel when you have just threatened him with a wife? He has a woman,' he confided, coming to stand right behind her. 'A black-haired, ruby-eyed, golden-skinned Spaniard.' Reaching round with his hands, he slipped free the single button holding her jacket shut, then began to remove the garment. 'She dances the flamenco and famously turns up men's temperature gauges with her delectably seductive style.' His lips brushed the slender curve of her newly exposed shoulder. 'But Rafiq assures me that nothing compares to what she unleashes when she dances only for him.'

'You've seen her dance?' Before she could stop herself, Leona had turned her head and given him just what he had been aiming for, she realised, too late to hide the jealous green glow in her eyes.

A sleek dark brow arched, dark eyes taunting her with his

answer. 'You like to believe you can set me free but you are really so possessive of me that I can feel the chains tightening, not slackening.'

'And you are so conceited.' She tried to draw back the green eyed monster.

'Because I like the chains?' he quizzed, and further disarmed her.

It wasn't fair, Leona decided; he could seduce her into a mess of confusion in seconds: Ethan, the launch, her sense of righteous indignation at the way she was being manipulated at just about every turn; she was in real danger of becoming lost in the power he had over her. She tried to break free from it. From *her* chains, she recognised.

'I prefer tea to coffee,' she murmured, aiming her concentration at the only neutral thing she could find, which was the table set for breakfast.

The warm sound of his laughter was in recognition of her diversion tactics. Then suddenly he wasn't laughing, he was releasing a gasp of horror. 'You are bruised!' he claimed, sending her gaze flittering to the slight discolouring to her right shoulder that she had noticed herself in the shower earlier.

'It's nothing.' She tried to dismiss it.

But Hassan was already turning her round and his black eyes were hard as they began flashing over every other exposed piece of flesh he could see. 'Me, or the fall?' he demanded harshly.

'The fall, of course.' She frowned, because she couldn't remember a single time in all the years they had been together that Hassan had ever marked her, either in passion or anger, yet he had gone so pale she might have accused him of beating her.

'Any more?' he asked tensely.

'Just my right hip, a little,' she said, holding her tongue about the sore spot at the side of her head, because she could see he wasn't up to dealing with that information. '—Hassan, will you stop it?' she said gasping when he dropped down in front of her and began to unfasten her white trousers. 'It isn't that bad!'

He wasn't listening. The trousers dropped, his fingers were already gently lifting the plain white cotton of her panty line out of the way so he could inspect for himself. 'I am at your feet,' he said in pained apology.

'I can see that,' she replied with a tremor in her voice that had more to do with shock than the humour she'd tried to inject into it. His response was so unnecessary and so very enthralling. 'Just get up now and let me dress,' she pleaded. 'Someone might come, for goodness' sake!'

'Not if they value their necks,' he replied, but at least he began to slide her trousers back over her slender hip-bones.

It had to be the worst bit of timing that Faysal should choose that moment to make one of his silent appearances. Leona was covered—just—but it did not take much imagination for her to know what Faysal must believe he was interrupting. The colour that flooded her cheeks must have aided that impression. Hassan went one further and rose up like a cobra.

'This intrusion had better be worth losing your head for!' he hissed.

For a few awful seconds Leona thought the poor man was going to prostrate himself in an agony of anguish. He made do with a bow to beat all bows. 'My sincerest apologies,' he begged. 'Your most honourable father, Sheikh Khalifa, desires immediate words with you, sir.'

Anyone else and Hassan would have carried out his threat, Leona was sure. Instead his mouth snapped shut, his hands took hold of her and dumped her rudely into a chair.

'Faysal, my wife requires tea.' He shot Leona's own diversion at the other man. Glad of the excuse to go, Faysal almost ran. To Leona he said, 'Eat,' but he wasn't making eye contact, and the two streaks of colour he was wearing on his cheekbones almost made her grin because it was so rare that anyone saw Sheikh Hassan Al-Qadim disconcerted.

'You dare,' he growled, swooping down and kissing her

twitching mouth, then he left quickly with the promise to return in moments.

But moments stretched into minutes. She ate one of the freshly baked rolls a white liveried steward had brought with a pot of tea, then drank the tea—and still Hassan did not return.

Eventually Rafiq appeared with another formal bow and Hassan's apologies. He was engaged in matters of state.

Matters of state she understood having lived before with Hassan disappearing for hours upon end to deal with them.

'Would you mind if I joined you?' Rafiq then requested.

'Orders of state?' she quizzed him dryly.

His half-smile gave her an answer. Her half-smile accompanied her indication to an empty chair. She watched him sit, watched him hunt around for something neutral to say that was not likely to cause another argument. There was no such thing, Leona knew that, so she decided to help him out.

'Tell me about your Spanish mistress,' she invited.

It was the perfect strike back for sins committed against her. Rafiq released a sigh and dragged the *gutrah* from his head, then tossed it aside. This was a familiar gesture for a man of the Al-Qadim household to use. It could convey many things: weariness, anger, contempt or, as in this case, a relayed throwing in of the towel. 'He lacks conscience,' he complained.

'Yet you continue to love him unreservedly, Rafiq, son of Khalifa Al-Qadim,' she quietly replied.

An eyebrow arched. Sometimes, in a certain light, he looked so like Hassan that they could have been twins. But they were not. 'Bastard son,' Rafiq corrected in that proud way of his. 'And you continue to love him yourself, so we had best not throw those particular stones,' he advised.

Rafiq had been born out of wedlock to Sheikh Khalifa's beautiful French mistress, who'd died giving birth to him. The fact that Hassan had only been six months old himself at the time of Rafiq's birth should have made the two half-brothers bitter enemies as they grew up together, one certain of his high place in life, the other just as certain of what would never be his. Yet in truth the two men could not have been closer if they'd shared the same mother. As grown men they had formed a united force behind which their ailing father rested secure in the knowledge that no one would challenge his power while his sons were there to stop them. When Leona came along, she too had been placed within this ring of protection.

Strange, she mused, how she had always been surrounded by strong men for most of her life: her father, Ethan, Rafiq and Hassan; even Sheikh Khalifa, ill though he now was, had always been one of her faithful champions.

'Convince him to let me go,' she requested quietly.

Ebony eyes darkened. 'He had missed you.'

So did green. 'Convince him,' she persisted.

'He was lonely without you.'

This time she had to swallow across the lump those words helped to form in her throat before she could say, 'Please.'

Rafiq leaned across the table, picked up one of her hands and gave it a squeeze. 'Subject over,' he announced very gently.

And it was. Leona could see that. It didn't so much hurt to be stonewalled like this but rather brought it more firmly home to her just how serious Hassan was.

Coming to his feet, Rafiq pulled her up with him. 'Where are we going?' she asked.

'For a tour of the boat in the hopes that the diversion will restrain your desire to weaken my defences.'

'Huh,' she said, for the day had not arrived when anyone could weaken Rafiq in any way involving his beloved brother. But she did not argue the point about needing a diversion.

He turned to collect his *gutrah*. The moment it went back on his head, the other Rafiq reappeared, the proud and remote man. 'If you would be so good as to precede me, my lady. We will collect a hat from your stateroom before we begin…'

Several hours later she was lying on one of the sun loung-
ers on the shade deck, having given in to the heat and
changed into a black and white patterned bikini teamed with
a cool white muslin shirt. She had been shown almost every
room the beautiful yacht possessed, and been formally introduced to Captain Tariq Al-Bahir, the only other Arab as far
as she could tell in a twenty-strong crew of Spaniards. This
had puzzled her enough to question it. But 'Expediency,' had
been the only answer Rafiq would offer before it became
another closed subject.

Since then she had eaten lunch with Rafiq and Faysal, and
had been forced, because of Faysal's presence, to keep a lid
on any other searching questions that might be burning in
her head, which had been Rafiq's reason for including the
other man, she was sure. And not once since he'd left her at
the breakfast table had she laid eyes on Hassan—though she
knew exactly where he was. Left alone to lie in the softer
heat of the late afternoon, she was free to imagine him in
what would be a custom built office, dealing with *matters of
state*.

By phone, by fax, by internet—her mouth moved on a
small smile. Hyped up, pumped up and doing what he loved
to do most and in the interim forgetting the time and forgetting her! At other times she would have already been in
there *reminding* him that there was a life other than *matters
of state*. Closing her eyes, she could see his expression: the
impatient glance at her interruption; the blank look that followed when she informed him of the time; the complaining
sigh when she would insist on him stopping to share a cup
of coffee or tea with her; and the way he would eventually
surrender by reaching for her hand, then relaxing with a contented sigh...

In two stuffed chairs facing the window in his palace office—just like the two stuffed chairs strategically placed in
the yacht's stateroom. Her heart gave a pinch; she tried to
ignore what it was begging her to do.

*   *   *

Hassan was thinking along similar lines as he lay on the lounger next to hers. She was asleep. She didn't even know he was here. And not once in all the hours he had been locked away in his office had she come to interrupt.

Had he really expected her to? he asked himself. The answer that came back forced him to smother a hovering sigh because he didn't want to make a noise and waken her. They still had things to discuss, and the longer he put off the evil moment the better, as far as he was concerned, because he was going to get tough and she was not going to like it.

Another smothered sigh had him closing his eyes as he reflected back over the last few hours in which he had come as close as he had ever done to causing a split between the heads of the different families which together formed the Arabian state of Rahman.

Dynastic politics, he named it grimly. Al-Qadim and Al-Mukhtar against Al-Mahmud and Al-Yasin, with his right to decide for himself becoming lost in the tug of war. In the end he had been forced into a compromise that was no compromise at all—though he had since tried to turn it into one with the help of an old friend.

Leona released the sigh he had been struggling to suppress, and Hassan opened his eyes in time to see her yawn and stretch sinuously. Long and slender, sensationally curved yet exquisitely sleek. The colour of her hair, the smoothness of her lovely skin, the perfectly proportioned contours of her beautiful face. The eyes he could not see, the small straight nose that he could, the mouth he could feel against his mouth merely by looking at it. And—

Be done with it, he thought suddenly, and was on his feet and bending to scoop her into his arms.

She awoke with a start, saw it was him and sent him a sleepy frown. 'What are you doing?' she protested. 'I was comfortable there—'

'I know,' he replied. 'But I wish to be comfortable too, and I was not.'

He was already striding through the boat with a frown that

was far darker than hers. Across the foyer, up the three shallow steps. 'Open the door,' he commanded and was surprised when she reached down and did so without argument. He closed it with the help of a foot, saw her glance warily towards the bed. But it was to the two chairs that he took her, set her down in one of them, then lowered himself into the other with that sigh he had been holding back for so long.

'I suppose you have a good reason for moving me here,' she prompted after a moment.

'Yes,' he confirmed, and turned to look into those slumber darkened green eyes that tried so hard to hide her feelings from him but never ever quite managed to succeed. The wall of his chest contracted as he prepared himself for what he was about to say. 'You have been right all along.' He began with a confession. 'I am being pressured to take another wife...'

She should have expected it, Leona told herself as all hint of sleepy softness left her and her insides began to shake. She had always *known* it, so why was she feeling as if he had just reached out with a hand and strangled her heart? It was difficult to speak—almost impossible to speak—but she managed the burning question. 'Have you agreed?'

'No,' he firmly denied. 'Which is why you are here with me now—and more to the point, why you have to stay.'

Looking into his eyes, Leona could see that he was not looking forward to what he was going to say. She was right.

'A plot was conceived to have you abducted,' he told her huskily, 'the intention being to use your capture as a weapon with which to force my hand. When I discovered this I decided to foil their intentions by abducting you for myself.'

'Who?' she whispered, but had a horrible feeling she already knew the answer.

'Did the plotting? We are still trying to get that confirmed,' he said. 'But whoever it was they had their people watching your villa last night, waiting for Ethan and your father to leave for the party on the Petronades yacht. Once they had assured themselves that you were alone they meant to come in and take you.'

'Just like that,' she said shakily, and looked away from him as so many things began to fall into place. 'I felt their eyes on me,' she murmured. 'I knew they were there.'

'I suspected that you would do,' Hassan quietly commended. 'It is the kind of training we instilled into you that you never forget.'

'But this was different.' She got up, wrapped her arms around her body. 'I *knew* it felt different. I should have heeded that!'

'No—don't get upset.' Following suit, Hassan stood up and reached for her. She was as pale as a ghost and shaking like a leaf. 'My people were also there watching over you,' he assured. 'The car driver was my man, as was the man at the gate. I had people watching their people. There was not a single moment when you were not perfectly safe.'

'But to dislike me so much that they should *want* to take me!' Hurt beyond belief by that knowledge, Leona pushed him away, unwilling to accept his comfort. It had been hard enough to come to terms with it, when she'd believed he had snatched her back for his own purposes. But to discover now that he had done it because there was a plot against her was just too much to take. 'What is it with you people that you can't behave in a normal, rational manner?' she threw at him, eyes bright, hurt and accusing. 'You should have phoned *me* not my father!' she cried. 'You should have agreed to a divorce in the first place, then none of this would have happened at all!'

The *you people* sent Hassan's spine erect; the mention of divorce hardened his face. 'You are one of *my people*,' he reminded her curtly.

'No, I am not!' she denied with an angry shake of her head. 'I am just an ordinary person who had the misfortune to fall in love with the *extra*ordinary!'

'At least you are not going back to denying you love this

extraordinary person,' he noted arrogantly. 'And stop glaring at me like that!' he snapped. 'I am not your enemy!'

'Yes, you are!' Oh, why had she ever set eyes on this man? It would have been so much easier to have lived her life without ever having known him! 'So what happens now?' she demanded. 'Where do we go from here? Do I spend the rest of my days hiding from dark strangers just because you are too stubborn to let me go?'

'Of course not.' He was standing there frowning impatiently. 'Stop trying to build this into more than it actually is—'

More? 'Don't you think it is enough to know that I wasn't safe to be walking the streets in San Estéban? That my life and my basic human rights can be reduced to being worth nothing more than a mere pawn in some wretched person's power game?'

'I am sorry it has to come to this—'

Well, that just wasn't good enough! 'But you are no better yourself!' she threw at him angrily. 'Up to now you've used abduction, seduction and now you've moved onto intimidation to bring the wayward wife into line.' She listed. 'Should I be looking for the hidden cameras you are using so that you can show all of Rahman what a strong man you can be? Do I need to smile now?' she asked, watching his face grow darker with the sarcasm she tossed at him—and she just didn't care! 'Which way?' she goaded. 'Do I need to let Rafiq shroud me in an *abaya* again and even go as far as to abase myself at your exalted feet just to save your wretched face?'

'Say any more and you are likely to regret it,' he warned very grimly.

'I regret knowing you already!' Her eyes flashed, her body shook and her anger sparkled in the very air surrounding her. 'Next I suppose you will have me thrown into prison until I learn to behave myself!'

'This is it—' he responded, spreading his arms out wide in what was an outright provocation. 'Your prison. Now stop shouting at me like some undignified fishwife,' he snapped. 'We need to—'

'I want my life back without you in it!' Leona cut loudly across him.

What she got was the prince. The face, the eyes, his mood and his manner changed with the single blink of his long dark eyelashes. When his shoulders flexed it was like a dangerous animal slowly raising its hackles, and the fine hairs on her body suddenly became magnetised as she watched the metamorphosis take place. Her breathing snagged; her throat grew tight. He was standing perhaps three yards away from her but she could suddenly feel his presence as deeply as if he was a disturbing inch away.

'You want to live your life without me, then you may do so,' he announced. 'I will let you go, give you your divorce. There, it is done. *Inshallah.*' With a flick of the hand he strode across the room and calmly ordered tea!

It was retaliation at its most ruthless and it left her standing there utterly frozen with dismay. *Inshallah.* She couldn't even wince at what that single word represented. The will of Allah. Acceptance. A decision. The end. Hassan was agreeing to let her go and she could neither move nor breathe as the full power of that decree made its stunning impact.

She had not deserved that, Hassan was thinking impatiently as he stood glaring down at the telephone. She had been shocked, angry, hurt. Who would not be when they discovered that people they cared about, people they had tried to put before themselves, had been plotting to use them ruthlessly in a nasty game called politics? She had every right to vent her feelings—he had expected it! It was the reason why he had found them privacy before telling her the truth!

Or part of the truth, he then amended, all too grimly aware that there was yet more to come. But the rest was going to have to wait for a calmer time, for this moment might be silent but it certainly was not calm, because—

Damn it, despite the sensible lecture he was angry! There

was not another person on this planet who dared to speak to him as she had just done, and the hell if he was going to apologise for responding to that!

He flicked a glance at her. She hadn't moved. If she was even breathing he could see no evidence of it. Her hair was untidy. Long silken tendrils had escaped from the band she'd had it tied up in all day and were now caressing her nape, framing her stark white profile to add a vulnerability to her beauty that wrenched hard on his heart-strings. Her feet were bare, as were her slender arms and long slender legs. And she was emulating a statue again, only this time instead of art-deco she portrayed the discarded waif.

He liked the waif. His body quickened; another prohibited sigh tightened his chest. Curiosity replaced anger, though pride held his arrogant refusal to be the first one to retract his words firmly in place. She moved him like no other woman. She always had done. Angry or sad, hot with searing passion or frozen like ice as she was now.

Inshallah. It was Allah's will that he loved this woman above all others. Let her go? Not while he had enough breath in his body to fight to hold onto what was his! Though he wished he could see evidence that there was breath inside hers.

He picked up an ornament, measured the weight of the beautifully sculpted smooth sandstone camel then put it back down again to pick up another one of a falcon preparing to take off on the wing. And all the time the silence throbbed like a living pulse in the air all around them.

Say something—talk to me, he willed silently. Show me that my woman is still alive in there, he wanted to say. But that pride again was insisting he would not be the one to break the stunning deadlock they were now gripped in.

The light tap at the door meant the ordered tea he didn't even want had arrived. It was a relief to have something to do. She didn't move as he went to open the door, still hadn't moved when he closed it again on the steward he'd left firmly outside. Carrying the tray to the low table, he put it down, then turned to look at her. She still hadn't moved.

Inshallah, he thought again, and gave up the battle. Walking over to her, he placed a hand against her pale cheek, stroked his thumb along the length of her smooth throat then settled it beneath her chin so he could lift her face up that small inch it required to make her look at him.

Eyes of a lush dark vulnerable green gazed into sombre night-dark brown. Her soft mouth parted; at last she took a breath he could hear and see. 'Be careful what you wish for,' she whispered helplessly.

His legs went hollow. He understood. It was the way it had always been with them. 'If true love could be made to order, we would still be standing here,' he told her gravely.

At which point the ice melted, the gates opened and in a single painfully hopeless move she coiled her arms around his neck, buried her face into his chest and began to weep.

So what do you do with a woman who breaks her heart for you? You take her to bed. You wrap her in yourself. You make love to her until it is the only thing that matters any more. Afterwards, you face reality again. Afterwards you pick up from where you should never have let things go astray.

The tea stewed in the pot. Evening settled slowly over the room with a display of sunset colours that changed with each deepening stage of their sensual journey. Afterwards, he carried her into the shower and kept reality at bay by loving her there. Then they washed each other, dried each other, touched and kissed and spoke no words that could risk intrusion for as long as they possibly could.

It was Leona who eventually approached reality. 'What now?' she asked him.

'We sail the ocean on our self-made island, and keep the rest of the world out,' he answered huskily.

'For how long?'

'As long as we possibly can.' He didn't have the heart to

tell her he knew exactly how long. The rest would wait, he told himself.

It was a huge tactical error, though he did not know that yet. For he had not retracted what he had decreed in a moment of anger. And, although Leona might appear to have set the words aside, she had not forgotten them. Nor had she forgotten the reason she was here at all: there were people out there who wanted to harm her.

But for now they pretended that everything was wonderful. Like a second honeymoon in fact—if an unusual one with Rafiq and Faysal along for company. They laughed a lot and played like any other set of holidaymakers would. Matters of state took a back seat to other more pleasurable pursuits. They windsurfed off the Greek islands, snorkelled over shipwrecks, jet-skied in parts of the Mediterranean that were so empty of other human life that they could have had the sea to themselves.

One week slid stealthily into a second week Leona regained the weight she had lost during the empty months without Hassan, and her skin took on a healthy golden hue. When matters of state refused to be completely ignored, Rafiq was always on hand to help keep up the pretence that everything was suddenly and miraculously okay.

Then it came. One heat-misted afternoon when Hassan was locked away in his office, and Faysal, Leona and Rafiq were lazing on the shade deck sipping tall cool drinks and reading a book each. She happened to glance up and received the shock of her life when she saw that they were sailing so close to land it felt as if she could almost reach out and touch it.

'Oh, good grief,' Getting up she went to stand by the rail. 'Where are we, Rafiq?'

'At the end of our time here alone together,' a very different voice replied.

CHAPTER SIX

LEONA turned to find Hassan was standing not far away and Rafiq was in the process of rising to his feet. One man was looking at her; the other one was making sure that he didn't. Hassan's words shimmered in the air separating them and Rafiq's murmured, 'Excuse me, I will leave you to it,' was as revealing as the speed with which he left.

The silence that followed his departure pulsed with the flurried pace of her heartbeat while Leona waited for Hassan to clarify what he had just said.

He was still in the same casual shorts and shirt he had been wearing when she had last seen him, she noticed. But there, the similarity between this man and the man who had kissed the top of her head and strolled away to answer Faysal's call to work a short hour ago ended. For there was a tension about him that was almost palpable, and in his hand he held a gold fountain pen which offered up an image of him getting up from his desk to come back here at such speed that he hadn't even had time to drop the pen.

'We arrived here sooner than I had anticipated,' he said, confirming her last thought.

'It would be helpful for me to know where *here* is,' she replied in a voice laden with the weight of whatever it was that was about to come at her.

And come it did. 'Port Said,' he provided, saw her startled response of recognition and lowered his eyes on an acknowledging grimace that more or less said the rest.

Port Said lay at the mouth of the Suez Canal, which linked the Mediterranean with the Red Sea. If they were coming into the port, then there could only be one reason for it:

Hassan was ready to go home and their self-made, sea-borne paradise was about to disintegrate.

He had noticed the pen in his hand and went to drop it on the lounger next to the book she had left there. Then he walked over to the long white table at which they had eaten most of their evening meals over the last two weeks. Pulling out a chair, he sat down, released a sigh, then put up a hand to rub the back of his neck as if he was trying to iron out a crick.

When he removed it again he stretched the hand out towards her. 'Join me,' he invited.

Leona shook her head and instead found her arms crossing tightly beneath the thrust of her breasts. 'Tell me first,' she insisted.

'Don't be difficult,' he censured. 'I want you here, within touching distance when I explain.'

But she didn't want to be within touching distance when he said what she knew he had to say. 'You are about to go home, aren't you?'

'Yes,' he confirmed.

It was all right challenging someone to tell you the truth when you did not mind the answer, but when you did mind it— 'So this is it,' she stated, finding a short laugh from somewhere that was not really a laugh at all. 'Holiday over...'

Out there the sun glistened on the blue water, casting a shimmering haze over the nearing land. It was hot but she was cold. It was bright but she was standing in darkness. The end, she thought. The finish.

'So, how are you going to play it?' she asked him. 'Do you drop me off on the quay in the clothes I arrived in and wave a poignant farewell as you sail away. Or have I earned my passage back to San Estéban?'

'What are you talking about?' Hassan frowned. 'You are my wife, yet you speak about yourself as a mistress.'

Which was basically how she had been behaving over the

last two weeks, Leona admitted to herself. '*Inshallah*,' she murmured.

The small sarcasm brought him back to his feet. As he strode towards her she felt her body quicken, felt her breasts grow tight and despised herself for being so weak of the flesh that she could be aroused by a man who was about to carry out his promise to free her. But six feet two inches of pedigree male to her five feet seven was such a lot to ignore when she added physical power into the equation, then included mental power and sexual power. It really was no wonder she was such a weakling where he was concerned.

And it didn't stop there, because he came to brace his hands on the rail either side of her, then pushed his dark face close up to hers. Now she could feel the heat of him, feel his scented breath on her face. She even responded to the ever-present sexual glow in his eyes though it had no right to be there—in either of them.

'A mistress knows when to keep her beautiful mouth shut and just listen. A wife does her husband the honour of hearing him out before she makes wildly inaccurate claims,' he said.

'You've just told me that our time here is over,' she reminded him with a small tense shrug of one slender shoulder. 'What else is there left for you to say?'

'What I said,' he corrected, 'was that our time here *alone* was over.'

The difference made her frown. Hassan used the moment to shift his stance, grasp both of her hands and pry them away from the death grip they had on her arms. Her fingers left marks where they had been clinging. He frowned at the marks and sighed at her pathetically defiant face. Then, dropping one of her hands, he turned and pulled her over to the table, urged her down into the chair he had just vacated and, still without letting go of her other hand, pulled out a second chair upon which he sat down himself.

He drew the chair so close to her own that he had to spread his thighs wide enough to enclose hers. It was a very effective way to trap his audience, especially when he leaned forward and said, 'Now, listen, because this is important and I will not have you diverting me by tossing up insignificant comments.'

It was automatic that she should open her mouth to question that remark. It was predictable, she supposed, that Hassan should stop her by placing his free hand across her parted lips. 'Shh,' he commanded, 'for I refuse to be distracted yet again because the anguish shows in your eyes each time we reach this moment, and your words are only weapons you use to try and hide that from me.'

'Omniscient' was the word that came to mind to describe him, she thought, as her eyes told him she would be quiet. His hand slid away from her face, leaving its warm imprint on her skin. He smiled a brief smile at her acquiescence, then went so very serious that she found herself holding onto her breath.

'You know,' he began, 'that above all things my father has always been your strongest ally, and it is for him that I am about to speak...'

The moment he mentioned Sheikh Khalifa her expressive eyes clouded with concern.

'As his health fails, the more he worries about the future of Rahman,' he explained. 'He frets about everything. You, me, what I will do if the pressures currently being brought to bear upon me force me to make a decision which could change the rule of Rahman.'

'You mean you have actually considered giving up your right to succession?' Leona gasped out in surprise.

'It is an option,' he confessed. 'And one which became more appealing after I uncovered the plot involving you, which was aimed to make me do as other people wish,' he added cynically. 'But for my father's sake I assured him that I am not about to walk away from my duty. So he decided to fret about my happiness if I am forced to sacrifice you for the sake of harmony, which places me in a frustrating no-win situation where his peace of mind is concerned.'

'I'm sorry,' she murmured.

'I don't want your sympathy, I want your help,' he stated with a shortness that told her how much he disliked having to ask. 'He loves you, Leona, you know that. He has missed you badly since you left Rahman.'

'I didn't completely desert him, Hassan.' She felt pushed into defending herself. 'I've spoken to him every day via the internet.' Even here on the yacht she had been using Faysal's computer each morning to access her e-mail. 'I even read the same books he is reading so that we can discuss them together. I—'

'I know,' Hassan cut in with a wry smile. 'What you say to him he relays to me, so I am fully aware that I am a bully and a tyrant, a man without principle and most definitely my father's son.'

'I said those things to tease a laugh out of him,' she defended.

'I know this too,' he assured her. 'But he likes to make me smile with him.' Reaching up, he stroked a finger along the flush of discomfort that had mounted her cheeks. 'And let me face it,' he added, removing the finger, 'your communication with him was far sweeter than your communication with me.'

He was referring to the letters he'd received from her lawyer. 'It was over between us. You should have left it like that.'

'It is not over between us, and I *cannot* leave it like that.'

'Your father—'

'Needs you,' he grimly inserted. '*I* need you to help me ease his most pressing concerns. So I am asking you for a full and open reconciliation of our marriage—for my father's sake if not for yours and mine.'

Leona wasn't a fool. She knew what he was *not* saying here. 'For how long?'

He offered a shrug. 'How long is a piece of string?' he posed whimsically. Then, because he could see that the answer was not enough, he dropped the whimsy, sat right back in his seat and told her curtly, 'The doctors give him two months—three at most. In that period we have been warned to expect a rapid deterioration as the end draws near. So I ask you to do this one thing for him and help to make his passage out of this world a gentle one...'

Oh, dear heaven, she thought, putting a hand up to her eyes as the full weight of what he was asking settled over her. How could she refuse? She didn't even want to refuse. She loved that old man as much as she loved her own father. But there were other issues here which had not been aired yet, and it was those that kept her agreement locked inside.

'The other wife they want for you,' she prompted, 'am I to appear to accept her imminent arrival also?'

His expression darkened. 'Do me the honour of allowing me some sensitivity,' he came back. 'I have no wish to sacrifice your face for my own face. And I find it offensive that you could suspect that I would do.'

Which was very fine and noble of him but— 'She is still there, hovering in the shadows, Hassan,' Leona said heavily. She could even put a name to the woman, though he probably didn't know that she could. 'And taking me back to Rahman does not solve your problems with the other family leaders unless you take that other wife.'

'The old ones and I have come to an agreement,' he informed her. 'In respect for my father, they will let the matter ride while he is still alive.'

'Then what?'

'I will deal with them when I have to, but for the next few months anyway, my father's peace of mind must come first.'

And so, he was therefore saying, should it for her. 'Will you do this?'

The outright challenge. 'Did you really think that I would not?' She sighed, standing up and pushing her chair away so that she could step around him.

'You're angry.' His eyes narrowed on her sparkling eyes and set expression.

Anger didn't nearly cover what she was really feeling. 'In principle I agree to play the doting wife again,' she said. 'But in fact I am now going to go away and *sulk* as you like to call it. Because no matter how well you wrap it all up in words of concern, Hassan, you are as guilty for using me in much the same way my foiled abductors intended to use me, and that makes you no better than them, does it?'

With that she turned and walked away, and Hassan allowed her to, because he knew she was speaking the truth so had nothing he could offer in his own defence.

Within seconds Rafiq appeared with a question written into the hard lines of his face.

'Don't ask,' he advised heavily. 'And she does not even know the half of it yet.'

'Which half does she not know,' Rafiq asked anyway.

'What comes next,' Hassan replied, watching his half-brother's eyes slide over his left shoulder. He spun to see what he was looking at, then began cursing when he saw how close they were to reaching their reserved berth in Port Said. 'How long?' he demanded.

'You have approximately one hour before the first guests begin to arrive.'

A small hour to talk, to soothe, to plead yet again for more charity from a woman who had given enough as it was. 'You had better prepare yourself to take my place, Rafiq,' he gritted. 'Because, at this precise moment, I am seriously considering jumping ship with my wife and forgetting I possess a single drop of Al-Qadim blood.'

'Our father may not appreciate such a decision,' Rafiq commented dryly.

'That reminder,' Hassan turned to snap, 'was not necessary.'

'I was merely covering for myself,' his half brother defended. 'For I have no wish to walk in your shoes, my lord Sheikh.'

About to go after Leona, Hassan paused. 'What do you wish for?' he questioned curiously.

'Ah.' Rafiq sighed. 'At this precise moment I wish for midnight, when I should be with *my* woman in a hotel room in Port Said. For tonight she flies in to dance for visiting royalty by special request. But later she will dance only for me and I will worship at her feet. Then I will worship other parts of her until dawn, after which I will reluctantly return here, to your exalted service, my lord sheikh,' he concluded with a mocking bow.

Despite the weight of his mood, Hassan could not resist a smile. 'You should change your plans and bring her to dinner,' he suggested. 'The sheer sensation she would cause would be a diversion I would truly appreciate.'

'But would Leona?' Rafiq pondered.

Instantly all humour died from Hassan's face. 'Leona,' he predicted. 'is in no frame of mind to appreciate anything.'

And on that grim reminder, he went off to find *his* woman, while half wishing that he was the one treading in Rafiq's shoes.

He found her without difficulty, shut behind the bathroom door and hiding in the steam being produced by the shower. The fact that she had not bothered to lock the door spoke volumes as to her mood. Hassan could visualise the angry way she would have walked in here, throwing the door shut behind her then taking the rest of her anger out on the heap of clothes he could see tossed onto the floor.

So what did he do now? Go back to the bedroom and wait for her to reappear, or did he throw caution to the wind, strip off and just brave her fiery den?

It was not really a question since he was already taking off his clothes. For this was no time to be feeble. Leona had agreed *in principle*, so now she was about to learn the consequences of that. With a firming of his mouth he opened the shower-cubicle door, stepped inside and closed it again.

She was standing just out of reach of the shower jets with her head tipped back as she massaged shampoo into her hair. Streams of foaming bubbles were sliding over wet gold skin, collecting around the tips of her tilted breasts and snaking through the delightful valley in between to pool in the perfect oval of her navel, before spilling out to continue their way towards the chestnut cluster marking the apex with her slender thighs.

His body awoke; he allowed himself a rueful smile at how little it took to make him want this beautiful creature. Then she realised he was there and opened her eyes, risking soap burn so that she could kill him with a look.

'What do you want now?' she demanded.

Since the answer to that question was indubitably obvious, he didn't bother with a reply. Instead he reached for the container of foaming body soap, pumped a generous amount into the palm of his hand and began applying it to her skin. Her hands dropped from her hair and pressed hard against his chest in an effort to push him away.

'Thank you,' he said, and calmly pumped some soap onto his own chest as if it was a foregone conclusion that she would wash him. 'Sharing can turn the simplest of chores into the best of pleasures, do you not think?'

The green light in her eyes took on a distinctly threatening gleam. 'I think you're arrogant and hateful and I want you to get out of here,' she coldly informed him.

'Close your eyes,' he advised. 'The shampoo is about to reach them.'

Then, even as she lifted a hand to swipe the bubbles away, he reached up and directed the shower head at her so that the steamy spray hit her full in the face. While gasping at the shock, he made his next move, turned the spray away and replaced it with his mouth.

For a sweet, single moment he allowed himself to believe he'd made the easy conquest. It usually worked. On any other occasion it would have worked as a tasty starter to other ways of forgetfulness. But this time he received a sharp dig in the ribs for his optimism, and a set of teeth closed threateningly on his bottom lip until he eased the pressure and lifted his head. Her eyes spat fire and brimstone at him.

He arched an eyebrow and glided a defiant hand down to the silken warmth of her abdomen.

'You are treading on dangerous ground, Sheikh,' she warned him.

'I am?'

She ignored the message in his tone. 'I have nothing I want to say to you. So why don't you leave me alone?'

'But I was not offering to talk,' he explained, and boldly slid the hand lower.

'You are not doing *that* either!' Squirming away like a slippery snake, she ended up pressed against the corner of the cubicle, eyes like green lasers trying their best to obliterate him. One arm was covering her breasts, the other hand was protecting other parts. She looked like some sweet, cowering virgin, but he was not fooled by the vision. This beautiful wife of his possessed a temper that could erupt without warning. At the moment it was merely simmering.

'Okay.' With an ease that threw her into frowning confusion, he conceded the battle to her, pumped more soap onto his chest and began to wash while trying to ignore the obvious fact that a certain part of him was as hard as a rock and begging he do something about it. 'We did not really have time, anyway. Our guests arrive in less than an hour...'

'Guests?' she looked up sharply. 'What guests?'

'The guests we are about to transport to Rahman to attend the anniversary of my father's thirtieth year of rule, which will take place in ten days' time,' he replied while calmly sluicing the soap from his body as if he had not dropped yet another bomb at her feet. 'Here.' He frowned. 'Wash the shampoo from your hair before you really do hurt your eyes.' And he stepped back to allow her access to the spray.

Leona didn't move; she didn't even notice that he had. She was too busy suffering from one shock too many. 'How long have you known you were taking on guests?'

'A while.' Reaching up to unhook the shower head from the wall, he then pulled her towards him to began rinsing the shampoo from her hair for himself.

'But you didn't feel fit to tell me before now?'

'I did not feel fit to do anything but enjoy being with you.' Pushing up her chin, he sent the slick, clean pelt of her hair sliding down her spine with the help of the shower jet. 'Why?' He asked a question of his own. 'Would knowing have had any bearing on your decision to come back to Rahman with me?'

Would it? Leona asked herself, when really she did not need to, because she knew her answer would have been the same. He was rinsing the rest of her now and she just stood there and let him do it. Only a few minutes ago his smallest touch had infused her with that need to feel him deep inside her, now she could not remember what the need felt like. As she waited for him to finish administering to her wooden form, she noticed that his passion had died too.

'I suppose I had better know if there is anything else you haven't bothered to tell me,' she murmured eventually.

His pause before speaking could have been a hesitation over his answer, or it could have been a simple pause while he switched off the shower. 'Just the names of our guests,' he said. 'And that can wait until we have dealt with the more urgent task of drying ourselves and getting dressed.'

With that he opened the shower door and stepped out to collect a towel, which he folded around her before offering her another one for her hair. For himself he reached for a towelling bathrobe, pulled it on and headed for the door.

'Hassan...' she made him pause '...the rest of this trip and your father's celebration party—am I being put on public show for a specific purpose?'

'Some people need to be shown that I will not be coerced in any way,' he answered without turning. 'And my father wants you there. This will be his last anniversary. I will deny him nothing.'

At Hassan's request, she was wearing a calf-length white silk tunic studded with pearl-white sequins that shimmered when she moved. In accordance with Arabian tradition, the tunic had a high neckline, long sleeves and a pair of matching slender silk trousers that covered her legs. On her head she had draped a length of fine silk, and beneath it her hair had been carefully pleated into a glossy, smooth coronet. Her make-up was so understated you could barely tell it was there except for the flick of black mascara highlighting the length of her eyelashes and the hint of a gloss to her soft pink mouth.

Beside her stood the Prince. Dressed in a white silk tunic and gold silk top robe, on his head he wore a white *gutrah* ringed by three circles of gold. To her other side and one short pace behind stood Rafiq, dressed almost exactly the same as his brother only without the bands of gold. And as they waited in the boat's foyer, Leona was in no doubt that the way they were presented was aimed to make a specific statement.

Sheikh Hassan ben Khalifa Al-Qadim and his wife the Sheikha Leona Al-Qadim—bestowed upon her at her request, for the woman of Arabia traditionally kept their father's name—were ready to formally receive guests, whether those guests were friends or foes.

Rafiq was their guardian, their protector, their most respected brother and trusted friend. He possessed his own title, though he had never been known to use it. He possessed the right to wear the gold bands of high office, but no one had ever seen them circling his head. His power rode on the back of his indifference to anything that did not interest him. His threat lay in the famed knowledge that he would lay down his life for these two people standing in front of him, plus the father he loved without question.

His presence here, therefore, made its own loud statement; come in friendship and be at peace; come in conflict and beware.

Why? Because the first person to tread the gangway onto the yacht was Sheikh Abdul Al-Yasin and his wife, Zafina. Hassan and Rafiq knew that Sheikh Abdul was behind the plot to abduct Leona, but the sheikh did not know the brothers knew. Which was why he felt safe in taking the bait handed out for this trip—namely a meeting of the chiefs during a cruise on the Red Sea, in which his aim was to beat Hassan into submission about this second wife he was being so stubborn in refusing.

What none of them knew was that Leona suspected it was Sheikh Abdul who had planned her abduction. Because she knew about Nadira, his beautiful daughter, who had been held up to her many times as the one chosen to take that coveted place in Sheikh Hassan's life as his second wife.

'Ah—Hassan!' The two men greeted and shook hands pleasantly enough. 'You will be pleased to know that I left your father in better sorts than of late. I saw him this morning before I caught my flight to Cairo.'

'I must thank you for keeping him company while we have been away,' Hassan replied.

'No thanks—no thanks.' Sheikh Abdul refused them. 'It was my privilege—Leona...' He turned towards her next, though offered no physical contact as was the Arab way. He bowed instead. 'You have been away too long. It is good to see you here.'

'Thank you.' She found a smile, wished she dared search for the comfort of Hassan's hand, but such shows of weakness would be pounced upon and dissected when she was not there to hear it happen.

'Rafiq.' His nodded greeting was distinctly wary. 'You made a killing with your stock in Schuler-Kleef, I see.'

'My advice is usually sound, sir,' Rafiq replied respectfully. 'I take it you did not buy some for yourself?'

'I forgot.'

Through all of this, Sheikh Abdul's wife, Zafina, stood back in total silence, neither stepping forward to follow the line of introduction nor attempting to remind her husband of her presence. It was such a quiescent stance, one that Leona had grown used to from the women of Rahman when they were out in the company of their men.

But it was a quiescence that usually only lasted as long as it took them to be alone with the other women. Then the real personalities shot out to take you by surprise. Some were soft and kind, some cold and remote, some alive with fun. Zafina was a woman who knew how to wield her power from within the female ranks and had no hesitation in doing so if it furthered her own particular cause. It was due to her clever machinations that her son had married another sheikh's most favoured daughter.

She'd had Hassan marked for her daughter, Nadira, from the day the child had been born. Therefore, in her eyes, she had every reason to dislike Leona. And, tranquil though she might appear right now, Leona could feel resentment flowing towards her in waves.

'Zafina.' She stepped forward, deciding to take the polite stand. 'You are well, I trust? Thank you for taking time out of your busy life to join us here.'

'The pleasure is all mine, Sheikha,' the older woman replied. But then her husband was listening and so was the coveted Sheikh Hassan. 'You have lost weight, I think. But Sheikh Khalifa tells me you have been sick?'

Someone had told her at any rate, but Leona suspected it was not Hassan's father. Thankfully other guests began to arrive. Sheikh Jibril Al-Mahmud and his timid wife, Medina, who looked to her husband before she dared so much as breathe.

Sheikh Imran Al-Mukhtar and his youngest son, Samir, arrived next. Like a light at the end of a tunnel, Samir put the first genuine smile on everyone's face because he broke right through every stiff convention being performed in the yacht's foyer, and headed directly for Leona. 'My princess!' he greeted, picked her up in his arms then swung her around.

'Put her down,' his father censured. 'Rafiq has that glint in his eye.'

'Not Hassan?' Samir questioned quizzically.

'Hassan knows what belongs to him, Rafiq is merely over-protective. And everyone else simply disapproves of your loose ways.'

And there it was, tied up in one neat comment, Hassan

noted as he watched Leona laugh down into Samir's handsome young face. Al-Qadim and Al-Mukhtar set apart from Al-Mahmud and Al-Yasin. It promised to be an interesting trip. For the first time in two weeks they used the formal dining room on the deck above. White-liveried stewards served them through many courses, and the conversation around the table was pleasant and light, mainly due to Samir, who refused to allow the other men to sink into serious discussion, and even the other women unbent beneath his boyish charm.

But Leona was quiet. From his end of the table Hassan watched her speak when spoken to, smiling in all the right places. He watched her play the perfect hostess in that easy, unassuming way he remembered well, where everyone's needs were predicted and met before they knew they were missing something. But occasionally, when she thought no one was attending her, he watched the corners of her mouth droop with short releases of the tension she was experiencing.

Sad. Her eyes were sad. He had hurt her with his dripping-tap method of feeding information to her. Now here she sat, having to pretend everything was perfect between them, when really she wanted to kill him for waiting until the last minute to spring all of this.

His heart clenched when he caught sight of her impulsive grin as she teasingly cuffed Samir for saying something outrageous. She had not laughed with him like that since the first night they'd been together again. No matter how much she had smiled, played, teased—loved him—during the last two weeks, he had been aware of an inner reserve that told him he no longer had all of her. Her spirit was missing, he named it grimly. It had been locked away out of his reach.

I love you, he wanted to tell her. But loving did not mean much to a woman who felt that she was trapped between a rock and a hard place.

A silence suddenly reigned. It woke him up from his own thoughts to notice that Leona was staring down at the plate in front of her and Samir had frozen in dismay. What had he missed? What had been said? Muscles began tightening all over him. Rafiq was looking at him for guidance. His skin began to crawl with the horrible knowledge that he had just missed something supremely important, and he could not think of a single thing to say!

His half-brother took the initiative by coming to his feet. 'Leona, you will understand if I beg to leave you now,' he petitioned as smooth as silk, while Hassan, who knew him better than anyone, could see him almost pulsing with rage.

Leona's head came up as, with a flickering blink of her lashes, she made the mammoth effort to pull herself together. 'Oh, yes, of course, Rafiq,' she replied, having absolutely no idea, Hassan was sure, why Rafiq was excusing himself half-way through dinner, and at this precise moment she didn't care. It was a diversion. She needed the diversion. It should have been himself who provided it.

'I need a word before you leave,' he said to Rafiq, and got to his feet. 'Samir, do the honours and replenish my wife's glass with wine.'

The poor young man almost leapt at the wine bottle, relieved to have something to do. As Rafiq walked past Hassan, with a face like fury, Hassan saw Leona reach out and gently touch Samir's hand, as if to assure him that everything was all right.

'What did I miss in there?' he rapped out at Rafiq as soon as they were out of earshot.

'If I did not like Samir I would strangle him,' Rafiq responded harshly. 'Leona asked him how his mother was. He went into a long and humorous story about her sitting in wait for his sister to give birth. Leona dealt with that. She even laughed in all the right places. But then the fool had to suggest it was time that she produced your son and heir.'

'He cannot have known what he was saying,' Hassan said angrily.

'It was not the question which threw Leona, it was the resounding silence that followed it and the bleak expression upon your face! Where were you, man?' Rafiq wanted to know. It was so rare that he used that tone with Hassan, that the censure in it carried twice the weight.

'My mind had drifted for a few seconds,' he answered tensely.

'And the expression?'

'Part of the drift,' he admitted heavily.

'You were supposed to be on the alert at all times for attacks of this kind.' Rafiq was not impressed. 'It was risk enough to bring onto this boat the man who wishes her ill, without you allowing your mind to drift.'

'Stop spitting words at my neck and go to your dancer,' Hassan snapped back impatiently. 'You know as well as I do that neither Abdul or Jibril would dare to try anything when they are here for the specific purpose of talking me round!'

It's okay, Leona was telling herself. I can deal with it. I've always known that deep inside he cared more than he ever let me see. So, he had been caught by surprise and showed the truth to everyone. *I* was caught by surprise and showed it myself.

'Samir,' she murmured gently. 'If you pour me any more wine I will be sozzled and fall over when I have to stand up.'

'Hassan wants your glass kept full.' He grimly kept on pouring.

'Hassan was attempting to fill an empty gap in the conversation, not put me under the table,' she dryly pointed out.

Samir sat back with a sigh. 'I want to die a thousands deaths,' he heavily confessed.

Hassan arrived back at the table. Leona felt his glance sear a pointed message at her down the table's length. She refused to catch his eye, and smiled and smiled until her jaw ached.

After that, the rest of the dinner passed off without further incident. But by the time the ladies left the men alone and removed to the adjoining salon Leona was in no mood for a knife-stabbing session. So she was actually relieved that Medina and Zafina chose to stab at her indirectly by discussing Zafina's daughter, Nadira, whose beauty, it seemed, had multiplied during the last year. And as for her grace and quiet gentle ways—she was going to make some lucky man the perfect wife one day.

At least they didn't prose on about how wonderful she was with children, Leona thought dryly, as the conversation was halted when Hassan brought the men through within minutes of the ladies leaving them.

The evening dragged on. She thought about the other days and nights still to come and wondered if she was going to get through them all in one piece. Eventually the other two women decided they were ready to retire. A maid was called and within minutes of them leaving Leona was happy to follow suit. As she stepped outside, Hassan joined her. It was the first time he had managed to get her alone since the incident at the dinner table.

'I am at your feet,' he murmured contritely. 'I was miles away and had no idea what had taken place until Rafiq explained it to me.'

She didn't believe him, but it was nice of him to try the cover-up, she supposed. 'Samir wins hands down on apologies,' she came back. 'He wants to die a thousands deaths.'

With that she walked away, shaking inside and not really sure why she was. She got ready for bed and crawled between the cool cotton sheets, sighed, punched the pillow, then attempted to fall asleep. She must have managed it, because the next thing she knew a warm body was curling itself in behind her.

'I don't recall our new deal involving having to share a bed,' she said coldly.

'I don't recall offering to sleep elsewhere,' Hassan coolly returned. 'So go back to sleep.' The arm he folded around her aimed to trap. 'And, since I am as exhausted as you are, you did not need the silk pyjamas to keep my lecherous desires at bay...'

'I really hate you sometimes.' She wanted the last word.

'Whereas I will love you with my dying breath. And when they lay us in our final resting place in our crypt of gold it will be like this, with the scent of your beautiful hair against my face and my hand covering your lying little heart. There,' he concluded, 'is that flowery enough to beat Samir's one thousand deaths?'

Despite not wanting to, she giggled. It was her biggest mistake. The exhausted man became an invigorated man. His lecherous desires took precedence.

Did she try to stop him? No, she did not. Did she even want to? No, again. Did he know all of that before he started removing the pyjamas?' Of course he did. And there was something needle-piercingly poignant in this man losing touch with everything but this kind of loving as he came inside her, cupped her face with his hands and held her gaze with his own, as he drove them towards that other resting place.

CHAPTER SEVEN

MORNING came too soon, to Leona's regret. Although here, shut inside this room and wrapped in the relative sanctuary of Hassan's arms, she could let herself pretend for a little while longer that everything was perfect.

He was perfect, she observed tenderly as she studied the lean smooth lines of his dark golden face. He slept quietly—he always had done—lips parted slightly, black lashes lying still against the silken line of his cheekbones. Her heart began to squeeze and her stomach muscles joined in. This deep-rooted attraction he had always inspired in her had never diminished no matter what else had come in between.

She released a sigh that feathered his face and made his nose twitch. And it was such a nose, she thought with a smile, irresistibly reaching up to run a fingertip down its long silken length.

'Life can have its perfect moments,' a sleepy voice drawled.

Since she had been thinking much the same herself, Leona moved that bit closer so she could brush a kiss on his mouth.

Eyelashes drifted upward, revealing ebony irises packed with love. 'Does the kiss mean you have forgiven me for dropping all of this on you?'

'Shh,' she whispered, 'or you will spoil it.'

'Kiss me again, then,' he insisted. So she did. Why not? she asked herself. This was her man. Rightly or wrongly he was most definitely hers here and now.

It was a shame the ring of the telephone beside the bed had to intrude, or one thing would have led to another before they should have needed to face reality again. As it was, Hassan released a sigh and reached out to hook up the receiver. A few seconds later he was replacing it again and reaching out to touch her kiss-warmed mouth with a look of regret.

'Duty calls,' he murmured.

Ah, duty, Leona thought, and flopped heavily onto her back. Perfect moment over, pretence all gone. Stripped clean to his smooth dark golden skin, it was the prince who rose up from the bed and without saying another word disappeared into the bathroom.

He came out again ten minutes later, wrapped in fluffy white cotton and looking as handsome as sin. Wishing his pull wasn't as strong on her senses, she got up with a definite reluctance to face the day mirrored on her face, pulled on her wrap and went to take her turn in the bathroom.

But Hassan stopped her as she walked past him, his hand gently cupping her chin. He smelt of soap and minted toothpaste as he bent to kiss her cheek. 'Fifteen minutes, on the sun deck,' he instructed as he straightened again. 'For breakfast with an added surprise.'

The 'added surprise' made Leona frown. 'You promised me you had no more surprises waiting to jump out at me,' she protested.

'But this one does not count,' he said with a distinctly worrying gleam in his eye. 'So hurry up, wear something deliciously stylish that will wow everyone, and prepare yourself to fall on my neck.'

'Fall on his neck,' Leona muttered to herself as she showered. She had developed a distinct aversion to surprises since arriving on this wretched boat so she was more likely to strangle him.

In a pale blue sundress made of a cool cotton, and with her red hair floating loose about her shoulders—because she felt like wearing it as a banner, which made a statement about…something, though she wasn't absolutely sure what—Leona walked out onto the sun deck to find Rafiq there but no Hassan.

He looked up, smiled, then stood to pull out a chair for

her. He was back in what she called his off-duty clothes, loose-fitting black chinos and a white V-neck tee shirt that did things to his muscled shape no one saw when he was covered in Arab robes.

'Was your mother an Amazon, by any chance?' she enquired caustically, because his father was a fine boned little man and Rafiq had to have got his size from someone.

The waspishness in her tone earned her a sharp glance. 'Did you climb out of bed on the wrong side, by any chance?' he threw back.

'I *hate* surprises,' she announced as she sat down.

'Ah,' Rafiq murmured. 'So you have decided to take it out on me because I am unlikely to retaliate.'

He was right, and she knew it, which didn't help this terrible, restless tension she was suffering from. 'Where is Hassan?' She strove for a nicer tone and managed to half succeed. 'He said he would be here.'

'The pilot who will guide us through the Suez Canal has arrived,' Rafiq explained. 'It is an expected courtesy for Hassan to greet him personally.'

Glancing outwards, Leona saw Port Said sprawling out in front of them like a vast industrial estate. It was not the prettiest of views to have with your breakfast, even though they seemed to have got the best of the berths, moored way off to one side in a separate harbour that looked as if it was reserved for the luxury private crafts.

'And the rest of our guests?' she enquired next, aware that she probably should have asked about them first.

'Either still asleep or breakfasting in their suites.'

Mentioning sleep had a knock-on effect on him, and in the next moment Rafiq was stifling a yawn. It was only then that Leona recalled his slick retreat from the fray the evening before.

'Up all night?' The spike was back in her voice.

He didn't reply, but the rueful way his mouth tilted suddenly made her think of Spanish dancers. 'I hope she was good.' She took a tart stab in the dark.

'Delightful.' He smiled. It was yet another blow to her fragile ego that her one solid ally had deserted her last night for another woman. 'Here,' he said gently, and began to pour her out a cup of tea. 'Maybe this will help soothe your acid little tongue.'

Something needed to, Leona silently admitted as she picked up the cup. She had never felt so uptight and anxious, and it all was down to Hassan and surprises she did not want and people she did not want to be with and a marriage she did not—

The slightly sweet scent of Earl Grey suddenly turned her stomach. She must have gone pale because Rafiq began frowning. 'What is the matter?' he demanded.

'I think the milk must be off,' she explained, hastily putting the cup back on its saucer then pushing it away.

The sickly sensation left her almost as suddenly as it had hit. Problem solved in her mind, she wasn't convinced when Rafiq picked up the jug to sniff at the milk and announced, 'It seems fine to me.'

But he rose anyway and went to replace the milk with fresh from the cartons kept in the refrigerator situated just inside the salon. Then Hassan appeared and the incident was forgotten because, after dropping a kiss on her forehead, he went to pull out the chair next to Rafiq, who was just returning to the table with the fresh jug of milk. For a moment Leona was held captivated by how much alike the two men were. Even their clothes were similar, only Hassan wore beige chinos and a black tee shirt.

Men of beauty no matter what clothes they were wore, she mused a trifle breathlessly, knowing that she would be hard put to it to find two more perfect specimens. So why do I love them both so differently? she asked herself as she watched them sit down. Life would certainly have been a whole lot simpler if she'd fallen in love with Rafiq instead of Hassan. No strict calls to duty, no sheikhdom to rule, no onus to produce the next son and heir to his vast power and untold fortune.

But she loved Rafiq as a brother, not as a lover—just as he loved her as a sister. Plus, he had his mysterious dancer, she added wryly, as she poured herself another cup of tea in a clean cup, then reached for a slice of toast.

'You look pale. What's wrong?' Glancing up, she found Hassan's eyes were narrowed on her profile.

'She hates surprises.' Rafiq offered a reply.

'Ah. So I am out of favour,' Hassan drawled. 'Like the milk and the butter...' he added with the sharp eyes that should have been gold, like a falcon's, not a bottomless black that made her feel as if she could sink right into them and never have to come back out again.

'The milk was off, it turned my stomach, so I decided not to risk it or the butter,' she said, explaining the reason why she was sipping clear tea and nibbling on a piece of dry toast.

Keeping dairy produce fresh was an occupational hazard in hot climates, so Hassan didn't bother to question her answer—though Leona did a moment later when a pot of fresh coffee arrived for Hassan and the aroma sent her stomach dipping all over again.

Hassan saw the way she pushed her plate away and sat back in the chair with the paleness more pronounced, and had to ask himself if her pallor was more to do with anxiety than a problem with the milk. Maybe he should not be teasing her like this. Maybe no surprise, no matter how pleasant was going to merit putting her through yet more stress. He glanced at his watch. Ten more minutes. Was it worth him hanging on that long?

'You look stunning,' he murmured.

She turned her head, her wonderful hair floating out around her sun-kissed shoulders and the perfect heart-shape of her face. Her eyes were like emeralds, to match the one she wore on her finger, glowing with a passion she could never quite subdue no matter how low she was feeling. Kiss me, her small, soft, slightly sulky mouth seemed to say.

'I am *de trop*.' Rafiq broke through the moment and rose

to his feet. 'I will go and awaken Samir and drag him to the gym for an hour before I allow him breakfast.'

Neither bothered to answer even if they heard him, which Rafiq seriously doubted as he went to leave. Then a sound beyond the canvas awning caught his attention, diverting him towards the rail. A car was coming down the concrete quay towards them, its long black sleekly expensive lines giving him a good idea as to who was inside it.

This time he made sure he commanded attention by lightly touching Hassan's shoulder. 'Your surprise is arriving,' he told him, then left as Hassan stirred himself and Leona blinked herself back from wherever she had gone to.

Getting up, Hassan went to capture one of her hands and urged her out of her chair. 'Come,' he said, and keeping hold of her hand walked them down the stairs, across the foyer, out onto the shade deck and to the rail beside the gangway, just in time to watch a beautiful creature with pale blonde hair step out of the car and onto the quayside.

Beside him he felt Leona's breath catch on a gasp, felt the pulse in her wrist begin to race. 'Evie,' she whispered. 'And Raschid,' she added as Sheikh Raschid Al-Kadah uncoiled his long lean body out of the car.

'They're sailing with us?' Now her eyes were shining with true pleasure, Hassan noted with deep satisfaction. Now she was looking at him as if he was the most wonderful guy in the world, instead of the most painful to be around.

'Will their presence make your miserable lot easier to bear?'

Her reply was swift and uninhibited. She fell upon him with a kiss he would have given half of his wealth for. Though it did not need wealth, only the appearance of her closest friend and conspirator against these—arrogant Arabian men, as she and Evie liked to call Raschid and himself.

'After six years, I would have expected the unrestrained passion to have cooled a little,' a deep smooth, virtually accent-free voice mocked lazily.

'Says the man with his son clutched in one arm and his daughter cradled in the other,' mocked a lighter, drier voice.

Son and daughter. Hassan stiffened in shock, for he had not expected the Al-Kadahs to bring along their children on this cruise. Leona, on the other hand, was pulling away from him, turning away from him—hiding away from him? Had his pleasant surprise turned into yet another disaster? He turned to see what she was seeing and felt his chest tighten so fiercely it felt as if it was snapping in two. For there stood Raschid, as proud as any man could be, with his small son balanced on his arm while the beautiful Evie was in the process of gently relieving him of his small pink three-month-old daughter.

They began walking up the gangway towards them, and it was his worst nightmare unfolding before his very eyes, because there were tears in Leona's as she went to meet them. Real tears—bright tears when she looked down at the baby then up at Evangeline Al-Kadah before, with aching description, she simply took the other woman in her arms and held her.

Raschid was watching them, smiling, relaxed while he waited a few steps down the gangway for them to give him room to board the boat. He saw nothing painful in Leona's greeting, nor the way she broke away to gently touch a finger to the baby girl's petal soft cheek.

'I didn't know,' she was saying softly to Evie. 'Last time I saw you, you weren't even pregnant!'

'A lot can happen in a year,' Raschid put in dryly, bringing Leona's attention his way.

The tableau shifted. Evie moved to one side to allow her husband to step onto the deck so he could put his son to the ground, leaving his arms free to greet Leona properly. 'And aren't you just as proud as a peacock?' She laughed, defying the Arab male-female don't-touch convention by going straight into Raschid's arms.

What was wrong with Hassan? Leona wondered, realising that he hadn't moved a single muscle to come and greet their latest guests. She caught his eye over one of Raschid's broad shoulders, sent him a frowning look that told him to pull himself together. By the time he was greeting Evie Leona was squatting down to say hello to the little boy who now clutched his mother's skirt for safety. Dark like his father; golden-eyed like his father. The fates had been kind to these two people by allowing them to produce a son in Raschid's image and a daughter who already looked as if she was going to be a mirror of her mother.

'Hello, Hashim.' She smiled gently. They had met before but she was sure the small boy would not remember. 'Does that thumb taste very nice?'

He nodded gravely and stuck the thumb just that quarter inch further between sweetly pouting lips.

'My name is Leona,' she told him. 'Do you think we can be friends?'

'Red,' he said around the thumb, looking at her hair. 'Sunshine.'

'Thank you.' She laughed. 'I see you are going to be a dreadful flirt, like your papa.'

Mentioning his papa sent the toddler over to Raschid, where he begged to be picked up again. Raschid swung him up without pausing in his conversation with Hassan, as if it was the most natural thing in the world for him to have his son on his arm.

Tears hit again. Leona blinked them away. Hassan gave a tense shift of one shoulder and in the next moment his arm was resting across her shoulders. He was smiling at Evie, at her baby, at Raschid. But when Leona noticed that he was not allowing himself to so much as glance at Raschid's son it finally hit her what was the matter with him. Hassan could not bear to look at what Raschid had, that which he most coveted.

Her heart dropped to her stomach to make her feel sick again. The two men had been good friends since—for ever. Their countries lay side by side. And they shared so many similarities in their lives that Leona would have wagered everything that nothing could drive a wedge between their friendship.

But a desire for what one had that the other did not, in the shape of a boy-child, could do it, she realised, and had to move away from Hassan because she just couldn't bear to be near him and feel that need pulsing in him.

'May I?' she requested of Evie, holding out her arms for the baby.

Evie didn't hesitate in handing the baby over. Soft and light and so very fragile. It was like cradling an angel. 'How old is she?' she asked.

'Three months,' Evie supplied. 'As quiet as a mouse, as sweet as honey—and called Yamila Lucinda after her two grandmothers, but we call her Lucy because it's cute.'

At the sound of her mother's voice, Lucy opened her eyes to reveal two perfect amethysts the same as Evie's, and Leona found herself swallowing tears again.

You're so lucky, she wanted to say, but remarks like that were a potential minefield for someone in her situation. So she contented herself with lifting the baby up so she could feel her soft cheek against her own and hoped that no one noticed the small prick of tears she had to blink away.

A minute later and other guests began appearing on the shade deck to find out who else had joined them. Sheikh Raschid earned himself looks of wary surprise from some. From all he was awarded the respect accorded to a man who held absolute rule in his own Gulf state of Behran. His children brought down other barriers; the fact that Evie had achieved what Leona had not, in the shape of her small son, earned her warm smiles instead of stiffly polite ones that conveyed disapproval. Still, most of the tension from the evening before melted away in the face of the newcomers, and Leona was deeply grateful to them for succeeding in neutralising the situation.

When it was decided that they would move up to the sun deck, with its adjoining salon, to take refreshment and talk in comfort, Leona quickly shifted herself into hostess mode and led the way upstairs with her small bundle in her arms and her husband walking at her shoulder.

He didn't speak, and she could sense the same mood about him he had donned when he'd come face to face with Raschid and his son. It hurt. Though she strove not to show it. But his manner made such a mockery out of everything else he had said and done.

They arrived on the upper deck as the yacht slipped smoothly from its moorings and began making its way towards the mouth of the Suez Canal. Medina Al-Mahmud suddenly appeared in front of Leona and politely begged to hold the baby. She was a small, slight woman with nervous eyes and a defensive manner, but as Leona placed the little girl in her arms Medina sent her a sympathetic look which almost broke her composure in two.

She did not want people's pity. Oh, how she had come to hate it during her last year in Rahman when the rumours about her had begun flying. With a desperate need of something else to do other than stand here feeling utterly useless, she walked into the salon to pick up the internal phone and order refreshments.

It was really very bad timing for Hassan to follow her. 'I must offer you my deepest apologies,' he announced so stiffly it was almost an insult. 'When I arranged this surprise for you I did not expect the Al-Kadahs to bring their children with them.'

She was appalled to realise that even Hassan believed her an object of such pity. 'Oh, stop being so ultra-sensitive,' she snapped. 'Do you really believe that I could resent them their beautiful children because I cannot have them for myself?'

'Don't say that!' he snapped back. 'It is not true, though you drive me insane by insisting it is so!'

'And you stop burying your head in the sand, Hassan,' she returned. 'Because we both know that you know it is you who lies to yourself!'

With that she stalked off, leaving him to simmer in his

own frustration while she went to check that the accommodation could stretch to two more guests than they had expected. Faysal already had the matter in hand, she discovered, finding several people hurriedly making ready a pair of adjoining suites, while others unpacked enough equipment, brought by the Al-Kadahs, to keep an army of young children content.

On her way back upstairs she met Rafiq and Samir. Rafiq studied her narrowly, his shrewd gaze not missing the continuing paleness in her face. He was probably questioning whether one sniff at suspect milk could upset her stomach for so long when in actual fact it had never been the milk, she had come to realise, but sheer anxiety and stress.

Samir, on the other hand, noticed nothing but a target for his wit. By the time the three of them had joined the others, Samir had her laughing over a heavily embroidered description of himself being put through the agonies of hell in the gym by a man so fit it was a sin.

After that she played the circulating hostess to the hilt and even endured a whole ten minutes sitting with Zafina listening to her extol the virtues of her daughter, Nadira. Then Evie rescued her by quietly asking if she would show her to their room, because the baby needed changing.

With Hashim deciding to come with them, they went down to the now beautifully prepared twin cabins and a dark-eyed little nurse Evie had brought with them appeared, to take the children into the other room. The moment the two women were alone Evie swung round on Leona and said, 'Right, let's hear it. Why did Hassan virtually beg and bribe us to come along on this trip?'

At which point; Leona simply broke down and wept out the whole sorry story. By the time she had hiccuped to a finish they were curled up on the bed and Evie was gently stroking her hair.

'I think you are here to make me feel better.' She finally answered Evie's original question. 'Because anyone with eyes can see that the Al-Mahmuds and the Al-Yasins wish me on another planet entirely. Hassan doesn't know that I've always known that Nadira Al-Yasin is the people's preferred wife for him.'

'I've been there. I know the feeling,' Evie murmured understandingly. 'I suppose she's beautiful, biddable and loves children.'

Leona nodded on a muffled sob. 'I've met her once or twice. She's quite sweet,' she reluctantly confessed.

'Just right for Hassan, I suppose.'

'Yes,'

'And, of course, you are not.'

Leona shook her head.

'So why are you here, then?' Evie challenged.

'You tell me,' she suggested, finding strength in anger and pulling herself into a sitting position on the bed. 'Because I don't know! Hassan says I am here for this reason, then he changes it to another. He is stubborn and devious and an absolute expert at plucking at my heart strings! His father is ill and I adore that old man so he uses him to keep me dancing to his secret tune!'

'Raschid's father died in his arms while I held Raschid in my arms,' Evie told her sadly. 'Wretched though it was, I would not have been anywhere else. He needed me. Hassan needs you too.'

'Oh, don't defend him,' Leona protested, 'It makes me feel mean, yet I know I would have gone to his father like a shot with just that request. I didn't need all of this other stuff to make me do it.'

'But maybe Hassan needed this other stuff to let him make you do it.'

'I'm going to sit you at the dinner table between Mrs Yasin and Mrs Mahmud tonight if you don't stop trying to be reasonable,' Leona said warningly.

'Okay, you've made your point,' Evie conceded. 'You need a loyal champion, not a wise one.' Then, with a complete change of manner, 'So get yourself into the bathroom and tidy yourself up before we go and fight the old dragons together.'

Leona began to smile. 'Now you're talking,' she enthused, and, stretching out a long leg, she rose from the bed a different person than the one who'd slumped down on it minutes ago. 'I'm glad you're here, Evie,' she murmured huskily.

It was a remark she could have repeated a hundred times over during the following days when everyone did try to appear content to simply enjoy the cruise with no underlying disputes to spoil it.

But in truth many undercurrents were at work. In the complicated way of Arab politics, there was no natural right to succession in Rahman. First among equals was the Arab way of describing a collective of tribe leaders amongst which one is considered the most authoritative. The next leader did not necessarily have to be the son of the one preceding him, but choice became an open issue on which all heads of the family must agree.

In truth everyone knew that Hassan was the only sensible man for the job simply because he had been handling the modern thrusts of power so successfully for the last five years as his father's health had begun to fail. No one wanted to tip the balance. As it stood, the other families had lived well and prospered under Al-Qadim rule. Rahman was a respected country in Arabia. Landlocked though it was, the oil beneath its desert was rich and in plenty, and within its borders were some of the most important oases that other, more favourably placed countries, did not enjoy.

But just as the sands shifted, so did opinions. Al-Mahmud and Al-Yasin might have lived well and prospered under thirty years of Al-Qadim rule, but they had disapproved of Hassan's choice of wife from the beginning. Though they could not fault the dedication Hassan's wife had applied to her role, nor ignore the respect she had earned from the Rahman people, she was frail of body. She had produced no sons in five years of marriage, and then had made Hassan appear weak to his peers when she'd walked away from him of her own volition. Divorce should have followed swiftly. Hassan had refused to discuss it as an option. Therefore, a second wife should have been chosen. Hassan's refusal to pander to what he called the ways of the old guard had incensed many. Not least Sheikh Abdul Al-Yasin who had not stopped smarting from the insult he'd received when Hassan had not chosen his daughter, Nadira, who had been primed from birth to take the role.

With Hassan's father's health failing fast, Sheikh Abdul had seen an opportunity to redress this insult. All it required was for Hassan to agree to take on a second wife in order to maintain the delicate balance between families. It was that simple. Everyone except Hassan agreed that his marriage to Nadira Al-Yasin would form an alliance that would solve everyone's problems. Hassan could keep his first wife. No one was asking him to discard this beautiful but barren woman. But his first son would come from the womb of Nadira Al-Yasin, which was all that really mattered.

The alternatives? Sheikh Jibril Al-Mahmud had a son who could be considered worthy of taking up the mantle Hassan's father would leave vacant. And no one could afford to ignore Sheikh Imran Al-Mukhtar and his son, Samir. Samir might be too young to take on the mantle of power but his father was not.

This, however only dealt with the male perspective. As the sheikhs fought their war with words on each other during long discussions, ensconced in one of the staterooms, the women were waging a similar war for their own reasons. Zafina Al-Yasin wanted Leona out and her daughter, Nadira, in. Since Hassan was not allowing this, then she would settle for her daughter taking second place. For the power lay in the sons born in a marriage, not the wives. So critical remarks were dropped at every opportunity to whittle away at Leona's composure and a self-esteem that was already fragile due to her inability to give Hassan what he needed most in this world.

In the middle of it all stood Sheikh Raschid and his wife, Evie offering positive proof that west could successfully join with east. For Behran had gone from strength to strength since their marriage and was fast becoming one of the most influential States in Arabia. But they had a son. It was the cog on which everything else rotated.

It took two days to navigate the Suez Canal, and would take another five to cross the Red Sea to the city of Jeddah on the coast of Saudi Arabia. By the time they had reached the end of the Canal, battle lines had been clearly marked for those times when the war of words would rage or a truce would be called. Mornings were truce times, when everyone more or less did their own thing and the company could even be called pleasant.

In the afternoons most people took a siesta, unless Samir grew restless and chivvied the others towards more enjoyable pursuits.

'Just look at them,' Evie murmured indulgently one afternoon as they stood watching Samir, Rafiq, Raschid and Hassan jet-skiing the ocean like reckless idiots, criss-crossing each other's wash with a daring that sometimes caught the breath. 'They're like little boys with exciting new toys.'

They came back to the boat, refreshed, relaxed—and ready to begin the first wave of strikes when the men gathered to drink coffee in one of the staterooms while the women occupied another.

Dinner called a second truce. After dinner, when another split of the sexes occurred, hostilities would resume until someone decided to call it a day and went to bed.

Bed was a place you could neither describe as a place of war nor truce. It gave you a sanctuary in which you had the chance to vent all of the things you had spent the day suppressing. But when the person in the bed with you saw you as much the enemy as every one else did, then you were in deep trouble. As Hassan acknowledged every time he slid into bed beside Leona and received the cold shoulder if he so much as attempted to touch her or speak.

She was angry with him for many reasons, but angriest most for some obscure point he had not managed to expose. He was aware that this situation was difficult, that she would rather be anywhere else other than trapped on this yacht right now. He knew she was unhappy, that she was only just managing to hide that from everyone else. That she was eating little and looking contradictorily pale when in truth her skin was taking on a deeper golden hue with every passing day. He knew that Zafina and Medina used any opportunity presented to them to compare her situation unfavourably with Evie's. And he wished Raschid had shown some sensitivity to that prospect when he'd made the decision to bring his children along!

The children were a point of conflict he could not seem to deal with. This evening, for instance, when Raschid had brought his son into the salon to say goodnight to everyone, Hashim had run the length of the room with his arms open wide in demand for a hug from Leona. She had lifted him up in her arms and received all of his warm kisses to her face with smiles of pleasure while inside, Hassan knew, the ache of empty wishes must be torture for her.

When she hurt, he hurt. When he had no remedy to ease that pain, he had to turn away from its source or risk revealing to her the emptiness of helplessness he suffered whenever he saw her hugging a son that was not their own.

But in trying to protect Leona from himself he had forgotten the other pairs of eyes watching him. The Al-Mahmuds and the Al-Yasins had seen, read and drawn their own conclusions.

'A sad sight, is it not?' Abdul had dared to say.

Leona had heard him, had known what he'd been referring to, and had been shunning Hassan ever since.

'Talk to me, for Allah's sake.' He sighed into the darkness. 'Find another bed to sleep in.'

Well, they were words, he supposed, then sighed again, took the bull by the horns and pushed himself up to lean over her, then tugged her round to face him. 'What is it that you want from me?' he demanded. 'I am trying my best to make this work for us!'

Her eyes flicked open; it was like gazing into pools of broken ice. 'Why go to all this trouble when I am still going to leave you flat the first moment I know I can do it without hurting your father?'

'Why?' he challenged.

'We've already been through the *whys* a hundred times! They haven't changed just because you have decided to play the warlord and win the battle against your rotten underlings without giving an inch to anyone!'

'Warlord?' His brow arched. 'How very pagan.' He made sure she knew he liked the sound of that title in a very physical way.

'Oh, get off me,' she snapped, gave a push and rolled free of him, coming to her feet by the bed. Her hair floated everywhere, and the cream silk pyjamas shimmied over her slender figure as she walked down the room and dumped herself into one of the chairs, then dared to curl up in it as if he would allow her to sleep there!

'Come back here, Leona,' he commanded wearily.

'I regret ever agreeing to be here,' she answered huskily.

Husky meant tears. Tears made him want to curse for making a joke of what they had been talking about when any fool would have known it was no time for jokes! On yet another sigh he got out of the bed, then trod in her footsteps and went to squat down in front of her.

'I'm sorry,' he said, 'that this situation is so difficult for you. But my father insisted that the family heads must talk to each other. I have no will to refuse him because in truth his reasons are wise. You know I have no automatic right to succession. I must win the support of the other family leaders.'

'Stop being so stubborn and just let me go and you would not have to win over anyone,' she pointed out.

'You know...' he grimaced '...I think you are wrong

there. I think that underneath all the posturing they want me to fight this battle and win, to prove the strength of my resolve.'

She brushed a tear off her cheek. Hassan had wanted to do it for her, but instinct was warning him not to. 'Tonight Zafina asked me outright if I had any idea of the life I was condemning you to if I held onto a marriage destined to have no children.'

His eyes flashed with raw anger, his lips pressing together on an urge to spit out words that would make neither of them feel any better. But he made a mental note that from tomorrow Leona went nowhere without himself or Rafiq within hearing.

'And I saw your face, Hassan,' she went on unsteadily. 'I heard what Abdul said to you and I know why he said it. So why are you being so stubborn about something we both know is—'

He shut her up in the most effective way he knew. Mouth to mouth, tongue to tongue, words lost in the heat of a much more productive form of communication. She fought him for a few brief seconds, then lost the battle when her flailing fingers made contact with his naked flesh.

He had no clothes on, she had too many, but flesh-warmed silk against naked skin achieved a sensual quality he found very pleasurable as he lifted her up and settled her legs around his hips.

'You are such an ostrich,' she threw into his face as he carried her back to bed. 'How long do you think you can go on ignoring what—!'

He used the same method to shut her up again. By then he was standing by the bed with her fingernails digging into his shoulders, her hair surrounding him and her long legs clinging to his waist with no indication that they were going to let go. If he tried for a horizontal position he would risk hurting her while she held him like this.

So—who needed a bed? he thought with a shrug as his fingers found the elastic waistband to her pyjama bottoms and pushed the silk far enough down her thighs to gain him access to what he wanted the most. She groaned as he eased himself into her, and the kiss deepened into something else.

Fevered was what it was. Fevered and hot and a challenge to how long he could maintain his balance as he stood there with his hands spanning her slender buttocks, squeezing to increase the frictional pleasure, and no way—no way— would he have believed three nights without doing this could leave him so hungry. Twelve months without doing this had not affected him as badly.

'You're shaking.'

She'd noticed. He wasn't surprised. He wasn't just shaking, he was out of control, and he could no longer maintain this position without losing his dignity as well as his mind. So he lowered her to the bed with as much care as he could muster, pushed her hair from her face and stared blackly into her eyes.

'You tell me how I deny myself this above all things?' he demanded. 'You, only you, can do this to me. It is only you I want to do it with.'

The words were spoken between fierce kisses, between possessive thrusts from his hips. Leona touched his face, touched his mouth, touched his eyes with her eyes. 'I'm so very sorry,' she whispered tragically.

It was enough to drive an already driven man insane. He withdrew, got up, swung away and strode into the bathroom, slammed shut the door then turned to slam the flat of his palm against the nearest wall. Empty silences after the loving he had learned to deal with, but tragic apologies in the middle were one large step too far!

Why had she said it? She hadn't meant to say it! It was just one of those painful little things that had slipped out because she had seen he was hurting, and the look had reminded her of the look he had tried to hide from her when she had been cuddling Hashim.

Oh, what were they doing to each other? Leona asked

herself wretchedly. And scrambled to her feet as the sickness she had been struggling with for days now came back with a vengeance, leaving her with no choice but to make a run for the bathroom with the hope that he hadn't locked the door.

With one hand over her mouth and the other trying to recover her slipping pyjama bottoms, she reached the door just as it flew open to reveal a completely different Hassan than the one who had stormed in there only seconds ago.

'You may have your wish,' he informed her coldly. 'As soon as it is safe for me to do so, I will arrange a divorce. Now I want nothing more to do with you.'

With that he walked away, having no idea that her only response was to finish what she had been intending to do and make it to the toilet bowl before she was sick.

CHAPTER EIGHT

LEONA was asleep when Hassan let himself back into the room the next morning. She was still asleep when, showered and dressed, he left the room again half an hour later, and in a way he was glad.

He had spent the night stretched out on a lounger on the shade deck, alternating between feeling angry enough to stand by every word he had spoken and wanting to go back and retract what he had left hanging in the air.

And even now, hours later, he was not ready to choose which way he was going to go. He'd had enough of people tugging on his heartstrings; he'd had enough of playing these stupid power games.

He met Rafiq on his way up to the sun deck. 'Set up a meeting,' he said. 'Ten o'clock in my private office. We are going for broke.'

Rafiq sent him one of his steady looks, went to say something, changed his mind, and merely nodded his head.

Samir was already at the breakfast table, packing food away at a pace that made Hassan feel slightly sick—a combination of no sleep and one too many arguments, he told himself grimly.

Leona still hadn't put in an appearance by the time everyone else had joined them and finished their breakfast. Motioning the steward over, he instructed him to ring the suite.

'I'll go,' Evie offered, and got up, leaving her children to Raschid's capable care.

And he was capable. In fact it irritated Hassan how capable his friend was at taking care of his two children. How did he run a Gulf state the size of Behran and find time to learn how to deal with babies?

The sun was hot, the sky was blue and here he was, he acknowledged, sitting here feeling like a grey day in London.

'Hassan...'

'Hmm?' Glancing up, he realised that Sheikh Imran had been talking to him and he hadn't heard a single word that he had said.

'Rafiq tells us you have called a meeting for ten o'clock'

'Yes.' He glanced at his watch, frowned and stood up. 'If you will excuse me, this is the time I call my father.'

To reach his office required him to pass by his suite door. It was closed. He hesitated, wondering whether or not to go in and at least try to make his peace. But Evie was in there, he remembered, and walked on, grimly glad of the excuse not to have to face that particular problem just now. For he had bigger fish to fry this morning.

Faysal was already in the office. 'Get my father on the phone for me, Faysal,' he instructed. 'Then set the other room up ready for a meeting.'

'It is to be today, sir?' Faysal questioned in surprise.

'Yes, today. In half an hour. My father, Faysal,' he prompted before the other man could say any more. He glanced at his watch again as Faysal picked up the telephone. Had Leona stayed in their suite because she didn't want to come face to face with him?

But Leona had not stayed in their suite because she was sulking, as Hassan so liked to call it. She was ill, and didn't want anyone to know.

'Don't you dare tell anyone,' she warned Evie. 'I'll be all right in a bit. It just keeps happening, and then it goes away again.'

'How long?' Evie looked worried.

'A few days.' Leona shrugged. 'I don't think I've got any-thing your children might catch, Evie,' she then anxiously assured her. 'I'm just—stressed out, that's all.'

'Stressed out.' Evie was looking at her oddly.

'It's playing havoc with my stomach.' Leona nodded and took another sip of the bottled water Evie had opened for her. 'Who would not be feeling sick if they were stuck on this boat with a load of people they liked as little as those people liked them? You and your family excluded, of course,' she then added belatedly.

'Oh, of course.' Evie nodded and sat down on the edge of the bed, a bed with one half that had not been slept in. Hassan had not come back last night, and Leona was glad that he hadn't.

'I hate men,' she announced huskily.

'You mean you hate one man in particular.'

'I'll be glad when this is over and he just lets me go.'

'Do you really think that is likely?' Evie mocked. 'Hassan is an Arab and they give up on nothing. Arrogant, possessive, stubborn, selfish and sweet,' she listed ruefully. 'It is the moments of sweetness that are their saving grace, I find.'

'You're lucky, you've got a nice one.'

'He wasn't nice at all on the day I sent him packing,' Evie recalled. 'In fact it was the worst moment of my life when he turned to leave with absolutely no protest. I knew it was the end. I'd seen it carved into his face like words set in stone...'

'I know,' Leona whispered miserably. 'I've seen the look myself...'

Evie had seen the same look on Hassan's face at the breakfast table. 'Oh, Leona.' She sighed. 'The two of you have got to stop beating each other up like this. You love each other. Can't that be enough?'

Raschid was not in agreement with Hassan's timing. 'Think about this,' he urged. 'We have too much time before we reach dry land. Time for them to fester on their disappointment.'

'I need this settled,' Hassan grimly insisted. 'Leona is a mess. The longer I let the situation ride the more hesitant I appear. Both Abdul and Zafina Al-Yasin are becoming so over-confident that they think they may say what they please. My father agrees. It shall be done with today. *Inshallah*,' he concluded.

'*Inshallah*, indeed,' Raschid murmured ruefully, and went away to prepare what he had been brought here specifically to say.

An hour later Evie was with her children, Medina and Zafina were seated quietly in one of the salons sipping coffee while they awaited the outcome of the meeting taking place on the deck below, and Leona and Samir were kitting up to go jet-skiing when Sheikh Raschid Al-Kadah decided it was time for him to speak.

'I have listened to your arguments with great interest and some growing concern,' he smoothly began. 'Some of you seem to be suggesting that Hassan should make a choice between his country and his western wife. I find this a most disturbing concept—not only because I have a western wife myself, but because forward-thinking Arabs might be setting such outmoded boundaries upon their leaders for the sake of what?'

'The blood line,' Abdul said instantly.

Some of the others shifted uncomfortably. Raschid looked into the face of each and every one of them and challenged them to agree with Sheikh Abdul. It would be an insult to himself, his wife and children if they did so. None did.

'The blood line was at risk six years ago, Abdul.' He smoothly directed his answer at the man who had dared to offer such a dangerous reason. 'When Hassan married, his wife was accepted by you all. What has changed?'

'You misunderstand, Raschid,' Jibril Al-Mahmud quickly inserted, eager to soothe the ruffled feathers of the other man. 'My apologies, Hassan, for feeling pressed to say this.' He bowed. 'But it is well known throughout Rahman that your most respected wife cannot bear a child.'

'This is untrue, but please continue with your hypothesis,' Hassan invited calmly.

Flustered, Jibril looked back at Raschid. 'Even in your

country a man is allowed, if not expected, to take a second wife if the first is—struggling to give him sons,' he pointed out. 'We beg Hassan only take a second wife to secure the *family* line.' Wisely, he omitted the word 'blood'.

'Hassan?' Raschid looked to him for an answer.

Hassan shook his head. 'I have the only wife I need,' he declared.

'And if Allah decides to deny you sons, what then?'

'Then control passes on to my successor. I do not see the problem.'

'The problem is that your stance makes a mockery of everything we stand for as Arabs,' Abdul said impatiently. 'You have a duty to secure the continuance of the Al-Qadim name. Your father agrees. The old ones agree. I find it insupportable that you continue to insist on giving back nothing for the honour of being your father's son!'

'I give back my right to succession,' Hassan countered. 'I am prepared to step down and let one or other of you here take my place. There,' he concluded with a flick of the hand, 'it is done. You may now move on to discuss my father's successor without me...'

'One moment, Hassan...' It was Raschid who stopped him from rising. Worked in and timed to reach this point in proceedings, he said, 'I have some objections to put forward against your decision.'

Hassan returned to his seat. Raschid nodded his gratitude for this, then addressed the table as a whole. 'Rahman's land borders my land. Your oil pipeline runs beneath Behran soil and mixes with my oil in our co-owned holding tanks when it reaches the Gulf. And the old ones criss-cross our borders from oasis to oasis with a freedom laid down in a treaty drawn up and signed by Al-Kadah and Al-Qadim thirty years ago. So tell me,' he begged, 'with whom am I expected to renegotiate this treaty when an Al-Qadim is no longer in a position to honour his side of our bargain?'

It was an attack on all fronts. For Rahman was landlocked. It needed Behran to get its oil to the tankers that moored up at its vast terminals. The treaty was old and the tariffs laid down in it had not been changed in those thirty years Raschid had mentioned. Borders were mere lines on maps the old ones were free to ignore as they roamed the desert with their camel trains.

'There is no question of altering the balance of power here in Rahman,' It was Sheikh Jibril Al-Mahmud who declaimed the suggestion. He looked worried. Crown Prince Raschid Al-Kadah was not known as a bluffing man. 'Hassan has our complete loyalty, respect and support.'

'Ah,' Raschid said. 'Then I am mistaken in what I have been hearing here. My apologies.' He bowed. 'I believed I was hearing Hassan about to step down as his father's natural successor.'

'Indeed no such thing ever crossed our minds.' You could almost see Sheikh Jibril shifting his position into the other camp as he spoke. 'We are merely concerned about future successors and question whether it is not time for Hassan to consider taking steps to—'

'As the old ones would say,' Raschid smoothly cut in, 'time is but a grain of sand that shifts in accordance with the wind and the will of Allah.'

'*Inshallah*,' Sheikh Jibril agreed, bringing Sheikh Abdul's house of cards tumbling down.

'Thank you,' Hassan murmured to Raschid a few minutes later, when the others had left them. 'I am in your debt.'

'There is no debt,' Raschid denied. 'I have no wish to see the spawn of Sheikh Abdul Al-Yasin develop in to the man who will then deal with my son. But, as a matter of interest only, who is your successor?'

'Rafiq,' Hassan replied.

'But he does not want the job.'

'He will nonetheless acquire it,' Hassan said grimly.

'Does he know?'

'Yes. We have already discussed it.'

Raschid nodded thoughtfully, then offered a grim smile.

'Now all you have to do, my friend, is try to appear happy that you have achieved your goal.'

It was Hassan's cue to begin smiling, but instead he released a heavy sigh and went to stand by the window. Outside, skimming across the glass-smooth water, he could see two jet-skis teasing each other. Leona's hair streamed out behind her like a glorious banner as she stood, half bent at the knees, turning the machine into a neat one-hundred-and-eighty-degree-spin in an effort to chase after the reckless Samir.

'The victory could be an empty one in the end,' he murmured eventually. 'For I do not think she will stay.'

Raschid's silence brought Hassan's head round. What he saw etched into the other man's face said it all for him. 'You don't think she will, either, do you?' he stated huskily.

'Evie and I discussed this,' Raschid confessed. 'We swapped places with you and Leona, if you like. And quite honestly, Hassan, her answer made my blood run cold.'

Hassan was not surprised by that. East meets west, he mused as he turned back to the window. Pride against pride. The love of a good, courageous woman against the—

'In the name of Allah,' he suddenly rasped out as he watched Leona's jet-ski stop so suddenly that she was thrown right over the front of it.

'What?' Raschid got to his feet.

'She hit something,' he bit out, remaining still for a moment, waiting for her to come up. It didn't happen. His heart began to pound, ringing loudly in his ears as he turned and began to run. With Raschid close on his heels he took the stairs two at a time, then flung himself down the next set heading for the rear of the boat where the back let down to form a platform into the water. Rafiq was already there, urgently lowering another jet ski into the water. His taut face said it all; Leona still had not reappeared. Samir had not even noticed; he was too busy making a wide, arching turn way out.

Without hesitation he wrenched the jet-ski from Rafiq and

was speeding off towards his wife before his brother had realised what he had done. Teeth set, eyes sharp, he made an arrow-straight track towards her deadly still jet-ski as behind him the yacht began sounding its horn in a warning call to Samir. The sound brought everyone to the boatside, to see what was going on.

By the time Hassan came up on Leona's jet-ski, Rafiq was racing after him on another one and Samir was heading towards them at speed. No one else moved or spoke or even breathed as they watched Hassan take a leaping dive off his moving machine and disappear into the deep blue water. Three minutes had past, maybe four, and Hassan could not understand why her buoyancy aid had not brought her to the surface.

He found out why the moment he broke his dive down and twisted full circle in the water. A huge piece of wood, like the beam from an old fishing boat, floated just below the surface—tangled with fishing net. It was the net she was caught in, a slender ankle, a slender wrist, and she was frantically trying to free herself.

As he swam towards her, he saw the panic in her eyes, the belief that she was going to die. With his own lungs already wanting to burst, he reached down to free her foot first, then began hauling her towards the surface even as he wrenched free her wrist.

White, he was white with panic, overwhelmed by shock and gasping greedily for breath. She burst out crying, coughing, spluttering, trying desperately to fill her lungs through racking sobs that tore him to bits. Neither had even noticed the two other jet-skis warily circling them or that Raschid and a crewman were heading towards them in the yacht's emergency inflatable.

'Why is it you have to *do* this to me?' he shouted at her furiously.

'Hassan,' someone said gruffly. He looked up, saw his brother's face, saw Samir looking like a ghost, saw the inflatable almost upon them, then saw—really saw—the woman he held crushed in his arms. After that the world took on a blur as Rafiq and Samir joined them in the water and helped to lift Leona into the boat. Hassan followed, then asked Raschid and the crewman to bring in the other two men on the jet-skis. As soon as the jet-skis left the inflatable, he turned it round and, instead of making for the yacht, he headed out in the Red Sea.

Leona didn't notice, she was lying in a huddle still sobbing her heart out on top of a mound of towels someone had had the foresight to toss into the boat, and he was shaking from teeth to fingertips. His mind was shot, his eyes blinded by an emotion he had never experienced before in his life.

When he eventually stopped the boat in the middle of no-where, he just sat there and tried hard to calm whatever it was that was raging inside of him while Leona tried to calm her frightened tears.

'You know,' he muttered after a while, 'for the first time since I was a boy, I think I am going to weep. You have no idea what you do to me, no idea at all. Sometimes I wonder if you even care.'

'It was an accident,' she whispered hoarsely

'So was the trip on the gangway! So was the headlong fall down the stairs! What difference does it make if it was an accident? You still have no idea what you do to me!'

Sitting up, she plucked up one the towels and wrapped it around her shivering frame.

'Are you listening to me?' he grated.

'No,' she replied. 'Where are we?'

'In the middle of nowhere where I can shout if I want to, cry if I want to, and tell the rest of the world to get out of my life!' he raged. 'I am sick of other people meddling in it. I am sick of playing stupid, political games. And I am sick and tired of watching you do stupid madcap things just because you are angry with me!'

'Hassan—'

'What?' he lashed back furiously, black eyes burning,

body so taut it looked ready to snap in two. He was soaking wet and he was trembling—not shivering like herself.

'I'm all right,' she told him gently.

He fell on her like a ravaging wolf, setting the tiny boat rocking and not seeming to care if they both ended up in the water again. 'Four minutes you were under the water—I timed it!' he bit out between tense kisses.

'I'm accident prone; you know I am,' she reminded him. 'The first time we met I tripped over someone's foot and landed on your lap.'

'No.' He denied it. 'I helped you there with a guiding hand.'

She frowned. He grimaced. He had never admitted that before. 'I had been watching you all evening, wondering how I could get to meet you without making myself appear over-eager. So it was an opportunity sent from Allah when you tripped just in front of me.'

Leona let loose a small, tear-choked chuckle. 'I tripped in front of you on purpose,' she confessed. 'Someone said you were an Arabian sheikh, rich as sin, so I thought to myself. That will do for me!'

'Liar,' he murmured.

'Maybe.' She smiled.

Then the teasing vanished from both of them. Eyes darkened, drew closer, then dived into each other's to dip into a place so very special it actually hurt to make contact with so much feeling at once.

'Don't leave me—ever.' He begged her promise.

Leona sighed as she ran her fingers through his wet hair. Her throat felt tight and her heart felt heavy. 'I'm frightened that one day you will change your mind about me and want more from your life. Then what will I be left with?'

'Ethan Hayes is in love with you,' he said.

'What has that got to do with this?' She frowned. 'And, no, he is not.'

'You are frightened I will leave you. Well, I am frightened

that you will one day see a normal man like Ethan and decide he has more to offer you than I ever can.'

'You are joking,' she drawled.

'No, I am not.' He sat up, long fingers reaching out to pluck absently at the ropework around the sides of the boat. 'What do I offer you beside a lot of personal restrictions, political games that can get nasty enough to put your well-being at risk, and a social circle of friends you would not pass the day with if you did not feel obliged to do so for my sake.'

'I liked most of our friends in Rahman,' she protested, sitting up to drape one of the towels around her head because the sun was too hot. 'Those I didn't like, you don't particularly like, and we only used to see them at formal functions.'

'Or when we became stuck on a boat with them with no means of escape.'

'Why are we having this conversation in this small boat in the middle of the Red Sea?' she questioned wearily.

'Where else?' He shrugged. 'In our stateroom where there is a convenient bed to divert us away from what needs to be said?'

'It's another abduction,' she murmured ruefully.

'You belong to me. A man cannot abduct what is already his.'

'And you're arrogant.' She sighed.

'Loving you is arrogant of me?' he challenged.

Leona just shook her head and used the corner of the towel to dry her wet face. Her fingers were trembling, and she was still having a struggle to calm her breathing. 'Last night you promised me a divorce.'

'Today I am taking that promise back.'

'Here…' she held her arm out towards him. '…can you do something about this?'

Part of the netting she had been tangled in was still clinging to her wrist. The delicate skin beneath it was red and chafed. 'I'm sorry I said what I did last night,' he murmured.

'I'm sorry I said what I did,' Leona returned. 'I didn't even mean it the way it came out. It's just that sometimes you look so very…'

'Children are a precious gift from Allah,' Hassan interrupted, dark head sombrely bent over his task. 'But so is love. Very few people are fortunate enough to have both, and most only get the children. If I had to choose then I would choose, to have love.'

'But you are an Arabian sheikh with a duty to produce the next successor to follow on from you, and the choice no longer belongs to you.'

'If we find we want children then we will get some,' he said complacently, lifting up her wrist to break the stubborn cord with the sharp snap of his teeth. 'IVF, adoption… But only if *we* want them.' He made that fine but important point. 'Otherwise let Rafiq do his bit for his country,' he concluded with an indifferent shrug.

'He would give you one of his stares if he heard you saying that.' Leona smiled.

'He is an Al-Qadim, though he chooses to believe he is not.'

'He's half-French.'

'I am one quarter Spanish, and one quarter Al-Kadah,' he informed her. 'You, I believe, are one half rampaging Celt. I do not see us ringing bells about it.'

'All right, I will stay,' she murmured.

Dark eyes shrouded by a troubled frown lifted to look at her. 'You mean stay as in for ever, no more argument?' He demanded clarification.

Reaching up, she stroked her fingers through his hair again. 'As in you've got me for good, my lord Sheikh,' she said soberly. 'Just make sure you don't make me regret it.'

'Huh.' The short laugh was full of bewildered incredulity. 'What suddenly brought on this change of heart?'

'The heart has always wanted to stay, it was the mind that was causing me problems. But…look at us, Hassan.' She sighed 'sitting out in the middle of the sea in a stupid little boat beneath the heat of a noon-day sun because we would rather be here, together like this, than anywhere else.' She gave him her eyes again, and what always happened to them happened when he looked deep inside. 'If you believe love can sustain us through whatever is waiting for us back there, then I am going to let myself believe it too.'

'Courage,' he murmured, reaching out to gently cup her cheek. 'I never doubted your courage.'

'No,' she protested when he went to kiss her. 'Not here, when I can feel about twenty pairs of eyes trained on us from the yacht.'

'Let them watch,' he decreed, and kissed her anyway. 'Now I want the privacy of our stateroom, with its very large bed,' he said as he drew away again.

'Then, let's go and find it.'

They were halfway back to the yacht before she remembered Samir telling her about the planned meeting. 'What happened?' she asked anxiously.

Hassan smiled a brief, not particularly pleased smile. 'I won the support I was looking for. The fight is over. Now we can begin to relax a little.'

As a statement of triumph, it didn't have much satisfaction running through it. Leona wanted to question him about it, but they were nearing the yacht, so she decided to wait until later because she could now clearly see the sea of faces watching their approach—some anxious, some curious, some wearing expressions that set her shivering all over again. Not everyone was relieved that Hassan had plucked her out of the ocean, she realised ruefully.

Rafiq and a crewman were waiting on the platform to help them back on board the yacht. 'I'll walk,' she insisted when Hassan went to lift her into his arms. 'I think I have looked foolish enough for one day.'

So they walked side by side through the boat, wrapped in towels over their wet clothing. Neither spoke, neither touched, and no one accosted them on their journey to their stateroom. The door shut them in. Hassan broke away from her side and strode into the bathroom. Leona followed, found the jets in the shower already running. She dropped the towels, Hassan silently helped her out of the buoyancy aid that had not been buoyant enough and tossed it in disgust to the tiled floor. Next came her tee shirt, her shorts, the blue one-piece swimsuit she was wearing beneath.

It was another of those calms before the storm, Leona recognised as she watched him drag his shirt off over his head and step out of the rest of his clothes. His face was composed, his manner almost aloof, and there wasn't a single cell in her body that wasn't charged, ready to accept what had to come.

Tall and dark, lean and sleek. 'In,' he commanded, holding open the shower-cubicle door so that she could step inside. He followed, closed the door. And as the white-tiled space engulfed them in steam he was reaching for her and engulfing her in another way.

Think of asking questions about how much he had conceded to win his support from the other sheikhs? Why think about anything when this was warm and soft and slow and so intense that the yacht could sink and they would not have noticed. This was love, a renewal of love; touching, tasting, living, breathing, feeling love. From the shower they took it with them to the bed, from there they took it with them into a slumber which filtered the rest of the day away.

Questions? Who needed questions when they had this depth of communication? No more empty silences between the loving. No more fights with each other or with themselves about the wiseness of being together like this. When she received him inside her she did so with her eyes wide open and brimming with love and his name sounding softly on her lips.

Beyond the room, in another part of the yacht, Raschid looked at Rafiq. 'Do you think he has realised yet that today's victory has only put Leona at greater risk from her enemies?' he questioned.

'Sheikh Abdul would be a fool to show his hand now, when he must know that Hassan has chosen to pretend he had no concept of his plot to take her.'

'I was not thinking of Abdul, but his ambitious wife,' Raschid murmured grimly. 'The woman wants to see her daughter in Leona's place. One only had to glimpse her expression when Hassan brought them back to the yacht to know that she has not yet had the sense to give up the fight...'

CHAPTER NINE

LEONA was thinking much the same thing when she found herself faced by Zafina later that evening.

Before the confrontation the evening had been surprisingly pleasant. Leona made light of her spill into the sea, and the others made light of the meeting that had taken place as if the battle, now decided, had given everyone the excuse to relax their guard.

It was only when the women left the men at the table after dinner that things took a nasty turn for the worse. Evie had gone to check on her children and Leona used the moment to pop back to the stateroom to freshen up. The last person she expected to see as she stepped out of the bathroom was Zafina Al-Yasin, standing there waiting for her.

Dressed in a traditional jewel-blue *dara'a* and matching *thobe* heavily embroidered with silver studs, Zafina was here to cause trouble. It did not take more than a glance into her black opal eyes to see that.

'You surprise me with your jollity this evening.' The older woman began her attack. 'On a day when your husband won all and you lost everything I believed you stood so proudly for, I would have expected to find you more subdued. It was only as I watched you laugh with our men that it occurred to me that maybe, with your unfortunate accident and Sheikh Hassan's natural concern for you, he has not made you fully aware of what it was he has agreed to today?'

Not at all sure where she was going to be led with this, Leona demanded cautiously, 'Are you implying that my husband has lied to me?'

'I would not presume to suggest such a thing,' Zafina denied with a slight bow of respect meant in honour of Hassan, not Leona herself. 'But he may have been a little...eco-

nomical with some of the details in an effort to save you from
further distress.'

'Something you are not prepared to be,' Leona assumed.

'I believe in telling the truth, no matter the pain it may
course.'

Ah, Leona thought, the truth. Now there was an interesting
concept.

'In the interest of fair play, I do feel that you should be
fully informed so that you may make your judgements on
your future with the full facts at hand.'

'Why don't you just get to the point of this conversation,
Zafina?' Leona said impatiently.

'The point is…this…' Zafina replied, producing from inside the sleeve of her *dara'a* a piece of paper, which she
then spread out on the bed.

Leona did not want to, but she made herself walk towards
it, made herself look down. The paper bore the Al-Qadim
seal of office. It bore the name of Sheikh Khalifa.

'What is it?' she asked, oddly unwilling to read the closely
lined and detailed Arabian script that came beneath.

'A contract drawn up by Sheikh Khalifa himself, giving
his blessing to the marriage between his son Sheikh Hassan
and my daughter Nadira. This is my husband's copy. Sheikh
Khalifa and Sheikh Hassan have copies of their own.'

'It isn't signed,' Leona pointed out.

'It will be,' Zafina stated certainly, 'as was agreed this
morning at the meeting of the family heads. Sheikh Khalifa
is dying. His loving son will deny him nothing. When we
reach Rahman the signing will take place and the announcement will be made at Sheikh Khalifa's celebration banquet.'

He will deny him nothing… Of everything Zafina had
said, those words were the only ones that held the poison.
Still, Leona strove to reject them.

'You lie,' she said. 'No matter what this piece of paper
says, and no matter what you imply. I know Hassan. I know
my father-in-law, Sheikh Khalifa. Neither would even think
of deceiving me this way.'

'You think not?' She sounded so sure, so confident. 'In the eyes of his country, Sheikh Hassan must prove his loyalty to them is stronger than his desire to pander to your western principles.'

More certain on having said it, Leona turned ice-cold eyes on the other woman. 'I will tell Hassan about this conversation. You do realise that?' she warned.

Zafina bowed her head in calm acquiescence. 'Face him,' she invited. 'Tell him what you know. He may continue to keep the truth from you for his father's sake. He may decide to confess all then fall on your mercy, hoping that you will still go to Rahman as his loyal first wife to help save his face. But mark my words, Sheikha,' she warned, 'my daughter will be Sheikh Hassan's wife before this month is out, and she will bear him the son that will make his life complete.'

Stepping forward, she retrieved her precious contract. 'I have no wish to see you humiliated,' she concluded as she turned towards the door. 'Indeed I give you this chance to save your face. Return to England. Divorce Hassan,' she advised. 'For, whether you do or not, he will marry my daughter, at which point I think we both know that your usefulness will be at an end.'

Leona let her go without giving her the satisfaction of a response, but as the door closed behind Zafina she began to shake. No, she told herself sternly, you will not let that woman's poison eat away at you. She's lying. Hassan would not be so deceitful or so manipulative. He loves you, for goodness' sake! Haven't you both just spent a whole afternoon re-avowing that love?

I will deny him nothing... Hassan's own words, exactly as spoken only days ago. Her stomach turned, sending her reeling for the bathroom. Yet she stopped herself, took a couple of deep controlling breaths and forced herself to think, to trust in her own instincts, to believe in Hassan!

He would not do it. Hands clenched into tense fists at her

sides, she repeated that. *He would not do it!* The woman is evil. She is ambitious. She cannot accept failure.

She used your own inadequacies against you. How dare you so much as consider anything she said as worthy of all of this anguish?

You promised to believe in him. How dare you let that promise falter because some awful woman wants you out of his life and her daughter in it?

A contract. What was the contract but a piece of paper with words written upon it? Anyone could draw up a contract; it was getting those involved to sign it that was the real test!

She would tell Hassan, let him deny it once and for all, then she could put all of this behind her and—

No she wouldn't. She changed her mind. She would not give that woman the satisfaction of causing more trouble between the families, which was what was sure to happen if Hassan did find out what Zafina had said.

Trust was the word. Trust she *would* give to him.

The door opened. She spun around to find Hassan standing there. Tall and dark, smooth and sleek, and so heart-achingly, heart-breakingly, precious to her.

'What is wrong?' He frowned. 'You look as pale as the carpet.'

'N-nothing,' she said. Then, because it was such an obvious lie, she admitted, 'H-headache, upset stomach...' Two tight fists unclenched, one hand going to cover her stomach the other her clammy forehead. 'Too much food tonight. T-too much water from my dip in the sea, maybe. I...'

He was striding towards her. Her man. Her beautiful, grim-faced man. He touched her cheek. 'You feel like ice.' He picked up her chafed wrist between gentle finger and thumb. 'Your pulse is racing like mad! You need the medic.' He spun towards the telephone. 'Get undressed. You are going to bed...'

'Oh...no, Hassan!' she cried out in protest. 'I will be okay in a couple of minutes! Please...' she pleaded as he picked up the telephone. 'Look!' she declared, as he glared at her from beneath frowning black brows. 'I'm feeling better already. I—took something a few minutes ago.' With a mammoth gathering together of self-control, she even managed to walk over to him without stumbling and took the receiver from his hand.

'No,' she repeated. 'I will not spoil everyone's enjoyment tonight. I've caused enough fuss today as it is.' And she would not give Zafina a moment's smug satisfaction. 'Walk me back along the deck.' Firmly she took his hand. 'All I need is some fresh air.'

He wasn't sure. But Leona ignored his expression and pulled him towards the door. Actually the walk did her more good than she had expected it to do. Just being with him, feeling his presence, was enough to help reaffirm her belief that he would never, ever, do anything so cruel as to lie about a second wife.

He's done it before, a small voice inside her head reminded her.

Oh, shut up! she told it. I don't want to listen. And she pasted a bright smile on her face, ready to show it to their waiting guests—and Zafina Al-Yasin—as she and Hassan stepped back into the salon.

Zafina wasn't there, which in a way was a relief and in another was a disappointment, because she so wanted to outface the evil witch. She had to make do with shining like a brilliant star for those left to witness it, and she wondered once or twice if she was going to burn out. And she was never more relieved when it became time to retire without causing suspicion that this was all just a dreadful front.

Raschid and Imran had collared Hassan. So she was free to droop the moment she hit the bedroom. Within ten minutes she was curled up in bed. Within another ten she was up again and giving in to what had been threatening to happen since Zafina's visit. Fortunately Hassan was not there to witness it. By the time he came to bed she had found escape in sleep at last, and he made no move to waken her, so morning arrived all too soon, and with it returned the nauseous sensation.

She got through the day by the skin of her teeth, and was pleasant to Zafina, who was not sure how to take that. She spent most of her morning with Evie and her children, taking comfort from the sheer normality of their simple needs and amusements. It was while she was playing with Hashim that the little boy inadvertently brushed against her breasts and she winced at their unexpectedly painful response.

Evie noticed the wince. 'You okay?' she enquired.

Her shrug was rueful. 'Actually, I feel a bit grotty,' she confessed. 'I ache in strange places after my fight with the fishing net yesterday, and I think the water I swallowed had bugs.'

'The same bugs that got you the day before that?' Evie quizzed.

'Okay,' she conceded. 'So I'm still stressed out.'

'Or something,' Evie murmured.

Leona's chin came up, 'What's that supposed to mean?' she demanded.

It was Evie's turn to offer a rueful shrug, then Raschid walked into the room and the conversation had to be shelved when he reminded them that lunch was being served.

After lunch came siesta time. Or, for those like Hassan and Raschid, time to hit the phones and deal with matters of state. Leona had never been so glad of the excuse to shut herself away in her room because she was really beginning to feel ill by then. Her head ached, her bones ached, her stomach was objecting to the small amount of food she had eaten for lunch.

Maybe it was a bug, she mused frowningly as she drew the curtains across the windows in an effort to diffuse the light that was hurting her eyes. Stripping off her top clothes, she then crawled into the bed.

Maybe she should have steered well clear of Evie's children just in case she had picked up something catching, she then added, and made herself a promise to mention it to Evie later just before she slipped into a heavy sleep.

She came awake only as a scarlet sunset seeped into the room. The last sunset before they reached Jeddah, she recalled with relief. And found the reminder gave her a fresh burst of energy that she took with her into the bathroom where she indulged in a long leisurely shower then took her time getting ready for dinner. She chose to wear a calf-length tunic made of spearmint-blue silk with a matching pair of slender-cut trousers.

Hassan arrived in the room with a frown and his mind clearly preoccupied.

'Hello stranger,' she said.

He smiled. It was an amazing smile, full of warmth, full of love—full of lazy suggestions as he began to run his eyes over her in that dark possessive way that said, Mine, most definitely mine. It was the Arab-male way. What the man did not bother to say with words he could make up for with expressive glances.

'No,' Leona said to this particular look. 'I am all dressed up and ready to play hostess, so keep your lecherous hands to yourself.'

'Of course, you do know that I could easily change your mind?' he posed confidently.

Jokes. Light jokes. Warm smiles and tender communication. Would this man she knew and loved so well look at her like this yet still hold such terrible secrets from her?

No, of course he would not, so stop thinking about it! 'Save it until later,' she advised, making a play of sliding the silk scarf over her hair.

His eyes darkened measurably. It was strange how she only now noticed how much he liked seeing her dressed Arabian style. Was it in his blood that he liked to see his woman modestly covered? Was it more than that? Did he actually prefer—?

No. She stopped herself again. Stop allowing that woman's poison to get to you.

'Wait for me,' he requested when she took a step towards the door. 'I need only five minutes to change, for I showered ten minutes ago, after allowing that over-energetic Samir talk me into a game of softball on the sun deck.'

'Who won?' she asked, changing direction to go and sit on the arm of one of the chairs to wait as requested.

'I did—by cheating,' he confessed.

'Did he know you cheated?'

'Of course,' Hassan replied. 'But he believes he is in my debt so he allowed me to get away with it.'

'You mean you played on his guilty conscience over my accident,' she accused.

He turned another slashing grin on her. It had the same force as an electric charge aimed directly at her chest. Heat flashed across her flesh in a blanket wave of sensual static. Followed by another wave of the same as she watched him strip off western shirt and shorts to reveal sleek brown flesh just made for fingers to stroke. By the time he had replaced the clothes with a white tunic he had earned himself a similar possessive glance to the one he had given her.

See, she told herself, you can't resist him in Arab dress. It has nothing to do with what runs in the blood. She even decided to tease him about it. 'If there is one thing I have learned to understand since knowing you, it is why men prefer women in dresses.'

'This is not a dress,' he objected.

Getting up, she went to stand in front of him and placed her palms flat against the wall of his chest to feel warm skin, tight and smooth, and irresistible to seeking hands that wanted to stroke a sensual pathway over muscled contours to his lean waist.

'I know what it is, my darling,' she murmured seductively. 'It is a sinful temptation, and therefore no wonder that you don't encourage physical contact between the sexes.'

His answering laugh was low and deep, very much the sound of a man who was aware of his own power to attract. 'Remind Samir of that, if you will,' he countered dryly. 'He is very lucky I have not beaten him to a pulp by now for the liberties he takes with my wife.'

But Samir, Leona discovered as soon as they entered the main salon, was more interested in extolling the liberties Hassan had taken with him. 'He cheats. He has no honour. He went to Eton, for goodness' sake, where they turn desert savages into gentlemen!'

'Oh...' Leona lifted her head to mock her husband. 'So that's what it is I love most about you.'

'The gentleman?'

'The savage,' she softly corrected.

He replied with a gentle cuff to her chin. Everyone laughed. Everyone was happy. Zafina tried very hard to hide her malicious glare.

They ate dinner beneath the stars that night. Leona was surprised to see a bed of ice holding several bottles of champagne waiting on a side table. Some of her guests drank alcohol; some of them did not. Wine was the favoured choice for those who did imbibe. But even when there had been cause to celebrate yesterday evening champagne had not been served.

'What's going on?' she asked Hassan as he saw her seated.

'Wait and see,' he replied frustratingly, and walked away to take his own seat at the other end of the table.

Ah, the last supper, she thought then, with a pinch of acid wit. And, believing she had her answer, she turned her attention to her meal, while Rafiq continued his opinions of men in high positions who could lower themselves to cheat.

The first spoonful of what was actually a delicious Arabian soup set Leona's stomach objecting. 'Never mind,' she said to soothe Samir's dramatically ruffled feathers as she quietly laid aside her spoon. 'Tomorrow you and I will race on the jet-skis and I promise that I, as an English gentlewoman, will not cheat.'

'Not on this trip, I am afraid,' Hassan himself inserted smoothly. 'All water sports are now stopped until we can replace the buoyancy aids with something more effective.'

Leona stared down the table at him. 'Just like that?' she protested. 'I have an unfortunate and one-in-a-million-chance accident and you put a stop on everyone else's fun?'

'You almost drowned. The life jacket did not do what it is designed to do. A million-to-one chance of it happening again makes the odds too great.'

'That is the voice of the master,' Samir noted.

'You heard it too, hmm?' Leona replied.

'Most indubitably,' Hassan agreed.

After that the conversation moved on to other things. Soup dishes were removed and replaced with a fish dish she didn't even attempt to taste. A richly sauced Arab dish followed, with a side bowl each of soft and fluffy steamed white rice.

The rice she thought she could just about manage to eat, Leona decided, listening intently to the story Imran Al-Mukhtar was telling her as she transferred a couple of spoonfuls of rice onto her plate then added a spoonful of sauce just for show.

One spoonful of soup, two forkfuls of rice. No fish. No attempt to even accept a sample of the thick honey pudding to conclude. Hassan watched it all, took grim note, glanced to one side to catch Evie's eye. She sent him a look that said that she had noticed too.

'The Sheikha Leona seems a little...pale,' Zafina Al-Yasin, sitting to one side of him, quietly put in. 'Is she not feeling quite herself?'

'You think so?' he returned with mild surprise. 'I think she looks exquisite. But then, I am smitten,' he allowed. 'It makes a difference as to how you perceive someone, don't you think?'

A steward came to stand at his side then, thankfully relieving him from continuing such a discussion.

With a nod of understanding he sent the steward hurrying over to the side table where he and his assistants began deftly uncorking the bottles of champagne. Picking up a spoon, he gave a couple of taps against a wine glass to capture everyone's attention.

'My apologies for interrupting your dinner,' he said, 'but in a few minutes our captain will sound the yacht's siren. As you can see, the stewards are in the process of setting a glass of champagne before each of you. It is not compulsory that you actually drink it,' he assured with a grin for those who never imbibed no matter what the occasion, 'but as a courtesy, in the time-honoured tradition of any sailing vessel. I would be most honoured if you would stand and join me by raising your glass in a toast. For we are about to cross the Tropic of Cancer...'

With the perfect timing of a man who was adept at such things, the siren gave three short sharp hoots at the same moment that Hassan rose to his feet. On a ripple of surprise everyone rose up also. Some drank, some didn't, but all raised their glasses. Then there was a mass exodus to the yacht's rail, where everyone stood gazing out into the inky dark Red Sea as if they expected to see some physical phenomenon like a thick painted line to mark this special place.

Of course there was none. It did not seem to matter. Moving to place his hands on the rail either side of his wife, Hassan bent to place his lips to her petal-smooth cheek.

'See anything?' he questioned teasingly.

'Oh, yes,' she replied. 'A signpost sticking out of the water. Did you miss it?'

His soft laugh was deep and soft and seductive. As she tilted back to look at him the back of her head met with his shoulder. She was smiling with her eyes. He wanted to drown in them. Kiss me, they were saying. An Arab did not kiss in front of guests, so a raised eyebrow ruefully refused the invitation. It was the witch in her that punished him for that refusal when one of her hands slid backwards and made a sensual sweep of one of his thighs.

Sensation spat hot pricks of awareness like needles deep into his flesh. She was right about the *dishdasha*, he conceded, it had to be one of the ancient reasons why his culture frowned upon close physical contact with the opposite sex whilst in the company of others.

'I will pay you back for that later,' he warned darkly.

'I am most seriously worried, my lord Sheikh,' she replied provokingly.

Then, in the way these things shifted, the private moment was broken when someone spoke to him. He straightened to answer Jibril Al-Mahmud who, since the meeting had spent every minute he could possibly snatch trying to squeeze himself back into Hassan's good graces. Leona took a sip at her champagne. That dreadful intruder, Samir, claimed the rest of her attention. He was, Hassan recognised, just a little infatuated with Leona, which offered another good reason why he would be happy when their cruise ended tomorrow.

Jibril's timid little wife came to join them. She smiled nervously at him and, because he felt rather sorry for her, Hassan sent her a pleasant smile back, then politely asked about her family. Raschid joined in. Evie and Imran went to join Leona and Samir. Abdul and Zafina were the last to join his own group but at least they did it, he acknowledged.

Tonight there was no splitting of the sexes. No lingering at the table for the men. They simply mingled, talked and lingered together. And, had it not been for one small but important detail, Hassan would have declared the evening— if not the whole cruise—a more than satisfactory success.

That small but important detail was Leona. Relaxed though she might appear, content though she might appear, he could see that the strain of the whole ordeal in general had begun to paint soft bruises around her eyes. He didn't like to see them there, did not like to notice that every so often the palm of her hand would go to rest against the flat of her stomach, as if to soothe away an inner distress.

Nor had he forgotten that she had barely eaten a morsel of food all day. He frowned down at his champagne glass, still brimming with its contents. Tomorrow they reached Jeddah. Tomorrow he would take her to visit a doctor, he decided grimly. If there was one rule you were taught never to ignore when you lived in a hot country, it was the rule about heeding any signs of illness. Maybe it was nothing.

Maybe it was all just down to stress. But maybe she had picked up something in the water when she fell in. Whatever—tomorrow he would make sure that they found out for definite.

It was a decision he found himself firmly repeating when they eventually retired to their stateroom and the first thing that Leona did was wilt.

'You are ill,' he said grimly.

'Just tired,' she insisted.

'Don't take me for a fool, Leona,' he ground back. 'You do not eat. You are clearly in some sort of discomfort. And you *look* ill.'

'All right.' She caved in. 'So I think I have developed a stomach bug. If we have time when we reach Jeddah tomorrow I will get something for it.'

'We will make time.'

'Fine.' She sighed.

He sighed. 'Here, let me help you…' She even looked too weary to undress herself.

So he did it for her—silently, soberly, a concentrated frown darkening his face. She smiled and kissed him. It really was too irresistible to hold the gesture in check. 'Don't turn into a minx just because I am indulging you,' he scolded, and parted the tunic, then let it slide to her feet.

'But I like it when you indulge me,' she told him, her eyes lowered to watch him reach for the front clasp holding the two smooth satin cups of her cream bra together. As the back of his knuckles brushed against the tips of her breasts she drew back with a sharp gasp.

'What?' he demanded.

'Sensitive.' She frowned. He frowned. They both glanced down to see the tight distension of her nipples standing pink and proud and wilfully erect. A small smug smile twitched at the corner of his mouth. Leona actually blushed.

'I'll finish the rest for myself,' she decided dryly.

'I think that would be wise,' Hassan grinned, and pulled

the *dishdasha* off over his head to show her why he had said that.

'I don't know.' She was almost embarrassed by how fiercely one responded to the closeness of the other. 'I'm supposed to be ill and tired and in need of much pampering.'

A set of warm brown fingers gently stroked the flush blooming in her cheek. 'I know of many ways to pamper,' he murmured sensually. 'Slow and gentle. Soft and sweet…'

His eyes glowed darkly with all of those promises; hers grew darker on the willingness to accept. The gap between them closed, warm flesh touched warm flesh, mouths came together on a kiss. Then he showed her. Deep into the night he showed her a hundred ways to pamper a woman until she eventually fell asleep in his arms and remained there until morning came to wake them up.

At breakfast she actually ate a half-slice of toast with marmalade and drank a full cup of very weak tea—hopefully without giving away the fact that it was a struggle not to give it all back up.

Little Hashim came to beg to be allowed to sit on her lap. Leona placed him there and together they enjoyed sharing the other half of her slice of toast, while Hassan looked on with a glaze across his eyes and Evie posed a sombre question at her husband, Raschid, with expressive eyes.

He got up and stepped around the table to lay a hand on Hassan's shoulder. The muscles beneath it were fraught with tension. 'I need a private word with you, Hassan,' he requested. 'If you have finished here?'

The same muscle flexed as Hassan pulled his mind back from where it had gone off to. 'Of course,' he said, and stood up. A moment later both men were walking away from the breakfast table towards the stairs which would take them down to the deck below and Hassan's private suite of offices.

Most watched them go. Many wondered why Sheikh Raschid felt it necessary to take Sheikh Hassan to one side. But none, friend nor foe—except for Evie, who kept her attention firmly fixed on the small baby girl in her arms—came even close to guessing what was about to be discussed.

By the time Raschid came to search his wife out she was back in their suite. She glanced anxiously up at him. Raschid lifted a rueful shoulder, 'Well, it is done,' he said. Though neither of them looked as if the statement pleased them in any way.

Well, it is done. That more or less said it. *Well it is done,* now held Hassan locked in a severe state of shock. He couldn't believe it. He wanted to believe it, but did not dare let himself because it changed everything: the view of his life; the view of his marriage.

He had to sit down. The edge of his desk was conveniently placed to receive his weight, and his eyes received the cover of a trembling hand. Beyond the closed door to his office his guests and the tail end of the cruise carried on regardless, but here in this room everything he knew and felt had come to a complete standstill.

He couldn't move. Now his legs had been relieved of his weight, they had lost the ability to take it back again. Inside he was shaking. Inside he did not know what to feel or what to think. For he had been here in this same situation before— many times—and had learned through experience that it was a place best avoided at all costs.

Hope—then dashed hopes. Pleasure—then pain. But this was different. This had been forced upon him by a source he had good reason to trust and not to doubt.

Doubt. Dear heaven, he was very intimate with the word doubt. Now, as he removed the hand from his eyes and stared out at the glistening waters he could see through the window, he found doubt being replaced by the kind of dancing visions he had never—ever—allowed himself to see before.

A knock sounded at the door, then it opened before he had a chance to hide his expression. Rafiq walked in, took one look at him and went rock solid still.

'What is it?' he demanded. 'Father?'

Hassan quickly shook his head. 'Come in and close the door,' he urged, then made an effort to pull himself together—just in case someone else decided to take him by surprise.

Leona.

Something inside him was suddenly threatening to explode. He didn't know what, but it scared the hell out of him. He wished Raschid had said nothing. He wished he could go back and replay the last half hour again, change it, lose it—

'Hassan...?' Rafiq prompted an explanation as to why he was witnessing his brother quietly falling apart.

He looked up, found himself staring into mirrors of his own dark eyes, and decided to test the ground—test those eyes to find out what Leona would see in his eyes if she walked in here right now.

'Evie—Raschid,' he forced out across a sand-dry throat. 'They think Leona might be pregnant. Evie recognises the signs...'

CHAPTER TEN

SILENCE fell. It was, Hassan recognised, a very deathly silence, for Rafiq was already showing a scepticism he dared not voice.

Understanding the feeling, Hassan released a hard sigh, then grimly pulled himself together. 'Get hold of our father,' he instructed. 'I need absolute assurance from him that I will not be bringing Leona back to a palace rife with rumour attached to her return.' From being hollowed by shock he was now as tight as a bowstring. 'If he has any doubts about this, I will place her in Raschid's safekeeping, for she must be protected at all cost from any more anguish or stress.'

'I don't think Leona will—'

'It is not and never has been anyone else's place to *think* anything about my wife!' The mere fact that he was lashing out at Rafiq showed how badly he was taking this. 'Other people's thinking has made our life miserable enough! Which is why I want you to speak to our father and not me,' he explained. 'I will have this conversation with no one else. Leona must be protected from ever hearing from anyone else that I am so much as suspecting this. If I am wrong then only I will grieve over what never was. If I am correct, then she has the right to learn of her condition for herself. I will not take this away from her!'

'So I am not even to tell our father,' Rafiq assumed from all of that.

'He and Leona communicate daily by e-mail,' Hasssan explained. 'The old man may be too puffed up with excitement to hold back from saying something to her.'

'In the state you are in, all of this planning may well be a waste of time,' Rafiq remarked with a pointed glance at his watch. 'In one hour we arrive in Jeddah. If you do not pull yourself together Leona will need only to look at your face to know that something catastrophic has taken place.'

Hassan knew it. Without warning he sank his face into his hands. 'This is crazy,' he muttered thickly.

'It is certainly most unexpected,' his brother agreed. 'And a little too soon for anyone, including the Al-Kadahs, to be making such confident judgements?' he posed cautiously.

Behind his hands Hassan's brain went still. Behind the hands it suddenly rushed ahead again, filling him with the kind of thoughts that made his blood run cold. For Rafiq was right: three weeks was not long enough—not to achieve what he was suggesting. As any man knew, it took only a moment to conceive a child. But which man—whose child?

On several hard curses he dragged his hand down. On several more he climbed to his feet then strode across the room to pull open the door that connected him with his aide.

'Faysal!' The man almost jumped out of his skin. 'Track down my father-in-law, wherever he is. I need to speak with him urgently.'

Slam. The door shut again. 'May Allah save me from the evil minds of others,' he grated.

'I do not follow you.' Rafiq frowned.

'Three weeks!' Hassan muttered. 'Three weeks ago Leona was sleeping in the same house as Ethan Hayes! It was one of the problems which forced me into bringing her to this yacht, if you recall...'

Leona didn't see Hassan until a few minutes before they were due to arrive in Jeddah. By then most of their guests were assembled on the shade deck taking refreshment while watching the yacht make the delicate manoeuvres required to bring such a large vessel safely into its reserved berth in the harbour.

In respect of Saudi Arabian custom everyone was wearing traditional Arab daywear, including little Hashim, who looked rather cute in his tiny white tunic and *gutrah*.

Hassan arrived dressed the same way; Rafiq was less than a step behind him. 'Hello, strangers.' Leona smiled at both of them. 'Where have you two been hiding yourselves all morning?'

'Working.' Rafiq smiled, but Hassan didn't even seem to hear her, and his gaze barely glanced across her face before he was turning to speak to Samir's father, Imran.

She frowned. He looked different—not pale, exactly, but under some kind of grim restraint. Then little Hashim demanded, 'Come and see,' and her attention was diverted. After that she had no time to think of anything but the formalities involved in bidding farewell to everyone.

A fleet of limousines stood in line along the concrete jetty waiting to speed everyone off to their various destinations. Accepting thanks and saying goodbye took over an hour. One by one the cars pulled up and took people away in a steady rota. Sheikh Abdul and Zafina first—relieved, Leona suspected, to be getting away from a trip that had not been a pleasant one for them, though their farewells were polite enough.

Sheikh Imran and Samir were the next to leave. Then she turned to smile at Sheikh Jibril and his wife, Medina, who made very anxious weight of their farewell, reminding Hassan several times that he had complete loyalty. In Jibril's case money talked much louder than power. He had no desire to scrape his deep pockets to pay Sheikh Raschid for the privilege of sending his oil across his land.

Raschid and his family were the last ones to leave. As with everyone else it would be a brief parting, because they would come together again next week, when they attended Sheikh Kalifa's anniversary celebration. Only this time the children would be staying at home with their nurse. So Leona's goodbyes to them were tinged with a genuine regret, especially for Hashim, who had become her little friend during their cruise. So, while she was promising to come and visit with him soon, she missed the rather sober exchanges between the others.

Eventually they left. Their car sped away. Rafiq excused himself to go and seek out Faysal, and Hassan said he had yet to thank his captain and walked away leaving her standing there, alone by the rail, feeling just a little bit rejected by the brevity with which he had treated her.

Something was wrong, she was sure, though she had no idea exactly what it could be. And, knowing him as well as she did, she didn't expect to find out until he felt ready to tell her. So with a shrug and a sigh she went off to follow Hassan's lead and thank the rest of the staff for taking care of everyone so well. By the time they came together again there was only time left to make the dash to the airport if they wanted to reach Rahman before nightfall.

Rafiq and Faysal travelled with them, which gave Hassan the excuse—and Leona was sure it *was* an excuse—to keep conversation light and neutral. A Lear jet bearing the gold Al-Qadim insignia waited on the runway to fly them over Saudi Arabia and into Rahman. The Al-Qadim oasis had its own private runway. A four-wheel drive waited to transport them to the palace whose ancient sandstone walls burned red against a dying sun.

Home, Leona thought, and felt a lump form in her throat because this was home to her. London…England—both had stopped being that a long time ago.

They swept through the gates and up to the front entrance. Hassan helped her to alight. As she walked inside she found herself flanked by two proud males again and wanted to lift her head and say something teasing about *abayas*, but the mood didn't allow for it somehow.

'My father wishes to see us straight away.' Hassan unwittingly explained the sombre mood. 'Please try not to show your shock at how much he has deteriorated since you were last here.'

'Of course,' she replied, oddly hurt that he felt he needed to say that. Then she took the hurt back when she saw the old sheikh reclining against a mound of pillows on his favourite divan.

His sons strode forward; she held back a little to allow them the space to greet him as they always did, with the old sheikh holding out both hands and both hands being taken, one by each son. In all the years she had known Sheikh Kalifa she had never seen him treat his two sons less than equal. They greeted each other; they talked in low-toned Arabic. They touched, they loved. It was an honour and a privilege to be allowed to witness it. When the old sheikh decided to acknowledge her presence he did so with a spice that told her that the old spirit was still very much alive inside his wasted frame.

'So, what do you think of my two warriors, huh?' he asked. 'They snatch you back with style and panache. A worthy woman cannot but be impressed.'

'Impressed by their arrogance, their cheek, and their disregard for my safety,' Leona responded, coming forward now that he had in effect given her permission to do so. 'I almost drowned—twice—and was tossed down a set of stairs. And you dare to be proud of them.'

No one bothered to accuse her of gross exaggeration, because he laughed, loving it, wishing he could have been there to join in. Reclaiming his hands, he waved his sons away and offered those long bony fingers to Leona.

'Come and greet me properly,' he commanded her. 'And you two can leave us. My daughter-in-law and I have things to discuss.'

There was a pause, a distinct hesitation in which Hassan looked ready to argue the point. The old man looked up at him and his son looked down; a battle of the eyes commenced that made Leona frown as a strange kind of tension began to sizzle in the air. Then Hassan conceded by offering a brief, grim nod and left, with Rafiq making the situation feel even stranger when, as he left with him, he placed a hand on Hassan's shoulder as if to reassure him that it would be okay.

'What was all that about?' she enquired as she reached down to brush a kiss on her father-in-law's hollowed cheek.

'He worries about you,' the old sheikh answered.

'Or he worries about you,' she returned.

He knew what she was referring to and flicked it away with a sigh and a wave of a hand. 'I am dying,' he stated bluntly. 'Hassan knows this—they both do. Neither likes knowing they can do nothing to stop it from happening.'

'But you are resigned?' Leona said gently.

'Yes. Come—sit down here, in your chair.' Discussion over, he indicated the low cushion-stuffed chair she had pulled up beside his divan years ago; it had remained there ever since. 'Now, tell me,' he said as soon as she was settled, 'have you come back here because Hassan bullied you into doing so, or because you still love him?'

'Can it be both?' she quizzed him.

'He needs you.'

'Rahman doesn't.'

'Ah,' he scathed, 'that stupid man, Abdul, thought he could force our hand and soon learned that he could not.'

'So it was Sheikh Abdul who plotted to take me,' Leona murmured ruefully.

Eyes that were once a rich dark brown but were now only pale shadows sharpened. 'He did not tell you,' he surmised on an impatient sigh. 'I am a fool for thinking he would.'

'Maybe that is why he didn't want to leave me alone with you,' Leona smilingly replied. 'Actually, I had already guessed it,' she then admitted, adding quietly, 'I know all about Nadira, you see.'

The name had a disturbing effect on Sheikh Khalifa: he shifted uncomfortably, pulled himself up and reached out to touch her cheek. 'Rahman needs my son and my son needs you. Whatever has to happen in the future I need to know that you will always be here supporting him when I can no longer do so.'

Strange words, fierce, dark, compelling words that sealed her inside a coating of ice. What was he saying? What did he mean? Was he telling her that Nadira was still Hassan's only real option if he wanted to continue in his father's foot-steps?

But before she could ask him to elaborate, as after most brief bursts of energy, Sheikh Khalifa suddenly lay back exhausted against the cushions and, without really thinking about it, Leona slipped back into her old routine. She picked up the book lying face down on the table beside him and began reading out loud to him.

But her mind was elsewhere. Her mind was filling up with contracts and Hassan's method of feeding her information on a need-to-know only basis. She saw him as he had been that same morning, relaxed, at peace with both her and himself. Then Raschid had begged a private word. When he'd eventually reappeared later it had been as if he had changed into a different man—a tense, preoccupied and distant man.

A man who avoided eye contact, as if he had something to hide...

The old sheikh was asleep. Leona put down the book.

Doubts; she hated to feel the doubts return. It was no use, she told herself, she was going to have to tackle Hassan about what Zafina had said to her. Once he had denied everything she could put the whole stupid thing away, never to be dredged up again.

And if he didn't deny it? she asked herself as she left the old sheikh's room to go in search of the younger one. The coating of ice turned itself into a heavy cloak that weighed down her footsteps as she walked in between pale blue walls on a cool, polished sandstone flooring.

She didn't want to do this, she accepted as she trod the wide winding staircase onto the landing where pale blue walls changed to pale beige and the floor became a pale blue marble.

She didn't want to reveal that she could doubt his word, she thought dully as she passed between doors made of thick cedar fitted tightly into wide Arabian archways, the very last one of which led through to Hassan's private suite of offices.

Her head began to ache; her throat suddenly felt strange:

hot and tight. She was about five yards away when the door suddenly opened and Hassan himself stepped out. Slender white tunic, flowing blue *thobe*, no covering on his raven-dark head. He saw her and stopped, almost instantly his expression altered from the frowningly preoccupied to... nothing.

It was like having a door slammed in her face. Her doubts surged upwards along with her blood pressure; she could feel her pulse throbbing in her ears. A prickly kind of heat engulfed her whole body—and the next thing that she knew, she was lying on the pale blue marble floor and Hassan was kneeling beside her.

'What happened?' he rasped as her eyes fluttered open.

She couldn't answer, didn't want to answer. She closed her eyes again. His curse wafted across her cheeks. One of his hands came to cover her clammy forehead, the other took a light grasp of her wrist then he was grimly sliding his arms beneath her shoulders and knees and coming to his feet.

'Ouch,' she said as her breasts brushed his breastbone.

Hassan froze. She didn't notice because from absolutely nowhere she burst into tears! What was the matter with her? she wondered wretchedly. She felt sick, she felt dizzy, she hurt in places she had never hurt before! From another place she had never known existed inside her, one of her clenched fists aimed an accusing blow at his shoulder.

Expecting him to demand what he had done to deserve it, she was thrown into further confusion when all he did was release a strained groan from deep in his throat, then began striding back the way from which she had come. A door opened and closed behind them. Lifting her head from his shoulder, she recognised their old suite of rooms.

Laying her on the bed, he came to lean over her. 'What did my father say to you?' he demanded. 'I knew I should not have left you both alone! Did he say you should not have come back, is that it?'

Her eyes flew open, tear-drenched and sparkling. 'Is that what he thinks?'

'Yes—no!' His sigh was driven by demons. But what demons—? The demons of lies? 'In case you did not notice,
he does not think so clearly any more,' he said tightly.

'Sheikh Abdul was behind the plot to abduct me; there is
nothing unclear about that, as far as I can see.'

'I knew it was a mistake.' Hassan sighed, and sat down
beside her.

He looked tired and fed up and she wanted to hit him
again. 'You lied to me again,' she accused him.

'By omission,' he agreed. 'And Abdul's involvement
cannot be proved,' he added. 'Only by hearsay which is not
enough to risk a war between families.'

'And you've always got the ready-typed contract involving
Nadira if things really do get out of hand...'

This time she saw the freeze overtake him. This time she
got the answer she had been desperately trying to avoid.
Sitting up, Leona ignored the way her head spun dizzily.
Drawing up her knees, she reached down to ease the straps
of her sandals off the backs of her heels, then tossed them
to the floor.

'He told you about that also?' Hassan asked hoarsely.

She shook her head. 'Zafina did.'

'When?'

'Does it really matter when?' she derided. 'It exists. I saw
it. You felt fit not to warn me about it. What do you think
that tells me about what is really going on around here?'

'It means nothing,' he claimed. 'It is just a meaningless
piece of paper containing words with no power unless several
people place their signatures against it.'

'But you have a copy.'

He didn't answer.

'You had it in your possession even before you came to
Spain to get me,' she stated, because she knew it was the
truth even though no one had actually told her so. 'What was
it—firm back-up in case Raschid failed to bail you out of
trouble? Or does it still carry a lot of weight around with it?'

'You could try trusting me,' he answered.

'And you, my lord sheikh, should have tried trusting me, then maybe it would not be the big problem it is.' With that, she climbed off the bed and began walking away.

'Where are you going?' He sighed out heavily. 'Come back here. We need to—'

The cold way she turned to look at him stopped the words; the way she had one hand held to her forehead and the other to her stomach paled his face. 'I am going to the bathroom to be sick,' she informed him. 'Then I am going to crawl into that bed and go to sleep. I would appreciate it if you were not still here when I get to do that.'

And that, Hassan supposed, had told him. He watched the bathroom door close behind her retreating figure.

He got up and strode over to the window beyond which an ink dark evening obliterated everything beyond the subtle lighting of the palace walls.

So where do we go from here? he asked himself. When Zafina Al-Yasin had picked her weapon, she'd picked it well. For Hassan could think of nothing more likely to shatter Leona's belief in his sincerity than a document already drawn up and ready to be brought into use should it become necessary. She would not now believe that he had agreed to the drawing up of such a document merely to buy him time. Why should she when he had refrained from telling her so openly and honestly before she'd found out by other means?

Sighing, he turned to leave the room. It was simpler to leave her alone for now. He could say nothing that was going to change anything, because he had another problem looming, he realised, One bigger and more potentially damaging than all that had tried to damage his marriage before.

He had a contract bearing his agreement to take a second wife. He had a wife whom he suspected might be carrying his first child. Leona was never going to believe that the former was not an insurance policy to protect him against the failure of the latter.

'Faysal,' he said as he stepped into his aide's office, which guarded the entrance to his own, 'get Rafiq for me, if you please…'

'You look pale like a ghost,' the old sheikh remarked.

'I'm fine,' Leona assured him.

'They tell me you fainted the other day.'

'I still had my sea legs on,' Leona explained. 'And how did you find out about it?' she challenged, because as far as she knew no one but herself and Hassan had been there at the time!

'My palace walls are equipped with a thousand eyes.' He smiled. 'So I also know that when he is not with me my son walks around wearing the face of a man whose father is already dead.'

'He is a busy man doing busy, important things,' Leona said with a bite that really should have been resisted.

'He also has a wife who sleeps in one place while he sleeps in another.'

Getting in practice, Leona thought nastily. 'Do you want to finish this chapter or not?' she asked.

'I would prefer you to confide in me,' the old sheikh murmured gently. 'You used to do so all the time, before I became too sick to be of any use to anyone…'

A blatant plucking of her heartstrings though it was, Leona could see the concern in his eyes. On a sigh, she laid the book aside, got up to go and sit down beside him and picked up one of his cool, dry, skeletal hands to press a gentle kiss to it.

'Don't fret so, old man,' she pleaded gently. 'You know I will look after your two sons for you. I have promised, haven't I?'

'But you are unhappy. Do you think this does not fret me?'

'I—struggle with the reasons why I am here,' she explained, because she wasn't going to lie. It wasn't fair to lie to him. 'You know the problems. They are not going to go away just because Hassan wants them to.'

'My son wants you above all things, daughter of Victor Frayne,' he said, using the Arab way of referring to her, because by their laws a woman kept her father's name after marriage. 'Don't make him choose to prove this to you...'

CHAPTER ELEVEN

DON'T make him choose... The next day, those words played inside Leona's head like a mantra, because she had just begun to realise that Hassan might not be forced to choose anything.

Sickness in the morning, sickness in the evening, a certain tenderness in her breasts and other changes in her body that she could no longer ignore were trying to tell her something she was not sure she wanted to know.

Pregnant. She could be pregnant. She *might* be pregnant. She absolutely refused to say that she was *most definitely* pregnant. How could she be sure, when her periods had never been anything but sporadic at best? Plus it had to be too soon to tell. It had to be. She was just wishing on rainbows—wasn't she?

A month. She had been back in Hassan's life for a tiny month—and not even a full month! Women just didn't know that quickly if they had conceived, did they? She didn't know. At this precise moment she didn't know anything. Her brain was blank, her emotions shot and she was fighting an ever-growing battle with excitement that was threatening to turn her into a puff of smoke!

It was this morning that had really set her suspicions soaring, when she'd climbed out of bed feeling sick and dizzy before her feet had managed to touch the floor. Then, in the shower, she'd seen the changes in her breasts, a new fullness, darkening circles forming round their tips. She'd *felt* different too—inside, where it was impossible to say how she felt different, only that she did.

Instinct. What did she know about the female instinct in such situations?

163

Doubt. She had to doubt her own conclusions because the specialists had given her so little hope of it ever happening for them.

But even her skin felt different, her hair, the strange, secret glint she kept on catching in her own eyes whenever she looked in a mirror. She'd stopped looking in the mirror. It was easier not to look than look and then see, then dare— *dare* to hope.

I want Hassan, she thought on a sudden rocketing rise of anxiety.

I don't want Hassan! she then changed her mind. Because if he saw her like this he would know something really drastic was worrying her and she couldn't tell him—didn't dare tell him, raise his hopes, until she was absolutely sure for herself.

She needed one of those testing kits, she realised. But, if such a thing was obtainable, where could she get one from without alerting half of Rahman? There was not a chemist's in the country she could walk into and buy such an obvious thing without setting the jungle drums banging from oasis to oasis and back again.

But I need one. I *need* one! she thought agitatedly.

Ring Hassan, that tiny voice inside her head persisted. Tell him your suspicions, get him to bring a pregnancy testing kit home with him.

Oh, yes, she mocked that idea. I can just see Sheikh Hassan Al-Qadim walking into a chemist's and buying one of those!

Rafiq, then. No, *not* Rafiq! she all but shouted at herself. Oh, why could there not be some more women in this wretched house of Al-Qadim? Why do I have to be surrounded by men?

Maids. There were dozens of maids she could call upon— all of whom would be just as proficient at belting out the message across the whole state.

As if she'd conjured her up a knock sounded on the door and one of the maids walked into the room. She was carrying a dress that Leona had ordered to be delivered from one of her favourite couturier's in the city.

'It is very beautiful, my lady,' the maid said shyly.

And very red, Leona thought frowningly. What in heaven's name had made her choose to buy red? Made by a local designer to a traditional Arabian design, the dress was silk, had matching trousers and *thobe*, and shimmered with beautifully embroidered golden threads. And she never, ever wore red!

'The sheikha will shine above all things tomorrow night,' the maid approved.

Tomorrow night, Leona repeated with a sinking heart as the maid carried the dress into her dressing room. For tomorrow night was *the* night of Sheikh Kalifa's anniversary celebration, which meant she had a hundred guests to play hostess to when really all she wanted to do was—

Oh, she thought suddenly, where is my head? And she turned to walk quickly across the room towards the telephone which sat beside the bed.

Pregnant.

Her feet pulled to a stop. Her stomach twisted itself into a knot then sprang free again, catching at her breath. It was a desperate sensation. Desperate with hope and with fear and a thousand other things that—

The maid appeared again, looked at her oddly because she was standing here in the middle of the room, emulating a statue. 'Thank you, Leila,' she managed to say.

As soon as the door closed behind the maid she finished her journey to the telephone, picked up her address book, flicked through its pages with trembling fingers, then stabbed in a set of numbers that would connect her with Evie Al-Kadah in Behran.

Hassan was fed up. He was five hours away from home, on his way back from Sheikh Abdul's summer palace, having just enjoyed a very uncomfortable meeting in which a few home truths had been aired. He should be feeling happy, for the meeting had gone very much his way, and in his possession he now had the sheikh's copy of one ill-judged contract and the satisfaction of knowing the man and his wife now understood the error of their ways.

But it had required a five-hour drive out to mountains of Rahman to win this sense of grim satisfaction, which meant they now had to make the same journey back again. And Rafiq might feel *he* needed the physical exercise of negotiating the tough and challenging terrain but, quite frankly, so did he. He felt tense and restless, impatient to get back to Leona now that he could face her with an easy conscience.

So the flat tire they suffered a few minutes later was most unwelcome. By the time they had battled in soft sand on a rocky incline to jack the car up and secure it so they could change the wheel time was getting on, and the sun was beginning to set. Then, only a half-mile further into their journey, they became stuck in deep soft sand. And he couldn't even blame Rafiq for this second inconvenience because he had taken over the driving for himself. Proficient though they were at getting themselves out of such difficulties, time was lost, then more time when they were hit by a sandstorm that forced them to stop and wait until it had blown past.

Consequently, it was very late when they drove through the gates of the palace. By the time he had washed the sand from his body before letting himself quietly into the bedroom he found Leona fast asleep.

Did he wake her or did he go away? he pondered as he stood looking down on her, lying there on her side, with her glorious hair spilling out behind her and a hand resting on the pillow where his head should be.

She murmured something, maybe because she sensed he was there, and the temptation to just throw caution to the wind, slide into the bed and awaken her so he could confide his suspicions then discover whether she felt he was making any sense almost got the better of him.

Then reality returned, for this was not the time for such an emotive discussion. It could backfire on him and deeply hurt her. And tomorrow was a day packed with strife enough for both of them, without him adding to it with what could be merely a foolish dream.

Anyway, he had some damage limitation to perform, preferably before this new development came into the open—just in case.

So, instead of waking her, he turned away, unaware that behind him her eyes had opened to watch him leave. The urge to call him back tugged at her vocal cords. The need to scramble out of the bed and go after him to confide her suspicions stretched nerve ends in every muscle she possessed.

But, no, it would not be fair to offer him hope where there might be none. Better to wait one more day until she knew for sure one way or another, she convinced herself.

So the door between their two rooms closed him away from her—just as it had closed him away before, when he had decided it was better to sleep elsewhere than risk another argument with her.

Maybe he was right. Maybe the common sense thing to do was stay out of each other's way, because they certainly didn't function well together unless they were in bed!

They had a battleground, not a marriage, she decided, and on that profound thought she turned her back on that wretched closed door and refused to look back at it.

The next day continued in much the same fashion. He avoided her. She avoided him. They circulated the palace in opposing directions like a pair of satellites designed never to cross paths. By six o'clock Leona was in her room preparing for the evening ahead. By seven she was as ready as she supposed she ever would be, having changed her mind about what to wear a hundred times before finally deciding to wear the red outfit.

When Hassan stepped into the room a few minutes later he took her breath away. Tall, lean and not yet having covered his silky dark hair, he was wearing a midnight blue long tunic with a standing collar braided in gold. At his waist a wide sash of gold silk gave his body shape and stature, and the jewel encrusted shaft belonging to the ceremonial scabbard he had tucked into his waistband said it all.

Arrogance personified. A prince among men. First among equals did not come into it for her because for her he was it—the one—her only one. As if to confirm that thought her belly gave a skittering flutter as if to say, And me, don't forget me.

Too soon for that, too silly to think it, she scolded herself as she watched him pause to look at her. As always those dark eyes made their possessive pass over her. As always they liked what they saw.

'Beautiful,' he murmured.

Tell me about it, she wanted to say, but she couldn't, didn't dare say anything in case the wrong thing popped anxiously out.

So the twist his mouth gave said he had misread her silence. 'Forgiveness, my darling, is merely one sweet smile away,' he drawled as he walked towards her.

'But you have nothing to forgive me for!' she protested, glad now to use her voice.

'Throwing me out of your bed does not require forgiveness?' An eyebrow arched, the outfit, the coming occasion, turning the human being into a pretentious monster that made her toes curl inside her strappy gold shoes. With life, that was what they curled with. Life.

I love this man to absolute pieces. 'You left voluntarily,' she told him. 'In what I think you would describe as a sulk.'

'Men do not sulk.'

But you are not just any man, she wanted to say, but the comment would puff up his ego, so she settled for, 'What do they do, then?'

'Withdraw from a fight they have no hope of winning.' He smiled. Then on a complete change of subject, he said, 'Here, a peace offering.' And he held out a flat package wrapped in black silk and tied up with narrow red ribbon.

Expecting the peace offering to be jewellery, the moment

she took possession of the package she knew it was too light. So...what? she asked herself, then felt her heart suddenly drop to her slender ankles as a terrible suspicion slid snake-like into her head.

No, she denied it. Evie just would not break such a precious confidence. 'What is it?' she asked warily.

'Open it and see.'

Trembling fingers did as he bade her, fumbling with the ribbon and then with the square of black silk. Inside it was a flat gold box, the kind that could be bought at any gift shop, nothing at all like she had let herself wonder, and nothing particularly threatening about it, but still she felt her breath snag in her chest as she lifted the lid and looked inside.

After that came the frown while she tried to work out why Hassan was giving her a box full of torn scraps of white paper. Then she turned the top one over, recognised the insignia embossed upon it and finally realised what it was.

'You know what they are?' he asked her quietly.

'Yes.' She swallowed.

'All three copies of the contract are now in your possession,' he went on to explain anyway. 'All evidence that they were ever composed wiped clean from Faysal's computer hard disk. There, it is done. Now we can be friends again.' Without giving her a chance to think he took the gift and its packaging back from her and tossed it onto the bed.

'But it doesn't wipe clean the fact that it was written in the first place,' she pointed out. 'And nor does it mean it can't be typed up again in five short minutes if it was required to be done.'

'You have said it for yourself,' Hassan answered. 'I must require it. I do not require it. I give you these copies for ceremonial purposes, only to *show* you that I do not require it. Subject over, Leona,' he grimly concluded, 'for I will waste no more of my time on something that had only ever been meant as a diversion tactic to buy me time while I decided what to do about Sheikh Abdul and his ambitious plans.'

'You expect me to believe all of that, don't you?'

'Yes.' It was a coldly unequivocal yes.

She lifted her chin. For the first time in days they actually made eye contact. And it was only as it happened that she finally began to realise after all of these years *why* they avoided doing it when there was dissension between them. Eye contact wiped out everything but the truth. The *love* truth. The *need* truth. The absolute and utter *total* truth. I love him; he loves me. Who or what else could ever really come between that?

'I think I'm pregnant,' she whispered.

It almost dropped him like a piece of crumbling stone at her feet. She saw the shock; she saw the following pallor. She watched his eyes close and feared for a moment that *he* was actually going to faint.

For days he had been waiting for this moment, Hassan was thinking. He had yearned for it, had begged and had prayed for it. Yet, when it came, not only had he not been ready, the frightened little remark had virtually knocked him off his feet!

'I could kill you for this,' he ground out hoarsely. 'Why here? Why now, when in ten short minutes we are expected downstairs to greet a hundred guests?'

His response was clearly not the one she had been expecting. Her eyes began to glaze, her mouth to tremble. 'You don't like it,' she quavered.

'Give me strength.' He groaned. 'You stupid, unpredictable, aggravating female. Of course I like it! But look at me! I am now a white-faced trembling mess!'

'You just gave me something I really needed. I wanted to give you something back that you needed,' she explained.

'Ten minutes before I face the upper echelons of Arabian society?'

'Well, thanks for being concerned about how I am feeling!' she flashed back at him.

She was right. 'You've just knocked me for six,' he breathed unsteadily.

'And I might be wrong, so don't start going off the deep end about it!' she snapped, and went to turn away.

Oh, Allah, help him, what was he doing here? With shaking hands he took hold of her by her silk-swathed shoulders and pulled her against him. She was trembling too. And she *felt* different, slender and frail and oh, so precious.

He kissed her— What else did a man do when he was so blown away by everything about her?

'I should not have dropped it on you like this,' she murmured repentantly a few seconds later.

'Yes, you should,' he argued. 'How else?'

'It might come to nothing.' Anxiety was playing havoc with her beautiful eyes.

'We will deal with the something or the nothing together.'

'I am afraid of the nothing,' she confessed to him. 'I am afraid I might never get the chance to feel like this again.'

'I love you,' he said huskily. 'Can that not be enough?'

'For you?' She threw the question back at him, clinging to his eyes like a vulnerable child.

'We know how I feel, Leona,' he said ruefully. 'In fact, the whole of Rahman knows how I feel about you. But we hardly ever discuss how you feel about the situation I place you in here.'

'I just don't want you to have to keep defending my place in your life,' she told him. 'I hate it.'

Hassan thought about the damage-control exercise he had already set into motion, and wished he knew how to answer that. 'I like defending you.' His words seemed to say it all for him.

'You won't tell anyone tonight, will you?' she flashed up at him suddenly. 'You will keep this our secret until we know for sure.'

'Do you really think I am that manipulative?' He was shocked, then uncomfortable, because he realised that she knew him better than he knew himself. 'Tomorrow we will bring in a doctor,' he decided, looking for an escape from his own manipulative thoughts.

But Leona shook her head. 'It would be all over Rahman in five minutes if we did that. Look what happened when I went to see him to find out why I couldn't conceive?'

'But we have to know—'

'Evie is bringing me a pregnancy testing kit with her,' she told him, too busy trying to smooth some semblance of calmness into herself to notice how still he had gone. 'I rang her and explained. At least I can trust her not to say anything to anyone.'

'What did she say?' Hassan enquired carefully.

'She said I should make sure I tell you. Which I've done.' She turned a wry smile on him. 'Now I wish that I hadn't because, looking at you, I have a horrible feeling you are going to give the game away the moment anyone looks at you.'

Confess all, he told himself. Tell her before the Al-Kadahs tell her that you already suspected all of this, days ago. A knock at the door was a thankful diversion. Going to open it, he found Rafiq standing there dressed very much like himself—only he was wearing his *gutrah*.

'Our guests are arriving,' he informed him. 'You and Leona should be downstairs.'

Guests. Dear heaven. His life was in crisis and he must go downstairs and be polite to people. 'We will be five minutes only.'

'You are all right?' Rafiq frowned at him.

No, I am slowly sinking beneath my own plots and counter-plots. 'Five minutes,' he repeated, and closed the door again.

Leona was standing by a mirror, about to fix her lipstick with a set of very unsteady fingers. The urge to go over there and stop her so that he could kiss her almost got the better of him. But one kiss would most definitely lead to another and another. In fact he wanted to be very primitive and drag her off by her beautiful hair to his lair and smother her in kisses. So instead he stepped back into the other room and came back a moment later wearing white silk on his head, held by triple gold thongs, to find that Leona had also covered her hair with a gold-spangled scarf of red silk.

The red should have clashed with her hair but it didn't. It merely toned with the sensual colour on her lips. She lifted her eyes to look at him. He looked back at her. A different man, a different woman. It was amazing what a piece of silk laid to the head could do for both of them, because neither was now showing signs of what was really going on inside them.

His smile, therefore, was rueful. 'Showtime,' he said.

And showtime it was. As on the yacht, but on a grander scale, they welcomed heads of state from all over Arabia, diplomats from further afield. Some brought their wives, sons and even their daughters, and some came alone. Some women were veiled; all were dressed in the exotic jewelled colours favoured by Arabian women.

Everyone was polite, gracious, and concerned about Sheikh Khalifa's well-being. He had not yet put in an appearance, though he had every intention of doing so eventually. This was his night. He had in fact planned it as much as he could from his sick bed. Today his doctor had insisted he be sedated for most of the day to conserve his energy. But he had looked bright-eyed and excited when Leona had popped in to see him just before she had gone to get ready.

'Rafiq should be doing this with us,' Leona said to Hassan when she realised that his brother was nowhere to be seen.

'He has other duties,' he replied, then turned his attention to the next person to arrive at the doors to the great hall. A great hall that was slowly filling with people.

Sheikh Abdul arrived without his wife, Zafina, which seemed a significant omission to Leona. He was subdued but polite to her, which was all she could really expect from him, she supposed. They greeted Sheikh Jibril and his wife, Medina, Sheikh Imran, and of course Samir.

When Sheikh Raschid Al-Kadah and his wife, Evie, arrived, there were some knowing glances exchanged that made Leona want to blush. But the real blushing happened every time Hassan glanced at her and his eyes held the burning darkness of their secret.

'Don't,' she whispered, looking quickly away from him.

'I cannot help it,' he replied.

'Well, try.' A sudden disturbance by the door gave her someone new to divert her attention, only to have her heart stop in complete surprise.

Two men dressed in black western dinner suits, white shirts and bow ties. She flicked her eyes from one smiling male face to the other, then on a small shriek of delight launched herself into the arms of her father.

Tall, lean and in very good shape for his fifty-five years, Victor Frayne caught his daughter to him and accepted her ecstatic kisses to his face. 'What are you doing here? Why didn't you tell me? Ethan—' One of her hands reached out to catch one of his. 'I can't believe this! I only spoke to you this morning. I thought you were in San Estéban!'

'No, the Marriott, here.' Her father grinned at her. 'Thank your husband for the surprise.'

Hassan. She turned, a hand each clinging to her two surprises. 'I love you,' she said impulsively.

'She desires to make me blush,' Hassan remarked, and stepped forward, took his wife by her waist, then offered his hand to his father-in-law and to Ethan Hayes. 'Glad you could make it,' he said.

'Happy to be here,' Ethan replied with only a touch of dryness to his tone to imply that there was more to this invitation than met the eye.

Leona was just too excited to notice. Too wrapped up in her surprise to notice the ripple of awareness that went through those people who had dared to believe rumours about her relationship with her father's business partner. Then, with the attention to fine detail which was Hassan's forte, another diversion suddenly appeared.

People stopped talking, silence reigned as Rafiq arrived,

pushing a wheelchair bearing Sheikh Khalifa ben Jusef Al-Qadim.

He looked thin and frail against the height and breadth of his youngest son. A wasted shadow of his former self. But his eyes were bright, his mouth smiling, and in the frozen stasis that followed his arrival, brought on by everyone's shock at how ill he actually looked, he was prepared and responded. 'Welcome…welcome everyone,' he greeted. 'Please, do not continue to look as if you are attending my funeral, for I assure you I am here to enjoy myself.'

After that everyone made themselves relax again. Some who knew him well even grinned. As Rafiq wheeled him towards the other end of the room the old sheikh missed no one in reach of his acknowledgement. Not even Leona's father, whom he had only met once or twice. 'Victor,' he greeted him. 'I have stolen your daughter. She is now my most precious daughter. I apologise to you, but I am not sorry, you understand?'

'I think we can share her,' Victor Frayne allowed graciously.

'And…ah…' he turned his attention to Ethan '…Mr Hayes, it is my great pleasure to meet Leona's very good friend.' He had the floor, as it should be. So no one could miss the messages being broadcast here. Even Leona began to notice that something was going on beneath the surface here. 'Victor…Mr Hayes…come and see me tomorrow. I have a project I believe will be of great interest to you… Ah, Rafiq, take me forward, for I can see Sheikh Raschid…'

He progressed down the hall like that. As Leona watched, she gently slipped her arm around Hassan's waist. She could feel the emotion pulsing inside him. For this was probably going to be the old Sheikhs final formal duty.

But nothing, nothing prepared her for the power of feeling that swept over everyone as Rafiq and his father reached the other end of the hall where Sheikh Khalifa's favourite divan had been placed upon a raised dais, ready for him to enjoy the party in reasonable comfort.

Rafiq bent and lifted his father into his arms and carried the frail old man up the steps then gently lowered his father down again. As he went to straighten, the sheikh lifted a pale bony hand to his youngest son's face and murmured something to him which sent Rafiq to his knees beside the divan and sent his covered head down.

The strong and the weak. It was a painful image that held everyone in its thrall because in those few seconds it was impossible to tell which man held the strength and which one was weaker.

'Hassan, go to him,' Leona said huskily. 'Rafiq needs you.'

But Hassan shook his head. 'He will not thank me,' he replied. And he was right; Leona knew that.

Instead Hassan turned his attention to causing yet another diversion by snapping his fingers to pull a small army of servants into use.

They came bearing trays of delicately made sweets and Arabian coffee and *bukhoor* burners, which filled the air with the smell of incense. The mood shifted, took on the characteristics of a traditional *majlis*, and the next time Leona looked the dais was surrounded by the old sheikhs from the desert tribes sitting around on the provided cushions while Sheikh Khalifa reclined on his divan enjoying their company.

Hassan took her father and Ethan with him and circulated the room, introducing them to their fellow guests. The timid Medina Al-Mahmud attached herself to Leona's side like a rather wary limpit and, taking pity on her, Leona found herself taking the older woman with her as they moved from group to group.

It was a success. The evening was really looking as if it was going to be a real success. And then from somewhere behind her she heard Sheikh Abdul say, 'A clever ploy. I am impressed by his strategy. For how many men here would now suspect Mr Hayes as his lovely wife's lover?'

She pretended not to hear, smiled her bright smile and just kept on talking. But the damage was done. The evening was ruined for her. For it had not once occurred to her that her father and Ethan were here for any other purpose than because Hassan wanted to please her.

Evie appeared at her side to save her life. 'Show me where I can freshen up,' she requested.

As Leona excused herself from those she was standing with, a hand suddenly gripped her sleeve. 'You heard; I saw your face. But you must not listen,' Medina advised earnestly. 'For he has the bad mouth and his wife is in purdah after Sheikh Hassan's visit yesterday.'

Sheikh Hassan's visit? Curiouser and curiouser, Leona thought grimly as she took a moment to reassure Medina before moving away with Evie Al-Kadah.

'What was that all about?' Evie quizzed.

'Nothing.' Leona dismissed the little incident.

But from across the room Hassan saw the green glint hit her eyes and wondered what had caused it. Had Evie let the proverbial cat out of the bag, or was it the timid Medina who had dared to stick in the knife?

He supposed he would soon find out, he mused heavily, and redirected his attention to whoever it was speaking to him, hoping he had not missed anything important.

The evening moved on; the old sheikh grew tired. His two sons appeared by the side of his divan. He did not demur when Hassan gently suggested he bid goodnight to everyone. Once again Rafiq lifted him into his wheelchair with the same gentleness that would be offered a fragile child. His departure was achieved quietly through a side door, as the old Sheikh himself had arranged.

Leona was standing with her father and Ethan as this quiet departure took place. 'How long?' Victor asked her gravely.

'Not very long,' she answered, then chided herself because Sheikh Khalifa wished his thirtieth celebration to be an occasion remembered for its hospitality, not as his obituary.

It was very late by the time people began leaving. Even later before Leona felt she could dare to allow herself a sigh of relief at how relatively pain-free the whole evening had turned out to be.

Which suddenly reminded her of something she still had to do that might not be as pain free. Her heart began thudding as Hassan came to take her hand and walk her towards the stairs. She could feel his tension, knew that his mind had switched onto the same wavelength as her own. Hand in hand they trod the wide staircase to the floor above. The door to the private apartments closed behind them.

'Did Evie bring—'

'Yes,' she interrupted, and moved right away from him. Now the moment of truth had arrived Leona found she was absolutely terrified. 'I don't want to know,' she admitted.

'Then leave it for now,' Hassan answered simply.

She turned to look anxiously at him. 'But that's just being silly.'

'Yes,' he agreed. 'But tomorrow the answer will still be the same, and the next day and the next.'

Maybe it was a good thing that the telephone began to ring. Hassan moved away from her to go and answer it. Thirty seconds later he was sending her a rueful smile. 'My father is restless,' he explained. 'Over-excited and in need of talk. Will you mind if I go to him, or shall I get Rafiq to—?'

'No,' she said quickly. 'You go.' She really was a pathetic coward.

'You won't...do anything without me with you?' he murmured huskily.

She shook her head. 'Tomorrow,' she promised. 'W-when I am feeling less tired and able to cope with...' *The wrong answer*, were the words she couldn't say.

Coming back to her, Hassan gave her a kiss of understanding. 'Go to bed,' he advised, 'Try to sleep. I will come back just as soon as I can.'

He was striding towards the door when she remembered. 'Hassan... My father and Ethan were invited here for a specific purpose, weren't they?'

He paused at the door, sighed and turned to look at her. 'Damage limitation,' he confirmed. 'We may not like it. We may object to finding such a demeaning act necessary. But the problem was there, and had to be addressed. *Inshallah.*' He shrugged, turned and left.

CHAPTER TWELVE

INSHALLAH—as Allah wills. It was, she thought, the perfect throwaway answer to an uncomfortable subject. On a dissatisfied sigh she moved across the room to begin to prepare for bed.

Already tucked out of sight in the drawer of her bedside cabinet lay the offerings Evie had brought with her from Behran. Just glancing at the drawer was enough to make her shudder a little, because the pregnancy testing kit had too much power for her comfort. So she turned away to pull on her pyjamas, slid into bed and switched off the light without glancing at the cabinet again. Sleep came surprisingly quickly, but then it had been a long day.

When she woke up, perhaps an hour later, she thought for a few moments that Hassan must have come back and disturbed her when he'd got into the bed. But there was no warm body lying beside her. No sign of life in evidence through the half-open bathroom door.

Then she knew. She didn't know how she knew, but suddenly she was up and pulling on a robe, frantically trying the belt as she hurried for the door. It was as if every light in the palace was burning. Her heart dropped to her stomach as she began racing down the stairs.

It was the sheikh. Instinct, premonition, call it what you wanted; she just knew there was something badly wrong.

On bare feet she ran down the corridor and arrived at his door to find it open. She stepped inside, saw nothing untoward except that neither the sheikh nor Hassan was there. Then she heard a noise coming from the room beyond, and with a sickening thud her heart hit her stomach as she made her way across the room to that other door.

180

On the other side was a fully equipped hospital room that had been constructed for use in the event of emergencies like the one Leona found herself faced with now.

She could not see the old sheikh because the doctors and nurses were gathered around him. But she could see Hassan and Rafiq standing like two statues at the end of the bed. They were gripping the rail in front of them with a power to crush metal, and their faces were as white as the *gutrahs* that still covered their heads.

Anguish lurked in every corner, the wretched sound of the heart monitor pulsing out its frighteningly erratic story like a cold, ruthless taunt. It was dreadful, like viewing a scene from a horror movie. Someone held up a hypodermic needle, clear liquid sprayed into the air. The lights were bright and the room bare of everything but clinical-white efficiency.

No, she thought, no, they cannot do this to him. He needs his room, with his books and his divan and his favourite pile of cushions. He needed to be surrounded by love, his sons, gentle music, not that terrible beep that felt to her as if it was draining the very life out of him.

'Switch it off,' she said thickly, walking forward on legs that did not seem to belong to her. 'Switch if off!' she repeated. 'He doesn't want to hear that.'

'Leona…' Hassan spoke her name in a hoarse whisper.

She looked at him. He looked at her. Agony screamed in the space between them. 'Tell them to switch it off,' she pleaded with him.

His face caved in on a moment's loss of composure. Rafiq didn't even seem to know that she was there. 'Don't…' he said huskily.

He wanted her to accept it. Her throat became a ball of tears as she took those final few steps then looked, really looked down at the ghost-like figure lying so still in the bed.

No, she thought again, no, they can't do this to him. Not here, not now. Her hand reached out to catch hold of one of his, almost knocking the nurse who was trying to treat him.

He felt so cold he might have been dead already. The tears moved to her mouth and spilled over her trembling lips. 'Sheikh,' she sobbed out, 'you just can't do this!'

'Leona...'

The thin, frail fingers she held in her hand tried to move. Oh, dear God, she thought painfully. He knows what is happening to him! 'Switch that noise off—switch it off!'

The fingers tried their very best to move yet again. Panic erupted. Fear took charge of her mind. 'Don't you dare bail on us now, old man!' she told him forcefully.

'Leona!' Hassan warning voice came stronger this time. He was shocked. They were all shocked. She didn't care.

'Listen to me,' she urged, lifting that frighteningly cold hand up to her cheek. The fingers moved again. He was listening. He could hear her. She moved closer, pushing her way past the doctor—a nurse—someone. She leaned over the bed, taking that precious hand with her. Her hair streamed over the white pillows as she came as close to him as she could. 'Listen,' she repeated, 'I am going to have a baby, Sheikh. Your very first grandchild. Tell me that you understand!'

The fingers moved. She laughed, then sobbed and kissed those fingers. Hassan came to grasp her shoulder. 'What do you think you are doing?' he rasped.

He was furious. She couldn't speak, couldn't answer, because she didn't *know* what she was doing. It had all just come out as if it was meant to. *Inshallah*, she thought.

'He can hear.' She found her voice. 'He knows what I am telling him.' Tremulously she offered Hassan his father's hand. 'Talk to him,' she pleaded. 'Tell him about our baby.' Tears were running down her cheeks and Hassan had never looked so angry. 'Tell him. He needs to hear it from you. Tell him, Hassan, please...'

That was the point when the monitor suddenly went haywire. Medics lunged at the sheikh, Hassan dropped his father's hand so he could grab hold of Leona and forcibly drag her aside. As the medical team went down in a huddle

Hassan was no longer just white, he was a colour that had never been given a name. 'You had better be telling him the truth or I will never forgive you for doing this,' he sliced at her.

Leona looked at the monitor, listened to its wild, palpitating sound. She looked at Rafiq, at what felt like a wall of horrified and disbelieving faces, and on a choked sob she broke free from Hassan and ran from the room.

Back down the corridor, up the stairs, barely aware that she was passing by lines of waiting, anxious servants. Gaining entrance to their apartments, she sped across the floor to the bedside cabinet. Snatching up Evie's testing kit, trembling and shaking, she dropped the packet twice in her attempt to remove the Cellophane wrapping to get the packet inside. She was sobbing by the time she had reached the contents. Then she unfolded the instruction leaflet and tried to read through a bank of hot tears, what it was she was supposed to do.

She was right; she was sure she was right. Nothing—nothing in her whole life had ever felt as right as this! Five minutes later she was racing downstairs again, running down the corridor in between the two lines of anxious faces, through doors and into the sheikh's room and over to her husband.

'See!' she said. 'See!' There were tears and triumph and sheer, shrill agony in her voice as she held out the narrow bit of plastic towards Hassan. 'Now tell him! *Please…!*' she begged him.

'Leona…' Hassan murmured very gently.

Then she heard it. The silence. The dreadful, agonising, empty silence. She spun around to look at the monitor. The screen was blank.

The screen was blank. 'No,' she breathed shakily. 'No.' Then she sank in a deep faint to the ground.

Hassan could not believe that any of this was really happening. He looked blankly at his father, then at his wife, then at the sea of frozen faces, and for a moment he actually thought he was going to join Leona and sink into a faint.

'Look after my son's wife.' A frail voice woke everyone up from their surprise. 'I think she has earned some attention.'

Before Hassan could move a team of experts had gone down over Leona and he was left standing there staring down at the bit of white plastic she had placed in his hand.

She was pregnant. She had just told him that this red mark in the window meant that she was pregnant. In the bed a mere step away his father was no longer fading away before his eyes.

Leona had done it. She'd brought him back from the brink, had put herself through the trauma of facing the answer on this small contraption, and she'd done both without his support.

'Courage,' he murmured. He had always known she possessed courage. 'And where was I when she needed my courage?'

'Here,' a level voice said. 'Sit down.' It was Rafiq, offering him a chair to sit upon. The room was beginning to look like a war zone.

He declined the chair. Leave me with some semblance of dignity, he thought. 'Excuse me,' he said, and stepped through the kneeling shapes round Leona, and bent and picked her up in his arms. 'But, sir, we should check she is...'

'Leave him be,' the old sheikh instructed. 'He is all she needs and he knows it.'

He did not take her far, only to his father's divan, where he laid her down, then sat beside her. She looked pale and delicate, and just too lovely for him to think straight. So he did what she had done with his father and took hold of her hand, then told her, 'Don't you dare bail out on us now, you little tyrant, even if you believe we deserve it.'

'We?' she mumbled.

'Okay, me,' he conceded. 'My father is alive and well, by

the way. I thought it best to tell you this before you begin to recall exactly why you fainted.'

'He's all right?' Her gold-tipped lashes flickered upwards, revealing eyes the colour of a sleepy lagoon.

I feel very poetic, Hassan thought whimsically. 'Whether due to the drugs or your bullying, no one is entirely certain. But he opened his eyes and asked me what you were talking about just a second after you flew out of the room.'

'He's all right.' Relief shivered through her, sending her eyes closed again. Feeling the shiver, Hassan reached out to draw one of his father's rugs over her reclining frame.

'Where am I?' she asked after a moment.

'You are lying on my father's divan, ' he informed her. 'With me, in all but effect, at your feet.'

She opened her eyes again, looked directly at him, and sent those major parts that kept him functioning into a steep decline.

'What made you do it?'

She frowned at the question, but only for a short moment, then she sighed, tried to sit up but was still too dizzy and had to relax back again. 'I didn't want him to go,' she explained simply. 'Or, if he had to go, I wanted him to do it knowing that he was leaving everything as he always wanted to leave it.'

'So you lied.'

It was a truth she merely grimaced at.

'If he had survived this latest attack, and you had been wrong about what you told him, would that have been a fair way to tug a man back from his destiny?'

'I'm pregnant,' she announced. 'Don't upset me with lectures.'

He laughed. What else was he supposed to do? 'I apologise for shouting at you,' he said soberly.

She was playing with his fingers where they pleated firmly with hers. 'You were in trauma enough without having a demented woman throwing a fit of hysterics.'

'You were right, though. He did hear you.'

She nodded. 'I know.'

'Here…' He offered her the stick of white plastic. Taking it back, she stared at it for a long time without saying a single word.

'It doesn't seem so important now,' she murmured eventually.

'The proof or the baby?'

She shrugged then pouted. 'Both, I suppose.'

In other words the delight she should be experiencing had been robbed from the moment. On a sigh, he scooped her up in his arms again and stood up.

'Where are you taking me now?' she questioned.

'Bed,' he answered bluntly. 'Preferably naked, so that I can hold you and our child so close to me you will never, ever manage to prise yourself free.'

'But your father—'

'Has Rafiq,' he inserted. 'And you have me.'

With that he pushed open the door to the main corridor, then stopped dead when he saw the sea of anxious faces waiting for news.

'My father has recovered,' he announced. 'And my wife is pregnant.'

There, he thought as he watched every single one fall to their knees and give thanks to Allah, that has killed two birds with one single stone. Now the phones could start buzzing and the news would go out to all corners of the state. By the time they arose in the morning there would not be a person who did not know what had taken place here tonight.

'You could have given me a chance to break the news to my own father.' Leona showed that her own thoughts were as usual not far from his own.

'He knows—or suspects. For I told him when I asked him to come here tonight. That was while we were still sailing the Red Sea, by the way,' he added as he walked them through the two lines of kneeling bodies. 'Raschid alerted me at Evie's instigation. And I am telling you all of this because I wish to get all my guilty machinations out of the way before we hit the bed.'

'You mean that Evie knew you suspected when I called her up yesterday and she didn't drop a hint of it to me?'

'They are sneaky, those Al-Kadahs,' he confided as he trod the stairs. 'Where do you think I get it from?'

'And your arrogance?'

'Al-Qadim through and through,' he answered. 'Our child will have it too, I must warn you. Plenty of it, since you have your own kind of arrogance too.'

'Maybe that's why I love you.'

He stopped halfway up the stairs to slash her a wide, white rakish grin. 'And maybe,' he said lazily, 'that is why I love you.'

She smiled, lifted herself up to touch his mouth with her own. He continued on his way while they were still kissing—with an audience of fifty watching them from the floor below.

Why not let them look? Sheikh Hassan thought. This was his woman, his wife, the mother of his coming child. He would kiss her wherever and whenever. It was his right. *In-shallah.*

ETHAN'S TEMPTRESS
BRIDE

MICHELLE REID

CHAPTER ONE

PARADISE was a sleepy island floating in the Caribbean. It had a bar on the beach, rum on tap and the unique sound of island music, which did seductive things to the hot and humid late afternoon air, while beyond the bar's open rough-wood construction the silky blue ocean lapped lazily against a white-sand shore.

Sitting on a bar stool with a glass of local rum slotted between his fingers, Ethan Hayes decided that it didn't get any better than this. Admittedly it had taken him more than a week to wind down to the point where he no longer itched to reach for a telephone or felt naked in bare feet and shorts instead of sharp suits and highly polished leather shoes. Now he would even go as far as to say that he liked his new laid-back self. 'No worries,' as the locals liked to say, had taken on a whole new meaning for him.

'You want a refill for that, Mr Hayes?' The soft melodic tones of an island accent brought his gaze up to meet that of the beautiful brown girl who was serving behind the bar. Her smile held a different kind of invitation.

'Sure, why not?' He returned a smile and released his glass to her—without acknowledging the hidden offer.

Sex in this hot climate was the serpent in Paradise. As one's body temperature rose, so did that particular appetite, Ethan mused, aware that certain parts of him were suggesting he should consider the offer in the bar-girl's velvet-brown eyes. But he hadn't come to the island to indulge that specific pleasure, and all it took was the tentative touch of a finger to the corner of his mouth to remind him

5

why he was wary of female entanglement. The bruising to his lip and jaw had faded days ago, but the injury to his dignity hadn't. It still throbbed in his breast like an angry tiger in dire need of succour for its nagging wound. If a man had any sense, he wouldn't unleash that tiger on some poor, unsuspecting female; he would keep it severely locked up and avoid temptation at all cost.

Though there was certainly a lot of that about, he acknowledged, as he turned to observe the young woman who was hogging the small bare-board dance floor.

The serpent's mistress, he named her dryly as he watched her sensual undulations to the music. She was a tall and slender toffee-blonde with a perfect Caribbean tan, wearing a short and sassy hot-pink slip-dress that was an almost perfect match for the pink hibiscus flower she wore tucked into her hair.

Eye-catching, in other words. Too irresistible to leave to dance alone, so it wasn't surprising that the young men in the bar were lining up to take their turn with her. She had class, she had style, she had beauty, she had grace, and she danced like a siren, shifting from partner to partner with the ease of one who was used to taking centre stage. Her eager young cohorts were enjoying themselves, loving the excuse to get up close and personal, lay their hands on her sensational body and gaze into big green beautiful eyes or watch her lovely mouth break into a smile that promised them everything.

And her name was Eve. Eve as in temptress, the ruin of man.

Or in this case the ruin of these brave young hunters who were aspiring to be her Adam. For she was the It girl on this small Caribbean island, the girl with everything, one of the fortunate few. A daddy's girl—though in this case it was Grandpa's girl, and the sole heir to his fabulous fortune.

Money was one hell of an aphrodisiac, Ethan decided cynically. Make her as ugly as sin and he could guarantee that those same guys would still be worshipping at her dainty dancing feet. But as so often was the way for the fabulously wealthy, stunning beauty came along with this package.

She began to laugh; the sound was soft and light and appealingly pleasant. She pouted at her present young hunter and almost brought the poor fool to his knees. Then she caught Ethan's eyes on her and the cynical look he was wearing on his face. Her smile withered to nothing. Big green come-and-get-me-if-you-dare eyes widened to challenge his cynicism outright. She knew him, he knew her. They had met several times over the last year at her grandfather's home in Athens, Ethan in his professional role as a design-and-build architect renowned for his creative genius for making new holiday complexes blend into their native surroundings, Eve in her only role as her grandfather's much loved, much spoiled, gift from the gods.

They did not like each other. In fact mutual antipathy ran in a constant stream between them. Ethan did not like her conceited belief that she had been put on this earth to be worshipped by all, and Eve did not like his outright refusal to fall at her feet. So it was putting it mildly to say that it was unfortunate they should both find themselves holidaying in the same place. The island was small enough for them to be thrown into each other's company too often for the comfort of either. Sparks tended to fly, forcing hostility to raise its ugly head. Other people picked up on it and didn't know what to do or say to lighten the atmosphere. Ethan usually solved the problem by withdrawing from the conflict with excuses that he had to be somewhere else.

This time he withdrew by turning away from her, back to the bar and the drink that had just been placed in front of him. But Eve's image remained standing right there, dancing on the bar top. Proud, defiant, unashamedly provocative—doing things to other parts of him he did not want her to reach.

His serpent in paradise, he grimly named this hot and nagging desire he suffered for Theron Herakleides' tantalising witch of a granddaughter.

Eve was keeping a happy smile fixed on her face even if it killed her to do it. She despised Ethan Hayes with an absolute vengeance. He made her feel spoiled and selfish and vain. She wished he had done his usual thing of getting up and walking out, so that she wouldn't have to watch him flirt with the barmaid.

Didn't Ethan know he was treading on dangerous ground there, and that the barmaid's strapping great sailor of a lover would chew him up and spit him out if he caught him chatting up his woman? Or was it the girl who was doing the chatting up? Then Eve had to settle for that as the more probable alternative, because Ethan Hayes was certainly worth the effort.

Great body, great looks, great sense of presence, she listed reluctantly. In a sharp suit and tie he was dynamic and sleek; now simple beach shorts and a white tee shirt should have turned him into something else entirely, but didn't—dynamic and sleek still did it for her, Eve decided as she ran her eyes over him. She began at his brown bare feet with their long toes that were curling lovingly round one of the bar stool crossbars, then moved onwards, up powerfully built legs peppered with dark hair that had been bleached golden by the sun.

How did she know the sun had bleached those hairs? Eve asked herself. Because she'd seen his legs before— had seen *all* of Ethan Hayes before!—on that terrible night at her grandfather's house in Athens, when she'd dared to walk uninvited into his bedroom and had caught him in a state of undress.

Prickly heat began to chase along to her nerve ends at the memory—the heat of mortification, not attraction though the attraction had always been there as well. She had gone to Ethan's room to confront him over something he had seen her doing in the garden with Aidan Galloway. Bristling with self-righteous indignation she had marched in through his door, only to stop dead with her head wiped clean of all coherent thought when she'd found him standing there still dripping water from a recent shower, and as stark staring naked as a man could be—not counting the small hand towel he had been using to dry his hair. The towel had quickly covered other parts of him, but not before she'd had a darn good owl-eyed look!

Oh, the shame, the embarrassment! She could feel her cheeks blushing even now. 'I presume Mr Galloway ran back to his fiancée, so you thought you would come and try your luck here.' Eve winced as Ethan's cutting words came back to slay her all over again.

'Your foot, sorry,' her present dance partner apologised.

He had misinterpreted the wince. 'That's okay,' she said, smiling sweetly at Raoul Delacroix without bothering to correct his mistake—and wished she'd had the wits to smile sweetly at Ethan Hayes that night, instead of running like a fool and leaving him with *his* mistake!

But she had run without saying a single word to him in her own defence, and by the next morning embarrassment had turned to stiff-necked pride; hell could freeze over before she would explain anything to him! As a result he had become the conscience she knew she did not deserve, because all it took was a glance from those horribly critical grey eyes to make her feel crushingly guilty!

It wasn't fair, she hated him for it. Hated his dark good looks too because they did things to her she would rather they didn't. But most of all she hated his cold, grim, English reserve that kept him forever at a distance, thereby stopping her from beginning the confrontation that she knew would completely alter his perception of her.

Did she need to do that? Eve asked herself suddenly. And was horrified to realise how badly she did.

'Have dinner with me tonight…' Her present dance partner was suddenly crowding her with his too eager hands and the fervent darkening of his liquid brown eyes. 'Just the two of us,' Raoul huskily extended. 'Somewhere quiet and romantic where no one can interrupt.'

'You know that's a no-no, Raoul.' Smiling to soften the refusal, she also deftly dislodged one of his hands from her rear. 'We're here as a group to have fun, not romance.'

'Romance can be fun.' His rejected hand lifted up to brush a finger across her bottom lip with a message only a very naïve woman would misinterpret.

Eve reached up and firmly removed the finger and watched his beautifully shaped mouth turn down in a sulk. Raoul Delacroix was a very handsome French-American, with eyes dark enough to drown in and a body to die for— yet he did nothing for her. In a way she wished that he did because he was her age and her kind of person, unlike the disapproving Ethan Hayes who added a whole new meaning to the phrase, the generation gap.

And what was that gap—her twenty-three years to his thirty-seven? Big gap—yawning gap, she mocked it dryly. 'Don't sulk,' she scolded Raoul. 'Today is my birthday and we're supposed to be having lots of fun.'

'Tomorrow is your birthday,' he corrected.

'As we all know, my grandfather is arriving here tomorrow to help me celebrate, which means I will have to behave with proper decorum all day. So tonight we agreed that we would celebrate my birthday a day early. Don't spoil that for me, Raoul.'

It was both a gentle plea and a serious warning because he had been getting just a little bit too intense recently. Raoul Delacroix was the half-brother of André Visconte who owned the only hotel on the island. So like the rest of the crowd whose families owned property here, they'd all been meeting up for holidays since childhood. They were all good close friends now who'd agreed early on that romance would spoil what they enjoyed most about each others' company. Raoul knew the rules, so attempting to change them now was just a tiny bit irritating—and a shame because he was usually very good company—when he wasn't thinking of other things, that was.

'The beach is strewn with good prospects for a handsome Frenchman to play the romantic,' she teased him. 'Take your pick. I can guarantee they will swoon at your feet.'

'I know, I've tried one or two,' Raoul returned lazily. 'But this was only in practice, you understand,' he then added, 'to prepare myself for the woman I love.'

Implying that Eve was that woman? She laughed, it was so funny. After a moment, Raoul joined in the laughter, and the mood between them relaxed back into being playful. The music changed not long after, calypso taking the place of reggae, and Eve found Raoul's place taken by another admirer while he moved on to pastures new.

Viewing this little by-play via the mirror on the wall behind the drinks optics, Ethan wasn't sure he liked the expression on Raoul Delacroix's face as he'd turned away from Eve. Raoul's look did nasty things to Ethan's insides and made him curious as to what Raoul and Eve had been talking about. They'd parting laughing, but Raoul's turning expression had been far from amused.

None of your business, he then told himself firmly. Eve knew what kind of dangerous game she was playing with all of these testosterone-packed young men. My God, did she know, he then added with a contempt that went so deep it reflected clearly on his face when, as if on cue, Aidan Galloway walked into the bar. The darkly attractive young Irish-American paused, found his target and made directly for Eve.

The last time Ethan had seen Aidan Galloway had been a month ago in Athens when he had been a guest of Eve's grandfather, along with several members of the Galloway family. On the face of it, the younger man had only had eyes for the beautiful fiancée he'd had hanging from his arm. But since coming to this island, Ethan had seen no sign of the fiancée and Aidan Galloway now only had eyes for Eve.

Someone slid onto the stool next to him, offering him a very welcome alternative to observing the life and loves of Eve Herakleides. It was Jack Banning who managed the only hotel on the island for owner, André Visconte. Jack was a big all-American guy, built to break rocks against but as laid-back as they came.

'Marlin have been spotted five miles out,' Jack informed him. 'I'm taking a boat out tomorrow. If you're interested in some big-game fishing, you're welcome to come.'

'Early start?' Ethan quizzed.

'Think sunrise,' Jack suggested. 'Think deep yawns and black coffee and no heavy partying the night before if you don't want to spend your time at sea throwing up.'

The barmaid interrupted by appearing with a glass of

rum for Jack. The two of them chatted boss to employee for a few minutes, but the girl's eyes kept on drifting towards Ethan, and when she had moved away again Jack sent Ethan a very male glance.

'Considering a different kind of game?' Jack posed lazily.

'Not today, thanks.' Ethan's smile was deliberately benign as he took a sip at his drink.

'Or any day that you've been here, from what my sources say.'

'Was that an idle question or a veiled criticism of my use of the island's rich and varied hospitality?'

'Neither.' A set of even white teeth appeared to acknowledge Ethan's sarcastic hit. 'It was just an observation. I mean—look at you, man,' Jack mocked him. 'You've got the looks, you've got the body parts, and I know for a fact that you've had more than one lovely woman's heart fluttering with anticipation since you arrived, but I've yet to see you take a second look at any of them.'

He was curious. Ethan didn't entirely blame him. The island was not sold on its monastic qualities. The women here were, in the main, beautiful people and a lot of them had made it clear that they were available for a little holiday romance.

But Ethan was off romance, off women, and most definitely off sex—or at least he was in training to be off it, he amended, all too aware that his body was trying to tempt him with every inviting smile that came his way.

Then there was that other sexual temptation, the one that hit him hard in his nether regions every time he looked at Eve Herakleides and recalled an incident when she'd walked into his room to find him standing there naked. She'd looked—no *stared*—and things had happened to him that he hadn't experienced since he'd been a hormone-racked teenager. What was worse than the reaction was knowing she'd witnessed it.

So why his eyes had to pick that precise moment to glance in the mirror was something he preferred not to analyse. She was dancing with Aidan Galloway, and the body language was nothing like what it had been when she'd danced with the other men. No, this was tense, it was serious. It reminded him of that kiss he had witnessed in her grandfather's garden in Athens. The two of them had been so engrossed in each other that they hadn't heard his arrival—nor had they known they'd also been watched by Aidan's fiancée, who'd almost fainted into the arms of another young Galloway.

Eve was a flirt and a troublemaker, a woman with no scruples when it came to other women's men. Her only mission in life was to slay all with those big green you-can-have-me eyes.

Ethan loved those eyes...

The unexpected thought jolted him, snapped his gaze down from the mirror to his glass. What the hell is the matter with you? he asked himself furiously. Too much sun? Too much time on your hands? Maybe it was time he got back into a suit and unearthed a mobile telephone.

'And you?' He diverted his attention back to Jack Banning. 'Do you sip the honey on a regular basis here?'

Jack gave a rueful shake of his head. 'The boss would have my balls for trophies if I imbibed,' he murmured candidly. 'No...' picking up his glass he tasted the rum '...I have this lovely widow living on the next island who keeps me sane in that department.'

With no ties, and no commitment expected or desired, Ethan concluded from that, knowing the kind of woman

Jack was talking about because he'd enjoyed a few of them himself in his time.

'She's a good woman,' Jack added as if he needed to make that point.

'I don't doubt it,' Ethan replied, and he didn't. In the time he had been here, he had got to know and like Jack Banning. Being in the leisure business himself—though in a different area—he wasn't surprised that André Visconte had a man like Jack in place. In fact he was considering doing a bit of head-hunting because they could do with Jack running the new resort his company was in the process of constructing in Spain.

Though that idea was shot to pieces when Jack spoke again. 'Her husband was caught out at sea in a hurricane four years ago,' he said quietly. 'He left her well shod but heavily pregnant. Left her with a badly broken heart too.'

Which told Ethan that Jack was in love with the widow. Which in turn meant there was no hope of getting him to leave for pastures new.

'So what's your excuse for the self-imposed celibacy?' Jack asked curiously.

Same as you, Ethan thought grimly. I fell for a married woman—only her husband is very much alive and kicking. 'Too much of a good thing is reputed to be bad for you,' was what he offered as a dry reply.

Glancing at him, he saw Jack's gaze touch that part of Ethan's jaw where the bruising had been obvious a few days ago. He had been forced to wear the mark like a banner when he'd first arrived on the island. Speculation as to how he'd received the bruise had been rife. His refusal to discuss it had only helped to fire people's imagination.

But the expression in Jack's eyes told him that Jack had drawn a pretty accurate conclusion. He sighed, so did Jack.

Both men lifted their glass to their mouths and said no more. It had been that kind of conversation: some things had been said, others not, but all had been taken on board nonetheless. Turning on his stool, Jack offered the busy bar room a once-over with his lazy-yet-shrewd manager's eye, while Ethan studied the contents of his glass with a slightly bitter gaze. He was thinking of a woman with dark red hair, silk-white skin and a broken heart that was in the process of being mended by the wrong man, as far as he was concerned.

But the right man for her, he had to add honestly, felt the tiger stir within and wished he knew of a good cure for unrequited love.

'Try the sex,' Jack said suddenly as if he could read his mind. 'It has to be a better option than lusting after the unattainable.'

Unable to restrain it, Ethan released a hard laugh. 'Is that advice for me or for yourself?'

'You,' Jack answered. Then he grimaced as he added, 'Mine is a hopeless case. You see, the widow's son calls me Daddy.' With that he got up and gave Ethan's shoulder a man-to-man, sympathetic pat. 'Let me know about the Marlin trip,' he said and strolled away.

Turning to watch him go, Ethan saw Jack stop once or twice to chat to people on his way out of the bar. One woman in particular came to meet him. It was Eve the temptress. A quick look around and he found Aidan Galloway standing at the other end of the bar. He was ordering a drink and he didn't look happy. Join the club, Ethan thought, as his eyes then picked out Raoul Delacroix who was watching Eve with an expression on his face that matched Aidan Galloway's.

As for Eve, her long slender arms were around Jack's neck and she was pouting up at him in a demand for a kiss. Amiably Jack gave it and smiled at whatever it was she was saying to him. Without much tempting she managed to urge the manager into motion to the music, his big hands spanning her tiny waist, his dark head dipped to maintain eye contact. Like that, they teased each other as they swayed.

Suddenly Ethan knew it was time to leave. Downing the rest of his drink, he came to his feet, placed some money on the bar and wished the girl behind it a light farewell. As he walked towards the dancers he thought he saw Eve move that extra inch closer to Jack's impressive body.

Done for his benefit? he asked himself, then shot that idea in the foot with a silent huff of scorn to remind himself that Eve Herakleides disliked him as much as he disliked her.

Outside the air was like warm damp silk against his skin. The humidity was high, and looking out to sea Ethan could see clouds gathering on the horizon aiming to spoil the imminent sunset. There could be a storm tonight, he predicted as he turned in the direction of his beach house. Behind him the sound of a woman's laughter came drifting towards him from inside the bar. Without thinking he suddenly changed direction and his feet were kicking hot sand as he ran toward the water and made a clean racing dive into its cool clear depths.

'Don't even think about it,' Jack cautioned. 'He's too old and too dangerous for a sweet little flirt like you.'

Dragging her eyes away from the sight of Ethan Hayes in full sprint as he headed for the ocean, Eve looked into Jack Banning's knowing gaze—and mentally ran for cover. 'I don't know what you're talking about,' she said.

Jack didn't believe her. 'Ethan Hayes could eat you for a snack without touching his appetite,' he informed her without a hint of mockery to make the bitter pill of truth an easier one to swallow.

'Like you, you mean,' she said with a kissable pout, which was really another duck-and-run. 'Big bad Jack,' she murmured as she moved in closer then began swaying so provocatively that he had to physically restrain her.

He did it with a white-toothed, highly amused, grin. 'Minx,' he scolded. 'If your grandfather could see you he would have you locked up—these messages you put out are dangerous.'

'My grandpa adores me too much to do anything so primitive.'

'Your grandfather, my little siren, arrives on this island tomorrow,' Jack reminded her. 'Let him see this look you're wearing on your face and we will soon learn how primitive he can be…'

CHAPTER TWO

ETHAN took his time swimming down the length of the bay to come out of the water opposite the beach house he was using while he was here. It belonged to Leandros Petronades, a business associate, who had understood his need to get away from it all for a week or two if he wasn't going to do something stupid like walk out on his ten-year-strong working partnership with Victor Frayne.

Victor... Ethan's feet stilled at the edge of the surf as the same anger that had caused the rift between the two of them rose up to burn at his insides again.

Victor had used him, or had allowed him to be used, as a decoy in the crossfire between Victor's daughter, Leona, and her estranged husband, Sheikh Hassan Al-Qadim. In the Sheikh's quest to recover his wife, Leona and Ethan had been ambushed then dragged off into the night. When Ethan had eventually come round from a knockout blow to his jaw, it had been to find he'd been made virtual prisoner on Sheikh Hassan's luxury yacht. But if he'd thought his pride had taken a battering when he'd been wrestled to the ground and rendered helpless with that knockout blow, then his interview with the Sheikh the next morning had turned what was left of his pride to pulp.

The man was an arrogant bastard, Ethan thought grimly. What Leona loved about him he would never understand. If *he* had been her father, he would have been putting up a wall of defence around her rather than aiding and abetting her abduction by a man whom everyone knew had been about to take a second wife!

Leona had been out of that marriage—*best* out of that marriage! Now she was back in it with bells ringing and—

Bending down he picked up a conch shell then turned and hurled it into the sea. He wished to goodness he hadn't had that conversation with Jack Banning. He wished he could stuff all of these violent feelings back into storage where he had managed to hide them for the last week. Now he was angry with himself again, angry with Victor, and angry with Sheikh Hassan Al-Qadim and the whole damn world, probably.

On that heavily honest assessment, he turned back to face land again. Leandros Petronades had been his saviour when he'd offered him the use of this place. Not that the Greek's motives had been in the least bit altruistic, Ethan reminded himself. As one of the main investors in their Spanish project, Leandros had been protecting his own back, plus several other business ventures his company had running with Hayes-Frayne. A bust up between Ethan and Victor would have left him with problems he did not need or want. So when he'd happened to walk in on the furious row the two partners had been locked in, had seen the huge purple bruise on Ethan's face and had heard enough to draw his own conclusions as how the bruise got there, Leandros had immediately suggested that Ethan needed a break while he cooled off.

So here he was, standing on the beach of one of the most exclusive islands in the Caribbean, and about the lush green hillside in front of him nestled the kind of properties most people only dreamed about. The Visconte hotel complex occupied a central position, forming the hub around which all activities on the island revolved. Either side of the hotel stood the private villas belonging to those wealthy enough to afford a plot of land here. André Visconte himself owned a private estate. The powerful

Galloway family owned many properties, forming a small hamlet of their own in the next bay. But if the size of a plot was indicative of wealth, then the villa belonging to Theron Herakleides had to be the king.

Painted sugar-pink, it sat inside a framework of ancient date- and fabulous flame-trees about halfway up the hill. From the main house the garden swept down to sea level via a series of carefully tended terraces: sun terraces, pool terraces, garden terraces that wouldn't be believed to be real outside a film set. There were tennis courts and even a velvet smooth croquet lawn, though Ethan could not bring himself to imagine that Theron Herakleides had ever bothered to use it. Then there were the guest houses scattered about the grounds, all painted that sugar-pink colour which came into its own with every burning sunset. Almost on the sand sat the Herakleides beach house, the part of her grandfather's estate that Eve was using while she was here.

It had to be the worst kind of luck that the Petronades and the Herakleides estates were beside each other, because it placed her beach house right next door to his, Ethan mused heavily, as he trod the soft sand on his way up the beach. Other than for Eve's close proximity he was happy with his modest accommodation. The beach houses might be small but they possessed a certain charm that appealed to the artist in him. Nothing grand: just an open-plan living room and kitchen, a bathroom and a bedroom.

All he needed, in other words, he acknowledged as he came to a stop at the low white-washed wall that was there to help keep the sand back rather than mark the boundary to the property. Set into the wall was a white picket gate that gave access to a simple garden and the short path that led to a shady veranda. Next to the gate was a concrete tub overhung by a freshwater shower head. Pulling his wet tee shirt off over his head he tossed it onto the wall, then stepped into the tub and switched on the tap that brought cool water cascading over his head.

His skin shone dark gold in the deepening sunset, muscles rippled across his shoulders and back, as he sluiced the sand and salt from his body. Standing a few short yards away on the hot concrete path that ran right around the bay, Eve watched him with the same fascination she had surrendered to the last time she had chanced upon Ethan Hayes like this.

Only it wasn't the same, she reminded herself quickly. He was dressed, or that part of him which caused her the most problems was modestly covered at least. But as for the rest of him—

Water ran off his dark hair down his face to his shoulders. The hair on his chest lay matted in thick coils that arrowed down to below his waist. She hadn't noticed the chest hair the last time—hadn't noticed the six-pack firmness of his abdomen. He was lean and he was tight and he was honed to perfection, and she wished she—

'You can go past. I won't bite,' the man himself murmured flatly, letting her know that he had seen her standing here.

Fingers curling into two fists at her sides, Eve released a soft curse beneath her breath. I hate him, she told herself. I *really* hate him for catching me doing this, not once but *twice*!

'Actually I quite like the view,' she returned, determined not to let him embarrass her a second time. 'You strip down quite nicely for an Englishman.'

More muscles flexed; Eve's lungs stopped working. She wished she understood this fascination she had for his body, but she didn't. She could not even say that he possessed the best body she had ever seen—mainly because it was the *only* one she had seen in its full and flagrant entirety. That, she decided, had to be the cause of this wicked fascination she had for Ethan Hayes. It fizzed through her veins like a champagne cocktail, stripped her mouth of moisture like crisp dry wine. Tantalising, in other words. The man was a stiff-necked, supercritical, over-bearing boor, yet inside she fluttered like a love-struck teenager every time she saw him.

The shower was turned off. He threw one of those cold-eyed looks at her then slid it away without saying a word. He was going to do his usual thing and walk away as if she didn't exist, Eve realised, and suddenly she was determined to break that arrogant habit for good!

'You've missed a bit,' she informed him.

He turned a second look on her. Looks like that could kill, Eve thought as, with a scrupulously bland expression, she pointed to the back of his legs where beautifully pronounced calf muscles were still peppered with fine granules of sand.

Still without saying a word he turned on the shower again. A sudden urge to laugh brought Eve's ready sense of humour into play and she decided to have a bit of fun at the stuffy Ethan Hayes' expense.

'Jack just warned me off falling for you,' she announced, watching him wash the sand off his legs. 'He thinks you're dangerous. The eat-them-for-a snack-as-you-walk-out-of-the-door kind of man.'

'Wise man, Jack.' She thought she heard him mutter over the splash of water, but she couldn't be sure.

'I laughed because I thought it was so funny,' she went on. 'I mean—we both know you're too much the English gentleman to do anything so crass as to love them and leave them without a backward glance.'

It was not a compliment and Ethan didn't take it as one.

'You keep taking a dig at my Englishness, but you're half English yourself,' he pointed out.

'I know.' Eve sighed with mocking tragedy. 'It worries the Greek in me sometimes that I could end up falling for a die-hard English stuffed-shirt.'

'Fate worse than death.'

'Yes.'

He switched the shower off again and Eve rediscovered her fascination with his body as he turned to recover his wet tee shirt; muscles wrapped in rich brown flesh rippled in the red glow of the sunlight, droplets of water clung to the hairs on his chest.

Ethan turned to catch her staring. The prickling sensation between his thighs warned him that he had better get away from here before he embarrassed himself again. Yet he didn't move, couldn't seem to manage the simple act. His senses were too busy drinking in what his eyes were showing him. He liked the way she was wearing her hair twisted cheekily up on her head with a hibiscus flower helping to hold it in place. He liked what the pink dress did for her figure and the slender length and shape of her legs. And he liked her mouth; it was heart-shaped—small with a natural provocative yen to pout. He liked her smooth golden skin, her cute little nose, and those eyes that had a way of looking at him as if she…

Go away, Eve, he wanted to say to her. Instead he dragged his eyes away, and looked for something thoroughly innocuous to say. 'I thought you were all off to a party this evening.' Flat-voiced, level-toned, he'd thought he'd hit innocuous perfectly.

But Eve clearly didn't. She stiffened up as if he had just insulted her. 'Oh, do let's be honest and call it an orgy,' she returned. 'Since you believe that orgies are more my style.'

Time to go, he decided, and opened the picket gate.

'While you do what you're probably very good at, of course,' she added, 'and play whist with the cheese and wine set at the hotel.'

He went still.

Eve's heart stopped beating on the suspicion that she had finally managed to rouse the sleeping tiger she'd always fancied lurked within his big chest. Sometimes— usually when she was least expecting it—Ethan Hayes could take on a certain quality that made her think of dangerous animals. This was one of those times, and her biggest problem was that she liked it—it excited her.

'How old are you?' he asked.

He knew exactly how old she was. 'Twenty-three until midnight,' she told him anyway.

He nodded his wet head. 'That accounts for it.'

This was blatant baiting, Eve recognised, and foolishly took it. 'Accounts for what?'

'The annoyingly adolescent desire to insult and shock.'

He was so right, but oh, it hurt. Why had she willingly let herself fall into that? Eve had no defence, none at all and she had to turn to stare out to sea so that he wouldn't see the sudden flood of weak tears that were trying to fill her eyes.

And who was the adolescent who made that cutting comment? Ethan was grimly asking himself, as he looked at her standing there looking like an exotic flower that had been cut down in its prime. Oh, damn it, he thought, and walked through the gate, meaning to get the hell away from this before he—

He couldn't do it. Muscles were tightening all over his body on wave after wave of angry guilt. What had she ever done to him after all? If you didn't count a couple of teasing come-ons and letting him catch her in a heated clinch with someone else's man.

She'd also caught him naked and had had a full view of his embarrassing response, but he didn't want to think about that. Instead he took in a deep breath and spun back to say something trite and stupid and hopefully less—

But he found he was too late because she had already walked off, a tall slender figure with a graceful stride and a proud yet oddly vulnerable tilt to her head. Still cursing himself for the whole stupid conversation, Ethan made himself walk up the path. Though, as he reached the shade of the veranda, he couldn't resist a quick glance sideways and saw Eve was about to enter her house. One part of him wanted to go after her and apologise, but the major part told him wisely to leave well alone.

Eve Herakleides could mean trouble if he allowed himself to be sucked in by her frankly magnetic appeal. He didn't need that kind of stimulation. He didn't want to end up in the same fated boat he had been in before with a woman just like her.

What was it that Jack had called it? 'Lusting after the unattainable.' Eve was destined to higher things than a mere architect had to offer—as her grandfather would be happy to tell him. But it was the word lust that made Ethan go inside and firmly close his door.

CHAPTER THREE

EVE tried to enjoy the party. In fact she threw herself into the role of life and soul with an enthusiasm that kept everyone else entertained.

But the scene with Ethan Hayes had taken the edge off her desire to enjoy anything tonight. And she was worried about Aidan. He had been drinking steadily since he'd arrived at the bar on the beach late this afternoon and his mood suited the grim compulsion with which he was pouring the rum down his throat.

Not that anyone else seemed to have noticed, she realised, as she watched him do his party trick with a cocktail shaker and bottle of something very green to the laughing encouragement of the rest of the crowd, whereas she felt more like weeping.

For Aidan—for herself? In truth, she wasn't quite sure. On that low note she surrendered to the deep doldrums that had been dogging her every movement tonight and slid open one of the glass doors that led onto the terrace. Then she stepped out into the warm dark night, intending to walk across the decking to the terrace rail that overlooked the sea—only it came as a surprise to discover that she was ever so slightly tipsy, so tipsy in fact that she was forced to sink onto the first sunbed she reached just in case she happened to fall down.

Well, why not? she thought with a little shrug, and slipping off her shoes she lifted her feet up onto the cool, cushioned mattress, then relaxed against the raised chair back with a low long sigh. The air was soft and seductively

27

quiet, the earlier threatened storm having passed them by. Reclining there, she listened to the low slap of lazy waves touching the shore, and wondered dully how much longer she needed to leave it before she could escape to brood on her own terrace without inviting comment here?

At least Aidan was already in the right place for when he eventually sank into a drunken stupor, she mused heavily. This was his home, or the one he liked to call home of several the family had dotted around this tiny bay. With a bit of luck he was going to slide under a convenient table soon and she could get some of the guys to put him to bed, then forget about him and his problems for a while and concentrate on her own.

She certainly had a few, Eve acknowledged through the mud of her half-tipsy state. Ethan Hayes and his horrible attitude towards her was one of them. Her grandfather in his whole, sweet, bullying entirety was another. The older he got, the more testy he became, and more determined to run her life for her. She smiled as she thought that about him though, and allowed her mind to drift back to the last conversation she'd had with him over the phone before she'd flown out here from her London flat.

'Grandpa, will you stop trying to marry me off to every eligible man you happen to meet?' she scolded, 'I am only twenty-three years' old, for goodness' sake!'

'At twenty-three you should be suckling my first grand-son at your breast while the next grows big in your belly,' he complained.

'Barefoot I presume, while making baklava for my very fat husband.'

Eve hadn't been able to resist it, she chuckled into the night at the outrageous scenario.

'Spiridon is not fat.'

'But he is twice my age.'

'He is thirty-nine,' the old man corrected. 'Very hand-some. Very fit. The ladies worship him.'

'And you ought to be ashamed of yourself for trying to foist me off with the most notorious rake in Greece,' she rebuked. 'I thought you loved me better than this.'

'You are the unblemished golden apple of my eye!' Theron Herakleides announced with formidable passion. 'I merely want you to remain that way until I see you safely married before I die.'

'Die?' she repeated. He was bringing out the big guns with that remark. 'Now listen to me, you scheming old devil,' she scolded, 'I love you to bits. *You* are the love of my life! But if you stick one—*just one*—eligible man in front of me I will never speak to you again—under-stand?'

'*Ne*,' the old man answered, gruff-voiced and tetchy. 'Yes, I understand that you bully a sick and lonely old man.'

Sick, she did not believe, but lonely she did. 'See you soon, Grandpa,' she softly ended the conversation.

And she would do—sooner than she'd thought too—because her grandfather was making a flying visit here tomorrow just to spend her birthday with her. The prospect softened her whole face. She loved that stubborn, bad tempered old man almost to distraction. He had been both her mother and father for so many years now that she could barely recall the time when she hadn't looked to him for every little thing she might need.

But not a husband, she quickly reminded herself. That was one decision in her life out of which he was going to have to learn to keep his busy nose!

Why a sudden image of Ethan Hayes had to flash across her eyes at that moment, Eve refused to analyse, but it put a dark frown upon her face.

'Here, try this...' Glancing up she found Raoul Delacroix standing beside her holding out a tall glass full of a pinkish liquid decorated with just about everything, from a selection of tropical fruit pieces to several fancy cocktail sticks and straws.

'What's in it?' she asked warily.

'Aidan called it tiger juice with a bite,' Raoul replied.

Tiger juice, how appropriate, Eve mused dryly, thinking of Ethan Hayes again.

'I'm game, if you are,' Raoul said, bringing her attention to the other glass of the same he was holding. 'It might help take the scowl from your face that you seem to have been struggling with all evening.'

Had her bad mood been that apparent? Eve accepted the glass without further comment, but as Raoul lowered himself onto the sunbed next to hers, she felt a fizz of anger begin to bubble inside because she knew whose fault it was that she was feeling like this!

If she didn't watch out, Ethan Hayes could be in danger of becoming an obsession.

'*Salute.*' Raoul's glass touching the edge of hers brought her mind swinging back to where it should be.

'Cheers,' she replied, unearthed a curly straw from the rest of the pretty junk decorating the glass, put it to her lips and sucked defiantly.

The drink tasted a little strange but not horribly so. She looked at Raoul, he looked at her. 'What do you think?' she asked him curiously.

'Sexy,' he murmured with a teasingly lecherous grin. 'I can feel my toes tingling. I will now encourage the sensation to reach other parts.' With that he took another pull on his straw.

Laughing at his outrageousness, Eve did the same, and it became a challenge as to which of them could empty

the glass of Aidan's wicked brew first. After that she remembered little. Not the glass being rescued from her
clumsy fingers nor the light-hearted banter that went on
around her as the rest of the crowd discussed where the
birthday girl should be placed to sleep it off. Aidan offered
a bed, someone else suggested she was perfectly fine
where she was. Raoul reminded them that her grandfather
was due in on the dawn flight, so maybe the wisest place
for him to find her tomorrow was in her own bed. This
drew unilateral agreement because no one wanted to explain to Theron Herakleides why his precious granddaughter had been so rolling drunk she hadn't even made it
home. Raoul offered to deliver her there since it was on
the way to his villa, and he'd only had one glass of alcohol.
Everyone agreed because no one else felt sober enough to
make the drive.

It was all very relaxed, very light-hearted. No one
thought of questioning Raoul's motives as they watched
him carry Eve to his car. They were all such long-standing
friends after all. All for one, one for all.

CHAPTER FOUR

ETHAN came shooting out of a deep sleep to the sound of a woman's shrill cry. Lying there in his bed with his heart pounding in his chest he listened for a few moments, uncertain that it hadn't been someone screaming in his dream.

Then the second cry came, and he was rolling out of bed and landing on his feet before the sound had come to a chillingly abrupt halt. Grabbing up a pair of beach shorts he pulled them on, then began moving fast out of his bedroom, across the sitting room and through the front door, where he paused to look around for some clue as to where the cries had come from.

It was pitch black outside and whisper-quiet; nothing stirred—even the ocean was struggling to make a sound as it lapped the shore. Peering out towards the sea, he was half expecting to see someone in difficulties out there, but no flailing silhouette broke the moon-dusted surface. The cries had been close—much closer to house than the water.

Then it came again, and even as he swung round to face Eve's beach house he saw the shadowy figure of a man slink down the veranda steps.

Eve was the screamer. His heart began to thump. 'Hey—!' he called out, startling the figure to a standstill halfway down the veranda steps. It was too dark to get a clear look at him but Ethan had his suspicions. He sure did have those, he thought grimly, as he began striding towards the boundary wall that separated the two properties. The name Aidan Galloway was burning like a light bulb inside his head. 'What the hell is going on?' he demanded, only to prompt the other man to turn and make a sudden run for it.

His skin began to crawl with a sense that something was really wrong here. People didn't run unless they had a reason to. Thinking no further than that, he gave chase, sprinting across the dry spongy grass and vaulting the wall without even noticing. Within seconds the figure had disappeared around the corner of Eve's beach house. By the time Ethan rounded that corner all he saw were the red tail-lights of a car taking off up the narrow lane which gave access to the beach from the road above.

On a soft curse he then turned his thoughts to Eve. Spinning about, he stepped onto her veranda and began striding along its cool tiled surface until he came to the door. It was swinging wide on its hinges and he stepped warily through it into complete darkness.

'Eve—?' he called out. 'Are you all right?'

He received no answer.

'Eve—!' he called again, more sharply this time.

Still no reply came back at him. He had never been in here before so he had to strain his eyes to pick out the shapes of walls and pieces of furniture as he began moving forwards. He bumped into something hard, found himself automatically reaching out to steady a table lamp by its shade and had the foresight to switch it on. Light suddenly illuminated a floor plan that was much the same as his own. He was standing in the sitting room surrounded by soft-cushioned cane furniture; there was an open-plan kitchen in one corner and two doors which had to lead to a bathroom and the only bedroom.

'Eve?' he called out again as he wove through the cane furniture to get to the other two doors. One was slightly ajar; warily he lifted a hand and widened the opening enough to allow light to seep into the darkened room.

What he saw brought him to a dead standstill. The room looked like a disaster area, with Eve sitting in the middle of it like a discarded piece of the debris. Lamp light shone onto her down-bent head and her hair was all over the place, forming a tumbling screen of silk that completely hid her face. She was hugging herself, slender arms crossed over her body, long fingers curled like talons around the back of her neck. The tattered remains of the hot-pink dress lay in a crumpled huddle beside her on the floor.

'God in heaven,' he breathed, feeling his heart drop to his stomach when he realised what had clearly been going on here.

'Go away,' she told him, the whimpered little command almost choked through a throat full with tears.

Grimly ignoring the command, Ethan walked forward, face honed into the kind of mask that would have scared the life out of Eve if she'd glanced up and seen it. He came to squat down in front of her. He might not be able to see her face but he could feel her distress pulsing out towards him.

'Are you hurt?' he asked gruffly, reaching out with a hand to lightly touch her hair.

Her response was stunning. In a single violent movement she rose to her feet, spun her back to him, then began trembling as her battle with tears began to be lost.

Ethan took his time in rising to his full height and trying to decide what his next move should be. It was as clear as day that some sort of assault had taken place here, that Eve was shocked and distressed and maybe—

'I hate you, do you know that?' she choked out suddenly. 'I really—really hate you for coming in here like this!'

'I heard a scream, came out to investigate and saw someone leaving here,' he felt compelled to explain. 'There was something in the way he moved that made me—Eve—' he changed tack anxiously '—you're shaking so badly you look like you're going to collapse. Let me—'

'Don't touch me,' she breathed, then quite suddenly her legs gave away on her and she sank, folding like a piece of limp rubber down onto the edge of the rumpled bed.

Standing there, Ethan was uncertain as to what to do next. She didn't want him near her, she wanted him to go, but there was no way he could do that without making sure she was fit to be left on her own. His eyes fell on the hot-pink dress, then the scrappy pink bra lying beside it. His skin began to crawl again in response to the horror that was painting itself into his head. The evidence suggested rape, or at the very least a bungled attempt.

A thrust of bloody anger had him bending down to scoop up a white cotton sheet from the tangle of bedding on the floor, then carefully draping the sheet around her trembling frame. It wasn't that she was naked, because he'd noticed the pair of pink panties when she'd risen to her feet. But, as for the rest... His teeth clenched together as he lowered himself into a squatting position in front of her again.

She was clutching the sheet now, face still hidden, hunched shoulders trembling like mad. 'What happened here, Eve?' he questioned grimly.

'What do you think?' she shot back on a bitter choke. 'I suppose you think I deserved it!'

'No,' he denied that.

'Liar.' She sobbed and lifted the sheet up to use it to cover her face.

'Eve—nobody of sane mind would believe a woman deserves what appears to have happened here,' he insisted soberly.

'I'm drunk,' she admitted.

He could smell the alcohol.

'It was all my fault.'

'No,' he said again, his hands hanging limp between his spread thighs, though they desperately wanted to reach out and touch her.

'I can't feel my legs. I don't even know how I got here. I think he spiked my last drink.'

'Possibly,' Ethan quietly agreed, willing to feed her answering remarks if it helped him to understand just what had happened here.

She moved at last, rubbing the sheet over her face then slowly lowering it so he could get his first look at it. Her lips were swollen and he could see chafe marks from a man's rough beard. His jaw became a solid piece of rock as he noticed other things and tried to keep that knowledge off his face.

Maybe she saw something—he wasn't sure, but she released the sheet and rubbed trembling fingers over the side of her neck, then lifted the fingers higher to push back her hair and clutched at her head as she began to rock to and fro again.

Ethan's fingers twitched; she saw it happen. 'I'm all right,' she said jerkily. 'I just need to—'

Get a hold on what has happened to me, he finished for her mentally. 'How bad was it?' He had to ask the question even though he knew she did not want to answer it. But this could well be the kind of scene that required a doctor and the police to investigate.

But Eve shook her head, refusing to answer. Then, from seemingly out of nowhere, a huge sob shook her from shoulders to feet and she was suddenly gulping out the tears with a total loss of composure.

A silent sigh ripped at the lining of his chest. 'Look, Eve, will you let me hold you? You need to be held but I don't want to—'

'You hate me.' She sobbed.

'No, I don't.' This time the sigh was full-bodied and heavy. 'I'll go and call the police.' He went to get up.

'No!' she cried, and without any warning she slid to the ground between his spread knees and landed heavily against his chest, almost knocking him over in the process.

As he flexed muscles to maintain his balance, she began sobbing brokenly into his shoulder. It was a dreadful sound—the sound nightmares were made of. Her arms went around his neck and began clinging tightly. The sheet began to slip, and with his jaw locked like a vice against the gamut of primitive emotion building inside him, Ethan caught the sheet, replaced it over her shoulders, then took a chance and wrapped his arms round her to just hold her while she cried herself out.

Her tears began to wet his shoulder and neck, mingling with her breath as she sobbed and quivered. She smelt of alcohol and something much more sweetly subtle, and he hoped she hadn't noticed that her naked breasts were pressing against his equally naked chest. She felt warm and soft and so infinitely fragile it was like holding a priceless piece of art. As his eyes took in the debacle of their surroundings, he couldn't think of a less likely setting or situation to discover that he was holding the perfect woman in his arms.

The unexpected thought stopped his train of thought. Maybe he tensed; he was certainly shocked enough to have turned into a pillar of rock. Whatever, the sobbing grew less wretched, the grip on his neck began to ease. Old tensions erupted, defensive barriers began to climb back into place. He could actually feel Eve taking stock of the situation. The sobs quietened, silence came and within it her distress changed to a self-conscious embarrassment.

She had noticed the intimacy of their embrace.

Untangling her fingers from round his neck, Eve lifted her head out of his shoulder, then drew away from him just enough to gather the sheeting around her front. She couldn't believe she had done that—couldn't believe she had just sobbed her heart out on Ethan Hayes of all people, nor that she had done it with her bare breasts flattened against his naked chest.

So now what did she do? she asked herself helplessly, and put a hand up to cover the aching throb taking place behind her heavy eyes. He didn't speak, though she wished he would because she just didn't know what to say to him.

'I'm sorry,' were the weak words that eventually left her.

'Please don't be,' he returned, sounding so stiff and formal that she wanted to shrivel up and die.

But at least he moved at last by sitting back on his ankles to place some much needed distance between them, and Eve dared herself a glance at that hair-covered chest she could still feel warm and prickly against her breasts. She liked the sensation, just as she liked the way she could taste the moist warmth of his skin on her lips.

Oh—what is happening to me? In trembling confusion brought the sheet up to cover her face again. Beyond her hiding place the silence in the room throbbed. What was he thinking? What did he really want to do? Get up and leave? Wishing he hadn't come in here at all? Why not? She knew what Ethan Hayes thought of her. She knew he was seeing only what he would have expected to see.

In his eyes she was a flirt, a man-teaser with no scruples

to stop her from going that step too far. Well, Mr Hayes, she thought behind the now damp sheet. Here I am where you probably always predicted I would end up, hoisted by my own petard.

'Say something!' she snapped out. She couldn't bear the silence.

'Tell me what happened here.'

'I don't remember!' The words and their accompanying sob drove her to her feet. Only, her legs wouldn't support her; they felt like two rubber bands stretched so taut they quivered. And how he knew that, she didn't understand! But he was on his feet and using a hand on her arm to support her as he guided her down onto the edge of the bed.

She was in shock. In one part of her wretched head, Eve was aware of that. She was even able to appreciate that Ethan did not quite know what to do in the situation he found himself in.

'I'm sorry,' she said again. 'I can't seem to th-think straight.' Taking a deep breath she made a concerted effort to be rational. 'W-we were all at Aidan's beach house. It was my birthday party and I suppose we were all a little bit tipsy. Aidan was mixing cocktails...'

Her voice trailed off, her mind drifting back over the following few minutes when Raoul had sat down beside her and they'd talked and had drunk...

After that she could remember nothing until she'd found herself back here and Raoul had been undressing her. 'It's okay, Eve.' She echoed Raoul's soothing words back to herself, unaware that what had come before had only been replayed inside her head. 'You are back home. I am putting you to bed...'

Bed. Her stomach revolted, forcing her back to her feet and off that dreadful piece of furniture! On her rubber-band legs she stumbled, her hand went out to grab at something to steady herself with and it had to be a rock-solid bicep belonging to Ethan Hayes. The worst of it was, she didn't want to let go again. She *never* wanted to let go! Why was that? she asked herself dizzily. Why was it that this man with this cold hard expression that so disapproved of her, could fill her with such a warm feeling of strength of trust?

She didn't know. In fact she didn't think she knew anything for certain any more. 'I believed him.' Staring up at Ethan's mask-like face, her own revealed a shocked lack of comprehension at her own gullibility. 'How could I have *done* that?' she cried. 'How could I *not* have known there was more to his motives than...?'

'He spiked your drink,' Ethan gently reminded her. 'Don't knock yourself over something I don't believe you had any control over.'

Swallowing she nodded and clutched more tightly at his arm. 'I m-must have passed out again,' she went on shakily. 'Next thing I remember, I was being kissed. I thought it was a dream...' She stopped to swallow thickly, put trembling fingers up to her swollen lips and her expression crumpled on a wave of pained and frightened dismay because it had been no dream. 'I th-think I screamed. I th-think I hit him. I think I m-managed to scramble off the bed. I *know* I screamed again because I can still hear it shrilling inside my h-head—'

The stumbling words were halted by the way Ethan wrapped her close to him again. It was the sweetest, most comforting gift he could have given her right then.

But Ethan wasn't thinking of gifts, he was thinking of murder. He was seeing Aidan Galloway's handsome face and how it was going to look when he had restructured it. He was thinking about how this proud, feisty woman had been reduced to this, because one spoiled lout didn't know how to control his libido. He was also thinking about the way she came into his arms without hesitation, how she was nestling here.

'I thought he was my friend.'

Ethan recognised the pained feeling that went into that wretched comment. 'We all make poor judgements of people now and then.'

She nodded against his breastbone—he wished she wouldn't do that he thought, as other parts of him began to respond. He wished he understood it, wished he knew why this woman had the power to move him in ways he'd never previously known. It wasn't just the sex thing, he made that clear to himself. But he liked the way she clung to him, and how, despite the ordeal she had just been through here, she could trust him enough to cling.

'You're being too nice to me.'

'You would prefer it if I tore into you about the dangers of flirting with one too many young and sexually healthy men?'

'Like you just did, you mean?' Lifting her head she looked at him through eyes turned almost black by fright and whatever drug was swimming in her blood.

Vulnerable, he thought. Too—too vulnerable. It made him want to kiss away her fears— What he didn't expect was for Eve to suddenly fall on his neck and start kissing him!

Shock leapt upon him like a scalded cat with its claws unsheathed. Those claws raked a pleasurable passage across his senses before he found the wits to prize his mouth free from hers. He had to use tough hands on her waist to prize the rest of her away from him. 'What the *hell*?' he ground out forcefully as she stood staring up at him through those wide black unseeing eyes. By now he

was feeling so damn shaken he was almost on the point
of running himself! 'Dear God, Eve, what do you think
you're playing at?'

The rough-cut rake of his voice brought her blinking
back from wherever she had gone off to. She stared at him
in horror then in dawning dismay. 'Oh,' she gasped out in
a shaken whimper, and then it was she who tried to make
a mortified bolt for it. But the moment she tried her legs
gave away once more.

On a muttered curse Ethan caught her up, then dumped
her unceremoniously back onto the bed. The whole thing
was taking on a surreal quality. Standing there he stared
down at her as if she was some kind of alien while she
rocked and groaned with a hand flattened across her horrified mouth. It was then as he watched her that it really
began to dawn on him that the swine must have spiked her
drink with something pretty potent and it was still very
much at work in her blood. 'I'm sorry,' she was saying
over and over. 'I don't know what came over me. I
don't—'

'You need a doctor,' Ethan decided grimly.

'No!'

'We need to call in the police and get them to track that
bastard down so that we can find out what it is he's slipped
you.'

'No,' she groaned out a second time.

But Ethan wasn't listening. He was too busy looking
around for the telephone. As Eve saw him take a stride
towards one sitting on a low table across the room, she
erupted with a panic that flung her anxiously to her feet.

'No, Ethan—please—!' she begged him. 'No police. No
doctor—I'm all right!'

Virtually staggering in her quest to put herself between him and the phone, she stood there trembling and looking pleadingly up at him while he looked down at her with an expression that grimly mocked her assurance.

'I *will* be all right in a minute or two!' she temporised, saw him take another determined step and felt the tears begin to burn in her eyes as fresh anxiety swelled like a monster inside. 'Please—' she begged again. 'You don't understand. The scandal, my grandfather—he will blame himself and I couldn't *bear* to let him do that!' I can't bear to know that he will never look on me in the same way again, Eve added in silent anguish. 'Look...' at least Ethan was no longer moving, and the panic had placed the strength back in her legs '...I was drunk. It was my own f-fault—'

'There is no excuse out there to justify date rape, Eve,' Ethan toughly contested.

'B-but it didn't get that far. I m-managed to stop him before he could—' The words dried up. She just couldn't bring herself to say them and had to swallow on a lump of nausea instead. 'I'll get over this—I will!' she insisted. 'But *only* if we can keep it a secret between you and me; please, Ethan—please—!' she repeated painfully.

She was pleading with him as if she was pleading for her life here, but Ethan could see the lingering horror in her eyes, see the shock and hurt and bewildered sense of betrayal, see the swollen mouth and the chafed skin, and the effects of some nasty substance that had turned her beautiful eyes black and had left her barely able to control her actions.

Did she really expect him to simply ignore all of that? In an act of frustrating indecision he sent his eyes lashing around the room. It looked like exactly what it was: the scene of some vile crime. The man was dangerous; he needed to be stopped and made to pay for his actions.

Flicking his gaze back to Eve, Ethan opened his mouth to tell her just that—then stopped, the breath stilling in his lungs when he saw the tears in her eyes, the trembling mouth, the anxiety in her pale face that was now over-shadowing the incident itself. His mouth snapped shut. A sigh rattled from him. Surrender to her pleas arrived when he acknowledged that she was in no fit state to take any more tonight.

'Okay,' he agreed with grim reluctance. 'We will leave the rest until tomorrow. But for now you can't stay here on your own…'

He deliberately didn't add, '…in case he comes back'. But he saw by her shuddering response that Eve had added the words for herself. 'Thank you,' she whispered.

He didn't want thanks. He wanted a solution as to what he was going to do next. Glancing at Eve in search of inspiration, he found himself looking at a wilting flower again, only she was a slender white lily this time, covered as she was in the cotton sheet.

A sad and helpless slender white lily, he elaborated, and the image locked up a blistering kind of anger inside his chest. 'How are you feeling?' he asked gruffly. 'Do you think you can manage to get yourself dressed?'

'Yes,' she whispered.

'Good.' He nodded. At least she was managing to stand unsupported at last. 'Do that, then I'll walk you up to the main house,' he decided, aware that there was a small army of live-in staff up there to watch over her.

'No, not the house.' Once again she vetoed his sugges-tion. 'The staff will report to my grandfather and…' Her voice trailed away, and those big eyes were suddenly pleading with him again. 'Could I come and stay with you?' she asked. 'Just for the rest of tonight. I promise I won't be any more trouble, only...'

Again that voice trailed away to nothing, and that dark, sad, vulnerable look cut into him with a deeply painful thrust. Hell, how was it he seemed to attract these kind of situations? he wondered, racking his brain for an alternative solution only to find there wasn't one. Beginning to feel a bit as if he'd been run over by a bus, he lifted up a hand in a hopeless gesture. 'Sure,' he said.

Why not? he asked himself fatalistically. He had conceded to just about everything else.

He was just about to leave her to it when he saw her mouth open to offer yet another pathetic thanks. 'Don't say it,' he advised grimly.

'No,' she mumbled understandingly. 'Sorry,' she offered instead.

His shoulder muscles rippled as they flexed in irritation. 'Don't say that either,' he clipped out tightly. 'I don't want your thanks or your apologies.' What he really wanted, he thought as he turned for the bedroom door, was to close his hands around Aidan Galloway's throat.

He was angry, Eve realised. She didn't blame him. She had probably managed to thoroughly ruin his holiday with all of this. Feeling sick to her stomach, as weak as a kitten, and still too shocked and dizzy to really comprehend even half of what had happened to her tonight, she turned away from him with the weary intention of doing as she'd been told and finding some clothes to put on—only to go still on a strangled gasp when she found herself confronted with her own reflection in the mirror on the opposite wall.

The sound brought Ethan's departure to a halt. Glancing back, he followed her gaze, found himself looking at her reflection in the mirror and instantly understood.

She'd seen her swollen mouth, her chafed skin—had

caught sight of the telling discolouration on the side of her neck that Ethan had been trying very hard to ignore from the moment he'd seen it himself. And perhaps most telling of all was the pink hibiscus still trying its best to cling to her hair.

The tears bulged in her eyes. 'I look like a harlot,' she whispered tremulously, lifting shaking fingers to remove the poor flower.

A sensationally beautiful, very special harlot, he silently extended, and on that provoking thought he threw in the metaphorical towel. 'Blow the clothes,' he decided harshly and walked back to her side. His arm came to rest across her sheet swathed shoulders. 'Let's just get you out of here.'

With that he grimly urged her into movement. Still shocked at the sight of herself, Eve tripped over the trailing sheet. On a muttered curse, Ethan went the whole hog and scooped her up high against his chest.

'I can walk!' she protested.

'Enjoy the ride,' was his curt response, as he began carrying her out of the bedroom and out of the house with his cast-iron expression brooking no argument.

Neither saw the dark figure standing in the shadows, whose eyes followed their journey from one beach house to the other by the conventional route of paths and gates. Eve's attention was just too occupied with that old fascination, which was this man called Ethan Hayes and the structure of his—she was thinking, handsome, but the word was really too soft to describe such a forcefully masculine face. His chin was square and slightly chiselled, his eyelashes long and thick. His eyebrows were two sternly straight black bars that dipped a little towards the bridge of his nose and added a disturbing severity she rather liked. She liked his eyes too, even with that a dark steely glint they were reflecting right now, and she loved his mouth, its size, its shape, its smooth firm texture— Her lips began to pulse with the sudden dark urge to taste him in that same wild, uncontrolled way she had done a few minutes ago.

Had she really done that? Shock ricocheted through her. *Why* had she done it? What kind of substance could Raoul have stirred into her drink that had had the power to make her do such an outrageous thing? She shifted uncomfortably, disturbed by the knowledge that such an out-of-control person could actually be lurking inside her, seemingly waiting the chance to leap out and jump all over a man. What must he be thinking about it, and her, and—?

'About that kiss earlier...' she said, approaching the subject tentatively.

Long eyelashes flickered, steely grey irises glinting as he glanced down at her upturned face. 'Forget it,' he advised, and looked away again because Ethan was trying not to think at all.

It was hard enough trying not to be aware that what he was carrying was feather-light and as slender as a reed, and that the warm body beneath the sheet was shapely and sleek. He didn't need the added provocation of looking into her beautiful face, nor to be reminded of that unexpected kiss.

So he concentrated his mind on the different ways he could make Aidan Galloway sorry for what he had done to Eve tonight. Date rape—for want of something to call it—and the use of sexually enhancing drugs to get what he desired, made Galloway the lowest form of human life.

That was where Eve's kiss had come from, he reminded himself. Nothing more, nothing less, therefore not worth a second thought.

So why can you still feel the imprint of her mouth against your own? he asked himself grimly.

Because she was beautiful, because she was dangerous, and—heaven help him—he liked the danger Eve Herakleides represented. It was called sexual attraction, and he would have to be a fool not to be aware that Eve felt the same pull. That little wriggle she'd just performed had been full of sexual tension—though he had to concede that the drink probably had had a lot to do with it too.

Either way, it was a danger he could not afford to be tempted by. His life was complicated enough without the tempting form of Eve Herakleides.

So what do you think you are doing now? he then scoffed to himself as he carried Eve in through his own front door. And discovered it was not a question he wanted to answer right now, as he lowered her feet to the floor then turned to close the door.

CHAPTER FIVE

THE beach houses were all very picturesque outside, but very basic inside; just one bedroom, a bathroom, small kitchen and a sitting room. Really they were meant for nothing more than a place to cool off during a day spent on the beach. Or as in Ethan case, the perfect place for the single person to use for a holiday. Problems only arose when the single person doubled to two.

It was a problem that only began to dawn on Eve as she watched Ethan close the door. The fact that it had dawned on him too at about the same moment became apparent when, instead of turning to face her, he went perfectly still.

A thick and uncomfortable silence settled between them. Clutching the sheet to her throat, Eve tried to think of something to say to break through the awkward atmosphere. Ethan tried to break it by taking off round the room to switch on the table lamps.

The light hurt her eyes, forcing her to squeeze them shut. He noticed. 'Sorry,' he murmured. 'I didn't think—'

'It's okay.' She made herself open them again. She didn't look at him though—she couldn't. Instead she made a play of checking out her surroundings—surroundings she already knew as well as she knew her own, because she had been in and out of the Petronades beach house since early childhood.

'Bedroom through that door, bathroom the other...'

She looked and nodded. Her mouth felt paper dry.

'Would you like a drink? Something hot like tea or coffee?'

Yes—no, Eve thought in tense confusion. Her head was beginning to pound, a sense of disorientation washing over her in ever increasing waves. She felt strange, out of place and—

'This was a mistake,' she pushed out thickly. 'I think I had better—'

One small step in the direction of the front door was all that it took for the whole wretched nightmare to come crashing back down upon her head. She swayed dizzily, felt her legs turn back to rubber; she knew she was going to do something stupid like drop to the floor in a tent of white sheeting.

Only it never happened, because he was already at her side and catching hold of her arms to steady her. She was trembling so badly her teeth actually chattered.

'Are you frightened of being alone here with me, or is this a delayed shock reaction?' he questioned soberly.

Both, Eve thought. 'Sh-shock, I think,' was the answer she gave out loud. Then she confessed to him shakily, 'Ethan, I really need to sit down.'

'What you need is a doctor,' he clipped back tautly.

'No,' she refused.

Sighing at her stubbornness. 'Bed, then,' he insisted. 'You can at least sleep off the effects there.'

He was about to lift her back into his arms when Eve stopped him. 'W-what I would really love to do is take a shower,' she told him. 'W-wash his touch from my skin...'

There was another one of those tense pauses. 'Eve, he didn't—?'

'No,' she put in quickly. 'He didn't.' But the tremors became shudders, and neither of them bothered to question why she was suddenly shuddering so badly.

'The bathroom it is, then,' he said briskly, and the next thing she knew Eve was being lifted into his arms again and carried into the bathroom. He set her down on the lowered toilet seat, then turned to switch on the shower. 'Stay right there,' he instructed then as he was disappearing through the door.

His departure gave Eve the opportunity to sag weakly. He was back in seconds, though, forcing her to straighten her backbone before he caught her looking so darn pathetic.

'Fresh towels,' he announced, settling them on the washbasin. 'And a tee shirt of mine.' He placed it on her lap. 'I thought it might be more comfortable to wear than the sheet.'

It was an attempt to lighten the thick atmosphere with humour, Eve recognised, and did her best to rise to it. 'White was never my colour,' she murmured, referring to the sheet.

The tee shirt was white. They both stared down at it. It was such a stupid, mild, incidental little error that certainly did not warrant the flood of hot tears it produced. Ethan saw them—of course he did—when had he missed a single thing since he'd barged into her bedroom?

He came to squat down in front of her. 'Hey,' he murmured gently. 'It's okay. I am not offended that you don't like my tee shirt.'

But she did like it. She liked every single thing about this man, every single thing he had done for her. And the worst of it was that he had done it all even though he actively disliked her! 'I'm so very sorry for dumping on you like this.' The sheet was covering her face again.

'I thought we'd agreed that you were not going to apologise,' he reminded her.

'But I feel so wretched, and I know you have to be hating this.'

'I hate what happened to you to put us both in this

situation,' he tempered. 'And the rest I think is best left until tomorrow when you should be feeling more able to cope.'

He was right. Eve nodded. 'I'll take that shower now,' she said bracingly.

'You will be okay on your own? You won't fall over or—?'

'I'll be okay.' She nodded.

He didn't look too sure about that. His eyebrows were touching across the bridge of his nose as he studied her, and his eyes were no longer steely but dark and deep with genuine worry and concern. Could she *ever* look more pathetic than this? Eve wondered tragically. And did it *have* to be Ethan Hayes who witnessed it?

The sheet was used as a handkerchief again, and they weren't her fingers that lifted it to wipe the tears from her cheeks, they were his gentle fingers. The caring act was almost her complete undoing.

'I'll be fine!' she promised in near desperation. Any second now she was going to throw herself at him again if she didn't get him out of here! 'Please go, Ethan—please,' she repeated plaintively.

Maybe he knew because he rose up to his full height. 'Don't lock the door,' was his final comment. 'And if you need me, shout.'

But Eve didn't shout, and while he waited for her to reappear, Ethan prowled the place. He was like a pacing tiger guarding his territory—he likened his own tense and restless state. In the end he put his restless energy to use and tidied the bedroom, remade the bed and, as a belated thought, pulled another clean tee shirt out of the drawer and slid it over his head, then went to make a pot of tea. He had just been placing a tray down on the coffee table when the bathroom door opened.

He glanced up. Eve paused in the doorway. She had a towel wrapped around her hair and she was wearing the tee shirt. It covered her to halfway down her thighs and the short sleeves almost brushed her slender wrists.

She was wrong about the colour, he thought, quickly dropping his eyes away. 'Tea?' he offered.

'I... Yes, please,' she answered and, after a small hesitation that told him Eve was as uncomfortable with this situation as he was, she walked forward and took the chair next to the sofa. Having been told how she liked her tea, Ethan poured and offered her the mug then folded himself into the other chair. Neither spoke as they sipped, and the atmosphere was strained, to put it mildly. Eve was the first to attempt to ease it. Putting the cup down on the tray, she removed the towel from her hair and shook out its wet and tangled length. 'Would you have a comb or something I could use?'

'Sure.' Glad of the excuse to move, he got up and found a comb. 'Hair-dryer's in the bathroom,' he said as he handed over the comb.

She nodded in acknowledgement of something he suspected she already knew. He sat down again and she began combing the tangles out of her hair. It was all very domestic, very we-do-this-kind-of-thing-all-the-time. But nothing could have been further from the truth.

'I'll take the couch,' she said.

'No, you won't,' he countered. 'I have my honour to protect. *I* take the couch.'

'But—'

'Not up for discussion,' he cut in on her protest. One brief glance at his face and she was conceding the battle to him. Suddenly she looked utterly exhausted yet so uptight that the grip she had on his comb revealed shiny white knuckles.

'Come on, you've had enough.' Standing up again, he swung himself into action which felt better than sitting there feeling useless. Taking hold of her wrist, he tugged her to her feet, gently prized the comb from her fingers, and began trailing her towards the bedroom.

'My hair...' she prompted.

'It won't fall out if you leave it to dry by itself,' was his sardonic answer. But really he knew he was rushing her like this because it was himself that had suddenly had enough. He needed some space that didn't have Eve Herakleides in it. He needed to get a hold on what was churning up his insides.

And what was that? he asked himself. He refused to let himself look for the answer because he knew it was likely to make him as bad as that swine Aidan Galloway.

The bedroom was ready and waiting, its shadows softened by the gentle glow from the bedside lamp. He saw Eve glance at the bed, then at the room as a whole, and her nervous uncertainty almost screamed in this latest silence to develop between them.

'You're safe here, Eve,' he grimly assured her, making that assurance on the back of his own sinful thoughts.

She nodded, slipped her wrist out of his grasp and took a couple of steps away. She looked so darn lost and anxious that he had to wonder if she was picking up on what his own tension was about.

Yet what did she do next? She floored him by suddenly spinning to face him. White-faced, big-eyed, small mouth trembling. 'Will you stay?' she burst out. 'Just for a few minutes. I don't want to be alone yet. I...'

The moment she'd said it, Eve was wishing the stupid words back. Just the expression on his face was enough to tell her she could not have appalled him more if she'd tried. Oh, damn, she thought and put a trembling hand up to cover her face. He didn't even like her; hadn't she always known that? Yet here she was almost begging him to sleep with her—or as good as.

'Pretend I never said that,' she retracted, turned away and even managed a couple more steps towards the wretched bed! She felt dizzy and confused and terribly disorientated—and she wished Raoul Delacroix had never been born!

The arm that reached round her to flip back the bed covers almost startled her out of her wits. 'In,' Ethan commanded.

In, like a child being put to bed by a stern father, she likened. *In* she got, curling onto her side like a child and let him settle the covers over her. When I leave here tomorrow I am *never* going to let myself set eyes on Ethan Hayes again! she vowed. 'Goodnight,' she made herself say.

'Shut up,' he returned and the next thing she knew he was stretching out beside her on top of the covers. 'I'll stay until you go to sleep,' he announced.

'You don't have to,' Eve responded with a hint of bite. 'I changed my mind. I don't—' The way he turned on his side to face her was enough to push the rest of her words back down her throat.

'Now listen to me, you aggravating little witch,' he said huskily. 'Any more provocation from you and I am likely to lose my temper. If you need me here, I'll stay, if you want me to go, I'll go. Your decision.'

Her decision. 'Stay,' she whispered.

Without another word he flopped onto his back and stared rigidly at the ceiling. Curled up at his side, Eve imagined his silent curses that were probably all very colourful ways of describing what he was feeling about this mess.

I'm sorry, she wanted to say, but she knew he didn't want to hear that, so she did the next best thing she could think of and shut her eyes then willed herself to fall asleep.

Five minutes, Ethan was thinking grimly. I'll give her five minutes to fall asleep then I'm out of here. With that, he took a look at his watch. Two o'clock.

A sigh whispered from her. Turning his head it wrenched at his heart to see the trace of tears still staining her cheeks. She had just endured a close encounter with what had to be a woman's worst nightmare and here he was putting a time limit on how long he was going to support her through the rest of this.

A sigh whispered from him. Eve liked the sigh. She liked the comfort she gained from hearing his closeness and the sure knowledge that if she was safe anywhere then it had to be right here with him.

Tomorrow was destined to be another thing entirely. By tomorrow, she predicted, it would be back to hostilities, with him backing off whenever she threatened to come close. But, for now, she was content to think of him as her guardian angel, and on that comforting thought she let herself relax into sleep.

Another five minutes, Ethan decided. She'd relaxed at last and her breathing was steady. He would give her another five minutes to slip into a deep slumber, then he would swap the comfort of the bed for the discomfort of the living-room couch.

His eyelids began to droop; he dragged them back up again and captured a yawn on the back of his hand. Eve moved and mumbled something, it sounded like, 'Don't.' He tagged on another five minutes because the last thing he wanted was for her to wake up in a strange bed alone and frightened. Another five minutes wouldn't kill him, would it?

Eve came thrashing up from a deep dark sleep to that halfway place where haunted dream mixed with confusing reality. A sound had disturbed her, though she wasn't sure what it had represented, only that it had made her pulse accelerate and had pushed up her eyelids so she found herself staring directly into the sleeping face of Ethan Hayes. He was lying kiss-close to her on the same pillow with his arms and legs wrapped warmly around her—or were her limbs wrapped around him? She didn't have time to consider the puzzle because the sound came again and even as she lifted her head off the pillow she was aware that Ethan was now awake also. They turned together to look towards the open bedroom doorway, then froze on a heart-stopping clutch of stunning dismay.

Theron Herakleides stood filling the doorway, looking like his favourite god, Zeus, with his thickly curling grey locks framing a rough, tough, lived-in face that was clearly preparing to cast thunderbolts down on their heads.

'Grandpa,' Eve only managed on a strangled whisper. Ethan hissed out a couple of quick curses beneath his breath. The old man flicked devil-to-pay black eyes from one to the other and conjured up an image of themselves, which showed them what he was seeing. It was so utterly damning neither found the ability to speak in their own defence.

Theron did it for them when hard as rock, he threw his first thunderbolt. 'One hour, in my study at the main house,' he instructed. 'I will expect you both there.'

Then he was gone, leaving them lying there in a tangle of limbs and white bedding, feeling as culpable as a pair of guilty lovers who'd been caught red-handed in the act of sex.

'Oh, dear God.' Eve found her voice first, groaning out the words as she fell back heavily against the bed.

Ethan went one stage further and snaked his legs free of the tangle then landed on his feet beside the bed. He did not want to believe that any of this was really happening.

'How did you get here?' Eve had the absolute stupidity to ask him.

'How did *I* get here?' Ethan swung round to lance at her. 'This is *my* bed!'

They'd both reacted on pure instinct. Now reality hit, clearing away the last muddy remnants of sleep. Eve began to remember. Ethan watched it happen in a slide-frame flicker, as she passed through last night's ordeal to this morning's shocked horror. She went as pale as alabaster, clamped a hand across her trembling mouth, and just stared at him through huge dark nightmare-ridden eyes that turned his insides into a raging inferno of anger and gave him a desire to break someone's neck.

His own at the moment, he acknowledged grimly, and released the air from his lungs on a pressured hiss. 'My fault,' he conceded. 'I fell asleep. I'll go and talk to him.'

Decision set in his mind, he was already turning towards the door when Eve's half hysterical, 'No!' hit his ears. 'He won't believe you. I have to do it!' She began scrambling shakily to the edge of the bed. All long limbs, flying hair and utterly shattered composure, she landed on her feet beside him and began searching the floor.

'Shoes,' she mumbled anxiously.

'You didn't come in shoes. I carried you, remember?'

The hand was at her mouth again as a second barrage of memories came flooding in. No shoes, no clothes; Ethan was seeing it all with her. He was also seeing another bed that had looked not unlike this one, with its covers lying in the same damning tangle, half on the floor half on the bed.

Had Theron Herakleides seen that other bed too? His skin began to prickle as he began to fully appreciate what the older man had to believe from the evidence. A passionate interlude spent in his granddaughter's bed before they'd transferred to this one to repeat the whole orgy all over again.

The air left his lungs on yet another hard hiss. This whole mad scenario was going to take some serious explaining. 'I'll do the explaining,' he grimly insisted. 'You can stay here while I—'

'Will you listen to me, Ethan—? He will not believe you!' Eve stated fiercely. 'Trust me. I know him. He has seen what he's seen.'

'The truth is out there, Eve,' he reminded her. 'It has a name and a face—and when I get my hands on him he will be happy to spill out the truth to your grandfather.'

While his eyes began to darken at the delightful prospect of bringing Aidan Galloway face to face with his sins, Eve's eyes did the opposite and turned bright green, glinting like the eyes of a witch who was busy concocting her next wicked spell. She started walking towards the door.

'Where are you going?' he demanded.

'To see Grandpa before you do,' she stated firmly.

'Eve—'

'No!' She turned on him. 'I said I will deal with it!' The eyes were now glinting with tears, not wicked spells. 'Y-you don't understand. You will *never* understand!' And on that she was gone, running out of the room and leaving him standing there wondering what the heck that last outburst had been all about?

He'd understood! Of course he'd understood, he claimed arrogantly. From the moment he'd stepped into her bedroom last night, he'd understood without question what it was he'd been seeing!

Now it hurt that *she* didn't see that understanding. What did she think he was going to do? Paint her character all the lurid colours he could think of just to make his own part in this fiasco seem prettier?

Well, he was damned if he was going to slink away and hide in some dark corner while Eve fought his battles for him. Theron Herakleides was expecting the two of them to present themselves in his study and that was what would happen.

CHAPTER SIX

UNDERSTANDING anything about Eve Herakleides flew out of the window the moment Ethan found himself confronting her grandfather. Because Eve, he all too quickly discovered, had got in first with her version of events leading up to what Theron had witnessed. Now Ethan was angrily trying to make some sense of what it was he was supposed to have done.

Standing tall and proud behind his desk, Theron Herakleides looked on Ethan as if he was seeing a snake in the grass. 'You have to appreciate, Mr Hayes,' he was saying, 'that in Greece we expect a man to stand by his actions.'

'Are you implying that I wouldn't?' Ethan demanded stiffly.

The older man's brief smile set his temper simmering. 'You stand here claiming no intimacy between yourself and my granddaughter,' he pointed out. 'Are those not the words of a man who is trying to wriggle off the hook he finds himself caught upon?'

'We were not intimate,' Ethan insisted angrily.

A pair of grey-cloud eyebrows rose enquiringly. 'Now you expect this old man to question what his own eyes have already told him?'

Not only his own eyes, Ethan noted, as he sent a murderous glance at Eve who was standing quietly beside her grandfather. Gone was the seductress in sexy hot-pink. Nor was there any sign of the broken little creature he'd taken under his wing. No, from the neatly braided hair to the clothes that had been chosen with modesty in mind, here stood a picture of sweet innocence wearing a butter-wouldn't-melt-in-her-mouth smile that told clearly that he was going to be made the scapegoat here!

'Of course,' Theron Herakleides broke into speech again, 'you could be attempting to protect Eve's reputation, in which case I most sincerely apologise for implying the opposite. But your protection comes too late, I'm afraid,' he informed him gravely. 'For what I saw with my own eyes had already been substantiated by one of the men that guard my property. He saw you carry my granddaughter from our beach house to your beach house covered only by a sheet, you see...'

Damned by his own actions, Ethan realised. Then he said frowningly, 'Just a minute. If your guard was watching the beach house, then where was he when Eve—?'

Eve moved, drawing his glance and lodging the rest of his challenge in his throat when he found those eyes of hers pleading with him to say no more. Anger erupted as he glared at her and felt frustration mount like a boiling lump of matter deep within his chest.

I should stop this right here, he told himself forcefully. I should tell Eve's grandfather the unvarnished truth and finish this craziness once and for all. But those pleading eyes were pricking anxiously at him, reminding him of the conversation he and Eve had had the night before.

Ethan looked back at her grandfather, and Eve held her breath. If he talked, it was over. If he talked, her life was never going to be the same again.

'I think it's time you explained to me where you are going with this, Theron,' Ethan invited very grimly.

A deep sense of relief relaxed the tension out of Eve's shoulders. Thank you, she wanted to say to him. Thank you from the bottom of my heart for this.

'I am going to give you the benefit of the doubt,' her grandfather smoothly announced, 'and presume that your intentions towards my granddaughter are entirely honourable...'

It wasn't a question but a rock-solid statement. Eve watched nervously as Ethan's full attention became riveted on the older man's face. Her heart stopped beating in the throbbing silence, her mouth running dry, as she tried to decide whether to jump in and take over before Ethan said something ruinous or to remain quiet and keep praying that he didn't let her down.

Ethan didn't know what he was doing. The word 'honourable' was playing over and over inside his head while he stared at Theron's perfectly blank expression. Then he switched his gaze to Eve who was standing there looking like a diehard romantic who'd just had her dearest wish voiced out loud.

I've been well and truly set up, he finally registered, and the knowledge was threatening to cut him off at the knees.

Eve came to his rescue—if it could be called a rescue. Leaving her grandfather's side she rounded the desk and came to thread her fingers in with his then had the gall to lean lovingly against him like an ecstatic bride. 'You guessed our secret.' She pouted at her darling grandpa. 'I'm so happy! This is turning out to be the most wonderful birthday of my entire life.'

Slowly turning his dark head Ethan looked down at her through narrowed, steely I'm-going-kill-you eyes. 'Oh, don't be cross.' She pouted at him also. 'I know you wanted to wait a while before we told anyone about us. But Grandpa can keep a secret—can't you, Grandpa?' It was Grandpa's turn to receive the full spell-casting blast of her wide green witch's eyes.

The old man smiled. It was an action that smoothed

every hard angle out of him. 'But why be secretive, my little angel?' he quizzed fondly. 'You are in love with each other. Don't hide it, celebrate! We will announce your betrothal in front of the family when we return to Athens next week...'

He's remembered he hates me, Eve realised nervously. Ethan had washed and changed before coming up to the main house, but even wearing a smart blue shirt and grey trousers she could still see the man sitting in the beach bar feeding her his utter contempt.

'Please, Ethan,' she said, panting as she hurried after him down the path that led the way back to the beach. 'Let me explain—'

'You set me up,' he rasped. 'That doesn't need explaining.'

'It was the only way I could think of to—'

'Get a marriage proposal?' he cut in contemptuously.

'You're not that good a catch!' she retaliated.

He stopped striding and swung round to face her. Sensational, Eve thought with an inner flutter. Ethan Hayes in the throws of a blistering fury was exciting and dangerous and—

'Then, *why* me?' he bit out.

'He dotes on me...'

Ethan responded to that with a hard laugh. 'Now tell me something I haven't worked out.'

'He's built this shining glass case around me that he likes to believe protects me from the realities of life.'

'Take my advice, and smash the case,' Ethan responded. 'Before someone else comes along and smashes it for you.' On that he turned and started walking again.

So did Eve. 'That's the whole point,' she said urgently. 'I know I need to smash the case, but gently, Ethan!' she pleaded with him. 'Not with a cold hard blow of just about the ugliest truth I could possibly think of to hurt him with.'

'He deserves the truth,' he insisted. 'You are insulting him by protecting him from it!'

'No.' Her hand gripping his arm pulled him to a stop again, like a miniature tyrant she stepped right in front of him to block his path. Her eyes pleaded, her mouth pleaded, the fierce grasp of her fingers pleaded. 'You don't understand. He's—'

Eve watched him go from sizzling fury to another place entirely. His shoulders flexed, his teeth gritted together, his wide breastbone shifted on an excess of suppressed air. 'Don't tell me again that I don't understand,' he bit out roughly, 'when all I need to understand is that you are using me, Miss Herakleides. And that sticks right here.' He stabbed two long fingers at his throat.

'Yes, I can see that...' she nodded '...and I'm sorry...'

'Good. Now let me pass so I can go and do what I need to do.'

'Which is what?' she asked warily.

The morning sun dappling through the tree tops suddenly turned his face into a map of hard angles that made her insides start to shake. 'Find the cause of this mess and make him wish he'd never been born before I deliver him into the hands of your grandfather,' Ethan answered grittily and went to step around her.

'You can't!' Once again Eve stopped him. 'H-he isn't here!' she exclaimed. 'H-he left the island by launch at first light. I know because I checked before I went to see Grandpa. H-he must have known I—'

'You checked,' Ethan repeated, his eyes narrowing on her pale features and her worriedly stammering lips. 'Now, why should you want to go and do that?' he questioned silkily.

'I w-wanted to talk to him, f-find out why he did it,' she explained. 'I really needed to know if I had brought it all upon myself! H-he was a friend—a long-standing friend. Friends don't do that to each other, do they? So I had to at least try to find out why!'

Ethan really couldn't believe he was hearing this. 'After everything he put you through last night.' Grimly he stuck to the main issue here. 'You went to confront him—on your own?'

Anxiety was darkening those big green eyes again. 'If I'd asked you to come with me, I knew you would want to kill him!'

Time to stop looking in those eyes, he decided. 'And you don't want him dead,' he persisted.

'No,' she breathed. 'I'm trying to avoid trouble not stir it up! A war will erupt between the two families if what happened last night ever got out.'

But that wasn't the real reason, Ethan thought grimly. She was hiding something, he was sure of it.

Then that something was suddenly clawing its way up his spine and attacking the hairs at the back of his neck. It was written all over her, in those big green apprehensive eyes, in the unsteady tremor of her lovely mouth—in the very words she had said!

'You're in love with the bastard.' He made the outright accusation. No wonder she'd felt compelled to find out why he had done what he had done! Why she didn't want Ethan to go anywhere near him—why she was trying to protect the swine now!

Her chin shot up. 'I'm what?' she questioned in shrill surprise.

But Ethan was no longer listening. 'I can't believe what a fool I've been,' he muttered. For him it was like lightning striking twice! First, he had got embroiled in Leona's love problems. Now he found himself embroiled in Eve's!

'How dare you?' she gasped out, dropping the surprise for indignant fury.

'No.' Ethan hit back by turning on her furiously. 'How dare *you* get me mixed up in your crazy love life?'

He was angry; she was angry; the old hostile sparks began to fly. The air crackled with them, 'That's rich,' Eve mocked, 'coming from a man who is only here on this island because he's in hiding after being caught red-handed with another man's wife!'

The sparks changed into a high-voltage current. It was unstable—very unstable. 'Who told you that?' Ethan demanded.

Eve shrugged. 'Leandros Petronades is a relative of Grandpa's. He told Grandpa, and Grandpa thought I should know before I committed myself to you.'

'It's a lie,' he declared.

Eve didn't believe him. 'Don't insult my intelligence,' she denounced. 'Do you think I didn't notice the bruise on your face when you arrived on the island? Everyone noticed it. In fact it was the source of much speculation.'

'And the bruise on your neck?' Ethan went in with the metaphorical knife and took some satisfaction from seeing her snap her hand up to cover the mark.

'I forgot!' she gasped out in impressive horror.

Ethan didn't believe her. The brazen hussy hadn't even bothered to cover the damn thing up! 'How many more people have seen it and been equally imaginative about how it was put there?'

She blushed and looked uncomfortable. Ethan released a harsh laugh. 'My God,' he breathed, 'you are unbeliev-able! Take my advice, Eve,' he offered as his grim farewell. 'Go back up to the house and tell your grandfather the truth before I do it for you.'

'You wouldn't...'

He was turning away when she said that. It brought him swinging back again. 'I would,' he promised. 'And you know why I would do it? Because you are a danger to yourself,' he told her. 'You flirt with every man you come into contact with, uncaring what your flirting is doing to them. Then you have the rank stupidity to fall in love with a piece of low life like Aidan Galloway— And even after what he tried to do to you last night, you are *still* standing here protecting him! That makes you dangerous,' he concluded, and tried to ignore her greyish pallor, the hint of tears, the small shocked jerk she made that somehow cut him so deeply he almost groaned out loud.

Instead he walked away, striding down the path towards the beach with so much anger burning inside him he had to reign in on just about every emotion he possessed, or he'd be doing something really stupid like—

Like going back up the path and taking back every rotten, slaying word he'd spoken, because he knew what it was like to be in love with the wrong person, didn't he?

At least Leona was warm and kind and unfailingly loyal to her husband, he grimly justified his reason for not turning back. Aidan Galloway was a different kind of meat entirely. He was poison; he needed exposing before he tried the same thing with some other woman.

From a window in the main house, Theron Herakleides observed the altercation on the path down to the beach through mildly satisfied eyes. He wasn't quite sure what the altercation was actually about, but he had a shrewd idea. Ethan Hayes had just been well and truly scuppered by his enterprising granddaughter and he was now in the middle of a black fury.

Served him right for seducing her, Theron thought coldly. If he hadn't been so sure that Eve truly believed she was in love with the rake, the hell being wrought down there on his path would have been happening right here at his own orchestration.

But if his beautiful Eve thought he was going to let her throw herself away on a man like Ethan Hayes, she was so wrong it actually hurt him to know that he was going to have to show her just how wrong she was. So what if the man was an outstandingly gifted architect? So what if he, Theron Herakleides, had actually held him in deep respect until today? By tomorrow Ethan Hayes would be out of the picture, Theron vowed very grimly, and Eve was going to learn to recover from her little holiday romance.

With those thoughts in mind, Theron turned away from the window to pick up the telephone. 'Ah—*yassis*, Leandros,' he greeted pleasantly, and fell into light conversation with his nephew while glancing back out of the window to see the way Eve had been left standing on the path, looking like a thoroughly whipped peasant instead of the proud and brave goddess he believed her to be.

Ethan Hayes would pay for that, he vowed coldly. He was going to pay in spades for playing with the heart of a sweet angel when everyone knew he was in love with Leona Al-Qadim!

'I am about to call in that favour you owe to me,' he warned Leandros Petronades, then went on to explain what he required of him. 'The sooner the better would be good for me, Leandros…'

Standing there on the sunny path, feeling as if she had just been reduced to dust by a man angry enough to tear down a mountain, Eve was carefully going over everything Ethan had tossed at her so she could be certain she had heard him correctly.

Aidan— 'Oh, good heavens,' she gasped as the whole thing began to get even more confused and complicated. Ethan believed it was Aidan, not Raoul, who'd been with her in her bedroom last night!

The telephone was ringing as Ethan let himself into the beach house. He stood glaring at the contraption, in two minds whether to ignore it. He didn't want to speak to anyone. He did not want to do anything but stew in the juices of his anger.

But, in the end, he gave in and picked up the receiver, if only to silence its persistent ring. It was Victor Frayne, his business partner, which did not improve his mood any. 'What do you want, Victor?' he questioned abruptly.

'Still as mad as hell at me, I see,' Victor Frayne drawled sardonically.

Mad as hell at the world, Ethan grimly extended. 'What do you want?' he repeated with a little less angst.

Victor went on to tell him that they had an emergency developing in San Estéban and that Leandros Petronades wanted Ethan back there to sort it out.

'Can't you see to it?' Ethan snapped out impatiently. He had no will to feel accommodating towards Victor nor Leandros Petronades for that matter, the latter being the spreader of gossip about his rich and varied love life!

'It's a planning dispute with the Spanish authorities,' Victor explained. 'Apparently we've breached some obscure by-law and they are now insisting we pull down the new yacht club and rebuild it somewhere else.'

'Over my dead body,' Ethan pronounced in fatherly protection of what happened to be one of his proudest achievements in design. 'We have not breached any bylaw. I know because I checked them all out personally.'

'Which makes you the man with the answers, Ethan,' Victor relayed smoothly. 'Therefore, it makes this your fight. I have to warn you that they are threatening to bull-doze the place themselves if we refuse to do it.'

'I'll be on the next plane,' Ethan announced, and was surprised to discover how relieved he felt to reach that decision. Now he could get the hell out of paradise and leave the serpent to look for a fresh victim to mesmerise before she bit!

'Have you heard from Leona?' he then heard himself ask, and could have bitten himself for being so damned obvious.

'She's fine,' Leona's father assured him. 'She is cruising the Med as we speak and thoroughly enjoying herself, by the sound of it.'

Which puts me right in my place, Ethan thought as he replaced the receiver. Out of sight, out of mind and where I belong.

'Damn,' he muttered. 'Damn all women to hell.' And, on that profound curse, he picked up the telephone again with the intention of reserving a seat for himself on the three o'clock plane to Nassau, where he could catch a con-necting flight to London, and then on to Spain. Only he didn't get quite that far because a movement at the door caught his eye.

CHAPTER SEVEN

SHE looked pale and fragile, as if someone had come along with an eraser and had wiped out all that wonderful animation which made Eve Herakleides the fascinating creature she was. His heart dipped. Had he done that? Or was the white-faced frailty Aidan Galloway's handiwork, and it was just that he had been too angry with her earlier to remember that she had been put through one hell of an ordeal only the night before.

No, he then told himself as a softening in his mood began to weaken his firm stance against her machinations. Eve is trouble. You've done enough. Send her packing and get out of here.

'What now?' he demanded in a hard, grim tone that told Eve he only had to look at her now to see trouble standing at his door.

But Eve wasn't Ethan Hayes' real trouble, she'd just come to realise. No, his trouble had been evident in the deep dark husky quality of his voice when he had spoken that other woman's name.

Suddenly she wanted to run, she wanted to hide, she wanted to pretend she had not overheard his conversation, because she knew for sure now that Ethan had lied before, and he was tragically, painfully in love with Leona Al-Qadim.

At that precise moment she felt like trouble because she had this blistering urge to knock some sense into him! Would someone like to tell her, please, how a man like Ethan Hayes could allow himself to fall in love with a very married woman? Was she a witch? Had she cast a spell over him? Had they been such passionate lovers that he'd been blinded by the sex and he couldn't see it took a certain type of woman to cheat on her husband?

No wonder the Sheikh had bruised his jaw for him! He deserved it, the fool! And she only hoped to goodness that the lovely Leona had received her just desserts too!

'Speak, Eve,' Ethan prompted, when she still hadn't managed to say anything. 'I'm in a rush. I have a plane to catch.'

A plane to catch, she silently repeated. Well, didn't that just about say everything else about him! Her eyes turned to crystal, backed by an ocean of burning green anger. 'So.' She stepped forward into his house and into his life with the grim intention to sort it out for him. 'You're going to leave the island and drop me in it because of one stupid phone call.'

The burning accusation flicked him like a whip. Ethan fielded it with the kind of small mocking smile that further infuriated Eve. 'That one stupid phone call was from my business partner informing me of an emergency that has developed on one of our projects in Spain,' he explained. 'And you dropped yourself in it,' he then coolly reminded her, 'by telling a pack of lies to your grandfather.'

'You had the chance to refute those lies. You didn't,' Eve pointed out. 'So now I'm afraid you are stuck with me.'

'As my future wife? Not in this life, Miss Herakleides,' he informed her. 'You know already what I think you should do, but if you still can't bring yourself to *drop* Aidan Galloway *in it* with your grandfather, then, with my speedy exit from here, at least you won't have to worry about me destroying your grandfather's trust in your honesty.'

With that cutting bit of arrogance he turned to walk away from this conversation—as if Eve was going to let him!

'Oh, you're so pompous sometimes.' She sighed as she trailed him across the sitting room. 'Do you ever stop to listen to yourself? I have no wish to be the wife of anyone,' she announced as she arrived in the bedroom doorway in time to see him settle a suitcase out on the bed. 'But, while we are on the subject of marriage, I'll point out that at least I am at liberty to be your wife if I wanted to be!'

The remark made him turn. Eve felt her skin start to prickle as she was reminded of wild animals again. 'Meaning—what?' he demanded.

She offered a shrug, that warning prickle forcing her to backtrack slightly. 'Meaning I don't have the wish, so why are we arguing about it?'

He knew she had backed out of what she had been going to say. It was there, written in the way she lowered her eyes from his—which in turn had his own narrowing threateningly. 'I don't know,' he incised. 'You tell me.'

His was an outright challenge for her to get off her chest whatever was fizzing inside it. He knew she knew about Leona. He knew she'd overheard his discussion with Victor just now.

But Eve was discovering that she just did not want to discuss his very married lover with him. She wanted to discuss *them*. 'Aidan Galloway,' she prompted, watching his face toughen up like a rock. 'I came here, because something you said on the path just now made me realise we seem to have been talking at cross purposes about what actually happened last night.'

Some of the challenge leaked out of him. 'He attempted to rape you.' Ethan named it.

'No.' Eve frowned. 'It wasn't—'

Ethan spun his back to her and walked over to the wardrobe to begin removing clothes from their hangers. 'Still protecting him, I see,' he drawled.

The comment stung. 'No,' she denied the charge. 'I don't need to protect Aidan. Not in this context anyway,' she felt pressed to add. 'And will you stop *doing* that and listen to me!' she snapped out, when he continued to pack his suitcase as if she wasn't even there.

Ignoring her demand, he made to walk back to the wardrobe. On a fit of irritation she went to stand directly in his path. She felt like a mouse challenging a giant and, the worst of it was, it excited her. Her insides came alive as if sparkling diamonds were showering her with the urge to reach out and touch.

'I am trying to tell you that Aidan Galloway was *not* the one who spiked my drink last night!' she told him furiously. 'You've been blaming the wrong man!'

Looking down into those rich green earnest eyes, Ethan had to wonder how such beautiful eyes could lie as well as they did? For some unaccountable reason the way she was still insisting on defending the bastard made him want to kiss that lying little mouth senseless.

Instead he released a very soft, very deriding laugh, took hold of her stubborn chin between finger and thumb and gave it a condescending shake. 'But you would say that, being so in love with him,' he taunted softly, then he side-stepped her and continued with what he was doing.

I knew I hated him, now I remember why, Eve thought, and took in a deep breath of air to give her the will to continue when really she wanted to beat out an angry tattoo on his back!

'We were at Aidan's beach house. It was my birthday party and we were all enjoying ourselves...' Except for me, because I was brooding over you! she added silently.

'Aidan was the one who was mixing the drinks. But it was *not* Aidan who slipped something potent into my drink. It was *not* Aidan who brought me home and—did what he did!'

'Who then?' he shot at her.

Ah, Eve thought, and snapped her lips shut. Having seen his burning desire to rip Aidan from limb to limb, she decided it might be wise to keep the name of the real culprit to herself for now. 'Who it was doesn't matter any more.' She therefore evaded the question. 'I just needed to tell you that it wasn't Aidan.'

'You're lying,' he pronounced with a withering glance at her.

'I'm not!' she denied. 'Aidan is one of the nicest people I know!' she insisted in defence of that look. 'And he's going through his own bit of hell right now—so he doesn't need you accusing him of something he would not think of doing in a million years!'

'Are we talking about the same man who could lose himself in the embrace of another woman while his fiancée, his cousin and myself, looked on from the sidelines?' he mocked. Then on a sudden burst of impatience, he tossed the clothes he had been holding onto the bed and took a hard grip her shoulders. 'Stop protecting him, Eve,' he shook her gently. 'The man just isn't worthy of it!'

'I am telling you the truth,' she insisted. 'If you will just shut up and listen, I will explain about the kiss—'

'You're in love with him,' he repeated the outright accusation. 'That doesn't need explaining.'

'You're in love with another man's wife,' Eve retaliated in kind. 'What does that say about your right to moralise over me?'

His eyes began to darken ominously. Eve's senses began to play havoc with her ability to breathe or think. His mouth was hard and tight and angry, hers was soft and quivery and hurt. He was too close—she liked it. Her hands even went up to press against his shirt front. She felt his heat, the pound of his heart, the elixir of sheer masculine strength.

She wanted him to kiss her so very badly that it hurt.

Damn it all, but he wanted to kiss some sense into her, so badly it actually hurt, Ethan was thinking helplessly. 'He bruised your mouth, here,' he murmured, making do with running a finger over the soft smooth padding where the slight discolouration was still evident.

'She let her husband bruise yours,' Eve responded with a mimicking touch of a finger to the corner of his mouth.

He wasn't listening. 'And here,' he continued, moving that same gentle finger to the mark at her throat. 'I want to kill him for doing this to you.'

'It wasn't Aidan.' Somehow, some way she managed to hang onto a thread of sanity long enough to say that, even though she was becoming more engrossed in the pleasure of touching him.

'It wasn't Leona's husband who put the bruise on my face.'

'I still want to kill her just for breathing,' she confessed with enough green-eyed jealousy to make him laugh.

It was a strained, low, husky sound though, thick with other things, that made her insides begin to melt. Then he wasn't laughing. Instead he was taking her trailing finger in his and feeding it slowly into his mouth. Moist heat enveloped each sensitised nerve end, then spread right down to her toes. She released a soft breath of air and watched his steel-grey eyes turn to smoke. He was going to kiss her.

Yes, please, she begged him silently, and let him lower

her hand back to his chest, let him lower his dark head, and parted her lips in readiness for when his met them.

Then he was kissing her, kissing her hotly, kissing her deeply, kissing her urgently like a man stealing something he knew he shouldn't take. But Eve wanted him to take. In fact she wholly encouraged him by sliding her hands up his shirt front until they joined at the back of his neck, then she parted her lips that bit more to invite him to take as much as he liked.

Heat poured from one to the other. One of them released a pent-up sigh—maybe both of them did. His hands left her shoulders and spread themselves across her slender spine, firm yet gentle in the way they urged her into closer contact with him. She liked it—loved it. This man had been threatening to ignite her like this from the first moment she had ever set eyes on him.

She was warm, she was sweet, she was seduction itself. She was everything he had been fantasising she would be for so long now he couldn't remember when it had begun. His hands felt enlivened merely by touching her. His body was slowly drowning in sensual heat. If she moved any closer, he'd had it, he was sure of it; that dragging sensation between his thighs was telling him he was ready to leap.

And the kiss? It just went on and on as a fascinating swim through a million pleasure zones. He didn't want it to end. Yet it had to end.

'What is this?' he murmured, against her mouth. 'Mutual consolation?'

He was trying to cool things, though Eve could tell he didn't really want to cool anything. So what if it was consolation to him? she asked herself. If the power of his hunger was anything to go by, Ethan Hayes was more than ready to be consoled. 'I'm game, if you are,' she therefore confided with enough breathy seduction to slay any man.

'Eve the flirt, Eve the temptress.' Ethan fought a hard battle between his desire to be tempted and a need to break free from her magic spell. But, in doing so, he hadn't realised he had said the words out loud.

Eve broke all connection. It was so abrupt he didn't even have time to respond. She turned away—walked away—then wrapped her arms around her body in a way he recognised all too well.

Eve trying to hug her pain away. He named it with a sense of bitter self-contempt for being the one to make it happen this time.

'I'm sorry,' he murmured. 'I didn't mean—'

'Yes, you did,' she cut in on him in a thin little voice.

A sigh eased itself from his body. 'All right,' he admitted it. 'So I think you like to tease men's senses.' She had been teasing his senses since the day they'd first met—was still teasing them! Even with whole chasms between them right now, he could still feel her lips and the impression of her body where it had pressed against his.

Damn it to hell! 'Aidan Galloway isn't the only man I've watched you turn inside out with a smile,' he added, angry with himself now for allowing that kiss to happen at all! 'Jack Banning isn't immune and neither is Raoul Delacroix.'

She stiffened sharply. 'Meaning what?' She spun on him. 'That I *did* get what I deserved last night?'

'I didn't say that.' Ethan sighed wearily. 'I will never say that!'

'But it's interesting that you're clocking up a whole list of men who could have been mad enough for me to want to spike my drink! We could even add your name, since you've just given in against your better judgement and kissed Eve the flirt!'

Ethan had no defence. 'I'm sorry,' was all he could say helplessly. 'But I was not making a judgement on you! If anything I was making a judgement on them! On me— it—oh, I don't know.' He sighed, heavily aware that he'd dug his own grave as deep as it needed to go.

'In other words the name doesn't really matter, just the one they revolve around,' Eve misunderstood him—deliberately he suspected.

'One name matters.' He grunted.

'As in, who tried the big seduction of Eve the flirt?' Ethan winced. Eve nodded, feeling that she'd more than deserved that telling wince. 'Well, let's go through all the candidates shall we?' She was beginning to warm to her sarcastic theme. 'We both know it wasn't you, so we can cross your name from the list. Jack Banning has a job to protect, so, even if it was him, he isn't going to come out and admit he so much as looked at me the wrong way. If it was Aidan, I'm in trouble because the Galloways are rich and powerful, and very clannish, they protect their own in ways you would not believe. As for André Visconte, he will defend his half-brother to his very last breath—as he has done on countless occasions before! Then there is my grandfather to consider—another rich man with too much power at his fingertips. If he finds out someone has dared to overstep the line, he will yell very loudly for the head of the man who tried to seduce his innocent granddaughter while she was under the influence of drink. War will be declared between the two involved families. But who do you think will come out of it with the damaged reputation? Me,' she threw at him. 'Eve the flirt. Eve the temptress. Eve the spoiled little rich girl who likes to lead men on for the fun of it and has finally received her just desserts!'

She was near to tears and didn't want him to know it, so she spun away again taking with her the image of him just standing there staring at her as if she'd just grown two heads. Well, maybe she had! She certainly felt as if she had two heads rocking on her neck. She was tired through lack of sleep, exhausted with lingering shock and whatever else was still permeating her bloodstream. And she was hurting inside because she still couldn't bring herself to understand why Raoul had believed he could do to her what he had tried to do! Nor could she quite manage to justify that she hadn't deserved what had happened.

That was the toughest pill to swallow. Self-contempt. She named it bleakly as she stared out of the window, while a deathly silence crowded in from behind. What was he thinking? she wondered painfully. What was now going on inside his cynical head?

Ethan was struggling to think anything much. She was amazing, was his one main impression, and that came from the gut not the brain. But, standing there with the light coming in from behind her, she seemed to shimmer like a proud goddess sent down from the heavens to mess up his life. No wonder her grandfather worshipped her. He was beginning to understand what that felt like.

He was also stunned by what she'd thrown at him. Worse, he wanted to refute what she'd predicted was bound to happen but knew that he couldn't. It was the way of the world. Since the beginning of time, woman had been cast in the role of temptress and man merely as a slave to her seductive wiles. He was as guilty as anyone of assuming the same thing about Eve. He'd even likened her to the serpent in paradise, when in truth the serpent had been his own desire to tap into that special magic that was Eve.

Man being man at the expense of woman, in other words, blaming her for his weakness.

It was not a nice thing to admit about oneself.

'So...' He sighed in what he knew was his surrender to the whole darn package that was Eve. 'Tell me what it is you want to do,' he invited.

Eve turned to look at him. All he saw was a pair of tear-washed wounded eyes. 'Do you mean it?' she asked him in an unsteady voice that finally finished him.

Ask me to bite the apple, Eve, and I will do it, he mused ruefully, well aware that man's oldest weakness was still very much alive inside him; after all he had just admitted to himself. 'Yes, I mean it,' he confirmed and even felt like smiling at his own downfall.

Her fingers released their comforting clutch on her arms. He watched them lower to her sides then turn themselves into two tight, hopeful little fists. He wanted to claim those fists. He wanted to prize those fingers open and feed them inside his shirt so they could roam at their leisure.

'Continue to play the charade—just for a few weeks,' she begged him. 'Give me time to let Grandpa down about this marriage thing—without my having to admit the truth to him.'

Well, he'd asked, now he knew. He was to play the love-struck lover of Eve until she decided it was no longer necessary. Why not? he asked himself. Why the hell not? At this precise moment he was even prepared to lie down on the floor and let her walk all over him.

Time to move, time to react. She was waiting for an answer. Dragging his eyes away from the inner vision of himself lying at her beautiful feet, he looked at his watch and tried to concentrate well enough to read it.

Twelve o'clock, he saw. 'You've got approximately two hours to pack a bag and say your farewells,' he announced with a smoothness that in no way reflected what was really happening inside him.

'Why, where am I going?'

Well, there's an interesting question, he mused. And wished he knew the answer. 'You can't come to despise me enough to jilt me while you're here in the Caribbean and I'm in Spain,' he pointed out. 'So you are going to have to come to Spain with me.'

CHAPTER EIGHT

EVE was late.

Standing by the car he aimed to return to the hire company at the tiny airport on the other side of the island, Ethan was beginning to wonder if she'd had a change of heart about coming away with him, when he caught sight of her coming along the path that led to the lane behind the beach houses.

She was pulling her suitcase behind her through the dappled sunlight cast by the shady overhang of the trees. Tall and slender, as always faultlessly sleek, gone was the sweet Miss Modesty look she'd created for her grandfather's benefit. Now the smooth and slinky siren was back in a misty-lavender skimpy camisole top edged with lace, and matching narrow skirt that did wonderful things to her figure as she moved. She had also let her hair down so it swung like spun toffee around her shoulders, and a pair of silver-framed sunglasses pushed up on her head held it away from her face.

A face that wasn't happy, Ethan noticed as she came closer. A face that was not just pale any more but sad and very grim.

'You're late,' he said as she reached him. 'I was beginning to think you weren't going to bother.'

'Well, I'm here, as you see.' And there was nothing loverlike, pretend or otherwise, in the way she flipped the sunglasses down over her eyes before she handed over her case then climbed into the car without offering another word.

Grimacing to himself, Ethan stashed the case then joined her. As they drove off up the lane he noticed that she didn't spare a glance for the sugar-pink gate posts that guarded her grandfather's property.

'He was okay about you leaving with me?' he dared to probe a little.

'Yes,' she answered, but he saw the tension line around her mouth and knew she was lying... Again, he tagged on, and wondered why it was that even the lies weren't bothering him any more.

'You surprise me,' he remarked mildly. 'Having flown in from Greece this morning specifically to spend your birthday with you, I expected him to be very annoyed that you were now walking out on him.'

'He didn't fly in from Greece, he flew from Nassau,' she corrected, 'where he always intended to return tomorrow, because his mistress is waiting there for him.'

Mistress. Ethan's opinion of the seventy-year-old Theron Herakleides altered slightly with that piece of information. 'I didn't know he had a mistress.'

'He has several,' his granddaughter supplied.

Ethan almost allowed himself a very masculine grin. 'Then, why not bring her here with him and save himself several island-hopping journeys?'

'A Greek male does not introduce his mistress to his family.'

'Ah.' Ethan began to see the light. 'And neither should a Greek woman introduce her lover to her family?'

'You are not my lover.'

'He thinks I am.'

'He also thinks you are only marrying me for my money,' she responded tartly. 'Says a lot about my personal pulling power, don't you think?'

It said a lot about his character too, Ethan noted grimly,

and stopped the car. Turning towards her he viewed her profile through a new set of eyes, and released a heavy sigh. 'You fed him a very carefully constructed catalogue of lies to save his feelings and he disappointed you by not appreciating the gesture,' he deduced.

She didn't answer, but those hands were locked into fists again.

It made him wonder if she was having second thoughts about this and was being just too stubborn to admit as much. 'If you would rather stay,' he offered. 'I can understand if you—'

'No, you don't understand,' she suddenly flashed at him. 'And, like it or not, I am coming with you!'

'Then why are you so angry?'

'I am not angry,' she denied.

Reaching over, Ethan whipped the sunglasses from her eyes.

'Okay,' she conceded, 'So, I'm angry. Grandpa is angry,' she tagged on with telling bite. 'He was lying before when he appeared to be sanctioning our relationship. He now claims that there is no way he is going to let you marry me.'

'Good for him,' Ethan commended. 'It means he has your best interests at heart. I admire him for that.'

Her chin came up. 'Do you also admire him for setting up this so-called emergency in Spain, just to get you off the island and away from me?'

No, Ethan did not admire Theron for stooping that low. 'Are you sure about that?'

'He told me himself,' Eve confirmed.

'Oh, what a tangled web we weave…' Ethan murmured, then sat back in his seat with a sigh. 'Go back and tell him the truth, Eve,' he advised heavily. 'This has gone too far.'

'I will have my tongue removed before I will tell him

the truth now!' she exclaimed. 'This is my life, Ethan! I have the right to make my own choices without interference from anyone!'

'So do I,' he announced with a sudden resolve that had him starting the car engine again.

'W-what are you doing?'

'Going back,' he said.

'Why?' she challenged. 'Because you've suddenly realised that he might decide to take the Greek project away from you if you let me step on that plane with you?'

Ethan stilled again. 'He threatened to do that?'

Her mutinous expression gave him his answer. Without another word he turned the car round and drove back down the lane and in through the sugar-pink gate posts, then along the driveway to pull up outside the palatial frontage of the Herakleides holiday home.

He was angry now, burning with it. Getting out of the car he walked round to open the passenger door. 'Out,' he said, reaching down to take hold of Eve's hand so he could aid her arrival at his side.

'What are you going to do?' she asked.

'Call his bluff,' he declared. This was no longer a case of helping Eve out of a situation. It had become a case of his honour and integrity being placed into question, and he didn't like that.

In fact he didn't like it one little bit.

Eve wasn't sure that she was looking forward to what was coming. It was one thing *her* being angry with her grandfather, but it was quite a different thing entirely to discover that she'd managed to make Ethan angry with him too. She loved that cantankerous old man. She understood where he was coming from; Ethan did not.

'Don't upset him,' she burst out suddenly.

Pausing in the process of closing the car door, 'Are you going to tell him the truth?'

He looked down at her, and she looked up at him, her heart flipped over. He was so much her kind of man that Grandpa couldn't be more wrong about anything! 'No,' she answered mutinously.

His dark head nodded. Her hand was grasped. He began trailing her behind him up white marble steps set between tall pink pillars. The front door was standing open; Ethan took them inside. The house was quiet, so their footsteps echoed on the cool white tiling as they trod the way across the huge hallway to Theron's inner sanctum. The man himself was lounging behind his desk talking on the telephone. But the moment he saw them appear through the door, the phone call was severed and he was rising to his feet.

'So he brought you back. I expected as much.' The eyes of a cynic lanced Ethan with a dismissive look before they returned to his granddaughter. 'Which part did it, hmm? The part about me threatening to leave you nothing if he married you, or the part about the Greek project hanging in the balance?'

'Neither.' Striding forward with Eve still in tow, Ethan lifted up their linked hands and brought them down, still linked, upon Theron's desk. It was a declaration of intent, and Theron took it as such, his smug expression turning slightly wary as he looked at the other man.

'My submission for the Greek project is now formally withdrawn,' Ethan announced. 'Written confirmation will arrive on your desk as soon as I can have it typed up. As for your money—tell him Eve...'

Tell him Eve... Tell him what? A current of communication was running between them via those firmly linked hands, but for the life of her she didn't know what it was Ethan was expecting her say. Her grandfather was looking at her, Ethan was keeping his eyes fixed on her grandfather, and her mouth had gone dry as the idea sank in that Ethan was waiting for her to come clean with the whole nasty truth, so her grandfather would know then that this was all nothing but a terrible sham.

'Ethan doesn't want your m-money,' she began, having to moisten her lips with the tip of her tongue before she could find the will to speak. 'M-money isn't what this is about. He only w-wanted to—'

'Love a woman whom I think is worthy of being loved for herself,' Ethan took over. 'But you don't seem to agree,' he informed the older man. 'So while I provide written confirmation of my withdrawal from the Greek project, I suggest you protect Eve from my evil intentions and provide formal notice that none of your money can be accessed or offered in any way shape or form, to me.'

He meant it—he really meant it! 'Ethan—no!' Eve cried out. 'I can't let you throw away your livelihood because I—'

He kissed her to shut her up—did he kiss her! In front of her grandfather and without compunction, he kissed her until her knees went weak.

Theron watched that kiss, saw its passion, and felt its intensity like the pulsing beat of a drum. Eve emerged in a state of blushing confusion. Ethan Hayes was black-eyed, tight-jawed—and hot. If it wasn't for that troubling rumour about a certain married lady, Theron would be convinced that Ethan Hayes was as much in love with Eve as she clearly was with him!

But there was that niggling rumour, the old man reminded himself. Which then made him wonder if Ethan Hayes was executing one very convincing bluff here? Was he now expecting Theron to withdraw all threats, then sit back and think that all was right in his granddaughter's world?

'I will have all the relevant documentation drawn up and ready for you to sign when you reach Spain,' Theron announced, smoothly calling a double bluff.

It took the two lovers a long moment to respond. Their eyes were still locked, as were those dramatically clasped hands. Ethan Hayes stood one very handsome dark head taller that his sweet Eve, and Theron was willing to admit that they made a strikingly fetching pair.

'Why should I go to deal with an emergency that never was?' Ethan prompted.

Theron merely gave an indolent shrug. 'The emergency is real,' he confessed. 'The difference being that your business partner was attempting to deal with it himself without breaking into your holiday. Apparently my request for help to get you off this island merely tied in with what your people were already intending to do.' He even grimaced at the irony. 'So go and catch your plane,' he invited as a form of dismissal, 'for we have nothing left to discuss on this subject, other than to confirm that I will expect to see you both in Athens in two weeks for the formal announcement of your betrothal.'

Unless Mr Hayes had found a way to wriggle out of it by then, was the silent addition Theron kept to himself. Ethan Hayes was frowning down at him, unconvinced by his all-too easy climb-down. On the other hand, his beautiful Eve was breaking his heart with angry daggers for eyes.

'I don't want your money,' she announced.

Theron just smiled a silky smile. 'But you are getting it, my sweet angel,' he returned. 'Every single hard-earned drachma. And not one coin will be spent on him.' Theron looked at Ethan, bluff and counter-bluff stirring spice into his old blood. 'Perhaps you can recommend one of your competitors to take over the Greek project?' he intoned.

'You already had the best, and you know it,' Ethan countered. 'So be sure to inform Leandros that you've chucked me off the job. I can promise you that he is going to be absolutely ecstatic.'

With that neat and final arrogantly confident cut, Ethan turned to Eve. 'Say your goodbyes properly,' he commanded. 'I don't want you with me if you're going to be angry with him.'

Then he kissed her fully on the mouth again and strode away, leaving grandfather and granddaughter staring after him as if they could not quite believe he was real.

Ethan himself didn't know if he was real. He certainly felt different—alive, pumped up, energised, as if someone had slipped him the elixir of life.

That kiss with Eve perhaps?

Oh, shut up, he told himself frowningly. This is all just a sham, remember?

Just a great sham. Think of Aidan Galloway, he reminded himself. Whatever Eve liked to pretend, she had something going on with the Irishman. Love, sex—call it whatever—it was there, a throbbing pulse that said it was of a lot more than mere friendship.

'Watch him,' Theron advised, forcibly dragging Eve's attention away from the long, straight-shouldered stride of Ethan's retreat. 'He has your measure, my girl, and I don't think you are going to like that.'

Like it? She loved it. In fact it was tumbling around inside like a barrow load of sins desperately trying to get out. She wanted to run after him, take his hand again, laugh up into his arrogant face. She wanted to wind her arms around his neck and kiss him to heaven and back.

'You mean, *you* don't like it.' She turned a wry, knowing smile on this other man. She knew *he* had her measure, and wondered if he had guessed that all of this was just a sham?

A sham. Yes, a sham, she reminded herself, and felt the smile fade away like day turning to night. 'Grandpa—don't spoil this for me,' she heard herself say tremulously.

'He's dangerous,' Theron stated.

'I know.' Her eyelashes flickered. 'I like it.' It was a terrible confession to make.

'He is in love with another woman.' The reminder was supposed to be deadly to fragile emotions.

'I know that too.' Eve nodded. 'But he's what I want. I can make him love me instead of her, given a bit of time and space.'

'So this isn't just a ploy to bring poor Aidan Galloway to his senses about you?'

Aidan? Eve blinked. Her grandfather as well—? 'Aidan is still in love with Corin!' she protested, as if he had just suggested something terrible.

Theron took his time absorbing that declaration. It worried him, because if it wasn't Aidan, then this was exactly what it seemed to be. Yet his instincts were picking up all kinds of messages that conflicted with what he was being shown here. He couldn't work it out. He needed to work it out.

Getting up from his chair, he reached into a drawer then came round the desk to stand in front of Eve. In his hand he held a gaily wrapped package. 'Happy birthday, my angel,' he murmured softly as he fed the package into her hands then placed tender kisses on both of her cheeks.

He received his reward with the kind of unfettered shower of affection he'd come to expect from Eve. 'I love you, Grandpa.'

'I know you do, child.' And he did know it. It was the

substance his whole life had been built upon since she'd been a shocked and grief-stricken child of ten years' old. 'Now, go catch your plane,' he told her. He had been going to say go catch your man, but something held him back.

Eve left with a promise to call him as soon as she arrived in Spain. As the door closed behind her, Theron was already reaching for the telephone.

'Ah—*yassis*, Giorgio,' he greeted. 'I have a job for you to do for me, my friend. Write this name down: Ethan Alexander Hayes. *Ne.*' He nodded. 'Anything you can find. Dig hard and dig deep and do it quickly.'

CHAPTER NINE

EVE felt so stupidly shy when she settled into the passenger seat next to Ethan. 'Thank you for that,' she said a trifle self-consciously. 'I would have hated to leave him angry with me.'

Ethan made no response. Eve shot him a wary glance. His profile looked relaxed enough, but there was something about the shape of his mouth that suggested he was angry about something.

With her, with her grandfather, or with himself for allowing himself to become so embroiled in her problems?

The car engine came to life, the air-conditioning kicked in and began circulating cool air filled with the scent of him. His knuckle brushed her thigh as he shifted the gear stick. Suffocation seemed imminent, and Eve didn't know whether it was due to that so seductive scent, or to the sensation of his accidental touch which had left her body thickened.

Or maybe it had more to do with knowing that her grandfather was right. I'm letting myself in for a lot of heartache here, she mused. He doesn't love me, he loves someone else. Eve put a hand up to her trembling lips and felt Ethan's lips there instead. Her hand was pulled down again; it was trembling too.

'Say something, for goodness' sake.' The words left her lips on a shaken whisper.

Say what? Ethan thought frustratedly. I don't know what I'm doing here? I don't know what you are doing, coming away with me like this? You should be back there, home

94

safe with your grandfather, because you certainly aren't safe here with me!

'What's in the packet?' Did he really just offer something as benign as that?

His fingers flexed on the steering wheel. The afternoon sunlight was shining on her bent head, threading red highlights through spun toffee like fire on silk. He'd never noticed the threads of fire before. Why was he noticing them now? Her skirt had rucked up, showing more thigh than he wanted to see. He could still feel the touch of her smooth skin against his knuckle and he wanted to feel more of it. All of it. Hell, damn it—everything.

'Grandpa's birthday present,' she answered huskily.

Husky was seductive. It was vibrating along almost every skin cell like a siren's melody. 'You haven't opened it.'

His voice had a rasp to it that was scraping over the surface of her skin like sand in a hot seductive breeze. 'He doesn't like me to open presents in f-front of him, just in case I don't like what he's chosen and he sees the disappointment on my f-face.' She was stammering. Stop stammering! Eve told herself fiercely.

She was stammering. Was she crying? Ethan couldn't tell because she had her head bent and her hair was hiding her face. 'Does it happen often?' Now he sounded husky, he noticed heavily.

'Never.' She shook her head. 'I always love anything he gives to me. You would think he had worked that out by now.' Another soft laugh and her fingers were gently stroking the present.

'Open it,' he suggested.

'Later,' she replied. She had enough to contend with right now without weeping all over Grandpa's gift as well.

They reached the top of the lane and turned onto the

only proper road on the island. It went two ways—to the lane they'd just left, or to the small town with its even smaller airport, passing the entrance that led into the Galloways' bay on its way.

Two ways, Eve repeated. Forward, or back the way they had come. Did she want to go back? Did he want her to go back?

'Eve—if you've changed your mind about this, I can soon turn around and—'

'I'm coming with you!' The words shot out like bullets from a gun, ricocheting around the closed confines of the car.

Ethan snapped his mouth shut. His fingers flexed again. Eve sat simmering in her own hectic fallout, and silence reigned for the rest of the way.

It took ten minutes to get there. Ten long minutes of throat-locking hell. Eve gripped her birthday gift. Ethan gripped the wheel. They slid into a parking spot by the car-hire shop and both of them almost tumbled out of the car in their eagerness to breath hot humid air.

The nine-seat Cessna was waiting on the narrow runway. A porter ran up to collect their luggage to take it to the plane. Ethan appeared out of the car-hire shop, still feeding his credit card back into his wallet as he came. His dark head was bent, his hair gleaming blue-black against his deeply tanned face. He was wearing another blue shirt with grey trousers, and over his arm lay a jacket to match. Eve clutched at the strap to her shoulder bag, over which hung the cardigan that matched her top—and wished she didn't find the man so fascinating to watch.

He looked up. She looked quickly away. She looked beautiful, and his heart pulled a lousy trick on him by squeezing so tightly it took his breath away.

Nassau was a relief. They had a two-hour stopover,

which meant they could both make excuses to go their separate ways for a while. Eve went window-shopping; Ethan went to hunt out somewhere he could access his website and download some documents so he could read them on the flight.

On his way back to find Eve, he spied a furry tiger with its tail stuck arrogantly in the air. He began to grin. Eve would never get the joke, but he couldn't resist going into the shop and buying if for her. While the toy was being gift-wrapped, he went browsing further down the line of shop windows and came back to collect the tiger with a strangely stunned expression on his face.

Eve was sitting with a fizzy drink can and a whole range of gifts packed into carrier bags. 'Souvenirs for my friends in London,' she explained. 'They expect it.'

Ethan just smiled and sat down beside her, then offered her his gift. 'Happy birthday,' he said solemnly.

She stared at him in big-eyed surprise. It was amazing, he mused, how much he adored those eyes. 'Open it,' he invited, tongue-in-cheek. 'I'm not at all sensitive to disappointment.'

He was smiling, really smiling, with his mouth, with the warm soft grey of his wonderful eyes. Eve smiled back, really smiled back, then handed him her can so she could give her full attention to ripping off the gold paper from her present. Meanwhile Ethan drank from her can and watched with interest as the tiger emerged.

There was a moment's stunned silence, an unexpected blush, then she laughed. It was that wonderfully light, delighted laugh he'd heard her use so often for other people but never for him before. 'Good old Tigger—you idiot.' She turned to him. 'How did you know I have a whole roomful of Tiggers back home?'

He hadn't known, but he did now, which rather sent his

private joke flat, because Tigger was not quite the animal he had been thinking about when he'd bought the furry toy. Still, did it matter? She liked it, that was enough.

'ESP,' he confided, tapping his temple.

With her old exuberance, Eve leaned over to kiss him, realised what she was about to do and hesitated halfway there. Wary eyes locked on his, and a black eyebrow arched quizzically over one of them. Her heart gave a thud. Irresistible, she thought. I'm falling head over heels and don't even care any more. She closed the gap, knowing by the dizzying curling sensation inside that a kiss was about the most dangerous thing she could offer right now, even here in the transit lounge of a busy airport with hundreds of people playing chaperone… Because he might think he was fatally in love with Leona Al-Qadim, but he fancies the pants off me!

And I'm available, very available, she added determinedly. Their lips met—briefly—and clung in reluctance to part.

Yes, Eve thought triumphantly, he does want me. 'Thank you,' she murmured softly.

'You're welcome,' he replied, but he was frowning slightly. Eve wished she knew what thoughts had brought on his frown.

Thoughts of Leona Al-Qadim? Was he sitting here with one woman's kiss still warm on his lips and daring to think of another? Like a coin flipping over, she went from smiling certainty of her own power to win this man, to dragging suspicion that the other woman would always win.

Tigger was receiving a mangling, Ethan noticed, and wondered what the poor tiger had done to deserve such abuse? Then he had to smother a sigh, because he knew it was him she was thinking about as she twisted the poor animal's tail round in spirals. They kept kissing when they shouldn't. They kept responding to each other when they shouldn't. He was not the right man for her, and she was most definitely *not* the right woman for him.

'Here, do you want this?' He offered the drink can back to her.

Eve shook her head. 'You can finish it if you want.'

He didn't want it, but he knew what he did want. On that grim thought he got to his feet, too tense and restless to sit still any longer in this—crazy situation that should never have begun in the first place!

Walking over to the nearest waste-disposal bin he dropped the can in it, took a deep, steadying breath, then turned to go back the way he had come. Eve was no longer sitting where he had left her. Alarm shot through his veins like an injection of adrenalin, that quickly changed to a kind of thick gluey stuff that weighed him down so heavily he couldn't move an inch.

Why? Because her hair lay like silk against her shoulders, her bags of shopping hung at her sides. Tall and tanned and young and lovely, she was drawing interested gazes from every man that passed her by because she had class, she had style. She was an It girl, one of the fortunate few—and right at the present moment in time she was looking in the same jeweller's window he'd stood looking in only minutes before. Same place, same tray of sparkling jewels, he was absolutely certain of it. His feet took him over there, moving like lead in time with the heavy pump of his heart.

'Which one do you like?' he asked lightly over her shoulder.

She jumped, startled, glanced up at him, then looked quickly away again, blushing as if he'd caught her doing something truly sinful. 'The diamond cluster with the emerald centre,' she answered huskily.

Husky was back, he noticed, and husky he liked. Reaching down, he took her bags from her then placed a free hand to the small of her back. 'Let's go and try it,' he murmured softly.

'What—? But we can't do that!'

She was shocked, she was poleaxed—he even liked that. The lead weights dropped away from his body; he sent her a wry grin that made her eyes dilate. 'Of course we can,' he disagreed. 'It's tradition.'

Tradition, Eve repeated and felt her mind start turning somersaults, as the hand on her back firmly guided her into the shop. Ethan placed her bags on the floor at his feet, kept her close and calmly asked for the tray of rings. It arrived in front of them, sparkling beneath the lights. Long, lean, tanned male fingers plucked the diamond and emerald cluster off its velvet bed. While the assistant smiled the smile used for lovers, Ethan lifted up her left hand and gently slid the ring onto her finger.

'What do you think?' he prompted softly.

Eve wasn't thinking anything, she discovered. 'It fits,' was all she could manage to come up with to say.

'But do you like it?' he persisted.

'Yes,' she answered, so gruffly she didn't know her own voice.

'Good. So do I,' Ethan said. 'We'll take it,' he told the smiling sales assistant.

'But—look at the price!' she gasped as the assistant went away with Ethan's credit card.

'A lady doesn't check the price,' he told her dryly.

'But I can't let you buy something that expensive! Can you afford it? We shouldn't even be doing it.' Eve was beginning to panic in earnest now, Ethan noted, feeling his few minutes of pure romanticism turned to ashes as she spoke. 'W-we told Grandpa we were going to keep all of this a secret.'

'There will be nothing secret about us living together in Spain, Eve,' he dryly pointed out, and earned a startled look from those eyes for saying that. Yes, he thought grimly, take a moment to consider that part about us living together, Eve. 'But if you really don't want the ring—'

'No— Yes, I want it!'

'Good.' He nodded. 'A sham is not a good sham without all the right props to go with it.'

Eve's heart sank to her shoes as reality came rushing in. Here she was thinking—while he was only thinking— a sham. She swallowed on the thickness of her own stupidity. 'Then we'll go halves on the cost,' she decided.

If she said it to hit back at him then she certainly succeeded, Eve noted, as he stiffened. 'You really do think that because I can't match your grandfather's billions I must be as poor as a church mouse, don't you.'

Eve gave a noncommittal shrug for an answer. 'I just don't want you to be out of pocket just because I dumped myself on you like this.'

'Well, think of how much relief you will feel on the day you throw it back at me.'

The assistant arrived back to finish the sale then. Maybe it had been a timely interruption, Eve thought, as she watched him sign the sale slip and receive back his passport and credit card, because the sardonic tilt to his tone when he'd made that last remark had been aimed to cut her down to size. When, in actual fact, she suspected they both knew it was Ethan Hayes who'd taken the blow to his ego.

But the ring had suddenly lost value, its sparkle no longer seemed so fine. Their flight was called, and in the time it took them to gather up their belongings the whole incident was pushed away out of sight, even as the ring winked on her finger every time she moved her hand.

The plane was full, but first-class was quiet, with new state-of-the-art seating that offered just about every comfort that might be required. As they settled themselves in for the long journey, Eve unearthed Tigger from her hand luggage and sat him on the arm between their two seats.

You were my favourite birthday present, she told the stuffed tiger—not counting Grandpa's present, of course, she then added loyally, which she intended to open when she wasn't feeling so miffed at Ethan Hayes. As for you, she looked down at the ring sparkling like a demon on her finger, you're just a prop, which means you are as worthless as paste.

Within an hour of taking off, Ethan was deep into a stack of printed literature he'd managed to get someone in Nassau to pull off his website. Eve wasn't talking. Now he was glad he hadn't confided in her that the ring was the very one he'd picked out himself only minutes before she'd picked it out. Silly stuff like that provoked curious questions. Questions provoked answers he didn't want to give. It had been a stupid gesture anyway. He wished he hadn't done it. Now the damn ring kept on sparkling at him every time she turned a page of the magazine she'd brought with her onto the plane.

'Would you like a refill for that, Mr Hayes?' the flight attendant asked him. Glancing up at the woman he saw the look in her eyes was offering a whole lot more than a second cup of coffee.

Spice of life, he mocked grimly and refused the offer. As she went to move away he saw the flight attendant glance at Eve, then at her finger. That's right, he thought acidly, I've already been hooked.

By a toffee-haired witch with a sulk to beat all female sulks.

'And you, Miss Herakleides?'

'No, thank you,' Eve refused. And keep your greedy eyes off my man, she thought.

A man who had a way with a black ballpoint pen that held her attention with the same rapt fascination she would have given to Picasso if she'd had the opportunity to watch him at work. It wasn't as if he was actually doing anything special—just drawing circles round sentences then scrawling comments over the printed words. He was sitting back against the seat with an ankle resting across his other knee. He stopped writing, frowned, used the pen to relieve an itch on the side of his chin; he used it to tap out an abstract drum beat; he drew another circle, then scrawled comments again.

He sighed at something. His chest moved, and as she glanced sideways at it she realised she could see glimpses of deeply tanned flesh in the gaps between shirt buttons. Nice skin, warm skin, tight let-me-touch skin, she thought.

Close your eyes, Eve, and stop this! she railed at herself.

It wasn't long after she closed her eyes that the magazine began to slip from her slackened grip. Ethan rescued it and folded it away, then rescued Tigger as he too began to slip off his perch.

Tigger: fun, bouncy, always in trouble—he wasn't so old that he couldn't remember the animal's appeal. He had to smile at the irony because *his* tiger was neither fun nor bouncy, but it certainly meant to cause him a lot of trouble where Eve Herakleides was concerned.

Reaching over he gently placed Tigger on Eve's lap, then sent him a wry man-to-man look. 'Lucky guy,' he told the toy, and pressed a button that would recline her into a more comfortable position for sleep. A sigh whispered from her as she resettled her body. A glance at her eyes to check if he had disturbed her showed him the fine bruising around the sockets, which told him she was still suffering the effects of last night.

He'd forgotten about that. How had he forgotten about that? Because his mind had become fixed on more lusty things, of which he really ought to be ashamed.

He returned to his papers for a little while, but not very much later succumbed to the need to sleep himself. Halfway across the Atlantic he woke up to find that Eve had curled up on her side facing him, and her hand was splaying across his chest. But that wasn't all—not by a long shot because a couple of her fingers had somehow found their way into the gap between his shirt buttons and were now resting against his warm skin.

He liked them there, had no wish to move them, even though a call of nature was nagging at him. So he closed his eyes again and saw his own fingers slipping down the front of her gaping top in a quest to caress the warm golden globe he'd caught sight of as he'd glanced at her.

Then he thought. No way. He forced his eyes back open—just in case he might do in sleep what he had been fantasising about while awake. Been there, done that once already today, he ruefully reminded himself. Instead he gave in to the other desire and gently removed her hand from his chest so that he could get up.

She was awake when he came back, and her seat had been returned to its upright position. 'Drink?' he suggested.

'Mmm.' She half yawned. 'Tea, I think, and can you see if they can rustle up a sandwich?'

'Sure.' He went off to find a flight attendant. When he came back Eve was not there and he presumed she'd gone where he'd just been. She slipped back into her seat as the flight attendant arrived with a china tea service and a plate of assorted sandwiches.

She'd freshened up, he'd freshened up, both looked a bit better for it. Ethan poured the tea while Eve checked the fillings between neat triangles of bread. 'Any preference?' she asked him.

You, he thought soberly. 'I don't mind,' he answered. 'I'm starving. We slept through dinner apparently.'

'You too?' she quizzed.

'Mmm,' he answered.

'Did you manage to finish your work before you slept?'

'Mmm,' he said again.

'Is that all you can say?' she mocked. 'Mmm?' It was like talking to a bumble-bee, Eve thought impatiently.

No, it wasn't all he could say, she discovered the moment he turned his head to look at her. Dark grey eyes locked with green, and the air was suddenly stifled by the kind of feelings that didn't belong in the cabin of an aeroplane. He wanted her. She wanted him. If they touched they would go up in a plume of fire and brimstone, it was so sinful what was happening to both of them.

They didn't touch. Eve looked away, picked up her cup and grimly drank the hot tea in the hope that it would outburn everything else. That damn ring flashed again and Ethan wished he hadn't put it there. It had been a mad impulsive gesture to make. This arrangement was a sham. The ring was a sham. But when he looked at that thing, Eve belonged to him.

CHAPTER TEN

THE rest of the flight was a lesson in how to avoid giving off the wrong kind of signals. They dropped down into Heathrow airport in the early morning local time, then had to hurry through transit to catch their connection to Malaga. That flight was full and noisy with excited children off on holiday to Spain. It was early afternoon by the time they cleared the formalities there.

Ahead of them lay a two-hour drive south to San Estéban, but one glance at Eve put the cap on that plan. Travel fatigue was casting a greyish pallor over her beautiful skin and she looked fit only to drop down and sleep where they stood.

Ethan had used a hand to guide her into a convenient seat in the airport arrival lounge. 'Sit,' he quietly commanded.

Subsiding without a single murmur, she watched him park their luggage trolley next to her through listless eyes and didn't even seem to notice that he then walked off without telling her where he was going.

He came back five minutes later to find her sitting more or less how he had left her. As he came to stand in front of her she looked up and, stifling a yawn, she pointed at their assorted luggage. 'Just think,' she said, 'how convenient it would be if we ever got married.'

Following the direction of her pointing finger, Ethan found himself looking at two sets of suitcases, both of which wore the same initials embossed on their leather like a sign from the devil of what the future held for them. He didn't like it. His mouth turned down in a show of dismay because those near-matching suitcases spoke of one giant step over that fragile line between, I can deal with this, and, The hell I can.

Eve saw he didn't like it. 'It was a joke, Ethan,' she sighed out wearily.

'Time to go,' was all he said—heavily.

Taking hold of her arm he pulled her to her feet when all Eve wanted to do was curl up in a dark corner some-where, go to sleep and not wake up again while he was still in her life!

Then what did he do to throw that last thought right out of her head? He placed an arm around her shoulders, gently urged her to lean against him then kept her that close while pushing the trolley in front of them as they walked outside.

I like him this close, she confessed to herself. I love it when he makes these unexpected gestures of concern. 'You've no sense of humour,' she muttered in grim rejection of her own weakness.

'Or your sense of timing is lousy,' he suggested sardonically.

Maybe he was right. Maybe it hadn't been the most diplomatic observation to make when they were in effect walking alongside a whole pack of lies. She released a sigh; he acknowledged it by giving her arm a gentle squeeze that could have been sympathising with that weary little sigh. And, because it felt right to do it, she slipped her hand around his lean waist—and leaned just that bit more intimately into him.

As the automatic exit doors slid open for them, a small commotion just behind them made them pause and glance back to see a group of dark-eyed, dark-suited Spaniards heading towards the doors with a pack of photographers on their trail. It was only as the group drew level with them that Eve realised the men were clustered around an exquisite looking creature with black hair, dark eyes and full-blooded passion-red mouth.

'Miss Cordero, look this way,' the chasing pack were pleading. Camera bulbs flashed. Miss Cordero kept her eyes fixed directly ahead as her entourage herded her towards the exit doors Eve and Ethan had conveniently opened for them. As they swept by, someone called out to Miss Cordero. 'Is it true that you spent the night in Port Said with your lover, Sheikh Rafiq?'

Eve felt Ethan stiffen. Glancing up at his face she saw a frown was pulling the edges of his brows across the bridge of his nose. 'What?' she demanded. 'Who is she?'

'Serena Cordero, the dancer,' he replied.

Eve recognised the name now. Serena Cordero was the unchallenged queen of classical flamenco. Her recent world tour had brought on a rash of Spanish dance fever, causing schools dedicated to the art to open up all over the place. It wasn't just classical dance she performed with sizzling mastery. Her gypsy fire dance could put an auditorium full of men into a mass passion meltdown.

None of which explained why Ethan was standing block-still with a frown on his face, she mused curiously. Unless… 'Do you know her?' she asked him, already feeling the sting of jealousy hit her bloodstream at the idea that Ethan might know what it was like to have the exotic Serena dance all over him!

But he gave a shake of his dark head. 'I only know *of* her,' he said, making the chilly distinction.

'Then why the frown?'

'What frown?'

He looked down at her. Eve looked up at him. The now familiar sting of awareness leapt up between the two of them. 'That frown,' she murmured, touching a slender long finger to the bridge of his nose where his eyebrows dipped and met. It was too irresistible not to trail that fingertip down the length of his thin nose. Her hand was caught, gently crushed into his larger hand and removed.

The question itself was no longer relevant: Serena Cordero had suddenly ceased to exist. Mutual desire was back, hot and tight and stifling the life out of everything else.

'Let's go,' Ethan murmured, striving to contain it.

He wanted her, she wanted him. It was going to happen some time, Eve was sure of it. 'Okay,' she said.

Attention returned to the exit doors, they stepped outside into the afternoon heat. Coming here from the Caribbean should have meant they were acclimatised to it by now. But the Spanish heat was so dry it scorched the skin, whereas the Caribbean heat was softened by high humidity and cooled slightly by trade winds coming off the sea.

The Cordero entourage had disappeared already. There was a chauffeur-driven car standing by the kerb waiting for them. Eve was glad to escape into the air-conditioned coolness of its rear seat. Having helped to stash their luggage in the car boot, Ethan joined her. The heat emanating from his body made her shiver, though she didn't know why it did.

Two hours of this, she was thinking breathlessly, as they took off with the smoothness of luxury. The prospect brought back the aching tiredness, the tiredness thankfully dulled the aching pulse of desire. Settling back into soft leather, Eve had just reconciled herself to this final leg of their journey when, to her surprise, they hadn't even left the airport perimeter before they were turning in through a pair of gates and drawing to a halt next to a gleaming white helicopter bearing the Petronades logo on its side.

'What now?' she asked curiously.

'Our transport to San Estéban, courtesy of your cousin, Leandros,' Ethan sardonically supplied. 'Having been so instrumental in getting us both here, I thought it was time he helped make this final part a bit easier.'

Easier, truly said it. Their two-hour drive south was cut by two-thirds. As they skipped over the top of a lush green headland, Ethan said, 'San Estéban.'

Glancing out of the window, Eve felt her heart stop beating in surprise. 'Oh,' she said, gasping in astonishment, unsure what it was that she had been expecting, but knew that it certainly wasn't this.

Her gaze took in the modern example of a Moorish castle guarding the hill top, then it flicked down the hill to a beautiful deep-water harbour with its mosaic-paved promenade that linked it to the pretty white-washed town. In the quest to create something magical, that same Moorish style repeated itself in a clever blend of modern with ancient. Nothing clashed—nothing dared. It was no wonder that her grandfather had been so eager to have Hayes-Frayne apply their magic touch to his project, she realised. From up here she could see the same sense of vision that must have inspired her grandfather when Leandros had suggested he come out here and take a look for himself.

Turning her face she looked into Ethan's grey eyes and saw a different man looking steadily back at her. The artist—the man with the vision that inspired others; the sensitive romantic who perhaps could fall in love with the unattainable, and maybe even go so far as to love *because* that person was out of his reach. It was a well-known fact that artists liked to suffer; it was a natural part of their persona to keep the creative juices flowing by desiring what could never be.

Was that part of her attraction? Eve then found herself

wondering curiously. With her grandfather openly stating that Ethan was not what he wanted for his only grandchild, had Theron unwittingly lifted her to the same desirable heights as the very married Leona Al-Qadim?

His eyes were certainly desiring her, she noted, but, for the first time, she didn't like what she could see. Don't raise me up onto a pedestal, she wanted to warn him, because she had no intention of remaining there, safely out of reach.

The helicopter dropped them onto a helipad custom-built to service the Moorish castle which, she realised, was really a hotel set in exquisite grounds. A car was waiting to transport them along the hill top that surrounded the bay where exclusive villas lay hidden behind screens of mature shrubs and trees. Eventually they pulled in through wide arched gates into a mosaic courtyard belonging to one of those villas.

Ethan unlocked the front door while the driver of their car collected their luggage and stacked it neatly by the door. Ethan knew the man; they'd chatted in Spanish throughout the short journey and continued chatting until the driver got back into his car and drove way.

Almost instantly silence tumbled down around them as it had done once before when they'd found themselves suddenly on their own like this.

'Shall we go in?' Ethan cut through it with his light invitation.

'Yes.' Eve made an effort to smile and didn't quite manage it as she walked into the villa while he brought the luggage inside then closed the door behind him.

Fresh tension erupted. Eve didn't quite know what to do next and Ethan didn't seem too sure himself, so they both started speaking at the same time.

'Is this one of your own designs?' she asked him.

'Would you like to freshen up first or—? No.' He answered her question.

'Yes, please.' She answered his.

He sighed, ran a hand round the back of his neck and looked suddenly bone-weary. Eve chewed nervously on her bottom lip and wished herself back in the Caribbean lying on a beach.

'Guest bedroom's this way…' Picking up her luggage he began leading the way over pale blue marble beneath arched ceilings painted the colour of pale sand. As they walked, they passed by several wide archways that appeared to lead to the main living space. But Eve was way beyond being curious enough to show any interest in what those rooms held. All she wanted was to be on her own for a while, to take stock, maybe even crash out on the large bed she'd caught sight of in the room Ethan was leading her into.

'Bathroom through that door,' he said as he placed her luggage on the top of a cedarwood ottoman. 'You can reach the terrace through there…' He pointed to the silk-draped full-length windows. 'Make yourself at home…' He turned toward the door, had seconds thoughts, and turned back again. 'I'll be working out on the terrace if you want me. Other than that…take your time…'

Lightly said, aimed to make her feel comfortable with whatever she wanted to do, he did not take into account that he hadn't once allowed his eyes to make contact with her eyes since they'd entered the villa.

Which meant that he was feeling as uncomfortable with this new situation as she was. 'Right. Fine,' she said.

He left her then; like a bat out of hell he got out of that room and made sure he shut the door behind him as he went. Eve wilted, had a horrible feeling that he was standing on the other side of that door doing exactly the same thing, and really, really wished she hadn't come.

Ethan was beginning to wonder if she'd made a run for it when, over an hour later, Eve still hadn't put in an appearance. At first he'd been glad of the respite, had taken a shower, had enjoyed a home-made pot of tea out here on the terrace with only the view and a dozen telephone calls to keep him company.

But as time had drifted on without him hearing a peep from Eve, he'd begun to get edgy. Now he felt like pacing the terrace because the tiger inside him was making its presence felt again.

What time was it? Six p.m., his watch told him. Two minutes later than it had been the last time he'd looked. He grimaced, then sighed to himself and walked over to the terrace rail to look down the hillside where San Estéban lay basking in the early evening sun. This time yesterday he had been sitting in the bar on the beach in the Caribbean drinking local rum and chatting with Jack Banning.

No, you were not, you were watching Eve dance with her eager young men and wishing you weren't there to witness it, a grim kind of honesty forced him to admit.

A sound further along the terrace caught his attention. His stomach muscles instantly tightened when he recognised the sound as one of the terrace doors opening. Eve appeared at last, wearing a plain straight dress with no sleeves, a scooped neck and a hemline that rested a quiet four inches above her slender knees.

Quiet—why quiet? he asked himself as he watched her walk over to the rail then stand looking out over the bay. There was nothing quiet about Eve Herakleides, not where he was concerned anyway. Her hair, her face, her wonderful figure— Even that sudden and unexpectedly shy expression on her face rang bells inside him as she turned and saw him standing there.

CHAPTER ELEVEN

'SORRY,' she murmured in apology. 'I fell asleep.'

'That's okay,' he replied, feeling all of that restlessness ease out of him to be replaced with—damn it—sex. The thought of it anyway. 'I've been working. Didn't notice the time.'

'This is a lovely view,' she remarked, turning her attention back to the bay. 'Nothing looks new or out of place; everything simply blends as if it's been like this for centuries.'

'That was the plan.' After a moment's hesitation he went to stand beside her and began to point out the different features the resort had to offer. She smelt of shampoo and something subtly expensive. Her voice, when she inserted a comment, played feather-like across his skin. 'We haven't even begun developing that area yet,' he said, indicating toward one of the farthest edges of the bay, and went on to describe what would be seen there within the next year or two.

His arm caught her shoulder, his voice vibrated along her flesh, raising goose-bumps on her skin as she listened to him—no—that she *absorbed* with a breathless kind of concentration every detail he relayed to her and wished she could remember a single one of them.

But she couldn't. It was the man who held her wrapped in fascination, the rest was just wallpaper pasted on for appearances' sake. 'Quite utopian,' she murmured eventually. 'And all your own?'

'No.' He denied that with a wry shake of his head. 'I

would love to say it was, but a very austere Spaniard called Don Felipe de Vazquez owns all the land. Victor and I are just the men who transformed his ideas into reality.'

'All of this doesn't reflect an austere temperament.' Eve frowned. 'I see the heart of a romantic at work here.'

'Maybe he has hidden depths.' But, by his tone, it seemed he didn't think so. 'It's more likely he has a good instinct for what will return a healthy dividend on his land.'

'You don't like him,' Eve said, presuming from that.

'It's not my place to like or dislike him.' Ethan took the diplomatic line.

Turning against the rail, Eve folded her arms beneath her breasts then looked up at him sagely. 'But you don't like him,' she repeated stubbornly.

Ethan laughed, it was a soft dryly rueful sound that brought his eyes down to meet with hers. It was a mistake; the wrong move. Things began to happen to him that he had been determined he would not let happen. Don Felipe was tossed into oblivion; San Estéban with all its beauty may as well have not been there at all. Eve the witch, the beautiful siren, was all that he was seeing. She had relaxed with him at last, was actually smiling with her eyes, with her lovely mouth. Don't spoil it, he told himself. Don't so much as breathe in case you ruin the mood.

This wasn't easy, Eve was thinking. Maintaining this level of relaxed friendliness was tough when what she really wanted to do was kiss him so badly that it was like a fire in her brain. She'd fallen asleep thinking of this man, had woken up thinking of this man and didn't dare look into what had gone on in between.

Dreams were ruthless truth-tellers, she mused. 'Don Felipe,' she prompted, though she wasn't interested in the slightest in the Spaniard; it was important that she kept the conversation going, or she might give in and make an absolute fool out of herself.

His eyelashes flickered—long dark silky things that made her lips tingle as if they'd flickered against them. He took in a measured breath that expanded his ribcage and made her breasts sting into peaks. His mouth parted to speak but it wasn't what he was going to say that held her captive.

'You have to know a man to draw a considered opinion as to whether you like him or not...' Ethan dragged his eyes away from her before he did something he shouldn't. 'He's a strange man: very private, cold and remote. Rumour has it that he was disinherited by his father in favour of his half-brother, and didn't take the decision very well. Went a bit mad for a while, got into a couple of fights, had an accident, which left him scarred in more ways than one. Since then he has been out to prove something—with this resort and all the other investments he has made during the last few years that have earned him a fortune big enough to throw in his family's face. But does all of that make him a romantic?' His tone was sceptical to say the least.

'Then you must be the romantic at work here,' Eve announced decidedly.

Me—a romantic? Sending a fleeting glance over San Estéban, Ethan shook his dark head. 'I'm just an architect who likes to leave a place looking as untouched as it was before I arrived...'

Another silence fell. It had probably had to, because neither of them were really thinking about the discussion in hand. Words were appearing from within the mists of other things.

'Drink,' Ethan said, filling the gap again.

'Yes,' she agreed. Relieved to have an excuse to move,

she straightened away from the rail at the same moment
that Ethan shifted his stance and made the fatal mistake of
looking down at her. That was all that it took to flip the
mood right into that one place they'd both been trying to
keep away from. Eve saw his eyes dilate, saw the breath
grow still in his chest. Her smile began to die along with
her relaxed manner, because she knew for certain now
what was really going on inside his head.

His tension began to fight with hers. 'And food,' he
added. 'We need to eat. The kitchen is stocked with all
the usual provisions, but we can eat out if you prefer.'

Eat in or out? Eve tried to make a decision, found she
couldn't because sexual desire lay too thickly in the atmosphere to think of anything else. It would take only one
more move, one tiny gesture from either of them, to lick
desire into a flame.

'In,' she said, choosing. 'I've had enough of crowded
places for one day.' She even managed to send him a semblance of a smile to accompany the reply.

But the smile was the gesture. It made him look at her
mouth. Eve released a soft gasp as if she'd just been surprised with a kiss. The flame was licked, her arms unfolded
and he was taking their place. They went into each other's
arms without another sane thought, and all it took was the
first light brush of their lips to plunge them right back to
where they'd cut off on the plane over the Atlantic.

Hungry and hot, it was the kind of kiss that worked on
every sense until she was trembling so badly she needed
to hang onto something. That something was his neck
where the tips of her fingers had curled and had dug in.
And he was no better, taking what she offered with an
urgency that fed the need. His hands explored her body,
his touch sure with knowledge, sensually driven by man

at his most practiced: He was not the fumbling boy Raoul had been the night before, a slave to his own urgent needs.

Eve knew the difference. And so Ethan should have understood that—being the sophisticated lover he was reputed to be. But he shot back so abruptly it was like being severed at the neck. 'What am I doing?' He began cursing himself. 'Great move, Ethan,' he told himself harshly. 'Great damn move!'

'You started it!' Eve threw at him as if he'd implied otherwise.

It swung him round. 'Do you think I don't know that?' he tossed back harshly. 'You suffered a bad experience only yesterday. If I took advantage of you now, it would make me no better than the bastard who did that to you! I apologise,' he clipped out. 'If I ever attempt anything like that again you have my permission to cry—'

Rape, Eve finished when he so obviously couldn't. And there it was, she realised. In one ill-thought-out sentence Ethan had brought this whole ugly situation back to where it really belonged.

So it is me who makes this happen, she realised. You don't get two men in one day thinking you're open to that kind of thing without you giving off something that tells them that!

'You're wrong, so stop thinking it,' he said.

'Why wrong?' He had to explain that or it meant nothing!

Ethan made himself look her in the eyes, made himself take the slap of those pained tears that glittered there. 'You wanted me,' he explained. 'You did not want him.'

It was true. Was it true? Too shaken to think straight, she looked away from his grim hard face, and down at her body where she could still feel the lingering pleasure of his touch. With Raoul she'd felt revulsion, only revulsion.

But that didn't mean she hadn't *asked* for what he'd tried to do! Did it make a difference that she hadn't known she'd been doing it? No, it did not. A flirt was a flirt. A tease was a tease. She looked back at Ethan through pain-bright eyes filled with a terrible self-disillusionment.

'No,' he denied, knowing what was raking around inside her head. 'No!' he repeated and walked back to take her by the shoulders and issue a gentle shake. 'With him, you screamed, Eve,' he pointed out gruffly. 'Even under the influence of whatever he gave you, you screamed loud enough to waken me.'

But that doesn't mean I didn't bring it on myself! she thought painfully.

'You're beautiful, stunning—irresistible in many ways,' he went on as if he could read the thoughts tumbling through her head. 'But ninety-nine per cent of the male population will resist you—unless you don't want them to.'

And I did not want you to resist me. 'But you stopped it anyway,' she whispered shakily.

'Because it was wrong. Because it is not what we're here for.'

'You pompous swine,' she said and turned to walk back to her room.

She didn't get very far. He exploded so spectacularly it came as a shock. 'What is it you actually want from me, Miss Herakleides?' he roared at her furiously as he strode towards her. 'I thought you wanted my help, so I gave it.' His hands found her shoulders. 'I thought you wanted my support with your lies, so I gave you that!' Those hands spun her round to face the fury he was giving out. 'You're here. *I'm* here, living a lie that should never have been allowed to start in the first place!' Cold steely eyes raked her face like cutthroat razors. 'Now I can't even honour that deal without you making me out to be some kind of rat!'

'I didn't mean—'

'Yes, you did,' he cut in thinly.

'I thought—'

'You don't think, Eve, that's your trouble!'

'Will you stop shouting at me,' she yelled back. 'I wanted what I thought you wanted! My mistake. I apologise. Now let go of me!'

He did. She staggered. His hands came back to steady her. She released a pathetic little sob. He muttered something. She looked up at him. Like lightning striking a volcano, a whole ocean of molten emotion came boiling out.

'He was there; he hurt me. You were the last person on earth I expected to understand! I liked it—your kindness, your caring, the strength that you let me lean on.' Stop trembling! she told herself. 'I liked the way you could be so stern with me, but make love to me with your eyes at the same time. You're doing it now!' she choked out shrilly. 'You're angry but you want me. I am *not* misreading the messages! How dare you imply that I am?'

It was a damning indictment. She was right, every word of it. Standing there, watching this beautiful woman shimmer with anger, hurt and a million other emotions beside, Ethan took it all full in the face and wondered what he was supposed to say or do now.

Then, he thought, oh to hell with it. He even released a short laugh because he knew what he was going to do with it. He was going to throw off his high moral stance and surrender to Eve—as he had been doing since this whole crazy thing had begun.

'Don't laugh at me,' she protested unsteadily, hurt tears sparkling across dark green irises.

'I'm not laughing at you,' he denied. 'I'm laughing at myself.'

'Why?'

Ethan kissed those tear-washed eyes, ran his lips down her cute little nose and settled at the corner of her trembling mouth. 'Because of this,' he murmured huskily, and made his surrender, falling into it without allowing himself another sane thought.

'If you're playing games with me, I'll—'

'No game,' he promised and, because they'd done enough talking, he moved his lips until they'd covered her own then gently parted them to receive the moist caress of his tongue.

It was different. Eve could feel it was different. Not just the kiss but the way he was holding her—not with anger nor that driving compulsion that had pulled their mouths together before. He was going to take what she had placed on such open offer, and for a fleeting, fleeting, moment Eve wondered if she had made a terrible mistake by making herself so easy for him. Then he lifted his head, and she saw the slightly awry smile he offered that told her he wasn't thinking this was easy at all.

'Beautiful Eve,' he murmured and covered her mouth again, picked her up and carried her down the terrace, into her bedroom and over to the bed before he let her feet slide down to the floor.

Shy, she felt agonisingly shy suddenly, which was stupid after everything that had gone before. He cupped her face, felt the burn in her cheeks, brushed his thumbs across them gently and felt her small tremor as he tilted her head back enough to receive his next kiss.

Only, not just a kiss but a deep and desirous prelude to what was about to come. It was a warm and unhurried

awakening of the senses that held her captivated and com-
pliant, wanting to go only where he led her.

He noticed, of course he did. 'A passive Eve?' he
mocked her gently.

'Yes,' she whispered. 'Do you mind?'

'No.' But that awry smile was on his lips again. 'Just
so long as it doesn't mean you're having second thoughts
and don't know how to tell me.'

'No second thoughts.' And to prove it, she wound her
arms around his neck and brought his mouth back to hers
again, then mimicked his long seductive kiss.

He led her through an erotic undressing by drawing the
zip of her dress down her spine with caressing expertise
that took her breath away. His fingers trailed feather-light
over exposed skin, sun-kissed shoulders, slender backbone,
the shockingly sensitised concaved arch at the nape of
back. She moved against him and could tell that he liked
that. It emboldened her into pressing the bowl of her hips
even closer to what was happening to him.

He released a sigh; it shook with feeling. Eve matched
that too, and he caught the sound on his tongue then fed
it back to her, while his hands drifted up her arms until
they reached her hands still locked around his neck. Drawing them downwards he encouraged her dress to slither
down her body, then laid her hands against his shirt front.
'Undress me,' he urged.

It was the calling song of a mating bird. Shy though she
still felt, Eve complied, while the caress of his hands and
his mouth urged her on. Did he know? she wondered mist-
ily. Could he tell she'd never done this before, and was
that why he was taking it all so slow and easy?

Shirt buttons slid from their buttonholes to reveal more
and more of that wonderful chest she loved to look at so
much. Now she allowed herself the pleasure of touching,

placing her fingers on his chest where dark hair coiled into the hollow between tight pectoral muscles. Then, because she couldn't resist, the moist tip of her tongue followed suit.

The air left his lungs on a heavy rush that brought her head up sharply. She looked up at him, he looked down at her, and the pace suddenly altered dramatically. They fell on each other's mouths with a series of deep hot kisses while his urgent hands stripped her flimsy scrap of a bra away and hers pushed the shirt off his back.

Then it was flesh on flesh, pleasure tangling up with pleasure as the whole thing shot off on its own natural journey. His arms were crushing her, his kiss was deep, their laboured breathing hissed into the warm golden light of the slow-dying day as he manoeuvred her down onto the bed. He came down with her, his skin was moist, she yearned to taste it but the kiss was just too good to break away from. His hands began caressing her with so much sensual expertise that she arched and flexed as sensation washed over her in waves and scraped restless fingernails over his shoulder blades with enough urgency to make him shudder in response.

'Sorry,' she whispered helplessly.

He released a thick laugh and said, 'Do it again.'

The exchange of words broke the kiss. Without the kiss she was free to indulge herself by tasting him. He liked her nails so she ran them down his back, loving the feel of his muscles flexing pleasurably, loving the groan he uttered just before he claimed one of her breasts with his mouth.

Desire stirred and writhed like an unleashed serpent deep within her abdomen. He must have known, because his hand was suddenly playing her stomach, moving downward, fingertips slipping beneath the scrappy fabric of her briefs. She knew he was going to touch her, knew that this was it, the moment she had been waiting for for what seemed the whole of her life. A tight and tingling breath-taking anticipation sent her still, which made him lift his head and send her a sharp questioning look.

'What?' he said.

'You,' she said in a sexually tense little voice.

He understood. His eyes went black, his features tightening into a very male, passionate cast. The hand slipped lower, fingertips drifting through dusky curls to seek out warm moist tissue that was the centre of her world right now. She groaned then gasped as pleasure licked with stunning intensity through to her toes and fingertips. He murmured something she didn't hear—it could have been her name or it could have been a curse because she knew she was rocketing right out of control here.

He encouraged her though. With the mastery of the seasoned lover, he orchestrated her pleasure trip through the senses. Did he know? He had to know. Surely no man took this much care to please the woman he was making love to without expecting some similar stimulation back by return, unless he knew that this was her first experience?

The last of her clothing was trailed away; she was vaguely aware of him ridding himself of his own. When his hands were busy elsewhere his mouth took up the burning seduction of her breasts, her navel, brushing hot moist kisses along the inner surface of her golden thighs.

Flesh burned against flesh; long restless limbs tangled in a love-knot caress. They rolled. He came above her, her hands locked around his neck. It was then that she felt the probing force of his masculinity and as her insides curled in anticipation she uttered his name on a sensual breath.

He liked it; she felt his response in the small shudder

that ripped through his body. She liked that, and responded with a lithe flexing of her hips that made her exquisitely aware of the power he was still keeping in check.

'Eve, give me your mouth.'

She gave him her mouth, willingly, hungrily. She gave him every little bit of herself that she could possibly give. He took it all. Like a man leaping into a fiery furnace knowing he was about to get severely burned, he made a single strangled sound in his throat then, swift and sure, he claimed the passage he had prepared for himself.

It was wild, it was shocking, it was shamelessly exhilarating. Barriers broke; she winced on a soft little gasp. He paused, touched her cheek with unsteady fingers, gently combed her hair away from her face.

'Eve,' he breathed.

She opened her eyes and made contact with the burning black density of his. He looked different, darker, masculine, more her man than ever.

'Yes,' she breathed, closed her eyes again, then made a single stretching movement that fastened her to him as a whole new hot probing journey held her in its spectacular thrall. He took her to places she hadn't known existed; he taught her things about her that held her trapped on the pin-piercing pinnacle of discovery for long agonising seconds before he tipped her over the edge with the sudden increased rush of masculine thrust. She learned what it was like to lose touch with everything but a swelling pulsing pleasure of the senses.

When it was over it was all she could do to hang onto him while he lay heavily on top of her with their pounding heartbeats throbbing all around.

He went to move. She stopped him. 'Wait,' she whispered. She didn't want to miss a single sense-soaring moment in this act of momentous importance to her. She had waited so very long for this to happen, had never been slightly tempted to experiment because she had been so determined to wait for the right man to come along—the one she would know instinctively was the one man for her. Marriage, wedding gowns, playing the shy virgin bride had never come into her perfect dream. It had just had to be the right man. She'd found that man, and nothing—no moment in time—was ever going to feel as special as this.

CHAPTER TWELVE

EVE'S sigh was soft against his shoulder; it whispered the pleasure still permeating her blood. Ethan knew the feeling; it was with him also. But that didn't mean he was feeling good about this.

What had he done—?

What the hell had he done? He didn't deserve this, he did not deserve one half second of what she had just given to him. Now he was desperate to move, to separate from this incredible creature so that he could take stock—come to terms with what this was going to mean to the both of them.

He felt her begin to stir beneath him. It became the most sensually evocative stretch of the female body that began at her shoulders and arched her slender spine and flexed the cradle of her hips where he received the full kick of the movement because they were still joined.

At least with that stirring she also gave him permission to move by slackening the grip her arms had around him. Using his forearms as braces to take his weight, he levered himself away from her, and shuddered at her soft quivering gasp as he withdrew other parts. The gasp didn't surprise him. He might be wishing himself a million miles away at this precise moment, but his body certainly wasn't agreeing.

It wanted more—already. It wanted him to begin the whole wildly exciting process all over again.

'Say something,' she murmured.

The soft sound of her voice brought his head round to

look at her. She was lying there beside him with her cheek resting on her forearm and gazing at him through shy, dark, vulnerable eyes. His heart pitched and rolled. She looked gloriously, stunningly, *achingly* lovely with her hair spreading out across the pillow and her face wearing that satiated bloom.

'I was your first lover.' It was the only thing rattling around his head that was fit to be said.

The bloom deepened, her eyelashes flickered down in a bid to hide away from that soul-blazing truth. But not for long; not this woman who had so much spirit; she wasn't going to let a bit of shy self-consciousness beat her. So the lashes rose up again, gave him a view of deep green, slightly mocking, eyes packed full of the new knowledge he had given to her. 'Thank you for making it such a memorable experience,' she said softly, and smiled.

That smile... He felt it reach right down inside and grasp hold of certain parts. The urge to roll towards her and recreate the whole magic again was so tantalising he could actually taste it.

Or taste Eve, he amended grimly, and sat up. 'You should have told me,' he censured.

There was a moment's silence, a moment's total stillness, a moment in which he felt muscles clench all over him because his gruff, curt attitude had just wiped the pleasure right out. He felt it leave like an actual entity, unfolding itself from their flesh and slipping silently through the open terrace window.

Not Eve though. She still lay beside him; he could see her slender bare feet, the sensual curl of her toes and the gold silk length of her slender legs.

'Why?' she challenged. 'Is there some unwritten rule somewhere that says all first-timers must announce that fact before proceeding?'

Put like that, he wanted to laugh. But the bottom line still read like ten vicious swear words. 'I had a right to know.'

'You believe you had a right of say over my virginity? Rubbish,' she denounced. 'For what purpose?' she demanded. 'So that you could make the decision as to whether you wanted to take it or not?'

'No.' This, Ethan realised, was not going to be easy.

'Then, what?'

The silky gold legs disappeared from his vision, the slender feet, the sensually curling toes. His eyes followed them as they slid across smooth white sheeting to snake out of his sight as she pulled herself up—not to sit but to kneel somewhere behind him. He felt her rise upwards, smelt the sweetly seductive scent of her skin, felt her sigh brush his nape, just before her arms appeared over his shoulders and long delicate fingers with nails painted hot-pink came to rest in the hair matting his chest. Her lips caught his ear lobe, her teeth gently bit, and sensation sprinkled through him like a thousand pinpricks, the tips of her breasts pressing like two hard buttons against his back.

'It wasn't your special moment, it was mine,' she told him. 'Go all Neanderthal on me and I might not let you teach me how good it can be the second time…the third…' She bit his lobe again. 'To infinity and beyond,' she whispered sensually.

His short huff of amused laughter found voice this time. Eve the flirt, Eve the temptress, Eve the serpent in paradise, whom he seemed to have transported with him across half the world. Now it was Eve the dangerous seductress. Though she might have just enjoyed her first experience in making love, even now he knew he could teach her nothing. She was a natural, born to it. Special and rare.

What had that small burst of laughter been for? Eve
wondered anxiously. Was he thinking she was incorrigi-
ble? Was he thinking she must be a real little hussy to
make so light of what they'd just done?

But Eve didn't feel light about anything. She was worried. She was scared in case he took the honourable path
and decided her virginity came with a price tag he might
be forced to pay, when all he'd really been doing had been
giving in to the temptation she'd so blatantly thrown his
way.

She loved him, she wanted him, but not without him
loving and wanting her above anything else.

Anything? she then questioned. One woman, she
amended. One unavailable woman, who had no right to
keep the heart she could never cherish. Well, move over,
Leona, she thought possessively. Because you've just lost
out and this beautiful man's heart is going to belong to
me!

'I need a shower,' she murmured huskily against that
tasty ear lobe. 'And so do you.'

Invitation—demand. Ethan stared down at the place
against his chest where his ring winked defiantly up at him.
She's all yours, mate, it seemed to be telling him. For now
at any rate.

Well, to hell with it—why not? he decided. He was a
big boy, he could take it when it was over and it was time
to get out! So he turned to look at her, dislodging her arms
in the process so she sat back on her haunches looking at
him through wide green wary eyes. She wasn't sure what
was coming but he knew.

He looked her over, his eyes stripping off a layer of skin
with their silver-bright possessive blast. Then he swung
himself off the bed, turned, and pressed Eve up against his
chest so that her eyes were level with his and her thighs

were clinging to his narrow waist. 'Your grandfather,' he said, 'should have locked you away years ago.'

She grinned; her eyes began to shine; she had the audacity to put out her tongue and lick the shape of his mock-stern mouth. 'Jack Banning said the very same thing,' she informed him. Then before he could respond, she kissed him—hell, did she kiss him! She kissed him all the way into the adjoining bathroom, then the shower and, as promised, beyond.

Eve was in the kitchen and was humming to herself as she waited for the toast to pop up from the toaster. Sunlight was pouring in through the open door which led onto the terrace and behind her lay the remnants of the meal they'd eaten in here the night before—though for the life of her she couldn't remember what that meal had consisted of.

It didn't matter. Nothing mattered, other than for the huggable knowledge that she had spent the night in Ethan's home, in Ethan's bed, in Ethan's arms, making wonderful love. She was now wearing Ethan's shirt as she prepared his breakfast, while his voice filtered into her from out on the terrace where he was sounding very smooth, very slick, very informed as he spoke in fluent Spanish to some authoritative body. She loved his voice; she loved its rich deep texture and what it did to her tummy muscles as she listened to him. She loved this feeling of complete contentment as she prepared breakfast for him.

He stopped talking as the toast popped up, his footsteps sounding on pale blue tiling as they brought him into the kitchen to look for her. She smiled as his hands came to cup her hips, crushing fine cotton against her cool flesh. 'Mmm, that smells good,' he said, then buried his mouth in the side of her throat.

It really was quite sinful the way she responded, turning

round in his grasp to demand that mouth for her own. His hands shaped her body and hers stroked the smooth clean surface of his freshly shaved face. Things would have moved onto something else if the telephone hadn't started ringing.

He was reluctant to let her go, Eve equally so. But she liked the evidence of frustration in his eyes as he dug his mobile out of his pocket and placed it to his ear.

'Ethan Hayes,' he announced in that deep smooth drawl that made her toes curl into the floor. He was wearing a light grey suit, white shirt and grey tie and was looking dynamic, again, she noticed with a wry little smile as she turned back to the toast while he discussed local by-laws.

The call ended just as she finished slotting triangles of toast into a toast rack. There was a short sharp silence that alerted her before she even turned round and saw his face.

He was gazing ruefully at the breakfast tray she had prepared ready to take out onto the terrace. 'You're going to be angry with me for this,' he warned her. 'But I'm afraid I'll have to miss breakfast. I have a meeting in ten minutes down at the yacht club.'

Disappointment curled inside her tummy but she kept it from showing on her face by hiding it behind an understanding smile. It was what he had rushed back here to Spain for, after all. 'So much for my display of domesticity,' she mocked.

'I shouldn't be long,' he assured her. 'You'll be all right here on your own until I get back?'

'I'll try my best not to go into too deep a decline while you're gone,' she promised.

'What about my decline?' he countered quizzically.

It was nice of him to say it, but he was in no danger of wasting away from not having her within touching distance. He was already pumped up and eager to go and take on the whole Spanish government.

Folding her arms beneath her breasts, Eve leaned against the worktop and sent him a dry look. 'Go,' she said.

'Right,' he said, but still didn't move. Instead he looked at her, really looked at her, with a slight tilt to his head and a slight frown to his brow, as if he was trying to work something out about her but couldn't quite grasp what that something was. Then he seemed to give up on it and, with a brief smile, he brushed a kiss across her cheek. 'I'll be as quick as I can,' he said.

Then he was gone, striding out of the kitchen and away from her with his car keys jangling in his hand as he made for the rear courtyard, where she'd noticed the set of four garages when they'd arrived the afternoon before.

Left on her own, breakfast lost some of its appeal, though the aroma of fresh coffee was too inviting to ignore. So she carried the tray out onto the terrace and sat at one of the tables there to drink it and watch San Estéban glitter with the early morning crystal-clarity that came with the promise of a perfect summer's day. After that she spent some time tidying the kitchen, then decided to take a long shower and dress before exploring the rest of the villa, since she hadn't bothered to notice anything much the day before.

She took the terrace route to her bedroom, noticed she hadn't even got around to unpacking her suitcase, and wondered if Ethan had unpacked his? A quick shower and she was just slipping into a short blue skirt and a white sun top, her next intention to explore the villa, when a telephone began ringing somewhere, it was the land-line kind that announced itself as such by its distinctive tone.

Ethan? she wondered, and felt her heart leap. He had only been gone a couple of hours yet he was missing her so much he had to give her a call? Hurrying out of the bedroom, she began to follow the sound down the wide arched hallway. The villa suddenly felt big and empty, and she wasn't sure she liked Ethan's taste in décor. It surprised her to think that because she liked just about every other thing about Ethan, she mused with a smile as she walked between pale sand walls on the same pale blue tiling that seemed to cover the floors throughout. It was all very cool, very Lawrence-of-Arabia, nothing shouted, nothing scarred the eyes. Yet...

She found the telephone in one of the reception rooms. As she moved towards it, it suddenly stopped ringing and the answering machine kicked in. As she waited to hear if it was indeed Ethan trying to contact her before she decided to pick up the receiver, she began to look around the room.

A stranger's voice suddenly filled the air space. Deep and smooth, it possessed the same rich English tones as Ethan's voice, only it lacked his toe-curling attraction.

'Ethan,' the voice said. 'It's Victor. When you get a spare minute, give me a call. I'm at the London office and that cantankerous devil, Theron Herakleides, has decided to go silent about the Greek project.'

Grandpa. Eve smiled at the cantankerous description, frowned at the part about the Greek project because she'd forgotten about her grandfather's threats. She remained standing there waiting for Victor Frayne to finish his message so that she could call up her grandfather and try and convince him he would be cutting off his nose to spite his own face if he pulled Hayes-Frayne's submission.

Maybe she shouldn't have come here. For the first time she began to have doubts about her own motives. Selfish, she was being selfish, and maybe she should let Ethan off the hook and tell her grandfather the truth about what had happened. It wasn't right; it wasn't fair that Ethan should be forced to make sacrifices just because she'd managed to wriggle her way beneath his tough façade and basically run rings around him.

Is that what she'd done? Yes, it was exactly what she'd done, she admitted. She'd wept, she'd fought, she'd begged and had seduced and had turned him upside down and inside out—and all in twenty-four wild and dizzying hours, too!

'Oh, by the way…' Victor Frayne's voice cut through her train of thinking at about the same moment Eve's eyes settled on a row of framed photographs sitting on a long low cedarwood sideboard. '…the door to Leona's bedroom is sticking. Can you get someone up there to take a look at it?'

The call to her grandfather was forgotten. A cold chill of dismay was settling on her skin. Ethan couldn't— surely—have brought her to stay at the home of Victor Frayne and Leona Al-Qadim?

CHAPTER THIRTEEN

THE meeting had taken longer than Ethan had expected but by the end of it Ethan was satisfied that the new yacht club building was no longer under threat. As he shook hands with the local planning officials, he was aware that his site managers were standing to one side waiting to do the usual post-mortem on the meeting, but he was eager to get away.

He kept thinking of Eve and how she'd looked when he'd left her, wearing nothing but his cast-off shirt and a becoming flush to her lovely face.

As soon as the officials departed, one of his managers stepped up. 'Victor has been trying to contact you,' the man informed him. 'Something to do with Theron Herakleides and the Greek project?'

Theron, Ethan began to frown. He had forgotten all about Eve's grandfather and his threats. 'I'll deal with it.' He nodded. He glanced at his watch, realised he'd been away from Eve for over two hours, and wished he knew at what point it had been that he had become so obsessed with her that she was virtually wrapped around his every thought. 'If everything is back on track here, can we rain check the post-mortem? I need to be somewhere else.'

He was talking to all three of his site managers, and they instantly developed distinct masculine gleams in their eyes. 'We heard all about the souvenir you brought back with you from the Caribbean,' one of them teased him lazily, telling him also that the company grapevine was still working efficiently.

This kind of man-to-man camaraderie was to be expected on building sites. One either sank or swam with it. Ethan usually swam.

'The *souvenir* goes by the name of Eve Herakleides,' he informed them dryly. 'And if you value your jobs here I would suggest you curb the joky comments, because she also happens to be my future wife.'

A stunned silence fell. Ethan looked at the three men and saw their slack-jawed trance. But their shock came nowhere near the shock that he found himself experiencing. He felt as if he had just stepped off a very high cliff.

Had he really said that? Yes, he had said that, he was forced to grimly face the fact.

They were looking at him as if they expected him to laugh now and withdraw what he'd said. After all, this had to be a classic example of building-site camaraderie where the jokes flew back and forth with quick-flitting wit that did not always need to tell the truth if the punch-line served got the right results?

So—okay, this was supposed to be part of an elaborate deception, he tried to reason. But it didn't feel like a lie. Was that why he was suddenly feeling as if he'd jumped into a free fall from a fatal height?

'Nothing to say?' he mocked, working like mad to keep the jaunty flow going now that he had opened his big mouth.

'Congratulations,' one man muttered uncomfortably. The others mimicked their colleague like puppets that had just had their strings well and truly jerked.

'Thank you,' he murmured, while thinking Eve would have loved to be here to witness this. It placed the act she'd put on for her grandfather the day before yesterday right into the shade. 'Be sure to make it a good whip-round for my wedding gift when the time comes.'

They should have laughed then—told him what a fool he was for getting caught after managing to stay single for all these years. But their expressions had now shifted to something else entirely.

What else? he puzzled. What exactly was now going on inside their heads while they stood there looking at him like that?

Then it hit him. Leona. His free fall through space stopped abruptly as cold anger erupted in his breast. Did everyone in San Estéban suspect his relationship with Leona had been something other than what it was?

Now he was glad that Eve wasn't here to witness this scene, or every single suspicion she had about him and Leona would be buzzing around her possessive head.

Oh, but he liked Eve possessive; he liked her weepy and vulnerable and high-tempered and snappy; he liked her wearing hot-pink, like the dress she'd had on in the bar on the beach, and she'd had painted onto the nails she'd drawn down his chest last night.

Where the hell did he think he was going with this kind of crazy thinking? Crazy really said it. The last twenty-four hours in their entirety had been one long walk through insanity! But in those twenty-four hours, he realised he'd come to care a great deal what Eve thought about him.

'So watch the snide remarks in her presence,' he cautioned more seriously. 'She's special. I expect her to be treated as special. Make sure you pass the warning on.'

And if this performance didn't convince them that he and Leona were not an item, then what would?

'Right, Boss,' they said in solemn unison.

As he left, Ethan wondered how long it would take for this juicy snippet of information to make it right round San Estéban?

Eve was standing in the sunny lounge holding a picture

frame between trembling fingers when she heard Ethan
return. She was trying to decide whether to be hurt, insulted or just plain angry. She'd certainly been hurt when
she'd picked up this frame, and had found herself staring
at the tableau it presented of a beautiful woman standing
with—not one—but *four* incredibly spectacular looking
men!

One of the men was Ethan. *All* of them looked ready
and willing to worship at the woman's feet. And why not?
she acknowledged. The lady was really quite something
special with her flowing red hair, exquisite face and the
kind of smile that dropped men to their knees.

'It was taken at Leona's civil wedding in England,'
Ethan's voice quietly informed her.

Looking up she saw him standing in the archway. The
jacket to his suit had gone but the tie still rested neatly
against his shirt front. As always, he looked heart-
stoppingly attractive, even with that guarded look he was
wearing on his face.

She looked away from him and back at the photograph.
'She's beautiful,' she murmured huskily.

His answering smile was more like a grimace as he
walked forward to glance down at the photograph. 'Victor
Frayne,' he indicated with a long finger. 'Leona, of course,
and Sheikh Hassan Al-Qadim. The giant is Sheikh
Hassan's brother, Sheikh Rafiq Al-Qadim—though he re-
fuses to acknowledge the title,' he added grimacing.

'Why?'

'Long story. Remind me to tell it to you sometime—
preferably before you meet him.' Said with humour, there
was nothing funny in the way he took the frame from her
then stood frowning down at it before putting it back in
its place.

'Is there a chance that I'll meet him?' Eve was already

stiffening her insides ready for the blow she thought was coming her way. If the Al-Qadim family were here in San Estéban... If they were staying in this same house then she was...

'Not really,' he murmured. 'He goes nowhere without his brother, and his brother is cruising the Mediterranean as we speak.'

'This is their villa, isn't it?' she stated.

Did he hear the accusation in her tone? If he did, his face didn't show it as he turned with what Eve read as reluctance from the photo to look at her. 'It's the company villa,' he corrected. 'Victor designed it, Leona furnished it. We all use it as a convenient place to live when we are here in Spain.'

Convenient, just about said it for Eve, and her mind was suddenly tripping over itself as it painted lurid pictures in her head of Ethan and Leona in their convenient love-nest with dear Papa along as one lousy chaperone!

'And where's Leona now?' she demanded.

'With her husband on their yacht. Victor flew back to London yesterday, once he knew I was coming here to take over for him.'

'So you thought, Why not bring Eve here and *conveniently* slot her in where Leona should be?'

Ethan's eyes narrowed at her waspish tone. 'What is that supposed to mean?'

'It means,' she lashed at him, 'that I do not appreciate playing substitute to anyone!'

'Substitute to who, exactly?'

He wanted her to spell it out for him. Well, she could do that! 'Leona's clothes hang in the wardrobe,' she told him. 'The next bedroom to yours as a matter of fact!'

'It bothers you?' he murmured.

'It bothers me.' She nodded. 'It more than bothers me

that you dared to bring me here to your sordid little love-nest and make love to me in the same bed in which you probably made love to her!'

His grey eyes narrowed some more and Eve was suddenly thinking about dangerous animals again, and felt the fizz of excitement leap inside.

She was trembling like mad, Ethan noticed, and he was angry! 'A small piece of advice,' he offered thinly. 'Loose talk is dangerous when the Al-Qadim family is involved. So hold your foolish tongue and listen. Leona and I are not, and never have been, lovers,' he stated it with ice-cold precision. 'Take that on board and heed it, Eve, because I won't repeat it again.'

But he would say that, wouldn't he, to protect his true love? Eve had never felt so used in her entire life. 'I'm leaving,' she decided.

He didn't say anything, but just stood there looking at her through cold hard gun-metal-grey eyes.

Her heart was bursting, because she didn't really want to go. But she turned anyway and began walking towards the archway the led to the hall.

'Back to Aidan Galloway?' he fed silkily after her. 'Back to the young bloods you can handle better than you can handle me?'

She stopped. 'At least Aidan cares about my feelings.'

'By spiking your drink so he can enjoy you without needing to put much effort into it?'

She swung round. 'I told you it wasn't Aidan that did that to me!'

'Ah, yes, the other nameless young blood,' he drawled, and Eve noticed that the cynicism was back. 'Funny how you remembered him only after I threatened to tear Galloway limb from limb.'

He still didn't believe her about Aidan! she realised. 'It

was Raoul Delacroix who spiked my drink!' she insisted furiously.

Raoul Delacroix. Any other name, Ethan was thinking, and he would have laughed in her lying face! But he was recalling the look on Raoul's face as he'd turned away from her in the bar at the beach. He was recalling the stinging sensation he'd experienced at the back of his neck, that reminded him he didn't like what he'd seen on the young Frenchman's face.

'And I don't know what right you think you have to throw my love life back at me when nothing could be more sordid than the set-up you have going here!'

'Leave Leona out of this,' he bit at her.

'Leave Aidan out of it!'

Stalemate. They both recognised it for what it was. She was standing there shimmering with offence and fury and he was standing there simmering in the midst of a jealous rage! He couldn't believe it. Couldn't bring himself to accept that in forty-eight short hours she could have actually brought him down to this.

'Go if you are going,' he said as the damning remark to come straight out of that last angry thought.

She turned—but not before he had seen that heart-shaped pink mouth that had a propensity to pout, quiver, and her eyes sparkle with the promise of tears. Hell, he cursed, when he knew what was going to happen: he was going to give in. He could feel it bubbling up inside him, hot and out of control.

'But—I'm coming with you.' The decision itself set his feet in motion. As he strode towards her he saw his ring sparkling on her finger when she lifted her hand up to brush a tear from her cheek.

My tears, my ring—my woman, he claimed possessively. He took all three, grabbing his woman around the waist, crushing the ring in the clasp of one of his hands, and spinning her about so that he could lick the tears from her cheek. 'Anywhere,' he murmured, while he did it. 'Hotel, an apartment in San Estéban. We can even take one of the other villas if that's what you prefer.'

Preference didn't really come into it, Eve thought helplessly. She preferred not to love him this badly. But she did. Bottom line. 'I would prefer it if Leona Al-Qadim didn't exist,' she told him honestly.

'Forget Leona,' he muttered impatiently.

'If you forget Aidan,' she returned, determined to maintain some level of balance around here.

She looked into his eyes; he looked into hers; both sets were angry because they were giving in. Their bodies liked it though, Eve noticed. They were greeting each other like hungry lovers.

'So, where are we going to go to continue this?' His voice rasped with impatience, his body pulsed with desire.

The fact that hers was doing the same thing made the decision for her. So she reached up, touched her mouth to his, and remained that close while she murmured, 'Here seems very convenient, don't you think…?'

CHAPTER FOURTEEN

THE little minx. An absolute witch, sent to torment the life out of him, Ethan was thinking irritably. There was nothing convenient about having Eve Herakleides running riot through his life.

The telephone rang. He picked it up. 'What?' he barked.

It was his secretary in London. Sitting there behind his desk, Ethan dealt with a list of queries while his angry gaze remained fixed on the little scene taking place outside his site-office window, where Eve stood laughing, surrounded by a whole rugby scrum of big, tough, very much hands-on builders wearing yellow helmets, dust-covered steel-capped boots, tight tee shirts and jeans.

And what was Eve wearing?

Hot-pink. It was her favourite colour, he had come to realise during the last ten days. Today it was hot-pink trousers that skimmed her hips and thighs and stopped just above her slender calf muscles, and a baby-pink top that left a lot of golden midriff on show.

Too much midriff. 'I don't know about that, Sonia,' he murmured. 'I can't be sure I'll be back in London to attend that meeting. You'd better ask Victor if he can do it.'

Eve's hair was up in a natty little twist that did amazing things to the length of her neck, and in profile she looked like the sweetest thing ever to be put onto this earth. Every time she moved he saw his ring flash in the sunlight. Every time she laughed he saw his men almost fall to their knees.

'I know they wanted me,' he rasped out testily. 'But they can't have me.'

I'm already engaged, he thought, to a woman with no sense of what's right or proper to wear on a building site! In the last ten days he'd also come to realise the full meaning of the term *engaged*.

'Heard anything from Theron Herakleides?' he thought to enquire.

There was another person who was irritating the hell out of him. Since their tough talk in the Caribbean, he hadn't had a single peep out of Eve's grandfather. His own letter formally withdrawing his submission for the Greek project had not been acknowledged. The promised contract making sure Ethan didn't get his greedy hands on the old man's money had never appeared. No one at Hayes-Frayne could get to speak to Herakleides, and even Leandros was complaining that the Greek had dropped off the face of the earth. As far as Ethan could make out, Theron was only answering calls from his precious granddaughter. She'd been talking to him every day, but even she couldn't get him to come clean as to what he was going to do about the Greek project. He'd just said, 'I'll see you in two weeks.' Then it had been one week. Now it was down to just a few days.

Their official betrothal. His ring on Eve's finger winked at him. 'Nothing,' he heard his secretary say.

The ring sparkled again as Eve lifted up her hand to brush some dry plaster from one man's bulging bicep. The guy grinned a very macho, very sexy, Spanish grin. Ethan felt his gut tighten up in protest. Abruptly finishing the telephone conversation, he stood up and knocked on the window-pane.

Eve turned. So did the men. She sent him a wide white brilliant smile. The men's smiles were more—manly, as in, You lucky devil, Mr Hayes.

'He wants his souvenir back,' he heard one man say to the others.

Eve laughed, as she had done from the first time she'd heard herself referred to as that. She liked it. Damn it, *he* liked it! He liked what it did to him when she sent him that teasing little smile that said, Some souvenir, hmm?

He was in love with her. He'd known it for days, weeks, maybe even months. She filled his every thought, his every sense, his every desire. He looked at her and felt a multitude of conflicting emotions, none of which on their own could adequately describe what he was having to deal with inside.

Bidding a light farewell to her macho fan club, she began walking towards his office door. He watched her come, watched her soft mouth take on a different look that was exclusively for him. It was a kiss, a sensual kiss, offered to him from a distance. She was a flirt; she was a tease; he found himself wearing an irresistible grin.

'What are you doing here?' he demanded though, the moment she came into the cool confines of his air-conditioned office. 'I thought we'd agreed you would keep away from the site so you don't cause accidents.'

She laughed; she thought he was joking, but Ethan wasn't sure that he was. Heads turned when Eve walked by. The fact that those heads were on bodies with feet balancing on ladders or on scaffolding made it dangerous.

'I needed to ask your advice about something.'

'Try the phone.'

'Oh, don't be a grouch.' She pouted up at him as she walked around his desk. Then she boldly pulled the cord that closed the sunblinds across the window and reached up to transform the pout into a kiss that wound its tentacles around him and left him wanting more.

I love this man, Eve thought, as she drew away again.

I love him so much that I daren't let myself think about Athens and the fact that we have only three days to go before we are expected there.

It was frightening. She held his cheek, looked deep into his eyes and wished she knew how much of what they relayed to her was just sexual desire and how much was still rooted in pretence. What she did know was that they had been so happy here. No spats, since the first day. No mention of anything likely to start a war.

Except for Grandfather, of course. He was discussed on a daily basis. But never in a way that could remind either of them of how this whole thing had started out.

'Was that it?' he prompted. 'You wanted my advice on how well you kiss?'

Eve refocused her attention and saw one of his eyebrows had arched and his mouth was wearing a lazily amused smile. It would be the easiest thing in the world to say yes, and leave it at that, keep the rest until later when he came home.

But keeping Ethan on his toes was her aim in life. So, she said airily, 'Oh, no. I already know what a great kisser I am.'

Stepping away from him, she applied her surprise tactics by unzipping her trousers and peeling them back from her hips. 'What do you think?' she asked innocently.

Innocent was not the word Ethan was thinking as he stared down at her silk-smooth abdomen. He was thinking, Minx, again. Outrageous and unpredictable minx. For there, nestling in the hollow of her groin, just above the tantalisingly brief panty line, and right on the spot of an erogenous zone he knew so well he could actually feel its response against the flat of his tongue, lay a heart. A small red painted heart.

'It's a tattoo,' he announced.

'What do you think?' she repeated.

'I think you're not safe to be let out on your own,' he replied. 'What were you thinking of, marking your lovely skin with something like that?'

'I thought you might like it.' The pout was back, Ethan noticed, the one that begged to be soothed into something else.

Well, not this time. 'You idiot,' he snapped. 'That's going to hurt like blazes by tonight.'

'No, it won't,' she denied. 'Because it isn't real. I found this amazing little shop down one of the back streets in San Estéban where they apply these temporary tattoos. It will disappear in about a month. I think its great.' Eve looked down to view her latest impulse. 'I might have it replaced with a permanent one next time.'

'Over my dead body,' he vowed, but he had to reach out to run his thumb pad over the painted heart. As he did so he heard her breath quiver in her throat and felt the sound replay itself in other parts of himself.

He knew that sound. He looked at her face and saw her innocent green eyes had darkened into those of an outright sinner. His body quickened; she saw it happen; her mouth stretched into a knowing smile. 'It will be interesting to see if you change your mind about that,' she taunted silkily.

It was no use, Ethan gave up—as he always seemed to do. Swinging his chair around, he sat himself down then drew her in between his spread thighs. 'No,' he refused, knowing exactly what she believed was going to come. Instead he tugged the zip shut on her trousers, then took a firm grip on both of her hips and brought her tumbling down on his lap. Kisses on the mouth were much less evocative than kisses elsewhere. This way at least he would manage to hang onto some of his dignity if anyone should happen to walk in here.

By the time the kissing stopped, her eyes were glazed—but then so were his. 'I'm going to send you packing now,' he told her huskily.

'But you would rather come with me.'

It was no lie. 'If that tattoo hurts later, we are going to have a row,' he warned.

'It won't,' she stated confidently.

The telephone on his desk began to ring. Maybe it was good timing on its part because it put a stop to what was still promising to develop into something else.

'Up,' he commanded, and used his hands to set her back on her feet, then urged her towards the door. 'Now go and don't come back.' On that brisk dismissal he reached out for the phone. 'And leave my labourers alone!' he added as she was about to walk out of the door.

She turned, sent him a look that stirred his blood. Then she caught him off guard, yet again. 'I did it for you, you know,' she softly confided. 'You're going to love it, I promise you.'

'Ethan Hayes,' he announced into the telephone, as he stood up to open the blinds so he could watch Eve walk towards the car he had hired for her to use.

The whole site had come to a stop. He watched it happen, watched her take no notice of any of the remarks that flew her way. He also saw her pause, look back and wave to let him know that she knew he was watching her. By the time she'd turned away again he knew that his own departure wasn't going to be that far away.

He was right, but for the wrong reasons. 'Ethan—' it was Victor '—you are not going to like this, but I need to ask you to do me a very big favour...'

Eve had been back at the villa for less than half an hour

when she heard Ethan come in through the door. Not expecting him for hours yet—even with the invitation she had left behind her earlier—she had just curled up in a shady spot on the terrace with the book her grandfather had given her for her birthday. It was a rare first edition of classical Greek love poems to add to the collection he had been building for her since her first birthday.

But the moment she heard Ethan's step, the book was forgotten, a look of surprised delight already lighting her face at this major triumph in managing to get him to come back early because he couldn't resist the invitation she'd so blatantly left him with.

'I'm on the terrace!' she called out and uncurled her feet from beneath her then stood up to go and meet him half-way. She reached the door through to the sitting room as he appeared in the arch leading into it from the hall. He stopped, she stopped. It took less than a second to make her welcoming smile fade from her face when she saw the expression on his. It was like being tossed back eleven days to that bar on the Caribbean beach, he looked so different.

CHAPTER FIFTEEN

'WHAT'S wrong?' she asked sharply, absolutely sure that something had to be, because no man changed so very much in such a short space of time without having a reason for doing so.

He didn't reply, not immediately anyway. Instead he built the tension by grimly yanking the tie loose from his collar and tossing it aside then releasing his top shirt-button before issuing a heavy sigh.

'We need to talk,' he said on the back of that sigh. That was all, no warm greeting, no teasing comment about the little red heart she was wearing for him.

Fear began to walk all over her self-confidence, 'W-what about?'

'You and me,' he replied, ran a hand round the back of his neck as if to attempt to ease the tension she could see he was suffering from. 'We've been living a lie for the last ten days, Eve. Have you ever stopped to think about that?'

Think about it? She lived with it! Ate, slept and made love to it!

'For me it stopped being a lie from the first time we made love, Ethan,' she answered. 'So maybe you had better tell me whether you've thought about it much recently.'

Her sarcasm hit a nerve, but instead of an answer he made a grimace that she just did not like. Something had happened; it had to have done to change the man she had left only an hour ago into this person who was so uptight she could actually feel his tension cutting through the air like a sharp knife. And worse: he had stopped looking at her.

'I have to go away for a few days,' he suddenly announced.

That was the root of all of this tension? 'Well, that's all right,' she murmured, unable to believe that was the answer to what was bothering him. Forcing herself to walk forwards on legs that weren't all that steady, she tried to look calm as she placed her book down on a nearby table then turned to look expectantly at him. 'Business?' she asked.

'Yes—no.' He changed his mind and began to frown. 'It's more an errand of mercy...' Then he muttered, 'Damn this, Eve—I'm trying to find out if you intend to still be here when I get back.'

Was that all? Staring at him, Eve couldn't believe the sense of relief that went flooding through her. 'Of course!' she exclaimed. 'Why ever not?'

For some bewildering reason, her reply only filled him with exasperation and he strode forward to grasp her left hand then lifted it up to her face. 'Because this ring,' he uttered tightly, 'will become a formal engagement ring on Saturday in Athens. So if you want out, you have to say so now.'

'Do you want out?'

'No.' He sighed. 'I do not want out. I just needed to know where I stand with you before I—'

'Well, I don't want out,' she cut in softly, and her smile came back to her eyes, to her slightly quivering mouth. 'I want you.'

He loved that mouth, Ethan reaffirmed something he already knew. He loved this woman. But was her 'I want you' enough to make him declare himself?

Was it enough to get him through the rest of what he

had to tell her. 'Enough to trust me?' he therefore had to ask.

'Trust you about what?'

Well, here it comes, he thought, the bottom line to all of this. He took a deep breath, let it out again, desperately wanted to kiss her first, but held back on the need and looked deep into her beautiful green eyes. 'Victor Frayne called me as you were leaving the office. He needs a very big favour from me. Due to unfounded rumours involving me and his daughter Leona, her marriage is under threat. So I am flying out to Rahman to help scotch those rumours—at her husband Sheikh Hassan's request.'

He added Hassan's name to give it all sanction. He hoped it would hold a lot of sway. But silence came back at him, though it wasn't really silence because Eve's eyes told him a lot; their warm green slowly froze over until they'd turned to arctic frost. Her kissable mouth became a hard cold untouchable line, and loudest of all, she snatched her hand out of his and curled it into a tight fist at her side.

'You're still in love with her, you bastard,' she whispered.

'No.' He denied it. 'Leona needs—'

'To know she still has you dangling on a string.'

Coming from the very woman who had him dangling, Ethan couldn't help but laugh at that.

Eve's response was to step around him and walk coldly away.

She had never felt so betrayed. He'd manoeuvred that discussion, worked it and her like a master conductor until he'd got her to say what he'd wanted to hear, before he'd told her what he'd known she had not wanted to hear.

And for what purpose? Had he received a telephone call from her grandfather also? Did he now know, as she did, that the Greek project was about to be awarded to Hayes-Frayne?

'Don't do this, Eve,' he threaded heavily after her.

She didn't want to listen—refused to listen, and just kept on walking out of the sitting room and down the hall into the bedroom. *Their* bedroom. The one they'd been sharing since the first night he'd brought her here. She hated him for that. She now hated him so very badly that she could barely draw breath over that burgeoning hate.

He arrived in the doorway just as she was flipping her case open on the bed. A sense of *déjà vu* washed over her; only, last time this scene had been played their roles had been reversed.

'Eve—this is important.' He tried an appeal.

She almost laughed at his choice of words, coming hard on the back of what she had just been likening this moment to.

'We are talking about an Arab state here—a Muslim state where women are held sacrosanct. The smallest hint of a scandal and she can be cast out into the wilderness without a single qualm. I have to go.'

'I'm not stopping you,' she pointed out.

'This is stopping me!' he rasped back angrily.

'Okay.' She turned on him in the midst of her own sudden fury. 'You don't go and I don't go!'

It was the gauntlet tossed down on the tiles between them. Ethan even looked down as if he could see it lying there—while Eve held her breath, though it didn't stop her heart from thundering madly in her ears, or fine tremors from attacking her flesh.

Because this was do or die. He chose her over Leona or it was finished for them. He knew that, she knew that.

His eyes lifted slowly, dark lashes uncurling to reveal stone-cold reservoirs of determined grey. 'The rumours are lies,' he stated. 'Just a cruel and ruthless pack of lies put about by Sheikh Hassan's enemies with the deliberate intention of forcing him to reject his wife and take another one. His father is dying. A power struggle is on. Leona is caught right in the middle because she cannot bear his child. Those who don't want to unseat Hassan from power are pressurising him to take a second wife who can give him that child. If you have one small portion of understanding what that must be like for her, then you will accept that I cannot turn my back on her need for my support now.'

'How does your going to Rahman scotch those rumours?' Eve questioned with an icy scepticism that made him release a short tight laugh.

'If you knew the ways of Arab politics you would know that no Arab would invite his wife's lover into his house,' he explained. 'I am to be placed on show.' The laughter died. 'Held up in front of Rahman's best and most powerful as a man Hassan trusts and admires. And if you think I'm looking forward to that, then you're wrong,' he grimly declared.

'So you love her enough to put her needs before your own pride,' Eve concluded. And that was what this was really all about. Not whether he went or whether he stayed. It was about whether he still loved Leona enough to do it. The rest was just icing to cover an ugly cake.

'I'm going home, to Athens,' she told him flatly. 'This is it. We are finished.'

Ethan released another very bitter laugh. 'Well,' he said, 'at least you managed to do what you set out to do. You gave yourself two weeks to get around to jilting me. You're even slightly ahead of time. Well done, Eve.'

With that, it was Ethan who walked away.

Why? Because he had his answer. If she'd loved him,

she would have trusted him. If she'd cared about anyone but herself, she would have understood why he had to go.

Funny really, he thought, when only five minutes later he walked out of the villa and climbed into his car. A bit of encouragement on Eve's part and he would probably have invited her to go to Rahman with him. She would have enjoyed the novelty of watching him be foisted up as a pillar of good old-fashioned gentlemanly honour, when she knew the real man could take a sweet virgin and turn her into a sex goddess.

Too late now. He didn't want a woman that couldn't trust his word, and she didn't want a man who didn't jump to her bidding every time she told him to. On that most final of thoughts on the subject of Eve Herakleides, he started the car and drove out of the courtyard then turned to skirt San Estéban so he could meet the main road to Malaga.

While Eve still stood where he had left her, staring at nothing, feeling nothing—was too scared to feel.

The sound of the front door closing only five minutes later came as a big shock though. She hadn't expected him to leave so soon. She hadn't realised the end was going to be so quick and so cold.

She even shivered, found herself staring at Tigger who was sitting where he always sat, on the table beside the bed. He was looking at her as if to ask what kind of fool she was.

Well, she knew she was a fool. She'd worked so very hard to bring Ethan to the point where he'd want her to keep his ring on her finger. Now she'd thrown it all away.

Was that good or bad? Staring down at the ring, she watched its sparkle grow dim behind a bank of tears, and knew her failure was not in making Ethan want her, but in failing to make him love her.

Malaga airport was packed as always. Ethan arrived just in time to catch his flight to London, where he would have time only to go to his apartment, catch a couple of hours' sleep then pack a bag before he was due to link up with Victor for their trip to Rahman.

Eve took the easier option, and rang her cousin Leandros to beg the use of his helicopter to take her to Malaga. Therefore she arrived long before Ethan got there, and had taken off for Athens by the time he pulled his car into a long-stay slot.

London was cold. He didn't mind; the heavy grey skies suited his mood. It wasn't until he thought to check his emails before shooting off to meet Victor, that he found a note from his secretary telling him that Theron Herakleides had come out of hiding and was now making hopeful mur-murings about Hayes-Frayne being awarded the Greek pro-ject.

'Well, shoot that in the foot,' he told the computer screen, and switched it off. As of now, Hayes-Frayne could kiss goodbye anything to do with Greece.

He wished he'd kissed Eve goodbye before he'd left...

Athens was hot, stifling beneath one of its famous heat-waves. Eve was glad to let the taxi cab drive her up into the hills where the air was more fit to breathe. Her grand-father's mansion house stood in a row of gracious old houses occupying one of the most prestigious plots the rambling city had to offer.

He was just sitting down to dinner when she walked in, unannounced. 'My angel!' he greeted in surprise, and got to his feet to come down the table for his expected em-brace.

He was not expecting her to burst into a flood of tears though. 'Oh, Grandpa!' She sobbed as she walked into his arms. 'I hate him. I hate him so much!'

CHAPTER SIXTEEN

THE palace of Al-Qadim made an impressive sight standing against a backcloth of a star-studded night sky. Its rich sandstone walls had been flood-lit from below and, as they drove through the arched gateway into its huge inner courtyard, Ethan was reluctantly impressed with the sheer scale and beauty that met his eyes.

But he didn't want to be here. He was angry and fed up with role-playing for other people's benefit. He was sick to his stomach with the Mr Honourable tab people seemed to like to stick on him. The Mr you-can-depend-on-me-to-bale-you-out label.

He grimaced. Somewhere back there across a large tract of land and an ocean, he was being summarily sacked from his latest role with the none too tasty word *jilted* to wear as an epitaph to that little affair. While here, he was about to become the focus of critical Arab eyes, when he received his second sacking in twenty-four hours from the role as wicked lover to the Sheikha Leona Al-Qadim.

'Ethan—if you don't want to go ahead with this, then say so,' Victor murmured beside him.

'I'm here, aren't I?' he answered tersely, but then his whole manner had been terse since he'd climbed into his car in Spain and had driven away from Eve.

Eve the flirt, Eve the temptress, Eve the serpent, who'd made the last two weeks a perfect paradise—before she'd reverted to her original form. And what was that? he asked himself. Eve, the spoiled little rich girl, who wanted everything to go her way.

He was best out of it. He should have known that before it began. He should have seen the idiot he was making of himself every time he let her weave her magic spells around him.

The trouble was, he'd liked it. He'd liked playing slave to Eve Herakleides and her whims. She turned him on, hard and fast. She made him feel alive.

She'd had a heart temporarily tattooed onto one of her most erogenous spots just to tease him out of his mind.

'Only, in this mood, you aren't what I would call sociable,' Victor inserted carefully.

'Watch me turn on when the curtain goes up,' he promised. 'I'll be so sociable with your son-in-law that they will start to wonder if it's Hassan I've been having the affair with.'

'Don't be facetious.'

Victor was getting angry. Ethan didn't particularly blame him.

'You should have brought her with you if you can't last a day out of her arms without turning into a grouch.'

'Who are we talking about?' Ethan's eyes flashed a warning glance at the other man.

Victor just smiled one of those smiles that people smiled around him these days. 'I might not have been to San Estéban recently, but even the London-office cleaner knows about the *souvenir* you brought back from the Caribbean.'

Souvenir from hell, he amended bitterly.

Then he saw her expression just before he'd turned his back on her for the last time, and his insides knotted into a tight ball. He'd hurt her with all of this. He'd known that he would. That's why he'd tried to find out where she'd wanted their relationship to go, before he'd told her about this trip.

He'd wanted her to understand. He'd wanted her to trust him. See, for goodness' sake, that he couldn't be in love with another woman when she possessed every single inch of him!

So—what now? What was he doing here? A sudden and uncontrollable aching tension attached itself to his bones. He should be back there, arguing with Eve, not snapping at Victor! She was right in a lot of ways: he should have put her feelings first!

Oh, hell, damn it, he cursed.

The car came to stop in front of a beautiful lapis-lazuli-lined dome suspended between pillars made of white marble. Beyond the dome he could see a vast entrance foyer glittering beneath Venetian crystal. Victor got out of the car. Ethan did the same. As they stepped towards the dome, he shrugged his wide shoulders and grimly swapped Eve-tension for play-your-part-tension—so he could get the hell out of here.

Dressed in black western dinner suites, white shirts and bow ties, he and Victor stood out in a room filled with flowing Arabian colour. He saw Leona straight away. She was wearing gold-threaded blood-red silk and she looked absolutely radiant. Beside her stood the man she had adored from the first moment she'd set eyes on him just over five years ago, Sheikh Hassan Al-Qadim—who looked unusually pale for a man of his rich colouring.

Had the strain of the last few weeks begun to get to him? Victor had relayed some of what had been going on. Hassan had been fighting the battle of his life to keep the wife of his choice by his side *and* retain his place as his father's successor as ruler of Rahman. He had achieved success on both fronts—by the skin of his teeth.

Other than for this one last thing...

The hairs on the back of Ethan's neck began to prickle.

A brief, smooth scan of the room showed him what he had expected to see. People were staring at him—in shock, in dismay, in avid curiosity.

Were they expecting a scene? Were they looking like that because they expected Hassan to call for his sword and have his head taken off?

The prickle at the back of his neck increased, when what had been meant as a bit of sardonic whimsy suddenly didn't seem that whimsical at all. Then common sense returned, because what use would it be to have his head severed from his shoulders when all that would do would be to prove that Hassan believed the rumours about his beautiful wife?

What he was doing was far more subtle. The man had style, Ethan was prepared to acknowledge when, on catching sight of him standing here next to Victor, Hassan did not reveal a hint of the old dislike that usually flashed between the two of them. Instead Ethan saw him smile, then gently touch Leona's arm to draw her attention their way.

Leona turned to towards them. By now the room was held enthralled. Her lovely face began to lighten. A pair of stunning green eyes, that somehow were not quite as stunning to him as another pair of green eyes, flicked from her father's face to his face then quickly back again. Then, on a small shriek of delight, she launched herself towards them.

It seemed as if the whole assembly took a step backwards in shocked readiness for her to reveal her true feelings for this western man. Tall, lean and in very good shape for his fifty-five years, Victor Frayne received his daughter into his arms and accepted her ecstatic kisses to his face while Ethan felt the room almost sag in relief, or disappointment, depending on whether they were friend or foe to Sheikh Hassan Al-Qadim.

'What are you doing here? Why didn't you tell me?' Leona was scolding her father through a bank of delighted tears.

'Ethan—' She turned those starry eyes on him next and reached out to capture his hand. 'I can't believe this! I thought you were in San Estéban!'

'I only spoke to you this morning in London.' She was talking to her father again.

'No, a hotel, here.' Her father grinned at her. 'Thank your husband for the surprise.'

Hassan appeared at Leona's side to lay a hand on her slender waist. Leona turned those shining eyes onto him. 'I love you,' she murmured impulsively.

'She desires to make me blush,' Hassan said dryly, then offered his hand first to his father-in-law then to Ethan. 'Glad you could make it,' he said congenially. 'We are honoured to receive you into our home.'

'The honour is all mine,' Ethan replied with a smile that held only a touch of irony to imply that there was more to this invitation than met the eye.

Hassan sent him a slight grimace, then looked down at Leona who was too excited to notice any of the undercurrents flowing around her.

She didn't know, Ethan realised. She had no idea that he was here to help save her reputation. His estimation of Sheikh Hassan rose a couple of notches in recognition of the lengths he was prepared to go to for his love of Leona.

Could he have ever loved her like that? Looking at her laughing, beautiful face, he found himself superimposing another laughing, beautiful face over the top of it, and had to ask himself if he'd ever loved Leona at all? For this other face didn't just laugh at him, it teased and flirted and sent him secret little come-and-get-me smiles that made his insides sing. This other face looked at him and loved him.

Loved him? He stopped to question that.

Loved him, he repeated. His legs almost went from under him as his heart sank like a stone.

It was there, he could see it. It was there. He'd been blind!

'Ethan, are you feeling okay?'

He blinked and found himself looking down at Leona's anxious face. 'Fine.' He smiled. 'I'm glad to see you looking so happy.'

Stupidly, utterly, totally blind!

'I am!' She smiled. 'Deliriously happy.'

I need to get out of here...

'Good,' he said. 'This time make sure you hang onto it.'

In solemn response, she linked her arm with Hassan's arm. 'Hanging on,' she softly promised him.

He was supposed to laugh so he did laugh. Half the room turned to stare at the two of them and because Hassan must have seen all his hard work going down the tubes, he suddenly laughed as well and so did Victor.

As if cued by this brief moment of danger, another diversion was suddenly grabbing everyone's attention. People stopped talking. Silence rained down on the whole assembly as Hassan's half-brother, Rafiq, appeared pushing a wheelchair bearing Sheikh Khalifa ben Jusef Al-Qadim.

Ethan had only met the elderly sheikh once before, five years ago at his son's wedding. But he still couldn't believe the changes wrought since then. The old man looked so thin and frail against the height and breadth of his youngest son—a wasted shadow of his former self. But his eyes were bright, his mouth smiling and, in the frozen stasis brought on by everyone's shock at how ill he actually looked, he was prepared, and ready to respond. 'Welcome—welcome everyone,' he greeted. 'Please, do not continue to look at me as if you are attending my wake, for I assure you I am here to enjoy myself.'

After that everyone made themselves relax again. Some who knew him well even grinned. As Rafiq wheeled him towards the other end of the room, the old Sheikh missed no one in reach of his acknowledgement. 'Victor,' he greeted. 'I have stolen your daughter. She is now my most precious daughter, I apologise to you, but am not sorry, you understand.'

'I think we can share her,' Victor Frayne replied smilingly.

'And...ah.' The old sheikh then turned to Ethan. 'Mr Hayes, it is my great pleasure to meet Leona's very good friend.'

He had the floor, as it should be, so no one could miss the message being broadcast. 'Victor...Mr Hayes...come and see me tomorrow. I have a project I believe will be of great interest to you... Ah, Rafiq, take me forward for I can see Sheikh Raschid...'

And there it was, Ethan saw. In a simple exchange of pleasantries, the rumours had been scotched, dismissed and forgotten, because there wasn't a person here who would continue to question Leona's fidelity after Sheikh Khalifa himself had made his own opinions so very clear.

The old sheikh moved on, the spotlight shifted. For the next couple of hours, Hassan consolidated on what his father had put into place by taking Ethan and Victor with him around the room and introducing them to some very influential people.

I'm going crazy, Ethan decided. Because here I am smiling and talking to a lot of people I don't even care about, when I could be somewhere else with someone I do care about.

And where was Eve? Was she still at the villa in San Estéban, or had she made good her word and gone back to Athens? He wanted to know. He needed to know. His mobile phone began to burn a hole in his pocket.

In the end he couldn't stand it. He left the throng and went outside to see if he could get a signal. It wasn't a problem, so he stabbed the quick-dial button that would connect him to the villa, then stood breathing in the jasmine-scented night air while he waited to discover what his fate was going to be. What he got was the answering machine, which told him exactly nothing.

Frustration began to war with tension in his breast. Someone came to stand beside him. It was Hassan, looking less the arrogant bastard that he'd always seen him to be.

'Thank you,' Hassan said. 'I owe you a great debt of gratitude for coming here like this.'

Where it came from, Ethan had no idea, but he was suddenly so desperate to be somewhere else entirely that he knew he couldn't stay here a single moment longer. 'Do you think that debt of gratitude could stretch to a quick exit from here?' he asked curtly.

Hassan stiffened. 'You dislike our hospitality?'

'No.' He laughed. Only, it wasn't a real laugh because it erred too close to the threshold of panic. 'I just need to be somewhere else.'

She was calling him. Like the witch she was, she was casting a spell somewhere, he was sure of it. He could feel her tugging him back to her like a dog on a lead. And he wanted to go back. He didn't even mind the lead he could feel tightening around his neck. He wanted his woman. He *needed* his woman.

Maybe he knew. Maybe Sheikh Hassan Al-Qadim

wasn't all self-centred arrogance. Because he simply glanced at him, just glanced, once, read something in his face—heartache, heartbreak, heart-something anyway—and with a click of his fingers he brought a servant running.

'Have my plane made ready for an immediate departure,' he instructed smoothly. 'Mr Hayes, your transport to...somewhere...awaits,' he then drawled sardonically.

CHAPTER SEVENTEEN

EVE was casting spells in the garden. They wound around a tall, dark, idiot Englishman with no heart worth mentioning.

She wasn't happy. Everyone in her grandfather's house knew that she wasn't happy. She'd rowed with Grandpa. No one had ever heard Eve row with her grandpa.

But, like the Englishman, she had come to realise that Theron Herakleides had no heart either. He'd let her down. When she'd needed his comfort and support more than she'd ever needed it, he had withdrawn both with an abruptness that shocked.

'No, Eve,' he said. 'I will not let you do this.'

'But you don't have a say in the matter!' she cried.

'On this point I do,' he insisted. 'I gave you two weeks to come to your senses about that man. When you did nothing but claim how much you adored him, I gave in to your wishes, soft-hearted fool that I am, and went ahead with planning tonight's party. You are not, therefore, going to make the Herakleides name look foolish, by cancelling at this late juncture!'

'But I no longer have a man to become betrothed to!'

'Then find one,' he advised. 'Or you will dance alone tonight, my precious,' Theron coolly informed her, 'with your honour lying on the floor by your pretty feet and the Herakleides pride lying beside it.'

'You don't mean it,' she denounced.

But he did mean it. Which was why she was sitting in the garden wondering what she was supposed to do about

a party she didn't want, meant to celebrate a betrothal she didn't want, to a man who wasn't here to share either even if she did want him!

Where was he?

Her heart gave a little whimper. Was he with Leona right now, worshipping the unattainable, while her long-suffering husband played the grim chaperone—just to save face?

I hope they've had him thrown into a dungeon, she decided savagely. I hope they've cast him out into the desert with no food and water and definitely no tent!

But *where* was he? her stupid heart cried.

Today was Saturday. Yesterday she'd left a message on the answering machine in San Estéban asking him to call her. Couldn't he have done that at least? He owed her that one small consideration for all the love she'd poured into him.

I want him back. I *don't* want him back. She stood up, sat down again, let her hands wring together, looked down to find the thumb from the right hand rubbing anxiously at a finger on the left where Ethan's ring used to be.

I miss it. I miss him. Come and get me, Ethan! Oh, good grief, she never knew anything could feel this wretched.

'Eve...'

'Go away, Grandpa.' She didn't want to speak to anyone.

'There was a telephone call for you—'

'From Ethan—?' She shot eagerly back to her feet. Seeing the pity in her grandfather's eyes made her wish the ground would open up and swallow her whole.

What have I let that man do to me?

'It was Aidan Galloway,' her grandpa told her. 'He is on his way from the airport. I said you would be glad to see him.'

'Why?' Her green eyes began to spark with aggression. 'Are you thinking that Aidan could stand in as substitute?'

It made her even angrier when he dared to laugh. 'That is not a bad idea, sweetness,' he mused lazily. 'He will be here in a few minutes. I will leave you to put the suggestion to him.' With that he strolled off, still grinning from ear to ear.

He was enjoying this, Eve realised. It amazed her that she hadn't realised before what a twisted sense of humour her grandfather possessed. Her life was on the line here— her one hope at happiness—and he thought it was funny to watch her tear herself apart?

Theron did pause for a moment to wonder whether he should put her out of her misery and tell her what he already knew. He had been in touch with Victor Frayne about the Greek project. Victor Frayne had, in turn, told him about Ethan's quick departure from Rahman.

If the man wasn't coming to claim his granddaughter, then his name wasn't Theron Herakleides. Keeping Eve unaware of this prediction was good for her character. Good things came too easily for Eve, he'd come to realise. She had sailed through her life without feeling the pangs that hunger breeds. She had wit, she had grace, she had charm and intelligence, and she knew how to use them all to reach her goals with ease. But love stood on its own as something that must be worked at if it was to develop into its fullest potential. Feeling the sharp-edged fear of losing love should make her appreciate and heed the fear of losing it again.

Why did he feel she needed to do that? Because Ethan Hayes was a man of hidden fibre, he'd discovered. To keep up with the sneaky devil she was going to have to learn dexterity and speed.

Ethan landed in Athens and had to utilise some dexterity

and speed to get through an airport that the rest of the
world had seemed to decide to use at the same time.

He managed to grab a taxi by jumping the queue with
the help of a British fifty-pound note. The drive through
the city set his teeth on edge. The heat, the crowded streets,
the knowledge that he had taken a chance and come here
directly from Rahman, instead of checking out San
Estéban, all helping to play on his stress levels. So, by the
time he passed through the gates of the Herakleides mansion, he was beginning to regret this madly impulsive decision to chase after Eve.

The taxi pulled to a halt in front of a stone-fronted residence built to emulate Greek classicism at its most grand.
A maid opened the door to him, smiled in recognition of
the times he had been here before. When he asked to see
Eve, she offered to take his suit bag from him then directed
him towards the garden at the rear of the house.

His heart began to pump with the adrenaline rush of
relief because he now knew his instincts had not let him
down and he had been right to miss out San Estéban to
come straight here.

It was mid-afternoon and as he stepped out onto the
wide stone-flagged terrace the air was just taking on the
warm golden glow that reminded him of the Caribbean.
Striding forward he paused at the head of a set of wide
shallow steps which led down into the garden. Standing
on a hill as the house did, the garden itself sloped away
from him in a riot of summer colour, so from up here he
should easily be able to pick out Eve.

He did so immediately. It would have been impossible
not to do when she was wearing a hot-pink stretchy top
with a short lavender skirt. She stood out in this garden of
colour like the most exotic flower ever created. As his
heart began to pound in response to wrapping all of that

vivid colour to him and never letting go of it again, he saw her move, realised that she wasn't alone, realised that she was also standing in the exact same spot he had seen her standing the last time he'd seen her here—and locked in the arms of the same man.

Aidan Galloway—she was locked in the arms of Aidan Galloway! Lightning was striking twice again, using a burning blast of cynical reality to hit him full in the face.

Aidan Galloway. It was a joke. He almost laughed. Only he didn't feel like laughing. Turn, he told himself. Leave, he told himself. Get away from here before she sees you and knows what a bloody fool you've made of yourself.

'Oh, Aidan,' Eve sobbed into his shoulder. 'I've made such a fool of myself!'

'Join the club,' Aidan said.

'He isn't going to come, and I've left this stupid message on his machine...'

'Now it's playing over and over in your head. I know.' Aidan sighed. 'Been there, done that, felt the agony.'

'I hate Ethan Hayes.' She sobbed into his shoulder.

'I wish I could learn to hate Corin,' Aidan murmured wistfully.

'Oh.' Eve touched his cheek. 'Is she still—?'

'Yes.'

Eve playing Eve, Ethan observed bitterly, as he watched her lift up her head and gaze into Galloway's eyes.

He felt his muscles go into violent spasm, as a need to go down there and commit murder swelled in his chest. He was about to take his first step towards assuaging that desire when a hand touched him on the shoulder, making him spin round and almost explode all that violence on Theron Herakleides instead.

'Come back inside, Mr Hayes,' Eve's grandfather said quietly.

'That's Aidan Galloway she's with,' he heard himself murmur hoarsely.

'Yes, I know it is.' Theron's steely head nodded. 'But angry men do not confront weaker men. So come inside,' he repeated the invitation. 'I have a matter I would like to discuss with you.'

Business, Ethan surmised, and shrugged the older man's hand from his shoulder. 'Keep your business proposals for someone else,' he said. He had taken enough from other people trying to direct his life. 'I'm leaving.' And he turned to stride back into the house.

Theron followed. 'Take care, Mr Hayes, what you say right now,' he quietly advised. 'For a man can still be chased through the courts here in Greece, for jilting his betrothed...'

There were several words used in that comment that stirred Ethan's blood. Jilting, was one of them, he chose to challenge another one. 'There was no betrothal,' he coldly denied. It was all just an elaborate sham thought up by the manipulating witch wearing hot-pink.

'How many witnesses do you think will I find in San Estéban who would be willing to swear the opposite to that?'

Ethan stopped walking, turned and looked at Eve's grandfather, aware that there was still more to come.

'Ah,' Theron said. 'I see you understand me. Then we will go in here and continue to discuss the small matter of a settlement...'

With that, Theron opened the door to his study and walked inside. After a small hesitation, Ethan followed him with the word settlement ringing warning bells in his head.

Theron's study was furnished to suit the man's big persona. Heavy furniture filled the floor space, heavy-framed portraits adorned the walls.

'So,' the big man began as he slotted himself behind his heavy oak desk. 'Did you really think that you could send my granddaughter back to me like used and broken goods without paying a heavy price?'

Broken. That word made Ethan release a hard mocking laugh. There had been nothing broken about the woman he'd seen wrapped in the arms of another man. 'Ask Aidan Galloway to pay the price,' he suggested. 'He has the money. You'll struggle to get a penny out of me.'

'Eve loves you.'

'Hell, damn it!' Ethan suddenly exploded spectacularly. 'Open your eyes, Theron! Eve only loves the thrill of the chase!'

Through the fine silk drapes covering the opened French window of her grandfather's study, Eve heard the deep rasping tones of Ethan's voice, froze for a split second, then spun around to stare at the house.

'Be assured that Aidan Galloway is more than willing to take your place tonight,' Theron smoothly replied. 'Oh, yes,' he confirmed at Ethan's sudden stillness. 'Eve's betrothal celebration will take place tonight whether or not it is you standing at her side. Eve is resigned to this. You've broken her heart, now she cares not about the man who will next share her bed.'

The words were used as well-aimed bullets that sank themselves deep into Ethan's head. Was that what Eve was doing out there—seducing Aidan Galloway to take his place? More bells began ringing, a red tide of anger came flooding in. He was very intimate with Eve's powers of persuasion. He knew only too well what it was like to fall into her sticky web.

'What do you want from me, Theron?' he demanded grimly.

'I want you to honour those promises you made to me in the Caribbean,' the big man said.

'I'll talk to her.' It was Ethan's only concession, though he was planning to do a lot more than just talk to Eve when he could get his hands on her. She played with men's feelings. She walked all over their self-respect. She made love like a natural-born seducer and he was damned if any other man was going to know how good that felt.

'Not without the right,' Theron smoothly said.

Ethan glared at him. 'Explain,' he insisted.

Theron went one better and slid several documents across the top of his desk. 'You know the score. Sign, and you can talk to my granddaughter. Don't sign, and you can leave her to Aidan Galloway's adequate care.'

Ah, Ethan thought. The contract to protect Theron's precious money. He almost laughed in the old man's face as he stepped up to the desk, picked up Theron's handy pen, and scrawled his signature in the allotted space.

'Now, if you will excuse me,' he concluded coldly.

'Don't you think you should have read what it is you've just put your signature to? It is an unwise man who signs a document without first ensuring himself that he has not just signed his entire wealth away.'

Wealth, Ethan thought. 'What wealth?' he mocked. His wealth stood outside in the arms of another man.

His wealth, his woman—hell, he was right back on track again; he felt so much better for realising that.

'You're a liar, Hayes,' Theron inserted, then suddenly let rip with a hearty laugh. 'Do you think I would let you seduce my granddaughter into marriage without having you thoroughly checked out? You are a Caledonian Hayes of the merchant shipping line. Your grandfather sold up in the sixties and died in the eighties, leaving you so much money you could even afford to buy me out!'

'Ah—my credentials,' Ethan acknowledged and the depth of his cynicism played havoc with his face. 'How long have you been planning this?' he demanded.

'Marrying you to my granddaughter? Two weeks ago you became worthy of consideration when my nephew, Leandros, let slip how much money you had invested in San Estéban,' Theron replied. 'A mere architect, no matter how gifted he is, could not earn that kind of money in a hundred years. I have an instinct for these things.' With a smugness that said he was enjoying himself, Theron touched a finger to the end of his nose. 'The nose twitched. So I decided to have you checked out for curiosity sake, you understand. And for Eve's sake, of course.'

Glancing down at the document he had just put his signature to, Ethan began to wonder what he had signed away. 'It won't do you any good,' he announced. 'I live off my earned income. Any money my grandfather left me is tied up in trusts for any children I might have.'

'Or my grandchildren.' Theron nodded. 'Exactly.'

So that was what this was all about. 'Eve is up for sale to the man with the biggest return.'

From sitting there wallowing in his own self-satisfied smugness, Theron was suddenly launching to his feet in a towering rage. 'Don't speak about Eve in that tone!' he bellowed. 'It is okay for you with your hidden millions to stand here mocking me whose wealth is well documented. But place yourself in Eve's shoes and tell me how *she* distinguishes between the man who will love her for herself and the one with love only for the money she will inherit one day!'

'So you think that by finding her a husband who is wealthier than herself, you are safeguarding her against disillusionment and a broken heart?' Ethan's tone poured contempt all over that concept as his own fury rose to match the older man's. 'Money in the bank is no guarantee for love, Theron!' he bit out furiously. 'It's just—money in the bank! I am as capable as the next man is of breaking her foolish, reckless heart!'

'If you were the kind of man to do that, you would not be standing here arguing with me about this!'

'She already thinks I'm in love with another woman!' he threw at Theron. 'Are you telling me that your investigation of me did not tell you that?'

'If it didn't, he knows now,' another quieter, heart-piercingly level voice inserted.

CHAPTER EIGHTEEN

BOTH men stiffened sharply, both turned to stare at the silk-draped window where Eve now stood. Both men went as pale as death.

'Eve, that wasn't said to—'

The flick of a hand silenced him; the expression on her face tore him apart. She was hurting, he was hurting. Ethan didn't even want to know what Theron was feeling like. Big, green how-could-you-both-hurt-me-like-this eyes flicked from one man to the other. She took in a breath of air. It seemed to pull all of the oxygen out of the room and left none for them to breathe.

Pale but composed, feeling as fragile as a lily about to snap in the soft warm breeze, Eve took a small step to bring herself into the very male-orientated surroundings of her grandfather's study, and announced. 'If you've both finished playing Russian roulette with my future. I would like to point out that women gained the right to choose for themselves some time during the last century.'

'You break my heart, child,' her grandpa told her painfully. 'I would be failing in my duty to you if I did not make this man formally declare his intentions.'

'He doesn't have any intentions!' Eve slashed at him.

'Yes, I do,' Ethan argued.

She turned on him, eyes burning like phosphorescence as they fixed themselves onto his. His chest swelled, his heart began to pump, other parts of him began to send taunting little signals out across his skin. She was waiting

178

to hear more. More was coming, if he could only get past the sight of her in Galloway's arms.

'Will you marry me, Eve?' There, he'd said it.

'Oh.' She choked, and her eyes filled with tears. 'How could you let him browbeat you into saying that?'

'I didn't.' He was shocked.

'I'll never forgive you for this—never.' She sobbed, turned and ran outside leaving Ethan staring after her in thundering dismay!

'I would go after her if I were you,' Theron smoothly advised while calmly reading the contract Ethan had just signed.

On an act of sheer frustration Ethan snatched the document out of Theron's hands. 'I am sick and tired of other people meddling in my life!' he announced, then turned and walked out of the study—by the conventional route of the door through to the hallway.

Outside he was a mass of offended dignity. Inside he was bubbling with angry offence at the way Eve had rejected him. He'd had enough. Eve was impossible. He was happy to let Aidan Galloway have her. He strode down the hallway with every intention of leaving this house and never stepping foot in it again.

As he crossed the foot of the stairs, he heard a door on the upper landing shut. His feet came to a stop. Bubbling offence had changed to something else entirely, and he knew he wasn't going anywhere but up those stairs to open her shut door.

On a lethal curse, he changed direction. As he took the stairs, two at a time, he had even reached the point of asking how he thought he could walk away, when he could feel that lead still attached to his neck.

She tugged, he went where it pulled him.

Eve stood in the middle of her bedroom and shook from

fingers to toes. She couldn't believe he'd said that. She couldn't believe she'd actually looked her dearest in the face then had turned and had walked away from it!

How could he—how *could* he stand there in her grandfather's study wheeling and dealing her life away? He was just like Grandpa: money orientated, power orientated! If she had any sense left she would get out of here. She would disappear somewhere so remote that she would never be found! She hated men—all men. Young, old, they were all the same: arrogant self-obsessed bullies who liked to think they were in control of everything.

The bedroom door suddenly flew open. She spun round to find Ethan standing there. 'If you've come to offer another proposal of marriage then don't bother!' she snapped.

'You will have to get down on your knees to get another one of those out of me,' Ethan grimly returned.

Her knees tried to buckle. Eve felt like screaming. He looked lean and hard, and tough and angry; the bitter expression on his face was spoiling its handsome lines. She liked it. It meant he was hurting. If he was hurting then it had to be because of her—didn't it?

'Then what do you want?' she demanded coldly.

'You,' he said, 'to explain to me what the hell were you doing wrapped in Galloway's arms the moment my back was turned!'

The door slammed shut. Eve's eyes began to fire. 'What were *you* doing leaving me to go to *her*, just because she crooked her little finger at you?' she countered furiously.

Eve folded her arms across her front. Ethan leaned back against the door and did the same. Stalemate. They'd been here before. Excitement began to fizz in the air. Green eyes flashed with it; grey glinted with it. She wanted to go over there and kiss him stupid.

'It was hell,' he pronounced. 'I didn't have any idea how

rife the rumours were until I saw the way my arrival was received. I half expected to die the death of a thousand cuts!' He released a short laugh.

'You are still in love with her,' she tossed at him in pained accusation.

'No, I am not,' he tossed right back. 'I am in love with you—God help me!'

'Oh,' she said.

'Yes,' he agreed in grim, tight mockery.

'Then you shouldn't have gone!'

'You should have come. You would have enjoyed the spectacle.'

'You should have invited me.'

'If you hadn't been so pig-stubborn, I probably would have done.'

'Oh,' she said again, and silence settled.

Eve wanted to fill it by throwing herself into his arms and kissing her way back into his good graces. Ethan wanted to fill it by throwing her on that bed he could see across the room and loving her absolutely senseless.

Instead they both looked at the papers he held in his hand. Eve recognised them for what they were; resentment began to flare again.

'Rip it up,' she told him.

'Why?' he asked. 'He's only got me to sign my life away.'

'I don't want your money.'

'I didn't say money, I said life!' He flashed her a hard look. 'Are you telling me you don't want that, either?'

Her chin went up. Two steps and she was snatching the contract from him just as he had snatched it from Theron.

Eve ripped it up. She tossed it to the ground. She placed hands on hips and waited for his eyes to move up from the torn contract to her provocative pose, to her mouth which was wearing its angry pout, and finally to her eyes shot through with challenge. 'Okay,' she announced. 'I'll take your life.'

Ethan reached out, pulled her hard up against him then kissed her... Why not? It was what they both needed. Eve didn't so much as attempt to pull away.

'Now, tell me why were you kissing Aidan Galloway,' he murmured some very satisfying seconds later.

'I wasn't kissing him,' Eve denied. 'I was sobbing on his shoulder because you weren't here and I wanted you to be.'

Ethan brought up a finger to gently touch the corner of her kiss-trembling mouth. 'And the last time I saw you with him like that?' he probed. 'You weren't sobbing then.'

'You misread what you saw that night,' she explained, slid out her tongue and licked his finger and watched as his eyes grew darker in response. 'Aidan had just seen Corin wrapped in a heated clinch with his cousin. They were childhood sweethearts; he's adored her all of his life. He was devastated, I was comforting him when I heard them coming towards us, and I just reacted by kissing Aidan to give Corin a taste of her own nasty medicine.'

'Impulsive as usual.' He sighed.

'Well, you should know.' She flashed. 'When I realised you'd seen us, I knew what you would be thinking. So as soon as I could safely leave Aidan, I *impulsively* went to your room to explain. Only...'

'You found me standing there stark-naked, and decided it was more fun to stare me into embarrassing myself?'

'If that's what you like to think.' She wasn't taking the bait. Instead she caught hold of his finger then fed it across the surface of his own mouth. Already moistened by the tip of her tongue the finger left a film of moisture on his lips.

He licked it off. Sex was suddenly alive in the air. 'You can't control yourself around me,' she informed him smugly, 'which is why you made sure you kept your distance from then on.'

His own hand came to remove her teasing finger. 'You tease and flirt without conscience,' he condemned.

'Your fault,' she blamed. 'The more you disapproved of me the more outrageous I became.'

'Dangerous is the word that comes to my mind.'

He was referring to Raoul Delacroix, Eve realised. It altered the mood so abruptly that Ethan gave a sigh of regret when she withdrew right away from him then walked over to stare out of the bedroom window with her arms crossed over her body in a gesture he recognised as Eve needing to protect Eve.

He followed, unwrapped her arms and replaced them with his own. 'I'm sorry,' he said. 'I didn't mean to resurrect bad memories.'

'I've known Raoul almost all of my life,' she murmured. 'We—all the crowd on the island have been meeting up for holidays there since we were small children. Flirting and teasing was part of the group culture but no one ever took it further than that.'

'But he decided to.'

'We hadn't seen him for a couple of years,' she explained. 'When he came back to the island this summer, he'd changed. We all noticed it, wondered why, but Raoul refused to talk about it. So we drew our own conclusions and decided it had to be a failed love affair or a fall-out with his brother, André, for whom he'd always nurtured a resentment. But never in my wild imaginings did I think he had changed so much that he was capable of pulling something like that.'

'Forget it, it's over.'

'But maybe it was my fault. Maybe I did lead him on.'

'You know that isn't true, so we aren't getting into that,' Ethan said firmly.

Eve pressed back against him and said no more. Beyond the window she watched her grandfather's car taking off down the driveway. The roof was folded away so she could see Aidan sitting next to him. They would be going to a local café where they would drink coffee while Aidan told her grandfather all his woes, and her grandfather would relay wise advice, previously discussed and decided upon with Aidan's older brother, Patrick. It was how it had always worked since Eve had lost her parents and Aidan had lost his in the same car accident, leaving Grandpa to play the role of wise counsellor to both families. Strange really, she mused. But, thinking about it, Raoul had shown signs of resentment to that closeness too.

'Where's your ring?'

Glancing down, she realised that her hands were lost in the clasp of his and his thumb was stroking her naked ring finger in much the same way as her own had been doing every since she'd taken the ring off.

'Tigger has it,' she said.

'And where is Tigger?'

'In my dressing room with his friends.' She went to move. 'Do you want me to go and—?'

'No.' He stopped her. 'We haven't finished here yet.'

'Finished what?' Foolishly she turned in his arms to face him—foolishly, because she should have guessed what was coming, but didn't; so his kiss when it arrived took her breath away.

It was fierce and it was greedy. It brought her hands

around his neck and placed his hands on her hip-bones so he could pull her close. She came alive for the first time in too many days to dare think about.

He whispered something into her mouth. 'Marry me,' he said.

'I'm not on my knees.'

'You can go there later. Just say yes.'

'Yes,' she said.

Ethan released a soft laugh. 'Now tell me you love me.' He was going for broke here.

'I love you,' she softly complied.

After that, things moved on a pace. They found the bed, they lost their clothes, Ethan found his little red-painted heart. 'We shouldn't be doing this here,' he thought to remark when it was already way too late. 'This is your grandfather's house. It shows a lack of respect.'

'I don't recall you being so sensitive when you seduced me in Victor Frayne's house,' Eve pointed out.

It more or less put the lid on his conscience so that he could sink himself into what he had started.

Later, much later, they lay in a tangle of satiated limbs. 'You do know I love you to distraction, don't you?' he told her solemnly. 'Leona was—' He stopped, then started the same sentence from a different place. 'I think I only ever loved the idea of loving someone like Leona.' He thought that said it best. 'But in Rahman, when I looked at her, I couldn't even see her face because your beautiful face insisted on imprinting itself over the top of hers. No, don't cry.'

'I'm not crying.' But there were tears in her beautiful eyes, nonetheless. 'I just needed you to say that.'

It cut him to the quick—which he knew he deserved. 'I'm sorry I didn't say it a long time ago.'

She wound her arms around him; he drew her close.

They sighed together as their mouths joined. No complicating sex this time, just love and caring and—'

'Get dressed,' he decided suddenly.

'Why?' she protested. Eve was perfectly happy where she was.

'We are going to play the rest of this relationship by the book. So we get dressed, then we will go out and find you something amazing to wear in hot-pink for our official betrothal tonight. Then we get married—next week,' he added as a frowning afterthought. 'Because I don't think we can behave ourselves for longer than that.'

'You won't last a week,' Eve informed him a short ten minutes later as they left her room and his hand was already checking out the smooth line of her bottom.

'I suppose you are going to make it your mission to prove yourself right.'

'Oh, yes,' she said airily. 'I love a good challenge.'

She won, but then she usually did. Eve the flirt, Eve the temptress, went to her marriage bed every night that week.

THE ARABIAN
LOVE-CHILD

MICHELLE REID

CHAPTER ONE

RAFIQ AL-QADIM climbed out of the back of a chauffeur-driven limousine and strode through the plate-glass doors that guarded the International Bank of Rahman. In the clenched fist of one hand he held a rolled-up newspaper, in his eyes glowed a look that foretold of hell to pay for some poor fool. Hurrying behind him, his newly appointed aide, Kadir Al-Kadir, was wearing an expression that suggested he might be that very unfortunate person.

As Rafiq struck a direct line for the row of steel lifts set into a wall of grey marble, people in his path took one look at him and began backing away to give the big man an uninterrupted passage to his target. He didn't notice; he was too consumed by the blinding fury that carried his intimidating six-foot-four-inch frame into the nearest vacant lift. A dark-suited arm shot out; a decidedly murderous finger stabbed at the button for the top floor. The lift doors shut out Kadir Al-Kadir and the sea of stunned faces. No one who'd had any dealings with Rafiq Al-Qadim had ever seen him appear anything but formidably controlled.

But he was not in control. Rafiq had never been so angry. Rage was literally bouncing inside him, fighting to get out and vent itself. The lift took less than fifteen seconds to reach its destination. The doors opened; he strode out. Nadia, his secretary, took one look at his face, paled and shot to her feet.

'Good morning, sir,' she greeted warily. 'There have been several messages for you and your first appointment arrives in—'

'No calls. Nothing.' He cut right across her and kept on walking, each of his powerfully constructed, sleekly toned muscles moving him with stallion-like grace to behind his office door, leaving Nadia staring after him in a state of near shock, for she too had never known Mr Rafiq to be anything but staunchly even-tempered and rigidly polite.

Rafiq's private office was a statement in architectural drama. High ceilings, marble floors, a window that was a wall of glass, in front of which a large slab of grey marble rested on legs of forged steel. As he moved across to it the pale sunlight of a London winter morning shot shards of cold steel through his black hair and added a sharpened cast to his lean dark profile that spoke of his ruthless Arab heritage.

Stepping around the edges of the slab of marble, he slammed the newspaper down on its smooth grey top. It unfurled on impact, showing him the inner-page headline that his aide had helpfully presented to him. It was Kadir's job to scour the world's newspapers, his job to mark those items he believed would be of interest to the acting head of the International Bank of Rahman. But Kadir would not be making the same mistake again very quickly, Rafiq mused as he glared at the reason for all of his anger. He had been duped, he'd been betrayed, he had been taken for a fool by a woman. And there it was, splashed all over the page of a Spanish tabloid: his private life uncovered, picked over and mocked at.

'SHOCK ANNOUNCEMENT,' block capitals proclaimed. 'SERENA CORDERO DROPS BILLIONAIRE SHEIKH TO MARRY HER DANCE PARTNER, CARLOS MONTEZ.'

His skin began prickling against his clothing, sharp white teeth setting behind the grim line of his mouth. Only two months ago she had been clinging to him like a limpet, adoring him, begging him, telling him she could never love anyone else.

The liar, the cheat, the unfaithful little slut. As far back as six months ago his brother Hassan had warned him about Serena and Carlos Montez. Rafiq had dismissed those rumours as mere publicity to add spice to the current world tour the two flamenco dancers were embarked upon. Now he knew the truth and he could taste the bitterness of his own conceit and arrogance at having believed that Serena could not have wanted another man while she could have had him. Only twice before in his life had he ever been betrayed by a woman: once by his mother, and once by the only woman he had ever let himself love. After that last bitter experience he had vowed he would never be betrayed like that again.

Yet here he stood, pulled into the betrayal trap by yet another woman, and he was so angry he could spit nails into the half-page picture of the beautiful Serena, smiling into her new husband's handsome face.

His mobile phone began to ring; dragging it out of his pocket he put it to his ear.

'*Querida*, please don't hang up. I need you to listen to me!'

His face, like his height and the tough, muscled build of his body, made no compromises at the best of times but the low dark sensual tones that hit his ear made his face take on properties as cold as the marble and steel that surrounded him.

'The tour is in trouble. We needed a sensation to put our names on people's lips. I love you, Rafiq. You know I do. But marriage between us was never a possibility. Can you not accept this situation for what it is?'

'You are someone else's wife. Do not call me again,' he incised, and broke the connection before tossing the phone from him as if it was contaminated.

Silence arrived, buzzing in his ears like a thousand wasp wings. In front of him lay the discarded phone and the damning newspaper. Behind him lay the rest of the world who would now be laughing at him. He was an Arab in every way you wished to look at him. Make an Arab look a fool and you win yourself a life-long enemy.

Eyes like black opals turned almost silver at the prospect. Picking up the newspaper, he flung it sideways and watched as it landed in the waste-paper bin. Serena Cordero's name would never reach his eyes again, he vowed as the other telephone sitting on his desk dared to start ringing. Black opals fired as a hand snaked down and long fingers closed round grey plastic as if it was someone's throat. 'I thought I said no calls!' he bit into the mouthpiece.

'By your tone I presume you have seen the news today,' a very dry voice drawled into his ear.

His half-brother, Hassan. He should have expected it. He swung himself down into his black leather desk chair. 'If you have called me to say I told you so, then take my advice and try silence,' Rafiq returned grimly.

'May I commiserate?' Hassan wryly suggested.

'You may mind your own business,' he snapped, then added tautly, 'Does our father know?'

'You think we swap gossip about your love life?'

'I don't have a love life,' Rafiq hit back with bite. This had been part of the problem with Serena. Finding a time when their busy schedules came to together had been almost impossible. If he had seen her twice in the last few months he could well be exaggerating, for while Serena had been travelling the world in one direction with her flamenco dance troupe he had been travelling in the other direction, attending to business duties that usually belonged to Hassan.

'How is Father?' he enquired as one thought led to another.

'He is well,' his brother assured him. 'His blood count is good and his spirit is high. Don't worry about him, Rafiq,' Hassan added gently. 'He means to meet his first grandchild, believe me.'

This time Rafiq's sigh was heavy. The last six months had been a trial for all of them. The old sheikh's illness had been long and miserable, spanning years of waste and pain. But six months ago it had almost taken him from them. With thanks to Allah, he had rallied on hearing the news about his coming grandchild. Now the disease was in remission, but no one could say how long it would remain that way. So it had been decided that from then on one of the two brothers must always be at home with their father. He needed the comfort of their presence. *They* needed to know that one of them would be there if his new-found strength should suddenly fade again. With Hassan's wife Leona in the latter stages of a much prayed for pregnancy, Hassan had elected to stay at home and deal with internal matters of state while Rafiq did all the travelling, taking care of the family's international business interests.

'And Leona?' he enquired next.

'Round,' her husband drawled satirically. But Rafiq could hear the pleasure there, the love and the pride. He wished he knew what those things felt like.

Then, he told himself forcefully, no, he was not going to go down that particularly rocky pathway, and turned the conversation to the less volatile subject of business. But when he rang off he continued to sit there seething and brooding and contrarily wondering why it was that he was so angry.

He had never loved Serena. She had been speaking the truth when she'd said marriage between them had never been a possibility. She was beautiful and hot—the perfect bed partner, in fact—but love had never been the engine that drove them through the passages of pleasure, even if she'd liked to use the word to him. It had been sex, good sex, but just sex for both of them. And sitting here wishing for love like his brother had was a damn fool's game.

But the small lecture brought him to his feet and sent him to stand staring out of the window. He was remembering a time when he had once thought he had found the kind of love Hassan was enjoying—had believed he held it in his hand like a precious diamond only to discover it was merely paste. Since then he had never looked for love;

he had no wish to feel its tortuous grip again, harboured no burning desire to pass on his genetic fingerprint. That delight belonged to Hassan and Leona, both of whom were worthy candidates to make the successful genetic mix. Whereas he…

That muscle within his chest called a heart gave a squeeze and he grimaced at the sensation. Alone. The sensation spoke to him of a bleak dark sense of aloneness that made him envy all of those people he could see moving about in the street below because they probably had good wholesome relationships to go home to at night, while he—

Well, he stood up here in his marble tower, personifying the rich and powerful and enviously privileged, when sometimes, like now, he felt as poor as any beggar you might pick out on any street corner—emotionally anyway.

Serena's fault? No, not Serena but that other woman, the one with hair with the same golden sheen he could see on the woman standing in the street below. Melanie had ruined him. With a calculation that belied her beauty, her shyness and innocence, she had taken a younger Rafiq, full of confidence and optimism, and had turned him into this hardened cynic he was today.

Where was she now? he found himself pondering sombrely. What had the last eight years done for Melanie? Did she ever think of him and what their affair had done to him? Or had she simply moved on, left him so far behind that she would struggle to remember his name if they had the misfortune to come up against each other again? He guessed the latter—he *knew* the latter. Melanie might have possessed the face of an angel but she owned the heart of a harlot. Harlots did not remember names; one merged in with the many.

Behind him his mobile phone burst into life again. It would be that other harlot, Serena, he decided. She was not the kind of woman to give up easily. Did he answer? Did he leave it? Had he dropped down so low in his own estimation that he was actually asking himself those questions? His teeth came together, gleaming white against the satin darkness of his olive-toned skin as he let the phone ring and glared down at the street where the woman with the golden hair was still hovering, as if she was unsure what she was doing or where she was going. He understood the feeling, could even sympathise with it.

In fact, the golden-haired stranger had more chance of getting him to answer her call than Serena did, was his final thought on the subject of female betrayal.

Standing on the pavement outside the imposing marble, glass and forged-steel frontage of the International Bank of Rahman, Melanie tried very hard to convince herself that she was doing the right thing by coming here. The building was big, and it was bold; it spoke of no compromises when she knew she desperately needed many compromises if her plan was to succeed.

Could it succeed? Was she wasting her time by coming here to see a man she knew from experience held no respect for her at all? Remember what he said, remember what he did, a small voice in her head cautioned. Turn around, Melanie, and walk away.

But walking away was the easy option. And easy options had never come to her. It was either do this or go home and tell Robbie nothing, she determined. And if those two options were not the same as being caught between a rock and a hard place, then she didn't know what was.

So, think of Robbie, she told herself firmly, and set her reluctant feet moving towards a giant pair of plate-glass doors reinforced by solid-steel tubing that defended the entrance to one of the most prestigious investment banks in the world. As she approached she glimpsed her own reflection in the polished glass doors and didn't much like what she saw: a too-slender woman with pale hair caught into a neat little topknot and an even paler complexion touched by strain. Her eyes looked too big, her mouth too vulnerable. Overall she looked just too darn fragile to be taking on an arrogant giant like Rafiq Al-Qadim. He'll step on you and not even notice, she warned her reflection. He'll do what he did to you the last time and freeze you out with his black opal stare.

No, he won't because you just won't let him, she told herself forcefully, and kept her feet moving as the pair of doors slid open with a stealthy silence that made her insides curl.

Like its exterior, the International Bank of Rahman's inside was a cavern of more glass, marble and steel. Glass walls for three floors gave her glimpses of open-plan office spaces flickering with busy computer screens and even busier people. Here in the foyer a marble fountain pushed moisture into the air while tall exotic plants tried and failed to soften the cold, cold atmosphere. People wearing statutory grey or black moved about with the confidence of those who knew exactly what they were doing here and where they were going.

It was sharp, it was sophisticated—it was everything she wasn't. A point that would have made her smile at any other time, because she knew who she was and she liked that person. The cut-throat world of high finance held no fascination for her. Never had, never would. But as she stood looking around she was forced to accept the grim truth that, hate all this though she might do, she had still dressed for the occasion in a sharp black suit that blended in perfectly here.

Deliberate? Yes, it had been deliberate. She answered her own question as her high-heeled shoes took her across the busy foyer towards the line of steel-faced lifts. She had dressed to impress, to make him stop and think twice before he tried throwing her out again. Melanie Leggett in jeans had never managed to do that, but Melanie Portreath in a designer suit might.

A stainless-steel plaque set between two of the lifts

listed the names of the departments and the floor on which each was situated. She hovered for a moment or two, unsure as to which department she should be making for, then realised that it could only be on the top floor, because high-powered executives liked to keep their minions firmly beneath them.

As she should know, having been there once upon a long time ago. She'd played the worshipping minion to a superior ego and had learned the hard way what it was like be walked all over. It wasn't the best memory she could have picked to take with her into the lift, Melanie realised as her heart began to pump unevenly. Pressing the top-floor button, she barely felt the lift move it was so efficient, so nerves were putting that sinking feeling in her stomach, she determined. Nerves and just the teeniest hint of excitement about what she was about to do.

Face the truth, an eight-year-old truth, a dark and potentially dangerous truth. The lift doors opened, her knees began to shake as she stepped out into yet another foyer; this one was much smaller and bore the refined trappings of luxury in the soft carpet covering the floor. A steel-framed desk stood in front of a floor-to-ceiling stretch of glass covered by vertical blinds. A dark-haired woman sat working at the desk. She glanced up at Melanie's approach, came to her feet and smiled.

'Mrs Portreath? How nice to meet you.' Her voice, like her smile, was warm and pleasant, the slight accent falling in with her dark and gentle Arabian looks. Coming out from behind her workstation, she presented Melanie with a hand. 'My name is Nadia,' she announced. 'I am Mr Al-Qadim's secretary. I am afraid Mr Al-Qadim is running a little late this morning,' she went on apologetically. 'And the information your lawyer sent ahead of you arrived on my desk only five minutes ago. Please...' she indicated towards several soft-leather chairs '...make yourself comfortable while I check if Mr Al-Qadim is ready for you.'

Not for me, he isn't, Melanie thought as she watched

Nadia walk towards another giant pair of doors, made of solid wood this time. The secretary paused, seeming to need a moment to gather herself before she knocked rather tentatively on the door, opened it, stepped through and closed it behind her.

That small hesitation left Melanie standing there having to deal with the next rush of uncertainty that attacked her resolve. Rafiq was on the other side of that door, and if his secretary had to steel herself to go anywhere near him then what chance did she have of meeting a sane and sensible man?

Arrogance; she was suddenly remembering the hardened arrogance that could add such cold condemnation to his lean face. He was a man who could freeze out the world by just standing in silence, a man who could shatter a person with just two small words: 'Get out.'

Her stomach muscles collapsed on the crippling memory. In the space of six short weeks he had wooed her into loving him. He had asked her to marry him and promised her the earth. He had told her that no one could ever love her as much as he did, then he had taken her to bed and wooed her of her innocence. Then, on the evidence of one cleverly constructed scene, he had simply turned his back on her with those now immortal words, 'Get out,' and had never looked at her again.

Did she really want to subject herself to that kind of humiliation again? she asked herself. Was she crazy to risk exposing Robbie to the same?

The urge to change her mind and just walk away while she still had the chance rose up to grab at her again; panic of the sort she hadn't experienced in a long time actually set her feet swivelling towards escape.

The door behind her opened. 'Mrs Portreath?' his secretary's smooth voice prompted.

Melanie froze—utterly. She couldn't move, not a muscle; she couldn't even bring herself to draw in breath. It was awful. For a horrible moment she wondered if she was going to faint.

'Mrs Portreath…?'

Remember why you are doing this, she tried telling herself. Think of Robbie. He loves you and he's suffering right now, feeling the vulnerability of his own mortality and, more significantly, yours. Rafiq does not know what he turned his back on eight years ago. He deserves this chance to know about Robbie, just as Robbie deserves this chance to know him.

But she was scared of what it was going to mean to all of them. Rafiq was from a different race and culture. He viewed things through different eyes than she did. He might not want to know about Robbie. He might fling this chance right back at her and…

'Mrs Portreath? Mr Al-Qadim will see you now.'

Mr Al-Qadim will see you, she repeated anxiously. Did it matter if he did toss Robbie aside? It would be his loss if he did. Robbie never needed to know about this visit, but if you'd asked him outright, he would say it was worth any risk. So do this one small thing for him and you might start to sleep nights.

Small. She almost laughed, because this was no small thing. It was huge, colossal, as big and unpredictable as the big man himself.

'Get out' her head echoed. What did those two cold words do but expose a man who was unwilling to face up to *his* responsibilities? Let him use them again, she decided as her chin lifted. She could take the rejection for Robbie. She had done it before, after all. Her conscience could be cleared and she could then walk away to get on with the rest of her life, and more importantly Robbie's life, knowing she had at least tried.

'Yes, thank you,' she heard herself murmur, and by the time she turned to face Rafiq's secretary she was back in control again, with her eyes clear and her slender shoulders set into a determined line. One of the doors to the office stood open. Nadia stood to one side of it, waiting for Melanie to step by. With only the smallest increase in her pulse-rate she walked towards that open doorway and through it, with her smile fixed and ready to meet fate full-on.

The room was just another play on steel and marble. It was huge, with high ceilings and wall-to-wall glass that framed a desk built of marble and steel. In front of the desk and standing slightly side-on stood Rafiq Al-Qadim. He was wearing a dark grey suit and was leaning over slightly with one big hand braced on the desk while he read the set of papers in front of him.

Her papers, Melanie recognised. Her requirements. Her nerves began to flutter. Had he seen? Did he know yet? A clammy sweat broke out on her skin as she stood just inside the door and waited for him to lift and turn his dark head so she could make that first stunning impact on eyes that, even after eight long years, still visited her in her dreams.

Rafiq was being deliberately slow in straightening to acknowledge Mrs Portreath. He was wishing he hadn't agreed to this meeting. The woman might have inherited the Portreath fortune, but even her healthy millions were small fry to an investment bank like this. Randal Soames, the executor of the Portreath estate, had talked him into this interview. He was doing it as a favour to Randal because the woman herself was being so stubborn about wanting to use the services of the bank and, more significantly, she had insisted on seeing Rafiq. In his mind, if she'd managed to get the hard-edged Randal Soames to go against his own better judgement it made her one very manipulative woman.

He despised that kind of woman. Was learning to despise the whole female sex with each betrayal they hung upon him. If he had a choice he would have them all locked up in harems to use only when necessary. They called them the weaker sex, the vulnerable sex, when really they were stronger and more dangerous than a whole army of men.

'Mrs Portreath to see you, sir,' Nadia prompted. It was a brave thing to do when his secretary was already aware that his mood was about as volatile as an active volcano.

But it also meant that he had taken too long to lift up his head. So, gritting his teeth together behind the flat-lined set of his lips, he attempted to put some semblance of a smile on them as he straightened up and made himself turn to face the woman he was already predisposed to dislike.

What he found himself looking at shut his heart down. What he saw standing not fifteen feet away made him have to wonder if he was actually losing his mind. He could not believe it. He had conjured her up. Any second now two more women were going to walk through the door and stand right beside her: Serena and his mother. The three witches.

As that dark head lifted Melanie felt her breath begin to feather, felt her pulse begin to accelerate. He hadn't changed, was her first breathtaking observation. He still had the build of a Roman gladiator and a proud cut to his jaw line that warned of no weakness anywhere. His hair was still as black as midnight, his hands as big and strong as she remembered them to be. He could fill a room like this with his size and the sheer electrifying force of his presence.

Yet his height and his size and his deep inner reserve had somehow always made her be very gentle with him. Why was that? Melanie asked herself now as she stood facing her past with the puzzled mind of maturity. It wasn't as if he was a vulnerable giant. If anything, he had been cruel and heartless, utterly ruthless in his method of discarding her.

Her eyes took their time lifting to clash with his eyes. She was expecting to be frozen by cold disdain but what she found herself dealing with shook her to the core. For she was looking at Robbie's eyes, Robbie's beautiful, almost black eyes that were looking back at her with the same sensational long eyelashes that could turn her insides to soft, loving butter. And Robbie's wonderful high slashing cheekbones, Robbie's perfectly, perfectly moulded mouth.

And the beauty, dear God, she'd forgotten the masculine beauty in those lean dark high-born features that could flip her heart over and set her senses singing to the kind of tune she'd experienced with no other man. It hurt, oh, it hurt, because she was standing here staring love in the face again.

How could she not love, when she was seeing the man who had shaped her son's image? she thought despairingly. It was like looking into the future and seeing her beloved Robbie as he would be thirty years on: the height, the riveting dark features destined to breaks hearts just as his father's had done. Did that forecast worry her, or did it touch to life maternal pride, knowing she was in the process of rearing a heartbreaker for a son? She didn't know, couldn't think, didn't even know why she was rambling over such ridiculous things when there were far more important issues to consider.

But her insides were a mass of shakes and tremors, her eyes stinging with the onset of tears. Tears for a lost love, a broken and irreparable love. She didn't want to feel like this; she hurt as badly as if it was only yesterday that he'd thrown her out of his life.

A movement behind her caught her attention. Rafiq's secretary was hovering, probably wondering what was going on. Neither she nor Rafiq had moved or even spoken. Rafiq was frozen, his face held by a shock so profound it was clear that he was in no fit state to say a word.

Which left that mammoth task to her, Melanie realised. She'd planned this moment, spent hours rehearsing it in her head. All she had to do was find the strength and the will to put her plan into action. But it wasn't easy. She had come here believing that Rafiq had killed everything she used to feel for him. Now she knew that wasn't the case, she accepted, as she set her feet moving across a vast space of marble until she came to a stop just an arm's reach away from him.

She looked up—had to—he was six feet four inches, a towering figure in comparison to her five feet eight. It wasn't a bad height for a woman, but compared to Rafiq she felt like a pocket miniature. He had shoulders that were three times the size of her slender ones, hands that could easily span her waist. His torso was lean and cased in hard muscle, and his legs—

No, stop it, she told herself fiercely as things began to stir inside that she just did not want to feel. She lifted her eyes, made contact with the dark, dark disturbing density of his still shocked eyes that seemed to want to pull her like a magnet into taking another step closer.

She resisted the urge, held it back with a fist-grabbing catch of control. Then, with every bit of sophistication she had acquired over the past eight years, she murmured, 'Hello, Rafiq,' and even managed to hold out a surprisingly steady hand. 'It's been a long time, hasn't it?'

CHAPTER TWO

IT CAME as a punch to his stomach. The truth—reality. Melanie was standing here in front of him. No ghost, no spectre dragged up from the depths of his own bitter memory. The same spun-golden hair, darker gold eyes, creamy smooth skin covering perfect features; the same small, soft kiss-needy mouth and that soft-toned sensually pitched voice which brushed across his senses like a long-remembered lover's caress.

Yet in other ways it was not the same Melanie. The clothes didn't match, nor the way she styled her hair. The old Melanie had worn jeans and battered old trainers, not handmade leather shoes with spindles for heels and a slender black suit that shrieked the name of its designer label. Her hair used to stream around her face and shoulders, freely and simply like a child's, though then she had been a twenty-year-old woman.

'What are you doing here?' he rasped out without any attempt to hide his contempt.

'You're surprised.' She offered a wry smile. 'Maybe I should have prewarned you.'

The smile hit his system like burning poison, seared through his bloodstream on a path that had no right to gather in his loins. He shifted, ignored the hand. 'You would not have got beyond the ground-floor foyer,' he responded with a gritty truth that sent her hand sinking to her side.

It also wiped the smile from her face, and with it Rafiq felt the heat in his body begin to dissipate. She shifted uncomfortably—so did someone else. Dragging his eyes across his office, he saw his secretary standing by the door.

20

Fresh anger surged, a burning sense of bloody frustration, because this was the second time today that Nadia had witnessed him behaving like an ill-mannered boor.

'Thank you, Nadia.' He dismissed her with icy precision.

His secretary left in a hurry. Melanie turned to watch her go. Give it an hour and the whole building was going to know that Mr Rafiq was undergoing a drastic change in personality, he was thinking grimly as Melanie turned back to face him.

'She's afraid of you,' she dared to remark.

'The word you mean to use is respect,' he corrected. 'But, in truth, your opinion of my staff does not interest me. I prefer to know how you dare to think you can safely walk in here masquerading as someone you most definitely are not.'

Eyes that reflected the winter pale sunlight streaming in through the window, widened. 'Oh, I'm sorry, Rafiq. I thought you knew who I was. Didn't you receive the papers from my lawyer's office?'

Since those very papers were lying on his desk in front of both of them, it was sarcasm at its infuriating best. But it also made its point. Rafiq's eyes narrowed. 'You mean you actually are the Melanie Portreath who inherited the Portreath fortune?' he demanded in disbelief.

'Don't sound so shocked,' Melanie responded dryly. 'Even poor little country girls can have a lucky change in fortune occasionally.'

'Marry it, you mean.'

The moment he'd said it Rafiq could have bitten his tongue off. It was hard and it was bitter and gave the impression that he might actually still care that she'd been seduced by his wealth.

'If you say so,' she murmured, and turned away to take an interest in her surroundings. As she did so he caught the delicate shape of her profile and felt something painful tug at his chest. Damn it, he thought. Don't do that to me.

'This place is as cold as a mausoleum,' she told him.

She was right, and it was. Leona was always telling him the same thing. His half-brother Hassan's office, which was next door to this one, had received a full makeover by Leona's gifted hand to make it more hospitable. But Rafiq refused to let her anywhere near his office because— because he liked mausoleums, having placed his life in one, he accepted with an inner sigh.

Maybe Melanie knew what he was thinking, because she turned suddenly and their eyes clashed again, golden light touching bleak darkness, and the years were falling away. She had once told him that he was incapable of feeling anything deeply, that his big test in life was to learn to trust his own feelings instead of deferring those judgements to others. 'You'll end up a cold and lonely cynic, Rafiq,' she'd predicted. 'Living on the fringes of real life.'

'What do you want, Melanie?' he demanded grimly.

'To sit down would be nice.'

'You will not be stopping long enough to warrant it.'

'It would be to your loss.'

'The door is over there,' he drawled coldly. 'My secretary will see you out.'

'Oh, don't be so arrogant.' She frowned at him. 'You could at least have the decency to hear what I have to say.'

'You can have nothing to say that I wish to listen to.' With that he turned and walked around his desk.

'Now you sound pompous.'

He swung on her so angrily that she took a shaky step back from the desk in alarm. 'I sound like a *cheated* man!'

The words rang in the space between them. Melanie looked into his face and felt her knees start to fail. Bold slashing features cast in bronze seemed to loom ever closer. Eyes spiked with bitterness threatened to shrivel her where she stood. His mouth was no longer a mouth, but a pair of parted lines between which a set of white teeth glinted with danger. And the cold slab of marble lying between them seemed to be the only thing holding him back from stretching out a large hand and taking hold of her by the scruff of her neck.

She was shocked. Oh, not because of the pulsing threat itself, but because she would never have believed that he could reveal so much of what was raging inside him. The man she'd used to know had been so fiercely controlled that it had taken him weeks to get around to admitting he was attracted to her. He'd used to haunt her family's farm on the pretext that he was considering investing money into it. He'd used to turn up in strange places like the tack room at the stables, or the hay barn, and would stand watching as she heaved bales of hay onto a low-loader ready for transport to the animals scattered about the outlying fields.

'You should not be doing this,' he'd said in husky disapproval.

'Why?' She remembered laughing at him. 'Because I'm a woman?'

'No.' He hadn't smiled back. 'Because you hate it.'

It had been a truth that had confounded her, because she hadn't realised her dislike had showed. She'd been living on the farm since she was ten year's old, had been expected to do her share of the many daily chores. But as for enjoying the life? No. She would have given anything to go back to how things used to be, when she'd lived in London with two loving parents instead of one bad-tempered uncle and his weak stepson.

'You cheated yourself,' she now returned unsteadily. 'And you have no idea how badly you—'

'Quit,' he warned thinly, 'while you still can.'

It was an outright threat. Instinct was telling her to heed it, but anger was already welling up from the dark pit where she'd stored it for the past eight long years.

'As you did when you preferred to believe lies about me, rather than give me a single minute to explain what you saw?' she flashed back at him. 'Is this my cue to come over all tomb-like and walk out of here, Rafiq? Will it make you feel better if I leave you alone with your righteous belief that you were the only one injured eight years ago?'

'Get out,' he incised.

And there they were. Those magic words, delivered with the same black-toned lack of emotion as before, that literally froze her blood. Melanie looked into the cold dark cast of his face and thought, Ten minutes. It had taken just ten short minutes for them to reach the same point where they had finished things eight years ago.

She laughed, though it was a shaky sound, and swung away, aware that she might have mocked herself about those two small words earlier, but they were still having that same crippling effect on her now as they'd had then.

Only there was a difference. The younger Melanie had run; this older version was made of stronger stuff. She swung back, faced him squarely. 'I have something important to tell you first,' she announced.

'I have no wish to hear it.'

'You might regret saying that.'

'Leave, Melanie,' he reiterated.

'Not until you hear me out.'

Where had that damn stubbornness come from? Rafiq glared at her with a mix of frustration and fascination. It had been a hard push to get the old Melanie to argue about anything. Now he could not shut her up!

The telephone on his desk began to ring, and glad of the diversion he picked it up. It was Nadia informing him that his next appointment had just cancelled. 'Thank you,' he murmured, and returned the receiver to its rest, then glanced at Melanie. 'I'm sorry but my next appointment has arrived,' he lied. 'Which means that your time is up.'

Melanie stared at him. He could have done without seeing the hurt glinting in her eyes. 'You never intended to give me a chance, did you?' she gasped.

'Even as Mrs Portreath?' He arched a cold black eyebrow. 'No,' he confessed. 'I have a congenital dislike of machinating women, you see, so using Randal Soames to get you into this room earned you no more extra time than if you had managed to get in here as Melanie Leggett.'

And that, Melanie realised, more or less said it. She had failed in her mission even before she'd arrived here. What a joke, what a sad little joke. For a few moments longer she continued to stand there, looking at this tall dark beautiful man with the romantic face of Arabia and eyes fit to turn a desert to ice, and seeing no sign at all that there was anything worth appealing to beyond those eyes she knew she was going to give up the fight.

'You know what I think, Rafiq?' she said quietly. 'I think you've just lost the only chance you will ever be given to turn yourself into a human being.'

And with that she turned to walk away. From his chance, from Robbie's chance. The threat of tears suddenly overtook her, because she knew deep down inside she was walking away from her own last chance to make this man understand the truth about her.

I was a fool for thinking I could do it, she railed at herself. Rafiq needed a heart before he could care enough to want to listen. Robbie didn't need a man without a heart cluttering up his life. He had already known the best. It would be an insult to William Portreath's memory to now offer her son the worst.

'Wait...'

Her hand had a grip on the door handle. Melanie froze like a statue with her eyes to the door. What next? What now? she wondered tensely. Did she even want to hear it?

Yet she didn't move. Bigger fool that she was, she just stood there and waited, with her teeth clenched tightly and her heart pumping heavily, while behind her there was... nothing. He didn't speak again, nor move, as far as she could tell. And where the silence before had held a smothering sense of failure, this silence screamed with hope. Weak and pathetic, pained and helpless—hope.

She was trembling; Rafiq could see it happening. So

much so that the knot of silk hair was threatening to come loose. Was she close to tears also? He had a suspicion that she was—just as he had a suspicion that he'd just made the biggest mistake of his life by stopping her from leaving here.

But her last remark had got to him; it had touched a raw nerve inside that went back eight years to when he'd regretted not listening to what she'd had to say. The human being part had pricked him, because if anyone knew he was only half-human then it had to be himself. But here stood the woman he blamed for that.

So why *had* he stopped her when she could have been gone by now? Confusion at his own actions set him frowning as he threw himself down into his chair and tried to decide what do next. As he did so his eyes fell on the stack of papers he'd only had time to glance at before Melanie had walked into the room.

'Tell me about William Portreath,' he invited.

Her shoulders sagged a little, her chin dipping towards her chest to expose the long slender length of her nape. A nape he could almost feel against his fingers—fingers that actually stretched out on cold smooth marble in a featherlike caress. He drew them into a fist, sat outwardly relaxed in his chair while inside every muscle he owned had knotted in an effort to cast out what had been daring to take a grip. His gaze dropped to where her hand still grasped the door handle. Like him, she was dubious about continuing this.

The tension rose along with the silence, and his heart began to pump unevenly in his chest. When his mobile phone began to ring he was so glad of the diversion that he answered it without even thinking about it.

It was Serena again. Of course it was Serena. She had just remembered who was financing her tour, and was using her most seductive voice to try and make him see sense.

At last Melanie moved. He didn't. In fact his eyes, ears,

his capacity to breathe had all been lost in a stress-loaded moment as he watched her fingers slacken and finally drop away from the handle altogether. She began to turn. It was slow and uncertain. She began walking back across the room with her eyes carefully lowered so he could not see what was going on behind them.

Serena was turning on the heat now, the fact that he hadn't cut the connection giving her encouragement. She wanted them to carry on as they had been. She wanted him to remember what it had been like for them.

But *he* was remembering what it had been like with Melanie. He watched her come towards him in her smart suit that skimmed her slender body like a smooth outer skin, but he saw tight faded jeans and a simple tee shirt, saw himself peeling both from her wonderful flesh with hands that worshipped what they found. He saw beautifully formed breasts with rose-tinted areolae and perfect nipples that tightened at the slightest caress. His eyelashes grew heavy as his gaze skimmed downwards to recall the flatness of her silk-smooth stomach with its perfect oval for a navel and gently rounded hips that loved to be cradled in his. Shy Melanie, virginal Melanie, with a soft mouth that had trembled because she had wanted him so badly, and eyes glowing like topaz, aroused and ready to offer him her one precious gift. If everything else she had ever offered him had been lies then he knew without question that wanting him so badly she had had to give him her virginity had been Melanie's one truth.

Should that count for something now? he pondered grimly. In his own country it would count for everything. They would have been man and wife on the strength of that one night alone. Indeed, his sense of honour had already made that decision before he had claimed his exquisite prize. It was a prize that still held a power over him as he sat here in the present listening to one woman beg for his passion while the other aroused him without having to try. He recalled a single afternoon spent upon an old-fashioned feather mattress beneath an eiderdown when her arms had clung to him and her body had accepted him with small soft gasps that had rolled his heart around. He had felt the barrier, could still feel it tempting the proud crown of his sex. 'Yes,' she had said in that soft breathy whisper, and it had stirred him beyond anything he could ever remember.

He was in agony, he noted ruefully. But while he sat here struggling with his own discomfort, he also had the satisfaction of seeing Melanie's cheeks grow warm and her eyelashes flicker in a way that placed a wry smile on his lips. She knew what he was thinking and was unable to look at him because she was feeling the effects of those memories just as strongly as he was.

It was sex, nothing more. He could deal with sex—as the beautiful Serena would agree.

If he didn't stop undressing her with his eyes she would change her mind and leave, Melanie decided as she sank down into the chair by the desk. He was daring to sit there looking as laid back as a man could look while listening to a telephone conversation, but his hooded eyes were burning through her clothing. Did he think she was too dense to know what he was doing?

A wry smile twitched his mouth. It was a mouth that should have looked mean and cold, but by some quirk of fate looked anything but. She sighed, dropped her eyes away from him and wished his expression did not reminded her of sex. One man, one afternoon, only that one experience to call upon—and she was certainly able to call upon it, she noted helplessly. All it had taken was a knowing glint in those eyes and she could see the man in all his naked glory. The breadth of his wide bronzed shoulders and long muscular torso peppered with soft dark hair and—no, stop right there.

Who was on the other end of the phone that could hold him in silence for so long? she wondered as she shifted restlessly on the chair. She wished he would speak, if only to break this terrible tension that was eddying in the air.

Sexual tension. The man had always had the power to turn her inside out with that heavy-lashed, steady stare. Perhaps he knew it, perhaps the call had finished ages ago but he was stretching out the silence on purpose just to extend the agony. Could he be that calculating?

Yes, she decided, of course he could. He had made it very clear that he didn't want her here, but then for some baffling reason had decided to give her a chance to say what she'd come to say. Perhaps she'd touched a nerve when she'd challenged his status as a human being, and this was his idea of payback. Rafiq had pride enough for ten men. He had an ego as big as...other parts.

Oh, stop it! she railed at herself as a second wave of heat crawled up her cheeks.

Rafiq saw the blush and was reminded of the first time he'd seen her, at a friend's country estate. He had been there as a weekend guest and Melanie had been one of the paid staff. She'd served him throughout dinner, quiet, shy, and wearing a perpetual blush to her cheeks. Every time she'd leant over his shoulder to serve him he'd inhaled the scent of her delicate perfume, had felt the soft brush of her breath and her silk hair brushing his cheek. Electric, clinging... He stopped breathing for a moment in dark recollection. Twice she'd caught his shoulder with a serving dish and had almost died with embarrassment. Twice he'd found himself making a joke about his own size in an attempt to deflect the wrath of his hostess.

'She's new—temporary,' Sally Maitland had explained with the condescending tone of someone who had lived her whole life being served only by the best. 'Leave it, Melanie!' she had snapped in annoyance while Melanie valiantly tried to remove spilled sauce from where it had landed on the tablecloth by Rafiq's plate. Her hand had been trembling, the heat from her cheeks hot enough to heat his own cheek as she leant across him. 'You just can't get the staff these days. Melanie is more used to feeding chickens than people.'

He smiled at the memory, though it was more like a grimace. Melanie had fed him a lot that weekend. She'd fed his mind and his senses by being everywhere he'd happened to be. Her perfume had lingered in his bedroom whenever he'd walked back into it after she'd been there tidying the bed; her shyly lowered eyes had followed him whenever she'd had the misfortune to be serving food. If they'd met on the stairs she'd blush like mad and scurry hastily away from him; if they'd brushed arms or shoulders she'd jump like a startled kitten and refuse, though he'd tried, to utter a single word to him. Nods and shakes had been all he'd got for his trouble.

Nods and shakes that had almost driven him out of his mind.

'Come on, *querida*. Forgive me and let us put this behind us. Carlos is not expecting fidelity from me and I—'

With a flick of the hand he cut the connection. Melanie lifted her face. 'You didn't speak a single word,' she said, almost accusingly.

'No words were required,' he drawled lazily, and smiled the kind of smile that made her feel threatened and edgy and eager to get out of here.

'About William,' she said firmly, 'I think I should start by—'

'Lunch,' he inserted.

'Lunch?' Melanie offered him a perfectly blank stare.

He offered a smile to her. 'I think we will take this conversation away from the business environment and place it in a more...congenial setting.'

'But you have another appointment waiting outside!'

His answer to that was to reach out and pick up the other phone. Several smooth words spoken in Arabic and as far as Melanie was concerned the problem of his next appointment had been consigned to the archives. The phone went back on its rest.

'Problem solved,' he murmured with lying smoothness.

'I really do prefer to deal with this right here.' It was almost a desperate little plea.

'Oh, come.' He stood up. 'Here I am attempting to show you my human side by offering to listen to you, and you throw this gesture back in my face?'

If he thought listening to her talk over lunch was going to be pleasant then he was in for a surprise, Melanie thought ruefully. And why did she feel as if she'd just come face to face with a slippery snake?

She watched him warily as he walked around the marble slab. The dig about his human side hadn't passed her by either, nor the fact that in the space of a one-way conversation with his mobile phone his whole manner towards her had taken a complete reversal. He arrived at the side of her chair. The hairs on the back of her neck began to stand on end. He was waiting for her to give in and stand up, but her eyes were level with a certain part of his anatomy and what she could see happening there sent a wave of shocked heat sweeping down her front.

This had nothing to do with lunch, or talking, or even him showing his human side! It was to do with sex. Let-me-rumble-you-on-the-nearest-bed kind of sex—for old times' sake.

'Stop this, Rafiq,' she uttered tensely.

'Stop what?'

'You *know* what!' Jumping up, she took an anxious step back. The chair was in the way, the marble desk blocking any other form of escape. 'Let me pass,' she insisted.

'Of course.' He took a step sideways.

Flustered beyond daring to think, Melanie went to slither between him and the desk. His hand snaked out, caught her by the waist to bring her to a standstill. It was the first time he'd touched her in eight long years and it turned her senses into live wires that forced her to draw in a sharp breath.

He laughed huskily. 'Sure you want to go?'

She lifted her face to spit out her answer at him. Eyes clashed with eyes, hot and elemental. She parted her lips on a shivering gasp. Rafiq dipped his dark head and covered them. She fell into his kiss like a suicidal lemming.

What shocked Rafiq more was that he did the same thing himself. He had no idea where it all came from. One minute he was toying with her just for the hell of it, the next he was locked into hottest, darkest, most sexually arousing kiss he had ever experienced in his life! He could feel every quivering inch of her as if they were already naked. Her perfume filled his head, and the desperate little groans she was making as she tried to fight what was happening and knew she did not stand a chance vibrated in every one of his nerve cells.

Melanie the harlot, he thought grimly as she arched compulsively then hungrily deepened the kiss. Well…why not? he asked himself as the anger still burning within the desire gave him the excuse to do what he liked. The desk was convenient. All it would take was a lift of his arm and he could be enjoying her on a slab of cold marble. Sex in a mausoleum, he thought grimly, sacrificial and pagan. It suited him very well.

A sound beyond the door infiltrated the madness. With a tug Melanie managed to separate their mouths, then took a jerky step back. Shocked and shaken by the whole experience, she slumped weakly against the edge of the marble and gasped like a sprinter while trying to clear the dizzy fog from her head.

'What made you do that?' she choked out when she could manage to say anything.

He laughed—harshly—as if she'd just told a really bad joke. But the really bad joke was the way he was standing there calmly fastening shirt buttons she must have unfastened! Horrified, she looked down, and saw her jacket was hanging open revealing her skimpy black lace bra. Pure vanity had made her decide to wear nothing else beneath the jacket, so as not to spoil its smooth line. But now she had to deal with the mortifying knowledge that he knew she had come here only half-dressed!

As if she was begging for it. She shuddered. She could almost hear him saying those derisory words out loud. Why not? She had fallen into that kiss like a love-racked teenager.

Her skin was flushed, her nipples hard. 'I don't believe this is happening,' she breathed shakily, while urgently redoing buttons with numb fingers and wishing she couldn't still feel his hands on her body.

'You should not have come here, Melanie,' Rafiq said grimly.

'I didn't come here for this!' she cried.

'Take my advice and get out of here.' Turning, he strode back round the desk. 'And if you have any sense at all you will not attempt to come back.'

Melanie nodded in complete agreement, tried swallowing down the lump in her throat and tried to stand without the aid of the desk. It didn't happen. Her legs refused to support her. It was the final humiliation and she had to put a trembling hand up to cover her burning eyes.

He was a ruthless, heartless, arrogant devil. How could she have let herself forget all of that?

But she hadn't forgotten it. She'd merely shelved it in a box marked, Has had time to change.

'I n-need my papers,' she stammered, and in a last-ditch attempt to leave with some dignity she forced her stupid legs to carry her weight.

He nodded coolly, and began gathering the papers together. Melanie stood at his side and waited in stiff silence for him to hand them over so that she could get out of here and never, ever come back.

'Your uncle is still running the farm?' he asked suddenly.

She frowned at the question, her head still too fluffy to think properly. 'He died five years ago in a farming accident.'

'I'm sorry, I had not heard.'

Melanie shrugged away his commiserations. There had never been any affection between her and her uncle. She was sorry he had died so tragically, but other than that, she still could not bring herself to forgive him for the part he had played in trying to ruin her life.

'And Jamie?'

Ah, he couldn't resist it, could he? A fresh wave of bitterness welled, putting the light of defiance back in her eyes. Her chin went up and she threw that defiance straight at him. 'My papers,' she prompted, holding a hand out.

To Rafiq, this was a challenge and a refusal to make any comment on the person she had betrayed him with. He lowered his gaze to the outstretched hand.

'You've changed,' he remarked. 'Grown more assertive.'

'Life has a habit of changing you.'

'And money.'

'And money.' She nodded in agreement.

'Which you would like me to invest for you?'

'Money is a devil to look after if you're not used to handling it,' she answered.

'Why me?' he asked, suddenly curious when Melanie no longer wanted him to be.

'Because Randal assured me that you were the best.' And that's all you're getting out of me, she added silently.

'Liar,' he drawled. '*You* suggested *me* to Randal.'

Oh, that shook her. She hadn't expected Randal to reveal that juicy bit of information. Still, she rallied. 'Are you trying to tell me that you *aren't* the best?'

His smile this time was disturbing. Disturbing because she'd seen Robbie use the exact same expression, but had never connected it with his father before. She knew that physical things, like the colour of eyes and hair and skin, came as part of the genetic package, but she hadn't realised that smiles did also.

'There you are, then.' She tried a smile. 'I was hoping

your business ethic would put you above bearing grudges. It seems I was wrong. My mistake. I'll find someone else.'

'To...' he glanced at the top piece of paper '''...invest one half of your inheritance in long-term options while the other half is locked into a trust fund,''' he read out loud.

A frisson of alarm disturbed her breathing. He was beginning to show interest when she no longer wanted him to. 'Randal is setting the trust fund up for me,' she said tensely, her eyes fixed on those long brown fingers set against the white paper that held the details of her entire life.

Her life and Robbie's life.

'For whom?' Rafiq questioned.

'Does it matter?' she countered stiffly.

'If you want me to work with you, it does,' he murmured quietly.

'But I don't any longer.'

He ignored that and went to sit down in his chair—taking her papers with him. 'Sit and explain,' he smoothly invited, then flipped to the next page.

'N-no,' she refused. 'I've changed my mind, Rafiq. I made a mistake to come to y-you. I know that now. You were right. I should leave. I'm s-sorry I intruded.'

Rafiq narrowed his eyes on her taut stature; something inside him went very still. She was afraid, white with it, suddenly no longer defiant but teetering dangerously on the edge of panic.

'For whom?' he repeated very quietly, and watched with deepening interest as her eyes flickered away, nervously scanning anything that did not include him. They settled on the illuminated numbers on the communications console.

'Lunch is out,' she announced jerkily. 'I have to be somewhere else at one.'

Rafiq said nothing. He just continued to sit there watching as her cheeks grew even paler and her tongue made a nervous pass across trembling lips. Lips that still pulsed

from his kiss, he noticed. Lips that seemed to have forgotten how to speak. She was tense, she was edgy, she
was so nervous he could see the fine tremors attacking her
flesh.

A sudden thought made his eyes narrow. She was
Melanie Portreath now, not the Melanie Leggett he'd used
to know. William Portreath had been in his nineties when
he'd died, making his widow very rich. Rafiq knew how
these things usually worked: wise men tended to protect
their money from the machinations of a trophy wife.

But protect it for whom? 'Answer me, Melanie,' he
commanded grimly.

She shimmered a glance at him then dragged it away,
swallowed, and murmured huskily, 'M-my son. The trust
is to be set up for my son.'

So, the old man had been capable of enjoying the
charms of his lovely young bride! Rafiq's skin began to
prickle at the very idea of it. She was now so pale her
eyes were bruising. Was it shame? Was she beginning to
realise that it was not as easy as she had expected to come
in here and admit that she had sold herself for a pot of
gold to a man old enough to be her grandfather?

Sickness was suddenly clawing at his stomach, disgust
climbing up the walls of his chest, as she stood there staring at him through eyes that seemed to beg him for some
kind of understanding. But all he saw was her beautiful,
smooth naked form lying beneath a withered old man.

Placing the papers on his desk, he stood up and was
amazed at the smoothness of the movement, was impressed
by the way his legs carried him around the desk. 'Come
with me,' he said, and was further impressed by the steadiness of his voice as he gave the instruction.

Melanie was looking slightly bewildered. He had no
wish to look into her face any longer so he turned and
walked away. As he strode towards the door he could hear
her following him. In the outer foyer Nadia was busy at
her computer, and Kadir was leaning against her desk

while talking on the telephone. He was speaking Arabic, but Rafiq had not a single clue what words were being spoken in his natural tongue.

'Kadir!' With a flick of a hand he brought his aide to attention and kept on walking towards the other side of the room, where the lift stood with its doors conveniently open and waiting for them.

Kadir arrived at Rafiq's side as he was silently indicating to his aide Melanie should precede him. She was frowning as she did so, eyeing Rafiq warily as she passed him by. He ignored her to indicate to Kadir to follow suit. Kadir entered the lift. Rafiq stepped in after them, but only for as long as it took him to hit the ground-floor button. He was taking no chances here.

'Escort Mrs Portreath off the premises,' he instructed Kadir. 'And ensure that she does not gain entrance to this building again.'

With that he walked away, hearing Melanie's shocked gasp as the lift doors put solid steel between them. As he strode past Nadia's workstation he ignored his secretary's stunned expression. With the easy flow of a man completely in control of his own actions, he stepped back into his office and closed the door.

Melanie was staring at the walls of her steel prison. Shock was holding her silent and still. Beside her, the dark-haired young Arab called Kadir was almost as frozen.

She found her voice. 'What happened?' she whispered.

He offered her a very formal bow. 'I'm afraid I do not know.'

Then, before either could say anything else, the doors were opening onto the ground-floor foyer and Kadir was politely carrying out his master's wishes by escorting her all the way to the giant glass doors and even beyond. In a daze of bewilderment Melanie found herself being offered another polite bow before the young man turned and retreated through the doors again, leaving her standing there in a state of utter disabling shock at the slick smooth way

Rafiq had just executed his revenge on her—if revenge was what it had all been about. She didn't know, didn't care. He had thrown her out—publicly. In all her life she'd never felt so humiliated.

Stunned beyond being able to function sensibly, she began moving and almost fell beneath the wheels of a passing car. The car horn sounded; she just stood watching as it brushed by within inches.

Up high, in his marble tower, Rafiq viewed her near-death experience through black eyes and with bone-crackingly clenched teeth. It was only as he stood there fighting a battle between fear for her life and a wish never to lay eyes on her again that he made the connection between Melanie and the golden-haired woman he had watched hovering in the street before.

If he had known then what he knew now she would not have got beyond the building's entrance doors, saving them both a lot of trouble.

The liar, the cheat, the little slut, he seethed in ice-cold silence. And he'd had the pleasure of experiencing two of her kind in a single day! All he needed now was for his mother to rise up from the grave and tell him exactly how much money she had squeezed out of his father before she'd agreed to carry his child full term.

Money. It always came down to money with women, he concluded, as he turned away from the window after watching one of their number safely cross the road. His mobile phone began to ring. Striding over to his desk, he picked it up, opened the back, removed the SIM card, then discarded the lot into the waste-paper bin where today's Spanish newspaper was already showing yesterday's news.

By tomorrow he would have pulled the plug on Serena's finances. And his mother had ceased to be an issue when she'd died on the day of his birth. Which left only Melanie—or Mrs Portreath, he amended bitterly as he picked up the stack of her papers with the intention of consigning those to the waste-paper bin along with everything else.

Only something caught his eye and he hesitated...

CHAPTER THREE

MELANIE had no idea how she managed to get home again. She had only a vague recollection of standing on an Underground train and being strangely comforted because she was just one more blank face amongst many. But now here she stood in her own warm kitchen, surrounded by everything that represented familiarity, comfort and security to her—and she felt like an alien.

An alien being in an alien place, present, yet not a part of. It was an odd sensation, because she recognised everything yet couldn't seem to connect with any of it. The old Aga set into the chimney-breast, for instance, the scrubbed table that took up too much space but was as much a part of the family as Robbie's pictures decorating the cork notice-board on the wall by the door. Assorted mugs hung from old-fashioned cup hooks suspended beneath one of the ancient wall cabinets, and at some point since coming home, she had set the old kettle to heat on the Aga, though she didn't remember doing it. It was puffing out steam in a gentle flow now, telling her the water was hot but not yet boiling. She had lost her shoes somewhere and was standing on cold quarry tiling in silk stockings that had cost her the absolute earth, though it felt as if she was floating above the floor.

Shock. She was suffering from shock. She understood that even if she couldn't seem to do anything about it. Every time she tried to think what had thrust her into this foggy state she experienced that awful sinking sensation of a lift swooping downwards and the claustrophobic sensation of being encased in steel. But what had happened before the lift and what had come after it was refusing to show itself.

She looked at the wall clock, saw it wasn't even one o'clock yet, and realised she'd done well to get back so quickly after...

That lift swooped her downwards again and she fumbled for a kitchen chair then sank onto it, put a cold hand up to cover her mouth and caught a brief flash of Rafiq's stone-like face. She blinked slowly as the part of her brain that stored pictures refused to connect with the part that stored emotion.

He'd thrown her out.

She dropped the hand onto the table, fingertips hovering in the air as if they knew that making contact with anything solid would cause some kind of horrible calamity.

He'd played with her like a cat with a mouse. He'd insulted her, kissed her, had brought her right there to the very edge of panic by suddenly showing an interest in things she'd no longer wanted him to know about. Then, quite calmly and precisely, he had thrown her out.

Her fingers began to curl down towards the table, her stomach muscles coiled into a ball, and at last blood began to pump more oxygen to her brain. Across the kitchen the kettle began to make hissing noises; the clock on the wall chimed the hour. The fingers touched base and she stood up; it was quick and tense and impulsive.

How could she have got it so wrong? How could she have talked herself into believing that he possessed a heart worth pleading with? Where had she ever got the stupid idea that he was a worthy father for her very precious son?

The telephone mounted on the wall behind her began ringing. Forcing herself to go and answer it took most of her self-control.

'I saw you come back,' a female voice said. 'How did it go?'

It was her neighbour, Sophia. 'It didn't go anywhere,' Melanie replied, then burst into tears.

Sophia arrived within minutes, banging on the back door with a demand to be let in after having come through the hole in the hedge that separated their two gardens. She was a tall, dark-haired, sex-seething bombshell with lavender eyes and a lush mouth that could slay the world. But inside the stunning outer casing lurked a legal mind that was a sharp as a razor and as tough as the glass ceiling she was striving to break through.

'Dry those tears,' she instructed the moment Melanie opened the door to her. 'He doesn't deserve them, and you know he doesn't.'

Half an hour later Melanie had poured the whole thing out to her over a cup of tea. By then Sophia's amazing eyes had turned glassy. 'It sounds to me as if you and Robbie have just had a very lucky escape. The man is a first-class bastard. I did tell you, you should have stuck with me, kid,' she added sagely. 'I'm a much better father-figure for any boy child.'

It was such a ludicrous thing to say that Melanie laughed for the first time. But in a lot of ways Sophia was speaking the truth, because her neighbour's curt, no-nonsense approach to life had always appealed to Robbie. When he was in need of something other than his mother's loving softness he would disappear through the hole in the hedge to search out Sophia. So did Melanie, come to that.

'What did your lawyer have to say when you told him?' Sophia asked curiously. 'The same as me—I told you so?'

Randal. Melanie's brain ground to a halt again; she went still, her eyes fixed and blank. Then—

'Oh, dear God,' Melanie breathed, then jumped up and made a dive for the telephone.

'What?' Sophia demanded anxiously. 'What did I say?'

'Oh—hello.' Melanie cut across Sophia with the tense greeting. 'I need to speak to Randal Soames, please. I'm M-Mrs Portreath... W-what do you mean he isn't there? I was supposed to be meeting him there for lunch!'

'Mr Soames was called out on urgent business, Mrs

Portreath,' his secretary told her. 'I was expecting you to arrive at any minute so I could offer you his apologies.'

She didn't *want* an apology. 'I have to speak to Randal!' She was becoming hysterical. 'When will he be back?'

'He didn't say...'

'W-well...' Melanie took in a breath and tried to calm herself '...I need you to get him on his mobile phone and tell him I have s-speak to him urgently.'

'Yes, Mrs Portreath. I will try to contact him for you but I can't promise. He tends to switch off his mobile when he's in a meeting, you see.'

Melanie placed the receiver back on its rest, then sank weakly against the wall and put a hand up to cover her aching eyes.

'What was all that about?' Sophia questioned.

'I left my papers on Rafiq's desk,' she breathed. 'How could I have been so *stupid*!'

The covering hand began to tremble. On a sigh, Sophia came to place an arm across her shoulders. 'Okay, calm down,' she murmured soothingly. 'I think you need to re-member that he didn't give you much chance to do other-wise,' she pointed out.

No, he hadn't, Melanie agreed. He'd just got rid of her. He'd heard enough—*had* enough—and had just got up and marched her out! Sophia almost copied him by marching her back to the kitchen table and sitting her down again, only her friend used a guiding arm to do it whereas Rafiq hadn't even spared her a glance, never mind touched her! As if she was unclean. As if he would have contaminated himself if he'd remained in her company too long.

A shudder ripped through her. 'Stop shaking,' Sophia commanded. 'The man isn't worth the grief.'

But Melanie didn't want to stop shaking. She wanted to shiver and shake and remember another time when he'd done almost the same thing. She had followed him back to London, had almost had hysterics in her desire to get inside his embassy and plead with him. What she'd met

with when she'd eventually been granted an audience had
been Rafiq locked into his Arab persona, about to attend
some formal function dressed in a dark red cloak, white
tunic and wearing a white *gut rah* on his head. He'd looked
taller and leaner, foreign and formidable. His face had
taken on a whole new appearance: harder, savage, honed
to emulate some cold-eyed, winged predator. 'Get out.'
He'd said those two immortal words then turned his back
on her to stride away.

'Melanie, if he still despises you as much as you think
he does, he will probably consign your papers to the bin
without bothering to read them.'

'Yes.' She liked that scenario.

'But would it be a very bad thing if he did read them?'
Sophia then dared to suggest. 'At least he would know
everything—which is what you wanted, remember? It was
why you decided to go to see him in the first place.'

Sophia was holding onto her hands while trying to talk
some good sense into the situation. But she hadn't been
there this morning; she hadn't seen the size of the mistake
Melanie had made. It had been huge; she'd been damned
by her own foolish optimism, letting the years soften
Rafiq's hard image until she'd actually begun to question
whether *she* had been fair to *him*.

William had helped by gently nudging her in this direction. Dear, sweet, gentle William who, like herself, hadn't
liked to see bad in anyone. But even William's advice had
only been wise with all the facts laid before him. If Rafiq
did decide to read those papers they would only tell him
half the story. As for the other half—

Well, that half belonged to his eagerness to believe
badly of her simply because people had told him to.

But, no. She sighed. There had been so much more to
it than words of poison spoken into his ear. He had *seen*
her with Jamie. It had all been so desperately damning.
And explainable, she reminded herself, if he had only
given her the chance to explain. He hadn't and still

wouldn't. That hadn't changed. He still looked at her and saw her through the unforgiving eyes of a half-Arab man with his feet firmly entrenched in cultural principles and a deep-rooted belief that all women were natural sinners.

And she no longer wanted a man like that to come anywhere near her son so he could contaminate him with his poisonous view of her.

'Melanie—'

No. She scrunched her hands free, then got to her feet. She didn't want to talk about it any more. For what was the use in talking when it was basically too late? All she could hope for now was that Randal would come through for her and manage to retrieve her stuff before Rafiq decided to feed his hatred by reading things that he really did not want to know.

'What are you doing at home at this time of the day, anyway?' she asked Sophia as an abrupt change of subject. 'I thought you were supposed to be wowing them all in some court or other.'

'The case was adjourned,' Sophia explained. 'And I'm off to wow them in Manchester tomorrow, so I decided to come home to pack a bag and catch a flight up there today. I've got friends there I haven't seen in ages—but I've changed my mind,' she then added swiftly. 'I'm going to stay here with you, just in case—'

'No, you're not.' Mouth set in a stubborn line, Melanie glared at her with a warning look. 'I had a bad experience today but I'm all right,' she insisted, and to prove it she gathered up the tea mugs and took them to the sink. 'Maybe I even needed it to help me move on from the past.'

'You believe you can do that?' Sophia sounded sceptical.

Maybe she was right to. 'I have no choice.' Just as soon as I've got my papers back, she thought with a shiver. 'Because I won't be repeating the same mistake twice.'

It was such a complete, final statement that Sophia

didn't even attempt to say another word. Ten minutes later she'd gone, leaving Melanie with the rest of the afternoon stretching out in front of her like a long dark road filled with nerve-stretching uncertainty—and a heartache she didn't want to feel.

She called Randal's office three times with no satisfaction. Actually picked up the phone to call Rafiq's secretary, only to change her mind when his final words came back to hit her full in the face. She would not even get beyond the main switchboard.

How could a man fester in such hatred that it could make him want to humiliate her like that? Tears threatened again; she swallowed them down and went upstairs to change out of her suit. As she removed the jacket she caught sight of herself in the mirror, saw the black lacy bra and relived the feeling of long brown fingers staking their claim. She shuddered, despising herself for being so easy, finished removing the suit and scrambled into a pair of faded old jeans and a roll-neck top that covered everything. By the time she walked downstairs a few minutes later she was the casual Melanie her son was used to seeing when he arrived home from school. No sign of designer clothes left anywhere for him to pick up on. No hint that she'd been doing anything today that was different from any other day.

Robbie arrived with a shout and a bump of his school bag against the polished hall floor. She turned from chopping vegetables at the sink to watch him come in through the kitchen door. His maroon and gold striped tie had flipped over his shoulder, and beneath his gaping school blazer she could see the white tails of his shirt hanging free from grey school trousers. One grey sock was up, the other was down, and his glossy black hair looked as if it had been in a fight.

Her heart dropped like a stricken bird, because even with his rumpled appearance he was hitting her hard with his father's image.

'Hi,' he said. 'Guess what we did today?'

'What?' she asked.

He frowned. 'Are you catching a cold?'

Melanie shook her head and tried swallowing the tears again. 'Just need to clear my throat.' Which she did. 'So what did you do today?' she prompted.

'We went to the park to collect fallen leaves that looked like skelintons, then took them back to press some into a books and draw round others.'

'Skeletons,' Melanie corrected.

'Skeletons,' he dutifully repeated. 'Do you want to see?'

'Of course I want to see,' she answered. 'But not before I get my hug.'

With a grin that could knock her eyes out he came towards her, a tall boy for his seven years. Melanie squatted down and opened her arms to receive him. As she hugged him close she felt another wave of emotion threaten. She must have sniffed, because Robbie jerked his head back.

Eyes as dark as his father's looked into hers, only they weren't the same, because this pair of eyes were darkened by love and warmth and concern whereas that other pair...

'Are you sure you're not catching a cold?' he demanded.

'Robbie,' she said firmly, 'I am not catching a cold, all right?'

It was a mother's voice, the I-know-everything voice. He continued to study her for a moment, then nodded his head. 'I'll go and get my bag.'

End of small developing crisis, Melanie thought with a sigh. Since William had died Robbie had lived in fear that she was going to follow him. Every sneeze, every twitch, every minor *ouch* could shake him to the core with fear.

They played with the leaves, drew some more, ate supper, watched some television then eventually went upstairs to play games in his bath before curling up on his bed to read stories. By eight o'clock he was fast asleep and Melanie had given up on expecting Randal to call.

For the next hour she tried to keep herself busy doing

the usual mundane chores. They'd used to employ a house-keeper, but she'd decided to retire when William had died and there seemed no point in employing another when there was only two of them to be looked after now. But the house was big—too big for both of them. A large Edwardian terraced home, with five bedrooms and four main reception rooms, it deserved a large noisy family to fill it, not two people who seemed to rattle around in it these days.

Melanie missed William, she missed Lucy the house-keeper, and she missed having only to open a couple of doors to find someone else there when she felt in need of company. As she felt now, she admitted, when she found herself standing in the front living room just staring into space.

Diversions, diversions, she told herself forcefully, and had just decided to go upstairs and indulge in a long hot bath in the hopes that it would ease some of the stress from her aching body when the sound of a car drawing up outside caught her ear. On legs that had suddenly turned very heavy she walked to the window and twitched back the edge of a curtain. As soon as she saw the low black monster crouching by the front gate she knew the long anxious wait was over.

Rafiq climbed out of his car and set the central locking system, then turned to view Melanie's home. It stood in the middle of an Edwardian terrace, brick-faced and solid-looking, with an iron gate leading to a small garden and a narrow porch with a half-stained-glass front door. One big bay window sat on each side of the porch and three flat windows faced the upper floor.

Did one of those windows belong to his son's bedroom?

Even thinking the word son threatened to lock him up inside. He saw a curtain twitch in a downstairs window, felt a cold winter gust of wind wipe what was left of the colour from his face.

An omen? he wondered, and had to accept that it probably was. This was not going to be easy. He was still in a deep state of shock and Randal had advised him to stay away until he had given himself time to recover. But Randal was not him. The other man could have no conception what was it was like to be him at this present moment. For how was he supposed to balance logic on the top of raging emotion? It was impossible. He was just swinging from one dark place to another with no respite in between. He had spent the whole afternoon with Randal Soames, swinging like that between a raging fury aimed entirely at Melanie and a heart-clutching sense of dismay at what he had almost tossed away today.

The curtain in a downstairs window gave a second twitch. Just before it fell back into place he caught a glimpse of Melanie's face. She had seen him. He must go in now. Had he actually been considering going away without doing so?

He didn't know, was no longer sure of anything. Half an hour ago he had been pacing his apartment; now he was here without recalling what had happened in between. He was the most controlled man he knew—prided himself on it—but control of any kind had completely deserted him. Pride, they said, usually came before a fall. Well, he was falling, had not stopped falling since he'd glanced at a piece of paper in his office and had seen the name Robert Joseph Alan Portreath typed in bold print in the middle of a blur of legal jargon.

Robert had been Melanie's father's name, but Joseph Alan belonged to him—Rafiq ben Jusef Al Alain Al-Qadim.

His throat moved on an attempt to swallow, his eyes growing glassy as he reached for the gate. It swung inwards with a creak of ageing wrought iron. As he stepped through it he caught sight of a figure through the stained-glass door and knew that Melanie was coming to open the door for him.

Don't touch the bell! Melanie prayed feverishly as she

made a last dash to get the door open before the shrill ring could fill the house and wake up Robbie.

It was like one of those nightmares where you opened the door to find yourself staring at the darkest force you could ever imagine. Big and broad and dressed entirely in black, Rafiq filled the narrow porch like a huge black shadow, blocking the light from the street behind him and taking the air from her lungs.

He believed. It was written there in every sharply angled feature, in the clench of his jaw and the muscle-locked stiffness of his big frame.

'Invite me in.'

His voice sounded like sawdust. Melanie tried to get a grip on her pounding heartbeat. 'It's late.' Like a coward she went for the easy route. 'I w-was just going to bed. W-why don't you come back tomorrow and we we'll—?'

'Invite me in, Melanie,' he repeated grimly.

'So that you can insult me again?'

'Probably.' He grimaced. 'I cannot be sure what I am going to do. I'm in shock,' he admitted.

Melanie could see it. 'All the more reason for you to come back tomorrow, when—'

His eyes gave a sudden flash. It was the only warning she got before she was being picked up by a pair of tough arms and bodily carried into the hall then into the living room.

'How dare you?' She gasped as he dropped her to her feet again.

He didn't bother to answer, instead he turned and strode back into the hallway, leaving her standing there shaking in her shoes and burning like fire down the front of her body where it had been crushed against his. She heard the front door click into its housing, heard his footsteps bringing him back this way. He stepped into the room, then closed this door also.

One look at his face here in the better light of the living room had her mentally backing away. Whatever all the hovering outside had been about, it hadn't communicated the anger she was being faced with now. He was in a rage, and a six-foot-four-inch male with a body to match his height was not what you wanted running loose in your house.

'I think y-you need to calm down a bit,' she stammered as he came towards her. 'You're in sh-shock, and you might not know w-what you're—'

'Shock,' he repeated so softly that she shivered. 'You think *this* is shock?'

'Angry, then,' she amended with a wary shrug and a gasp when the backs of her knees made contact with the arm of a chair. 'I can understand why you might feel you have the right to be. But—'

'Let us get one thing straight.' He cut across her. His mouth was thin and his eyes even narrower. 'I have the *right* to throttle the life from you for what you have done to me. But all I want from you are some acceptable answers!'

'Then back off—'

Back off? Rafiq stared down into her beautiful frightened face and blinked in complete astonishment. There was little more than an inch separating them. In fact he was standing so close she was arching her back in an effort to maintain the distance.

He was stunned. The red-hot rage had surged up out of nowhere, catching hold of him the moment he'd seen her standing at her door looking like the old Melanie, in jeans and worn-out old trainers. The years had fallen away and he'd found himself swapping new grievances for old grievances.

On a deep-throated curse he spun away from her, put a hand to the back of his neck and gripped. Behind him he could hear the uneven tug of her breathing, could feel her wariness, her fear. He closed his eyes and tried to get a hold on what was threatening to overwhelm him. He was a mess inside and the feeling was so alien that he didn't know how to deal with it.

'I apologise,' he muttered.

'It's all right,' she answered, but it was still the voice of fear.

He heard her movements as she edged warily sideways, heard the scrape of metal on metal and turned, a sense of pained horror filling him with dismay. She was standing by the fireplace and clenched in one hand was a brass poker. His eyes turned black and his stillness was suddenly electric. She believed him to be so dangerous that she armed herself against him.

'You don't need that, Melanie,' he said huskily.

He wasn't standing in her shoes, Melanie thought anxiously. He hadn't seen the look in his eyes just before he'd turned away. 'W-when you calm down I'll put it down,' she promised.

But she was shaking. Inside and out she was shaking. The way he ran those eyes over her she had a horrible feeling it would take him less than a second to disarm her if he decided to. He was big, he was strong, and he was also an expert in unarmed combat. She'd watched him in action once, in the Maitlands' all-purpose gym, when she'd gone in with a fresh stack of towels, only to find herself pulled to a complete standstill by the sight of him stripped to the waist and sparring with his brother. Sheikh Hassan had been stripped to the waist too, but she couldn't recall what he looked like. Only this man, moving with a speed and dexterous grace that belied his size and weight. He'd seen her standing there and had stopped to stare; within seconds he'd been flat on his back with his brother pinning him there. 'Such distraction is very unfair,' he'd sighed out complainingly and, as Sheikh Hassan had glanced up to see what he was talking about their positions had been smoothly reversed.

Man pitched against man, power against power, slick and smooth and so inherently masculine, with rippling muscles and the gleam of their bronzed flesh and the scent of the efforts permeating the air. She'd turned and run.

As Rafiq began walking towards her now maybe she should do the same thing, she told herself. But she couldn't run this time. This was her home. Her son lay sleeping upstairs. So she tightened her grip on the poker until her knuckles showed white, then made ready to defend herself.

His eyes were dark, his eyelashes lying thick against his cheekbones, his mouth a grim straight line. She sucked in a gulp of air as he reached out and closed a hand round the poker. With a gentle twist it was taken from her fingers.

'Never brandish point-on,' he said gravelly. 'The first thrust will tear your arm from its socket. Use it like this.' While she stood too dazed to stop him, he took hold of her hand, placed the poker back into it, angled it across her breasts, then, with a speed that set her gasping, he jerked the poker in a slashing arc towards his body. It came to stop with the point a breath away from his neck. 'This way you have a chance of doing me some damage.'

It was mad, really stupid, but her mouth began to wobble and tears suddenly filmed her eyes. 'I don't want to damage you,' she breathed shakily.

'I know.' He released his grip on the poker. 'It was my fault. I frightened you.' With that he turned and walked towards the door.

'Wh-where are you going?'

'You were right. I should not have come here tonight,' he answered grimly. 'I will go and leave you with your... safety.'

'N-no!' she cried, and wondered why. She wished she could stop trembling and tried to calm herself. 'Y-you're here now and...'

He stopped halfway across the room. Silence arrived. It pulled and it prodded. Melanie gripped the poker and tried to think of something to say that would not cause another eruption.

'Would you like a drink?' was her only inspiration. 'I can soon...'

'No—thank you,' he refused.

'Your jacket, then—let me take your jacket.' It was made of the softest kind of leather, his trousers of the smoothest suede. She swallowed thickly.

As she made to walk forward she was stopped when he turned to show her what was written in his eyes. 'I would really like to see my son.'

His son. The huskily possessive sound of his words had a creasing effect on her stomach. 'He's asleep. I don't want—'

'I was not intending to wake him, just...look upon him. Is that too much to ask?'

There was a bite to the last part. Without it she might well have given in, but the bite told her that his mood was still unpredictable. So she shook her head. 'He's a very light sleeper. The last thing he needs it to wake up and find a stranger standing over him.'

'Whose fault is it that I am a stranger?'

She ignored that. 'You need to understand a few things before we bring Robbie into this.'

'Such as the fact that you were never married to William Portreath?'

'I never said that I was,' she denied.

'You allowed me to assume it.'

'I don't recall being given the time to let you build any assumptions,' she countered coolly.

He took the criticism with a straightening of his shoulders. Melanie turned to put the poker back on its stand, but changed her mind and began stabbing at the fire log instead. Given a choice, he would rather be anywhere else than here in this room having this conversation with her, she reminded herself as wood sparks began to fly. In his eyes she was nothing, just a piece of low life he believed he had rid himself of once and for all today. Now he was being forced to backtrack, to be contrite and polite and civilised when he felt like being neither.

She made another hard stab at the fire log.

More sparks flew around the grate. 'You changed your name from Leggett to Portreath.'

'It pleased William to know that Robbie would carry on the Portreath name,' she explained.

The air was suddenly as tight at a bowstring, and Melanie knew why. He was thinking about Robbie's right to carry on *his* name. But, by the grim way he pressed his lips together, she realised he was not going to make any comment—for now at least.

Instead he stuck to his original subject. 'You call yourself *Mrs* Portreath,' he stated. 'Does this not signify a married status?'

'Why are *you* so struck by my marital status?' she countered, putting the poker back on its rest then turning to frown at him. 'I'm an unmarried mother with a son's feelings to consider,' she reminded him defensively. 'It made life simpler for Robbie if I invented a dead husband.'

'And a dead father.'

'I didn't say that,' Melanie denied. 'He knows about you. Of course he does. It would be unforgivable of me to pretend you were dead just because—'

'He knows who I am?' For such a dark-skinned man he suddenly looked ashen.

'Yes,' she confirmed. 'It was only natural that he should ask and only right that I should tell him the truth. But he—'

Rafiq's response shook her—she just didn't see it coming—so when he dropped down into one of the sofas then buried his face in his hands she was shocked.

'Rafiq...'

'No.' He shook his head. 'Leave me a moment.'

But he needed more than a moment to come to terms with what was suddenly raging inside him. His son knew about him. He knew he had a father who had never bothered to come and see him.

He couldn't make up his mind if it would have been less painful to think the boy had believed him dead!

'You have to understand. Robbie only—'

'Shut up,' he rasped, and found anger again, found strength in it, then lifted his dark head. 'I want to break your deceitful neck for keeping my son from me!' he ground out.

'You had your chance to be a father, Rafiq, and you blew it, not me.'

'When?' He was suddenly on his feet again. '*When* did you give me this chance?'

'When you threw me out of your embassy eight years ago!'

'You knew then and said nothing?'

Melanie laughed. 'You were the man who told me it was no use my saying a single word because you wouldn't believe me anyway!'

'And you could not bring yourself to stand your ground and *insist* I listen to you?'

Chin up, eyes bright, face white and body trembling, she still held her ground. 'For what purpose?' she demanded. 'You would have still called me a liar.'

A flick of a hand brought contempt back into the fight. 'You were sleeping with your step-cousin. Of course I would have questioned the boy's parentage!'

If Melanie had still had the poker in her hand she would have hit him with it. Who did he think he was, standing here trying to lay all the blame on her? 'What if I *had* come to you with your son in my arms, Rafiq?' she challenged. 'What if I'd said, Look, Rafiq, see for yourself that this child belongs to you?' She released a bitter little laugh. 'I'll tell you what you would have done. You would have taken him away from me. You would have used your filthy billions to split me from my child!'

'I would not!' He actually dared to look shocked.

Melanie wasn't impressed. 'Yes, you would,' she insisted. 'You believed I was a cheap little slut and a gold-digger who had made an utter fool out of you. You would have wanted revenge—probably still want it!' she flashed. 'But I have my own money with which to fight you now. I also have Robbie, who *loves* me, Rafiq. He loves *me*, as his mother, and he's old enough and wise enough to hate anyone who might dare to try and pull us apart!'

He went paler with every bitter word she tossed at him, until a white ring circled his taut mouth. 'If you feel like this, why have you decided to bring me into his life?'

'Because he needs you,' she whispered.

'And did not need me before?'

'No.' She shook her head. 'Before, he had William.'

CHAPTER FOUR

RAFIQ turned away as if her answer had cut him. His action more or less said it all for Melanie. Her anger fled, leaving her feeling weak and shaken, and she too turned away, putting a hand up to cover her trembling mouth, and waited for him recover from what she'd thrown at him. Because she knew it wasn't over, not by a long way.

Neither moved nor tried to speak again. In the drumming silence Rafiq was trying to decide how he felt about these latest revelations, and realised he was in no fit state to attempt the problem. Or was he being a coward and delaying the ugliness of truth?

And what was that truth? he asked himself. The truth was that Melanie had accused him of things he couldn't argue with. He would not have believed her son was his, unless presented with positive evidence. He would certainly have moved heaven and earth to remove his son from the clutches of a woman he believed unfit to rear his child.

He still believed it, which only helped to make the situation that bit uglier.

'I think I should leave,' he heard himself murmur.

'Yes,' she agreed.

'I think we should defer the rest until another time when we are both...calmer.'

'Yes,' she agreed again.

Yet he didn't move—he wanted to move but something was stopping him. A need to stay? To be here where his son was? Or was it Melanie who was holding him? He turned to look at her, at the fall of her pale hair against slender shoulders that were no longer straight with defiance but hunched and heavy. Her black woollen top clung to the gentle curves of her body and the jeans followed the lines of her hips and thighs. She held a hand to her mouth, he saw, which explained why her answers had sounded muffled, and the other hand was wrapped around her body, the fingernails trembling where they dug deep into black wool.

He turned away again, and looked at the room for the first time since he'd entered it. It came as a small surprise. The décor was old-fashioned, the furniture the same, mostly heavy dark pieces that spoke of another era, like the patterned red carpet that covered the floor and the dark red velvet curtain fabric that matched the upholstery covering the sofas and chairs. It was a man's kind of room, warm and solid, with the odd female touch, such as the jewel-coloured silk cushions heaped on the sofas and chairs.

He liked it, which further surprised him because he was so predisposed to dislike anything to do with Melanie right now.

Or was it William Portreath's taste he was reluctantly admiring? he then wondered suddenly, and felt the bitterness well up again, felt the hard cut of envy for a man who had loved another man's child enough to present him with his own name.

He didn't want to leave. Melanie could feel his reluctance wrapping round the room like a heavy dark cloud that stole all the oxygen. He was still steeped in shock. His son was here in this very house. He needed to see him, see the truth for himself. She understood that, and wished so much that things had worked out differently this morning, because they could have got all the fighting out of the way then and he could have happily met Robbie and have seen what a wonderful child they had made together. More importantly, Robbie would have met his father and would have known that he was no longer in danger of being left alone in this world if anything should happen to her.

Should she say something—hold out yet another olive branch? Should she tell him that she understood how he was feeling, but that she had to protect both herself and her son?

Would he listen? Was he ready to do that now?

A log dropped in the grate and sent out a spray of crackling sparks. As it did so the Westminster mantel clock chimed the hour. Then a floorboard creaked somewhere, making Melanie turn to look at the door. Sensing her doing it, Rafiq did the same thing. It came again; the pair of them went so still they could hear their hearts beating. Melanie knew every bump and creak in this old house; she knew every draught and whistle.

'What?' Rafiq asked.

'Robbie,' she said, and started walking. 'Stay in here,' she cautioned as she opened the door. Then she disappeared, closing the door behind her without seeing that Rafiq was incapable of going anywhere.

He had frozen into a posture only his brother would recognise. But even Hassan had only seen it happen when it involved their father and his battles with death that were sometimes too close to call. The name of it was fear—fear of losing a man he loved above all else in this world—only here he was experiencing the same paralysed fear of meeting his seven-year-old son.

Would she do that? Would Melanie bring the boy down here and present them to each other without any preparation to ease the—?

Another log fell in the grate and broke him free from his stone-like stasis. He turned his head and saw the log was in danger of rolling into the hearth.

Robbie was just coming out of the bathroom when Melanie arrived on the upstairs landing. 'Okay?' she asked softly.

'Mmm,' he murmured sleepily. 'I thought I heard voices.'

'The television, probably.' Melanie smiled through the

untruth and walked with him into his bedroom, then helped to tuck him into bed.

'I had a dream tonight, but it wasn't a bad one,' he told her.

'Good.' She stroked his silk dark head.

'There was a man on a big black stallion and he stopped and said, ''Are you Robbie?'' I said, ''Yes'' and he smiled and said, ''Next time, you can ride up here with me, if you like.'''

'Well, that was nice of him.' Melanie smiled, thinking she didn't like the idea of some stranger offering her son rides.

'Mmm.' His eyes were drooping; he gave a yawn. 'He was wearing one of those white robes and had a thing on his head, like Arabs wear.'

Melanie's stomach rolled over. She wasn't one of those people who believed dreams forecast the future, and Robbie knew about his Arabian side because William had spent hours with him in his study, filling his mind with all things Arabian. No doubt there had been a picture of an Arab on horseback at some time. But for her son to have the dream tonight of all nights disturbed her more than she liked.

'Go back to sleep,' she whispered.

'You won't go anywhere, will you?'

'No, I won't go anywhere,' she softly promised. 'Except back downstairs to watch television,' she added, just in case he was expecting her to remain right here, kneeling beside his bed for the rest of the night. It had happened before and probably would again, she mused bleakly.

But not tonight, she saw as he dropped back into sleep without another murmur. She waited a few minutes longer to make sure he was fully asleep, though, taking no chances in a situation that was hazardous enough as it stood without Robbie deciding to follow her downstairs as she knew he was quite capable of doing. But eventually she rose up and left him, silently closing the bedroom door behind her—just in case voices became raised again.

Walking back into the living room required her to take a deep breath for steadiness. What she found was that Rafiq had removed his jacket to reveal a black cashmere roll-neck sweater and was squatting down in front of the fire. His body twisted when he heard her come in, eyes fiercely guarded as they shifted across the empty spaces at her sides. Tension screamed from every muscle, from every flicker of an eyelash. He was looking for Robbie.

'He got up to use the bathroom,' she explained quickly. 'Then fell asleep again almost as soon as he'd climbed back into bed.'

With a nod of his head Rafiq turned away again, but not before she'd seen a war between desire and relief taking place upon his face, and her heart gave a twist of sympathy for this man who had to be struggling with just about every emotion available to him.

It was only as she began to walk forward that she noticed he held the hearth brush and pan in his hands. She also noticed the stretch of fine wool across expanded shoulder blades and remembered what it had felt like to press against them with the flat of her palms. Heat began to pool low down in her stomach; memories that really should not be so clear and sharp after all of these years sent her eyes on a journey down the length of his spine to the leanness of his hips and the power in his spread thighs.

'A log fell onto the hearth,' he said as she came up beside him. His voice sounded rough, like gravel. He wasn't actually using the brush and pan because he was just squatting there, staring at them as if they weren't there.

Coming down beside him, Melanie took them from his loose fingers and laid them aside. 'Rafiq...I'm sorry for saying what I said before. I was angry, and—'

'You needed to say those things, and I suppose I needed to hear them.'

But he wasn't sure. She watched the firelight play with

his taut features and enrich the dark olive tones of his skin. 'Here,' she said, and dipped a hand into the pocket in her jeans, then gently slotted a photograph into one of his hands. 'I thought you might like to have this.'

It was Robbie, looking all grown-up and smart in his school uniform and wearing that familiar rather sardonic half-smile. It had occurred to her as she was coming back down the stairs that Rafiq still had no conception of how like him his son was. If she had taken him into William's study he would have seen Robbie's face laughing back at him from photos on every available surface, because that was the way William had liked it and she hadn't yet got around to moving anything—hadn't had the heart to change anything anywhere in the house.

'It was taken in school only a few weeks ago,' she explained. 'He looks so much like you that it came as a shock when I walked into your office this morning and realised just...'

Her voiced trailed away, dying on words that did not need saying because she could tell from Rafiq's reaction that he was seeing it all for himself. His eyes were fixed on the simple four-by-four portrait. She could hear the strain in his shallow breathing, feel the tension in his body and the pulsing, stinging agony of his stress.

She tried to swallow, but found it impossible. She felt the sudden need to give him some space and privacy for what was battering him, but couldn't bring herself to get up and move away. Tears thickened her throat; her chest began to feel too tight. In desperation she reached out to pick up the hearth brush and pan and began carefully gathering up fine flakes of wood ash still scattered on the grate.

It was dreadful. Say something, she wanted to beg him. Shout at me, if you like! But I need to know what you think of this beautiful child we made together. I need—

His hands came out and took back the brush and pan. As her breathy gasp filtered through the air she watched him lay them carefully aside. She didn't know what was coming—was afraid of what was coming. Especially when long lean fingers curled around her upper arms and began drawing her to her feet. She felt small suddenly, overwhelmed by his superior height and size. He was standing too close, his touch achingly gentle yet frighteningly disturbing. The heat of his breath was on her face and his thighs were touching hers. Her arms felt soft and frail beneath the controlled power in his imprisoning fingers, and her breasts were tingling at the nearness of his chest.

Wary, she lifted her eyes to his, and the breath shivered from her lips at what she saw written in the dark glitter of his eyes.

No, she wanted to protest, but the denial just wouldn't come, and it would have been too late anyway because his dark head lowered and he was kissing her, though not hard or hotly as he had this morning. Nor even because he felt driven by a simple need to make physical contact with another human being right now. He was kissing her with reverence, gently crushing her against him, gently crushing her mouth with his.

Then he released her and turned away, dark head slightly lowered, wide shoulders set. He picked up his jacket, then just walked out of the room and, seconds later, out of the house, leaving Melanie standing right where he had left her, with the warmth of his kiss still pulsing against her lips and what she'd seen in his eyes before he turned away, quietly tearing her apart.

Tears, she'd seen the hot black glint of tears in the eyes of a man who'd gone way beyond the point of being able to contain the power of what it was he had been forced to deal with today.

She had done that. With her little plots and shock strategies she had managed to reduce a proud man to tears in front of her. She had never felt so ashamed of herself.

Rafiq sat in his office staring down at the neatly processed, finely detailed document he had spent the whole night working on. He was good at this, he acknowledged with absolutely no sense of pleasure. Concentrating his talents on the detached and inanimate was most definitely his forte. Money instead of emotions. The planning and arranging of someone else's finances instead of allowing himself to lie in his bed crucifying himself with his inadequacies as a fully paid up member of the human race.

The phone on his desk began to ring, halting the urge to put his head back and close his sleep-starved eyes. It was Randal Soames. 'Are you sure you want this?' the lawyer asked him.

'Exactly as I have set it out,' he confirmed.

He sounded dubious. 'You might marry some day, have more children.'

Not this man, Rafiq thought bleakly. 'Have you spoken to Melanie?'

Swift change of subject. He could almost hear Randal thinking it. 'She isn't there. There is some kind of function on at the boy's school, I seem to recall. I'll try again later.'

The boy's school. Some kind of function. Just two more things about his son he had no knowledge of.

Oh, damn. He got up and swung away from his chair, shoved his hands into his trouser pockets, then stood staring out of the window at a cold grey day. It had now begun to pour with rain.

Safely slotted into his wallet rested a miniature image of himself at the age of seven. Similar hair, similar eyes, similar slightly rueful expression which hid the same vulnerability he had suffered at the same age. He felt as if he knew this child of his inside out, yet he could not say which school his dark red uniform represented, nor what the boy ate for breakfast each morning.

His son even had his skin shading. So where were Melanie's genes? Where was his French blood? Where was there anything in the photograph to say that his son had not been cloned on a scientist's bench instead of conceived during the act of love?

Love. He cursed the word, hated it—despised it—and felt it grinding against his every muscle like a physical torture set up to make him accept that love could beat the hell out of any man's wish to feeling nothing.

He was in love with his son, but had made no attempt to go anywhere near him. He loved his father, his brother, and Hassan's lovely wife, Leona—but differently. With them he felt safe to love; with the boy he did not. Which was why he was standing here preferring to stare at the rain than take the bull by the horns and face uncertainty.

As for Melanie...

A sigh shot from him at this other reason why he had spent the past two days simmering in his own confusion. He had loved Melanie when they had conceived their son, but he would prefer not to be reminded of it. Now, what came next? Where were they supposed to go? Into one of those awful situations he had witnessed amongst so many friends with broken relationships, where they shared the children by cool agreement—when there was nothing damn cool about a child's feelings?

A knock sounded on his door; he swung round to watch Kadir walk in the room. As his aide offered a bow of apology for intruding Rafiq caught the sparkle of raindrops on the shoulders of his neat grey jacket. 'Been out in this filthy weather, Kadir?' he quizzed.

'Yes, sir.' Rafiq received another bow. 'A note has just arrived for you,' Kadir explained, and walked forward to hold it out to him.

Rafiq looked down at it without attempting to take it, wearily wondering, What now? Because this was no formal business note. The envelope was small and square, and its sender female, by the neatly scripted way his name had been written upon it. No address or postage stamp, which said it had been hand-delivered.

'Who is it from?'

Kadir cleared his throat. 'It arrived in another envelope addressed to me. This is all I know.'

All he knew. Frowning, Rafiq pulled his hands out of his pockets and accepted the letter, then he broke the glued seal. Still frowning, he took out the single sheet of paper and read the two short sentences written upon it. 'Can I come up? I'm standing across the street.'

His heart hit against his ribcage. He swung back to the window to stare down through sheets of rain to the street. A solitary figure stood against the building opposite, sheltering from the rain beneath a big black umbrella.

Melanie. Something burst into life inside him. With a twist of his body he snatched his jacket off the back of his chair. 'Have my car waiting,' he instructed Kadir as he headed for the door—then paused as his mind made a connection. 'Don't make a habit of lying to me, Kadir,' he advised.

Then he left, with Kadir's rather heavy, 'No, sir,' hanging in the air.

The lift took him downwards; his feet took him outside. The sheeting rain drenched him in the few seconds it took him to cross the street.

Melanie only realised he was there when she saw his feet appear in front of her. The umbrella was wrenched from her fingers, and was held higher, so he could join her beneath it. She looked up and saw the strain in his face, the tiredness, the frown. 'Are you mad?' he demanded. 'Why are you standing out here?'

'I didn't want your security people throwing me off the premises,' she explained. 'But I needed to talk to you.'

By the way he flattened his mouth she assumed he'd forgotten about his instructions regarding her and his bank. Then he noticed that she was shivering so much her teeth were chattering and, taking a grim hold on her arm, he hustled her into the nearest doorway, snapped the umbrella shut and laid it aside. Then he removed his jacket and swung it around her shoulders.

'You're freezing,' he muttered. 'I cannot believe you came here dressed like this.'

She was in her designer suit again. It had seemed appropriate when she'd made the decision to come. Now she was so grateful for the added warmth of his jacket that she huddled greedily into it. 'It w-wasn't raining this much when I left home and—and I'm not thinking very clearly right now...'

'I understand the feeling,' he murmured dryly.

'Now y-you're wet too,' she continued in an agitated rush. 'Y-you should have got Kadir to—'

'Run a few more messages?' he offered when she tried to swallow her runaway tongue.

She glanced up, met his eyes, saw the sardonic gleam in them and released a sigh. 'He told you. He promised he wouldn't. I didn't want him to get into trouble for colluding with me.'

'You believed I would be angry with him?'

'It's been two days...' Two days of waiting and pacing and jumping out of her skin every time the doorbell or telephone rang. In the end she hadn't been able to take the stress any longer and had come to find him. Now she wished that she hadn't because she was feeling like a fool.

'Kadir carried out your instructions to the letter,' Rafiq inserted. 'As for the rest...I guessed.'

He'd guessed. 'Mr Omnipotent,' she muttered.

To her surprise he laughed, it was a low deep sound that brought her eyes fluttering up to his again, which were warm and dark and concentrated on her. Things began to happen she just didn't want, like a pooling of warmth deep down in her abdomen and a breathlessness that tightened her chest.

Don't look at me like that, she wanted to protest, but too many things were leaping between them, such as the son they shared, not to mention shared kisses. Intimacy, in other words; too much of it that went back too many years yet could tug on her senses as if everything, including the events leading to Robbie's conception, had happened only yesterday.

'I needed time to think,' he murmured huskily.

Husky suddenly made her clothes feel too tight. 'I know you m-must be hurt, but I h-had to protect myself.'

'From the omnipotent Arab with revenge on his mind?' He smiled as he said it, but it was a grim smile.

'I'm sorry, but, yes,' she answered honestly. 'You—'

His hand lifted up to push a stray coil of damp hair away from her temple and she responded with a tense little jerk. Beyond the shelter of the doorway, the rain pounded on the pavements. The coil of hair left a trailing raindrop behind it so his finger moved to scoop it from her cheek.

Someone dashed into the doorway, stopped to shake out their umbrella, then, with a curious glance at them both, walked into the building, leaving Melanie with the disturbing impression that she must look like a wicked woman snatching a secret assignation with her tall dark lover.

Lowering her eyes, she huddled further into his jacket. It was big on her—huge—the slippery silk lining whispering softly against the thin fabric of her suit. She was picking up the scent of his aftershave from it, subtle and spicy, tantalisingly familiar. He couldn't stand much closer to her if he tried.

Maybe Rafiq was thinking along similar lines, because he released a short sigh. Her eyes became fascinated with his slender red tie and the way it lay down the length of his white shirt, covering muscular proportions that expanded and contracted with the sigh.

Her lips began to pulse, and it scared the life out of her. Things were happening here that really should not. 'I don't think this is an appropriate place,' she said a little wildly.

'No,' he agreed, but made no move to do anything about it.

One of those silences fell; it pumped up her heartbeat and dried out her mouth. His hands began to move, sliding beneath the lapel of his navy blue jacket until the backs of his fingers came to rest against her breasts. She pulled in a sharp breath; for a fine tight nerve-singing moment she thought he was going to lower his head and kiss her.

Then she shivered as genuine cold made itself felt again, and he was setting her free to reach for the umbrella. Opening it up, he urged her beneath it, then out into the pouring rain. Her stiletto shoes danced puddles as he hurried her across the street. Expecting to be ushered into the bank, she was surprised to find herself being bundled into the back of a car. It was big and plush, with a glass partition between them and the driver, and seats made of soft black leather.

Through shivering chatters she watched Rafiq toss the umbrella onto the floor of the car, then climb in beside her. His shirt was wet, showing patches of dark skin beneath its white fabric and his black hair was soaked and slicked to his head. He leant forward to pick up a telephone, uttered some terse command in Arabic, then sat back with a sigh.

'Where are we going?' she questioned.

'Somewhere we can talk.'

'Oh.' She took a pensive glance out of the window. 'I thought the bank...'

'No,' he said, and that was all. Her top teeth pressed into her bottom lip because she wasn't sure she liked the sound of that no.

'Rafiq—'

'Randal has been trying to contact you.'

A diversion. 'Has he?'

'He said you were out at some function or other.'

'First thing this morning, yes.' She nodded. 'Robbie's school is putting on a pantomime at Christmas. They're doing *Cinderella*. There were rehearsals this morning. I—helped out.'

'Which school?'

She told him. He pressed his lips together and nodded his dark head. Melanie shifted tensely, unsure of his mood now and even more uncertain that she wanted to be sitting here in such close confines with a man she couldn't read from one second to the next.

For all she knew he could be sitting here plotting her downfall—or her seduction. Because something improper had been running through his mind back there in the doorway. It had been running through hers too, she was forced to admit. It just wasn't fair. Only this man had ever been able to toss her into this hectic state of sexual awareness just by—being there.

She frowned at the rain-spattered window. That feeling had been there from the first time her arm had brushed against his shoulder when she'd been serving him at the Maitlands' dinner table. Twenty years old, as naive as they came, she'd caught his scent, the sound of his low dark laughter and the deeply smooth voice tones as he'd spoken to the person sitting next to him, and her response had been so primitively sexual that she'd spilled the sauce onto the tablecloth.

After that had come the humiliating dressing down from Sally Maitland, then her first real contact with his hand, when Rafiq had cornered her later and tried to make light of the embarrassing incident. He'd been dressed in a dinner suit, big and dark, suave and sophisticated, with an easy grace that had belied his size and a lazily worn self-confidence that aimed to charm.

'Watch him,' Sally Maitland had warned later. 'Arab men are notoriously attracted to slender young blondes. He'll take what you are putting on offer, Melanie, then despise you for it later.'

She had been right, too. Rafiq had pursued her like a man besotted until he'd finally managed to break down her defences. He'd promised her everything: love, marriage, the whole wonderful package. But the moment he'd taken what he had really been after he'd despised her for giving it. He'd seen a tramp then, a woman willing to give it out to all and sundry once she'd acquired the taste.

He moved. She stiffened and swung her head round to send him a hard, accusing glance.

'What?' He looked shocked by it.

'Nothing.' She looked away again, hoping to goodness that eight years of abstinence had given her some defence against him, though why did she think she needed it?

Because Rafiq still desired her. It had been there when they'd met in his office two days ago, there when he'd come to her home. It had been there just now in the door-way when he'd almost given in to it and kissed her.

Three meetings, two kisses, and one still hovering on the sidelines with time on its side to give it a chance.

As for defences, they were not much use when she only had to look at him to feel that old breathless, sensual pull.

The car drew to a stop outside a block of select apart-ments. Life took another worrying twist when she realised where they had to be. Rafiq opened his door and braved the rain again to stride round to her side of the car and open her door.

'I don't think...'

His hand found her wrist and the jacket began to slip from her shoulders as he tugged her into the rain. As she grappled to save the jacket from falling onto the wet pave-ment he pulled her inside the building before she had a chance to voice a bigger protest.

A man dressed in a security uniform sat behind a desk. He stood up and smiled. 'Good morning, sir...madam,' he greeted politely. 'Dreadful weather,' he opined with a glance at their rain-soaked clothes.

Rafiq murmured a reply; Melanie offered a nervous little smile and wondered what the man must really be thinking as Rafiq pulled her into the lift.

'I don't think this is a good idea,' she protested a trifle breathlessly.

'I do,' he countered, and one glance at him told her why he did. He wasn't even trying to hide it!

A wave of answering heat put her into a panic. 'No,'

she said, and tried to twist her wrist free from his grasp so she could turn and make a diving exit before the lift doors closed. But Rafiq was one step ahead of her; with only the gentlest of tugs he brought her hard up against his body at the same time as his other hand snaked out to hit the lift button.

To the man on the desk they must have looked like two people so hungry for each other they couldn't wait until they were alone. The lift doors closed while Melanie was still trying to recover from the shock contact with Rafiq's body. Eyes like hot coals burned his intention; her blood began to race, charged by her hammering heartbeat.

'How dare you?' she choked in shrill protest. 'This is supposed to be about Robbie!'

Rafiq laughed. Maybe she was right, but he didn't think so. For two long days he had prowled through his life trying to understand what it was that was holding him back from going to meet his son. For two aching days and sleepless nights he'd swung from one reason to another without hitting upon the right one. But one look at Melanie standing in the rain and the answer had lit up in his head like a beacon. He could not deal with the problem of his son until he'd dealt with the problem of his son's mother. He wanted her—all of her. He wanted every single thing he had walked away from eight years ago. He wanted her in his life, in his bed! And the best thing about it was that he meant to have it all, without the love thing cluttering up his reasoning.

'I am going to take you in my arms and kiss you stupid,' he informed her grittily. 'I am going to strip the clothes from your body and enjoy your exquisite flesh. I will take you to my bed and avail myself of every sweet, delectable inch of you,' he rasped with husky incision. 'I am going to take you out and buy you a ring which will say that you belong to me. Then, and only then, I will take you

with me to meet my son! You owe me this much, Melanie-
of-the-sweet-face-and-lying-little-heart. You owe me for
eight long years of bitterness, and seven years of never
knowing my son!'

CHAPTER FIVE

'YOU'RE crazy,' she breathed as she strained to get away from him.

'Maybe.' He shrugged, but the look in her eyes told him she was captivated by the whole exciting agenda, and she was quivering against him like a trapped little bird, mesmerised and enthralled.

'How long has it been for you, Melanie, since a man laid his hands on your body?' he questioned darkly. 'How long since you felt the burning thrust of a man's pleasure zone driving you mindless with need?'

Her mouth was trembling, her eyes were bright, her skin pale with what might have been mistaken for fear if it hadn't been for the seductive scent of her arousal sweetening the air. He knew that scent, had picked up on it at their first meeting, and it had never failed to be there every time they'd been near each other since. Eight years had not changed it; eight years had not diminished one small part of what it could do to him.

'Sex...' He leant close to whisper. 'It is all around us. You can feel it. Stop pretending.'

'If you don't stop this I am going to start screaming!'

His response was to clasp his free hand round her nape, his eyes glittering his intention just before he lowered his dark head and took what he wanted: her mouth, her hot, dry, trembling mouth, that opened without pause to welcome him. Her fingers grappled with his shirt front; her breasts heaved against his chest. And as her beautiful thighs arched in their eagerness to make contact with his, it was Melanie who plunged into the kiss.

She groaned as his tongue caressed moist tissue. He

laughed, low and throatily deep, pulsing with dark triumph that brought her nails clawing into his neck in punishment. He didn't care. He liked those sharp nails digging into him. They let him know this could be as wild and unbridled as he wanted it to be. They made him feel alive, energised! With Serena it had been sex. With this woman it was— regeneration of every single cell he possessed!

The lift doors slid apart. Without breaking the kiss, he swung her up into his arms and carried her towards his apartment door. Opening it with the key was a struggle when he was not prepared to release her mouth, but he managed it, stepped inside, kicked the door shut behind him then, with a satisfied grunt, began walking down the hallway towards the only room that mattered right now.

His jacket slipped from her shoulders, trailed its way to the ground and was left where it fell as he walked with unerring steps into the bedroom and shut this door too. Which left only them and a giant-sized bed, standing proud with its cover of royal blue silk. No soft feathers this time, no deep eiderdown, just a firm flat mattress dressed in the perfect colour on which to lay his prize.

When he lowered her feet to the floor she was trembling so badly she could barely stand upright unaided. Her eyes were big, glazed, and the colour of the richest gold, her mouth full and red and begging for his.

'Now tell me no.' He laid the silken words down like a challenge.

She couldn't answer. When all she did was reach out a hand to steady herself, he caught it and placed it onto his chest. Her eyes flickered down to absorb the fact that she was touching hair-roughened flesh. She had done it again. Without knowing it she'd unfastened his shirt during their walk down the hall!

'Yes,' he breathed in dark confirmation, and yanked his tie loose then tossed it aside. The last shirt button came undone at his throat and the shirt fell wide open to reveal a body built to carry the world if it was ever called upon to do so.

'Oh, dear God,' she managed to breathe in shaken realisation. By then his fingers were unfastening the buttons of her jacket to reveal a fitted top she had added to the ensemble that had not been there the last time.

Protection from him, or herself? The jacket slid from her shoulders; the top slipped over her head. As she lifted those dazed eyes back up to his he kissed her, fiercely, just in case she decided to try and stop this.

But Melanie was in no fit state to stop anything. She was lost in a gripping love affair with this man's body and the power of his kiss. Every time she breathed she drowned in the scent of him; every time she moved she felt the impact of his strength. His mouth consumed her with a voracious hunger; the stroke of his hands collapsed her brain. She had no sense, no will, no desire to do anything but be here, feeling the raging torment of a need so potent it overwhelmed her. The eight years since she'd been with him like this didn't seem to matter. Her senses remembered, desired and demanded she feed them with everything.

'This is mad,' she whimpered.

He didn't answer. His hands were ridding her of her bra. The black lace drifted away from full rounded breasts with nipples already tightly distended. He touched; she groaned and simply fell against him, then fell again, into a pit packed full of sensation. Sleek bronzed skin electrified her fingers; the rasp of curling hair excited her breasts. The kiss was a seduction on its own hot merits, and as he slid down the zip of her skirt she wriggled her hips to aid its journey to the floor. The powerhouse thrust of his erection jumped as she writhed against him. His breathing was rough, his body clenched by the ferocity of his desire. But when he slid his hands beneath the final piece of black lace to tug her more firmly against him, she was the one to fall apart.

It was a complete loss of control. She cupped his face, kissed it all over, urgently, desperately touching and tasting, and forcing tight, thick sounds to rasp from his throat. He belonged to her. This man, this glorious dark-skinned giant, belonged to her. She'd believed it eight years ago and she believed it again now. Part of her might be yelling, *Fool!* but at this precise moment she didn't care.

His hands spanned her hips and lifted her up against him; her arms wound around his neck. He began carrying her again, to lower her down onto the firm cool expanse of the large bed. Warm skin slid against the smoothness of silk; long limbs stretched sensually. Her eyes caught a glimpsing impression of ivory presented on a bed of blue, with her hair a golden halo as she watched him divest himself of the rest of his clothes. She watched in fascination as he drew in tight muscles in his abdomen then unclipped his trousers; her mouth ran dry as she watched him slide down the zip. Two seconds later he was naked, and her insides were curling on a mixture of excitement and stark, staring alarm until she remembered how it felt to absorb this man into her.

Then he was lowering his big frame down right next to her, reaching out to roll her against him. Skin met skin, stealing her breath away. His mouth claimed hers and his hands began to wreak magic, shaping her breasts, her stomach, the sensitive inner flesh of her thighs. She still wore silk stockings; deft fingers removed them. She still wore panties; they drifted away next. She moved and writhed to every clever stroke of his fingers. The kiss broke apart as she gulped greedily for breath. She was lost, gazing into eyes so black they drew her into them. Loving him, needing him.

'Do we stop?'

Do we stop…? she repeated dizzily, and tried to focus for the first time. His cheekbones stood out on a face taut with passion. His mouth wore the swollen bloom of desire gone wild. His beautiful bronzed body lay half across her and a hand was gently circling her navel.

'To continue means you accept my intentions.'

Intentions? Each time he spoke she had to work hard to grasp the words. 'Do you want to stop?' Long lashes blinked him a bemused look.

He touched his tongue to her lower lip. 'No,' he said.

'Then why ask?'

He smiled an odd smile, and used that tongue to circle the full pulsing beauty of her whole mouth. 'So be it,' he said.

She mimicked the stirring manoeuvre with an impulsiveness that for some unfathomable reason flung him over the edge. Passion roared like a lion, and the whole thing became a hot and seething whirl. He closed his mouth over one of her breasts, nipped her nipple with his teeth. As she drew in a sharp breath he sucked and played and tormented, with his mouth, with his hands. Then, with the glide of long fingers down the length of her, he descended into the cloud of gold at the apex of her thighs.

Pleasure became a greedy animal. Where he touched, she yearned for more. Her fingers dug and scraped and moulded rippling, trembling, slick male muscle. The whole thing grew like a mushroom, building pleasure on pleasure, and it made it all so much more exciting to know his breathing was ragged, that his heart was thumping madly and his body throbbing with a need as acute as her own.

I shouldn't be doing this. One single brief glimpse at sanity attempted to spoil it. She released a small whimper of distress. Then he was invading the soft tissue of her femininity with the touch of a master, and the door slammed on sanity, along with her ability to control anything, because she was flying, or as near as, her fingers clutching at him as she gasped out his name and begged him never to stop.

The ragged sound of his breathing filled her ears; the heat of his breath moistened her face. He moved over her, hair-roughened thighs parting her smooth ones. A hand slid beneath her hips to bring them towards him and she felt the first probe of his entry, then felt another set of fingers coil into her hair. He lifted her head from the bed, bringing her eyes flying open. Black heat blazed a path of fire right through her—compulsive, compelling, it warned of what was to come. Then he made that single surging thrust at the same moment his mouth smothered her cry.

It was possession in its fullest meaning. He moved, and she responded with pleasure-wracked sounds he claimed for himself. Each thrust sent him deeper, each withdrawal set her quivering in pleasurable response, each slide of damp flesh became an exquisite torment that heightened everything. When he increased the rhythm she just hung on and let him conduct the whole concert, and her imagination helped him by offering up picture flashes of pale skin against dark skin, slender white limbs clinging to majestic bronze. Darkness and sunlight became one glorious entity. He drove her into its seething depths then snapped the last thread of her control with a kiss that claimed every gasp and quiver as they came together as lost-souls in a black cavern that held back everything but the pin-sharp song of ecstasy.

He was lying beside her with his chest still heaving out the last throes of his own fulfilment. A brown hand covered his eyes. Melanie didn't move—couldn't. When she eventually managed to open her eyes it was to the grey day pouring into the bedroom and the chill that was already settling on her flesh. The ivory and blue room was about as cold a place as anyone could wish to enjoy a soulless tumble upon a strange bed. The slack-limbed languid aftermath was being replaced with reality, the dawning sense of horror, the flaying sense of dismay. What had she done—what had *they* done?

She wanted to die here, she decided. She just wanted to close her eyes and die rather than face what had to come next.

The truth. The cold, dark hollowness of truth. She'd expected him to seek revenge in one form or other, but she had not expected anything like this.

'I hate you,' she whispered as her mouth began to wobble.

He stopped breathing. The hand left his face.

'You did this on purpose. You meant to shatter me.' On a flood of tears she scrambled from the bed.

'In case you may not have noticed, I shattered too,' he fed after her quietly.

'That's different.' She began picking up her clothing. Every move, every grasp of her fingers shook with the agony of her distress. 'You're a man. You're allowed to behave like that.'

'Like what?'

'Animal!' she choked, searching the floor for her panties and not seeing them anywhere. Her cheeks were hot, yet her flesh felt so cold it was almost numb. 'Y-you look at me and see a western woman. Cheap to buy and easy to have!' she threw at him in shaken bitterness. 'You did this the last time. Y-you wanted and you took, then despised me for letting you!'

'I despised you for going from my arms into the arms of your cousin.'

'*Step*-cousin!' she corrected. 'And I am not going to discuss that with you!'

'Why not?' In a single lithe movement he snaked off the bed and came to stand over her. Naked, bold, so forcefully male, she almost sank beneath the swimming tide of her own response.

'Because you had your chance to listen eight years ago and decided it wasn't worth the effort.' Clutching her clothes to her front, she began looking wildly around her. 'Now hell will freeze over before I will defend myself to you—! Where's the bathroom?'

'Wait a minute—'

'No!' She swerved away from his reaching hands.

'Don't touch me—ever again!' The breakdown into tears was gaining momentum and she needed to get out before it happened. 'I adored you,' she whispered painfully. 'You know that I did. Y-you thought it a great hoot to relieve the besotted innocent of her virginity.'

'Hoot?' he repeated. His voice shook.

She made the mistake of looking at him.

He was laughing at her! It was the final humiliation. She turned and ran for the nearest door, found herself standing in a long wide hallway with a pale wood floor and walls painted pale blue. Where to now? Which door next? she asked herself frantically. Any door, she decided, and sped across the hall's width to the nearest one, opened it, fell inside, then closed it behind her.

It was a blue and ivory bathroom. She could not believe her one bit of good luck. With fumbling fingers she pulled her skirt up over her hips and fastened the zip. No bra, she realised, no stockings nor panties. The stretchy black top covered her naked breasts. Her nipples stung as the fabric slid across them; sparks of awareness set her teeth on edge. She pulled on the jacket and tugged it ruthlessly across her front. Then she turned to leave, caught sight of herself in a mirror and was suddenly left suspended by what she saw. Her eyes were so dark she could see no hint of gold anywhere; her mouth was swollen and pulsing and red. Her hair needing brushing. She looked wild and wanton. Cheap and easy! One kiss and you fall on him, she accused that hateful face.

Now she had a son to go home to and face, knowing what she had been doing here with his father. Nausea leapt to her throat. She spun, wondering dizzily where her bag had gone. She decided it didn't matter; she could walk home if necessary—anything so long as she could get out of here!

She tugged the door open to find him standing there waiting for her. He'd pulled on a robe, a dark blue thing that covered hardly anything. A blanket of awareness attacked each sensitised erogenous zone. 'Get out of my way,' she said through clenched teeth.

'You are not going anywhere.' A big shoulder made contact with the door frame. 'We agreed terms.'

'Terms?' She blinked. Narrowed eyes held hers with a warning glint. In a vague part of her mind she remembered words being spoken. 'Accept my intentions,' and, 'So be it.' Then he'd licked her mouth and—

'Oh, dear God,' she breathed.

'You remember?' he mocked. 'Well, that makes it easier.'

'I want to go home.' She was pale now; she could actually feel her skin turning cold and thin.

'Later,' he agreed, and a hand came out. 'Don't you want to put these on?'

He held her stockings, her bra and her panties, flimsy pieces of black silk and lace threaded through long, very male fingers that gave shamelessness a whole new edge.

But Rafiq hadn't finished with her yet—not by a long way. 'I have no objection to you choosing a ring without these on, you understand.' His dark-toned voice was remorseless. 'In fact I think it would be rather excitingly decadent to know that only you and I know you wear nothing beneath that smart suit. But the stockings, maybe, to protect your legs from the cold weather?'

'Ring?' she repeated. 'You were serious about the ring?'

Big and dark, lean and hard, he wore the face of an Arabian warlord in no mood for compromise. 'I was serious about everything,' he confirmed with silken emphasis. 'My possession of your body, the ring—my son. We will greet him as a single unit, marry with him at our side, and become a family.'

A family eight years too late. Some family, Melanie thought as the whole wretched debacle came tumbling down upon her head. Her legs went weak and she turned to lean against the inner edge of the door frame. Determined not to cry, she closed her eyes and covered her mouth with a hand.

Watching her lose the will to fight him had the odd effect of tearing at the seams of his heart. On a sigh that rid him of mockery, he tossed the scraps of silk aside. 'I do not think you cheap and easy,' he uttered grimly. 'If anything I think it is I who is guilty of being both of those things,' he admitted, with just enough bite to let his bitterness show. 'But we will put the past in abeyance and speak for now. And now demands that we pool our resources, for our son's sake.'

'You haven't even met him yet, and you're planning his life for him.'

'But I *know* him,' he declared. 'I know what it feels like to have only one parent. What it can do to his head to know that the other parent does not seem to care if he lives or he dies. I have been there before him.' It was tense, tight statement of grim factuality. 'He bleeds inside. He will bleed no longer.'

'William loved him.'

If she'd meant to hurt by saying that, then she'd succeeded. Rafiq stiffened away from the door frame. 'My half-brother, Hassan, loves me without question. But he could not be the mother I never met or fill the hole in my heart left by her.'

With that he turned and walked back into the bedroom, not liking how much of himself he had just revealed and liking even less the way that Melanie followed him when he now wished to be alone.

A familiar feeling, he noted with a tense flexing of his shoulders.

'Who was she?'

The question placed a bitter taste in his mouth. 'A Frenchwoman—Parisian,' he drawled with bite. 'Very dark, very beautiful, very much out to catch herself a rich Arab with the oldest tricks known to man.' He turned to look at her and saw a different kind of beauty standing in his bedroom doorway. A soft golden beauty—but the same flawed beauty nonetheless.

Okay, he argued with himself as he moved over to the bank of wardrobes that filled one wall. So Melanie had not blackmailed him with the child they'd made together—still was not doing that, he was forced to concede since it was he who was using the blackmail here. But she had seen her chance of marrying wealth and had been prepared to forfeit her childhood sweetheart for it.

Shame that he'd had to discover her duplicity, he thought angrily. Shame he had not married her anyway on a desire to punish her for the rest of her life. At least he would have known his child then, would have seen him grow big in her womb as Hassan was seeing his child grow. He would have been there at his son's birth, and would have loved him so much he would never have needed to know those bleak, dark little moments in life when rejection could tear at the soul.

'When she discovered that my father was already married, and his wife pregnant, she was not pleased.'

'I don't blame her,' Melanie responded. 'It sounds to me as if your father deserved the blame. He was playing with her, obviously.'

'True.' A glimpse of a hard smile touched his mouth as he pulled a clean shirt from a hanger. 'He was young, he was arrogant and unforgivably self-seeking. But when my mother decided to cut her losses and have an abortion he showed a different side to his nature by talking her out of it—or should I say that his money did the talking?' he offered cynically as he placed the shirt on the bed. 'It matters not.' He shrugged. 'She died giving birth to me.'

'I'm sorry,' Melanie murmured.

'Don't be.' The clean shirt was followed by a clean dark suit, still wrapped in a tailor's suit bag. 'The deal was that she hand me over to my father the moment it was legally possible to do so.'

'And you think that decision denies her the right to have

anyone feel sorry at her passing? That's mean and shallow, Rafiq.' He froze in the act of selecting fresh underwear. 'For all you know she might have changed her mind about you. It happens all the time. How can you condemn someone who was never given the chance to offer an opinion?'

He turned on her. 'As I was offered that chance with my child?'

She blinked, then lowered guilty eyes from him. For some reason it infuriated him to see her do that! He covered the distance between them in a few angry strides, then used his hand to capture her chin and make her to look at him. 'Yes,' he hissed at what he saw there. 'We come full circle, my unforgiving Melanie. We reach the point where this truly began. You denied me my chance just as I deny my mother her chance. It makes us two of a pair, does it not?'

'I'm giving you your chance now.' Reaching up she grasped his wrist in a useless effort to pull his hand away. 'But it doesn't have to come with a ring attached to it!'

'Yes, it does,' he insisted. 'Because my son will not remain a bastard. My son will be surrounded with love on all sides! *My* son will not be put at risk of you marrying another man who can treat him as a second-class member of his family!'

Her beautiful eyes darkened in horror. 'Who did that to you?'

He let go. 'It is of no matter.' And turned away again, cursing his own stupid mouth!

'Rafiq…' She touched his arm with sympathy.

Sympathy! The bubbling black mass of old hurts came thundering up to the surface. He turned back, knew he was losing it—*knew it* and could not stop it! 'Get out!' he breathed. 'Get out of here, Melanie, while you still can!'

What she did was step closer and wrap her arms around him like a mother would—like *she* would do with his son! 'I'm sorry,' she was saying. 'I'm sorry. I didn't know…'

He gripped her arms and tried to prise her free; he

needed to put a safe distance between them or he did not know what he would do! But she held on, lifted her face, lifted eyes that understood when he did not want anyone to understand!

'I am dangerous,' he grated. It was his final warning.

She reached up and kissed him. Blackness turned molten, molten spun itself into something else. She was amazing, fearless—foolish! She had to be to still be here when anyone with eyes must know he was about to slake all this emotion in the only way he knew how!

He caught that mouth with a kiss that blazed. He picked her up and pressed her back against the wall. Her skirt rose above her hips as he parted her legs and wrapped them around him. He entered her with no preliminary at all.

Bright fireballs of sensation propelled themselves at her senses; she clung to his shoulders and his mouth. It was all so intense that she barely noticed when he ejected into her with the shuddering groans of a man lost in hell. When it was over her feet slithered like melted wax onto the hard wood flooring. Shocked and dazed, and still caught by the pulsing aftermath of her own shimmering climax, she stared blindly at his chest, where damp whorls of black hair curled around his gaping robe.

Then once again the horror of reality hit: the knowledge that she could be so primitive! She choked on a sob as a stream of Arabic flooded over her, then hoarse thick English words of apology, of remorse and self-whipping disgust and disgrace as he picked her up in his arms and carried her out of the bedroom and down the hall.

Safety came with the neatness of a sitting room, apparently. He set her down in a low soft leather armchair, then muttered something she did not catch before striding away. A doorbell rang; he must have gone to answer it because she heard the sound of voices talking, then nothing until he came to squat down beside her and offered a glass to her trembling mouth. It was brandy; it burned as she swallowed. He took a gulp himself.

'I don't know what to say to you,' he pushed out thickly.

Her lashes flickered downwards as she made herself look into his face. He was as white as the chair she was sitting on, guilt-riddled and appalled with himself.

'I'll marry you,' she whispered. 'I'll marry you.'

'Why?' He couldn't have sounded more stunned if he'd tried.

Tears filled her eyes. It was all so—*basic!* She wanted him again so very badly it burned like a wound inside! He filled her with a thousand contradictions. Anger, hurt, resentment, confusion—desire! He ran cold, then hot, was ruthlessly hard and tough, yet so very vulnerable it almost broke her heart.

And then they came—the words that really mattered. She was still in love him, even after all these years and all the heartache and pain and the sense of betrayal. She still loved him no matter what or why. Realising that hurt more than anything else did. She couldn't tell him—would *never* tell him.

'Robbie needs you,' she said.

Robbie needs you. Once again they'd arrived back at the beginning. A different beginning in an ever-confusing spiral of beginnings.

He stood up. It was a withdrawal in many ways. 'Yes,' he said. 'Of course. I will go and dress. You may safely use the bathroom to—tidy yourself before we leave.'

CHAPTER SIX

HIS suit was a dark blue, almost black, in colour, the fabric an exquisite weave of silk. His shirt was white, his tie blue, and the whole ensemble blended perfectly with the man he had turned himself into.

Cleanly shaven face; neatly combed hair; raven eyelashes keeping a permanent guard over his eyes, and his mouth a beautifully defined example of sombre elegance. Melanie had to bite hard into her bottom lip so as not to say a word. If he'd dressed like this to put Robbie at his ease with him then he could not have got it more wrong. Her son was more likely to stand in awe than feel at ease. Rafiq was the ice man, a man who belonged in a palace built of glass, steel and marble.

She shivered and fiddled with the ring on her finger. It was made of gold and bright, flawless sparkling diamonds. She had chosen it from a luscious selection set on a black velvet tray in the privacy of his sitting room. Between her running for cover in the bathroom and their confrontation across its threshold he had called up a top London jeweller and had had them bring a selection to his apartment.

It was money wielding its awesome power. She shivered again; he shifted tensely and sent her a sharp look that scoured the skin from the part of her profile he could see. Sitting next to each other in this car was the closest they'd been to each other since he'd fed her the brandy. No eye contact nor body contact, words spoken as if through a glass wall. Why? Because they'd delved into a dark place they knew they should never have visited. It had exposed too much of an inner core that most preferred to keep hidden away.

89

Now here they were, driving towards her home where another ordeal was about to be enacted. Melanie tried to swallow and found that she couldn't. From the corner of her eye she caught sight of his hand where it rested on his thigh. The long fingers moved ever so slightly, but she could almost taste the tension that forced them to make that minuscule jerk. She dared a quick glance up from beneath her lashes and almost shattered on impact with the hard profile of a cold and aloof Arabian male: his long thin nose; his curling black eyelashes hovering against the firm glossy texture of his olive-toned skin; his jaw line taut and rock-like, the set of his mouth implacable and flat. If she superimposed Arab clothes over the suit she could be looking at the Arabian prince he was in everything but name.

But that memory belonged to another time, and it did nothing for her nerves to remember it now. Daunting as he was in his western sophistication, she preferred it to that other man she had met only once, when he'd torn her apart with his contempt.

This time she managed to contain the shiver. 'Robbie might mention your father,' she heard herself say as thoughts of his ruthless Arab side led her onto other things.

The dark head turned with frightening precision; eyes too dark to read fixed on her face. 'He knows about my father?'

It was too quietly and too smoothly spoken. Melanie tried that swallow again. 'W-William liked to keep him informed ab-about your country,' she explained. 'Your father's poor health is reported in the press occasionally, and a party six months ago was given quite a lot of coverage. A thirty-year anniversary?' she prompted.

He nodded. So did she, then dragged her eyes away to look down at the ring again. 'Robbie decided that your father's ill health m-must have kept you at home with him. H-he worries about things like that, so it suited him to give you that particular reason why you didn't come to London.'

The hand resting on his thigh gave that telling minuscule twitch once more. 'Without William Portreath's money, would you ever have told me about him?'

It wasn't harsh but it was coldly accusing. 'Robbie only started asking questions about you a year ago. He never asked to see you, but if he had done I'd like to think I would have done something about it.'

'You'd like to think?' he repeated.

'I had to protect both him and myself,' she reiterated.

'From me?'

'From this!' she cried, shattering the wall between them with a spectacular eruption, blasting away all of this nice polite civility. 'Look at what you've already done, Rafiq! Even with William's money as my so-called safeguard. I've been packed up and taken over! You did it before. You packed me up and took me over, then dropped me like a brick when I didn't come up to your high expectations!'

'You are twisting the truth.'

'No, I'm not.' Trying to make the eruption subside again was impossible. The bubble had burst and she suddenly didn't know what she was doing, sitting here next to him travelling towards calamity at what felt like the speed of light. 'If Robbie can't meet those same high expectations does he get dropped?' she pushed out thickly. 'Do you truly think I believe I am doing the right thing bringing you into his life? Because I don't! You're so hard and tough and unpredictable.' She sat upright on a raw flick of tension. 'You blow hot, then icy cold. I can't tell what you're going to do next, and I'm frightened I've made a huge error of judgement here. I feel like I'm playing Russian roulette with a child's life!'

'I will not drop him!' he raked at her. 'Nor you, for that matter,' he added with a lofty promise that aimed to put all the emotion back under wraps but didn't quiet make it. 'And if you still feel this way, why am I here at all?' he demanded, and brought the whole thing toppling down again.

Melanie looked down at her tightly clenched hands, then out of the car window while her chest grew tight on words she did not want to speak.

But time was beginning to run out. 'William's death had a profound effect on Robbie,' she told him. 'He suddenly realised that without William he had only me to take care of him. So he worries that I—'

'Might die too and leave him with no one.' Rafiq took over in a deep voice so drenched in bleak understanding that she glanced sharply at him.

He was sitting there with the same carved profile, but his eyes had come alive, burning with a personal knowledge that brought into hard focus the kind of childhood he'd experienced as a motherless son—a second son and an illegitimate one at that.

'Y-you had your brother,' she reminded him.

His tight smile mocked the remark. 'Hassan is six months older than I am. Every time his mother looked at me she saw the bitter proof of her husband's infidelity while she was heavily pregnant. Do you think she didn't yearn for the day when she could toss me out of her household? In the end she died before she could achieve her dearest wish, but as a child I learned to appreciate the vulnerability of my situation.'

'I'm sorry. I didn't know.'

'How could you?' He shrugged. 'These are not the kind of memories a man usually shares with other people.'

Not even with the woman he professed to love? If he had been a bit more open with her eight years ago maybe she would have stood a chance at understanding what had made him the man he was, and dealt with the situation of Robbie differently.

'So, he worries?' Rafiq prompted.

She nodded. 'He has nightmares about it,' she confessed, and watched in thick-throated distress as he turned his head so she could see those dark knowing eyes. 'He worries himself sick if I so much as sneeze. As I've been saying from the start, he—'

'Needs me,' Rafiq finished. 'As back-up,' he added.

It sounded so very cold put like that, but— 'Yes,' she confirmed.

'And if I had not come through with this back-up?'

She looked away and did not answer. But, being the man he was, he had already worked out what her alternatives were going to be. His hand snaked out to catch her chin, then he made her to look back at him. Hard eyes glinted into her eyes. 'As far as my son and his mother are concerned I will not be walking away,' he vowed very clearly. 'So you may put away any other options, Melanie. For the ring on your finger will be joined by another, and you will not need to look elsewhere for anything—understand?'

Yes. She nodded and let her eyelashes flutter onto her cheeks so he couldn't read her thoughts. Because she was beginning to understand an awful lot of things, and none of them helped her to feel less anxious about the situation. With every word he uttered, Rafiq was revealing an affinity with his son that promised to grow into a bond like no other. Who would become the expendable link then? She would, and on realising it she began to appreciate what it meant to feel so frighteningly vulnerable.

The car pulled up outside her house. Melanie was never so relieved for an excuse to escape. She went to pull her chin free of his fingers, but he held on until she surrendered and looked back up at him. The glow in his eyes was skin-piercingly covetous. It pricked at just about every nerve-end she possessed. The sexual pull was stunning; the emotional one threatened to strip her bare. Sparks flew; her breathing snagged; for a few blind seconds she had to fight the urge to turn her mouth into those cool fingers and say something calamitous like, I still love you, Rafiq.

She wanted to run and Rafiq didn't blame her. He could

not look at her without the sexual fallout drenching the air. The cool tips of his fingers slid against skin like fine satin, the inner recesses of his mouth sprang into life with a need to taste what he could feel. A driving compulsion to lean down and take what was throbbing in the atmosphere held him motionless, because he dared not even breathe in case he gave in to its magnetic pull.

He had revealed the absolute worst of himself to her today, yet she was still sitting here looking at him through those hungry eyes. Why was that? he asked himself. She was wearing his ring and was prepared to marry him when she had to know his arguments for marriage were a bluff, and that she possessed the resources to turn her back on him if she so pleased.

Was she doing this for their son? A son who had not even looked upon his father's face and who, when he did, might well decide he didn't like what he saw! What then— what did Melanie do then?

He removed his fingers and looked away from her, and heard her feather out a shaky breath. His driver opened the door for her. She scrambled out of the car and hurried up the path to fumble the key into the lock of her front door. The black suit skimmed her slender figure; her pale hair swung around her slender nape. His heart gave a tug. It was fear. He grabbed it and crushed it down again.

It had stopped raining but the air was cold and damp. As he stepped out of the car he felt it seep into his bones and had a sudden wish to be at home, standing beneath the relentless heat of the desert sun.

But first he had a son to meet and a relationship to build. His heart gave a different kind of tug, and he grimaced as he turned to dismiss his driver. Then he swung back to look at the house into which Melanie had already disappeared. The car moved away as he walked up the path. As he walked inside the house seemed to stir, like a sleeping monster awakening from a long dark slumber as its senses picked up on the scent of threat.

Threat to whom? To Melanie or his son? Was it William Portreath's ghost Rafiq could sense stirring in the shadows, watching Rafiq infiltrate his domain so he could see for himself if he was a worthy successor? He gave himself a mental shake. He wasn't usually prone to such superstitious nonsense, he grimly mocked himself.

A sound came from the living room and he stepped into it to find Melanie on her knees in front of the fire, putting a light to the logs neatly aligned in the grate. Flames leaped to life and she was on her feet, moving round the room lighting faded old lamps, plumping faded old cushions. 'Make yourself at home,' she invited. 'I need to go and change before— The fire should be okay, and I've switched on the central heating system so the house will heat up pretty quickly.'

For a man who had never walked into any of his many homes needing to think about what kept it heated—or cool, for that matter—Rafiq viewed all this brisk domesticity through vaguely shocked eyes. She disappeared into the hallway. He listened to her light footsteps as she ran up the stairs, and heard a door open and close. A few minutes later the clock on the mantelpiece chimed the half-hour. It was instinctive when he hitched back a snowy white shirt cuff to check the time on his state-of-the-art satellite-controlled wrist-watch and grimaced when he discovered that the old wooden-cased clock was accurate almost to the second.

Three-thirty, Melanie noted. That left them with ten short minutes before Robbie arrived back from school, and she tried not to predict what was going to happen as she scrambled out of her suit and into jeans and a pale blue sweater, then brushed her hair while avoiding any contact with a mirror because—

A ball of heat rolled in her stomach, then sank to the apex at her thighs. She caught her breath, then just stood there staring at the old-fashioned roses on the wallpaper while her head decided to play her some flashbacks from the last few hours just to make the feeling worse.

Oh, she'd behaved like an absolute wanton. What must he be thinking about her?

He—Rafiq ben Jusef Al Alain Al-Qadim. She gave him his name and was immediately hit with his naked image. Big, dark, muscular and sleek, with curling black hair following the contours of his long torso from his wide chest like an arrowhead pointing the way to the enthralling eminence of his, of his—

No. She blinked the image away, eyelashes fluttering with a terrible reluctance to let the image fade, which brought a flush to her cheeks as she slid her feet into a pair of lightweight flat shoes and tried very hard to concentrate her mind on what lay ahead of them instead of what lay behind.

She came down the stairs to the sound of a car engine idling outside the front gate. A door slammed; there was a child's shout of 'See you!' and her whole body froze on a moment's stark panic of what was about to happen.

The door was on the latch. She always made sure it was left on the latch so that Robbie could let himself in. His bag arrived first, swinging in through the door to land on the polished wood floor before he propelled himself inside. His tie was flying, as usual, his shirt collar curled up towards his chin.

'Hi,' he said, seeing her standing there as he closed the door behind him.

'Hi, yourself.' Her heart dipped and dived as she made herself walk forward on legs that felt hollow. 'Have you had a nice day today?'

'We've been making Christmas cards,' he informed her as she went down on her haunches in front of him. 'Mrs Dukes is going to print lots of copies so we can send them to our friends.'

'Well, that sounds like a good idea.' She smiled, or tried

to, while anxiously straightening his shirt collar and running shaky fingers through his ruffled hair.

'What are you doing that for?' Robbie frowned at her. 'I'm going to get changed in a minute.'

'Because I have a surprise for you,' she told him, feeling her tension hit its highest point, and feeling yet more tension coming at her in waves from inside the living room. She wondered what Rafiq was thinking, feeling—*doing*!

'A surprise?' Robbie prompted.

'Yes.' She smiled and straightened, then took hold of his hand. 'A really marvellous surprise. Come and see.'

With that she led him towards the living room, heart in her mouth as she brought him to a halt in the open doorway. She felt Robbie look up, felt him stiffen, then felt her own deep sinking sensation as she looked up into Rafiq's carved face. He was still standing where she had left him in the middle of the room, with the firelight flickering behind him. The air crashed with tension. It was sheer motherly instinct that made her swing her son to stand in front of her with his back to her, her arms wrapping themselves around him so she could feel his little heart pounding like a hammer drill.

'Rafiq, th-this is Robbie.' She made that first stammering introduction.

'Robbie,' she murmured gently to her son, 'this is—'

'My daddy,' the little boy said.

No one could have predicted he was going to say that. Melanie wasn't even aware how he knew what his father looked like; Rafiq just looked shell-shocked.

'I saw you in a picture William showed to me,' Robbie enlightened them. 'You were in Egypt with a lady, but you weren't dressed like that, though.' He frowned at the smart Italian suit. 'You had Arab clothes on and the lady had on a red frilly dress.'

As her son built a host of vivid pictures in his mother's head he also began slipping through her fingers, drawn towards Rafiq as if he'd known him since birth and had simply been waiting for him to come. Through eyes gone glassy with tears and a heart almost too swollen to manage to beat, she watched Rafiq observe with bottomless black fascination as his son approached him with his head tipped back so his eyes could maintain contact with his.

Move! Melanie wanted to shout at him. Make a response! Can't you see how brave he is being, coming to you like this? As if she'd shrieked the words out loud the stiffness faded from Rafiq's body and he lowered his big frame to his son's level.

'Hello,' he murmured rustily.

'Hello,' Robbie replied gravely. Black eyes searched black eyes for a few seconds. Then Robbie made his next courageous move and lifted up a hand and offered it to his father. Rafiq took it. Melanie watched through her tears as his large hand closed around her son's tiny one.

It was the first touch, first contact. She saw Rafiq's mouth move in response to it, then saw no more as tears blurred the rest of the tableau, and the silence throbbing all around them threatened to suffocate all three.

Then Robbie spoke again. 'Can you ride a camel?'

A camel, Melanie repeated to herself numbly as she listened to Rafiq's thickened reply. 'Yes.'

'William said you would know how. William said…'

She took the coward's way out, turned and made a dash for the kitchen, where she gave her legs permission to fold and slid into a huddle on the floor in a corner. She pressed her face into her knees, covered her ears with her hands and waited in trembling agony for the emotions trampling through her to subside.

The telephone began to ring, cutting through everything like an unwelcome intruder. She leaped up, wiped her eyes with trembling fingers, and made herself answer it.

It was Sophia, ringing to tell her she had decided to stay the weekend in Manchester with friends. 'How's it going?' she asked.

'Robbie is with his father in the other room,' she announced huskily.

'So he remembered to turn up.' Sophia had called Melanie every day to check on progress and had become more hostile with every day that Rafiq hadn't put in an appearance. 'If he hurts that boy, I'll—'

'They came together like long-lost friends!' Melanie said with a choke. 'Give them both a few minutes and they will have me all trussed up and labelled as the bad guy for keeping them apart!'

'Then don't let them do it,' Sophia said firmly. 'You know why you kept Robbie a secret from him. Just keep on reminding yourself that the rat dumped you without cause, on the hearsay of some very twisted people, and then left you alone and damn near destitute to carry his can of oats!'

His can of oats. Melanie couldn't help it; she laughed. 'Thanks,' she murmured.

'Don't mention it,' Sophia dismissed. 'I can still remember what you looked like when you turned up on William's doorstep as fat as a pig and looking like the original bag lady. Homeless, loveless and still trying to get a line of communication through to that arrogant fool sitting comfortably on his billions.'

'He doesn't know that.'

'Well, *tell* him!'

'No.' The stubborn lip protruded. 'That belongs in the past and I am determined to concentrate only on the future.' She paused, then decided to get the really bad news over with. 'We—we're getting married,' she added reluctantly.

'*What—?*'

Melanie winced. 'We decided it was the best thing for everyone. Robbie needs him—even you agree with that, Sophia! And marriage seems to be the best way to give him the security he—'

'Are you mad?' her friend shrieked. 'I'm coming home,' she decided.

'No!' Melanie cried. 'Don't do that, Sophia! I know what I'm doing, I—'

'You're a babe in arms when it comes to men, is what you are, Melanie Portreath!' the other woman derided. 'Have you stopped for one minute to think what his motives are for suggesting such a wicked thing?'

Oh, yes, Melanie thought, she'd stopped to think. The word HOT lit itself up in block capitals, followed by the word SEX!

'He will rush you to his desert hideout and lock you away there while he waltzes off with your son! It's the way they do things over there! Get behind me, woman, and all that!'

'He isn't like that,' she said, agitatedly twisting the ring on her finger.

'*All* men are like that if they think they can get away with it!'

'You don't know him—'

'Neither do you! You just slept with him once—'

Twice, Melanie silently corrected, then closed her eyes and thought—three times if you counted the last feverish grappling.

'Then he took off, with your virginity etched on his belt,' Sophia was saying, with no knowledge that Melanie had just taken off to a place she knew she should not be revisiting. 'And left *you* behind with the word *slut* etched on to your blasted forehead!'

Melanie blinked. Sophia was right. She had walked around for years thinking that word was branded on her brow. She hadn't dared trust herself with another man just in case he believed it and treated her the same way that Rafiq had done.

'Do me a favour, Melanie, and don't do anything stupid until I get back,' Sophia said urgently. 'Then we will grab your lawyer and sit down to talk through all of this.'

'Okay.' It made a lot of sense—more sense than she had been making all day, for that matter. 'But don't cut short your weekend or I won't forgive you!'

The call ended with Sophia reluctantly agreeing to wait until Monday before she began her crusade to save Melanie from a fate worse than death. Melanie put the telephone back on its rest, feeling a whole lot better for having had Sophia talk stubborn strength back into her.

It lasted only as long as it took her to prepare Robbie's favourite meal of pasta with tuna then to go in search of the two of them. She found them in William's study, and the moment she stepped through the door her new-found strength collapsed like a house of cards.

The room itself said everything about the man who had spent most of his life in it. The walls were lined with books, the furniture was so old it was threadbare. The fire wasn't lit and the two high-wing-backed chairs that flanked the fireplace looked as if they had been there for centuries. There was a chill in the air because the room was so rarely used these days, but someone had closed the heavy velvet curtains across the window and had switched on the faded table-lamps.

William's big old desk stood in the window. Robbie had pulled a chair up to it to kneel on while Rafiq stood beside him. Both of them had lost their jackets, both dark heads were close as they pored over the huge map that had been spread out across the top of the desk. Robbie was using an elbow to support his chin, Rafiq the flat of a hand as he listened to his son tell him all about the Arabian state of Rahman as if he had lived most of his life there.

'William said the river here keeps the valley fertile. And the mountains have snow on them in the winter,' Robbie was explaining casually. 'He said that you can walk for six days without seeing anything but sand, and that your daddy built this huge place—here—for the camel trains to use when they need to take a rest.'

His finger was pointing knowledgeably, but Rafiq

wasn't watching it. He was watching his son. The light from the desk lamp caught both sets of features, one young and smooth and contentedly serious, the other carved like wood to represent total infatuation.

'William said you have the biggest oasis in the country. Is that true?' He looked up, big brown eyes fixing on their older matching pair.

'It belongs to my father.' Rafiq nodded. 'It is called the Al-Qadim Oasis. My—home is there.'

'Yes.' The boy looked away again, graver now, worried a little. 'William said that your daddy is poorly. Is he feeling better? Is that why you've come to visit me?'

'I came because—yes...' Rafiq paused, then answered, 'he is a little better.'

'Good.' Robbie nodded. 'William was poorly for a long time before he— Shall we look at the photographs now?'

'How about some supper first?' Melanie inserted, trying hard to keep the thickening tears from sounding in her voice.

Both looked up; both straightened. One smiled at her; the other didn't. 'Hi,' Robbie said. 'I was just telling my daddy about Rahman.'

My daddy clutched at a tender spot inside her. 'That's nice.' She tried a smile but couldn't quite pull it off. 'But it's getting late. Why don't you go and get washed and changed now? It's your favourite for supper.'

'Tuna? Oh, great!' At once he was her little boy again, all beaming smiles and bouncing energy that had him leaping from the chair to land neatly on the faded carpet. He came towards her with a jaunty little stride—then stopped, the smile fading from his face as he turned to look at Rafiq. 'You won't go while I'm upstairs, will you?' he said cautiously.

'No, I won't go,' Rafiq promised him.

'Great,' Robbie said again, then grinned widely. 'Great!' he repeated, and was running out of the room, leaving two adults with a fallout he would never understand in a million years.

The moment they were alone Rafiq turned his back on her, broad shoulders like rods as he stared down at the map. 'I will never forgive you for this,' he breathed harshly.

'Won't forgive me for what?' she took the challenge head-on.

'*This*!' he rasped, waving a hand across the spread map. 'He knows more about Rahman than I know about it! He can plot a track across the desert from one of my homes to another!' he stated harshly. 'And he has learned it all from another man!'

'William—'

'Yes, *William*!' he incised, then gave his big shoulders a shrug, as if to rid them of whatever it was that was sitting on them. 'I think it is time you told me about William Portreath,' he demanded tightly.

Tension spun through every tight syllable, bitterness and anger and—yes, Melanie realised there was a burning jealousy for the love and affection Robbie felt for William.

CHAPTER SEVEN

RAFIQ did not know what he was feeling. He tried grabbing in a lungful of air in effort to control himself, but he was way past the point of controlling anything. The last hour had been heaven and hell wrapped in one package. He had never felt such instant attachment to another human being, and all that person could talk about was William Portreath.

He turned to glare at Melanie. She was standing in the doorway looking wary and stubborn, and it was clear she did not want to have this kind of discussion with him.

'Please,' he ground out from his chest like the rattle of a pistol.

With a little jerk she swung the door almost shut behind her, her fingers still clutching at the handle and her shoulders straight and tense.

'Okay,' she agreed reluctantly. 'What is it that you want to know?

His teeth gritted at the reluctance, and his chest clenched at the rebellious expression on her beautiful face. But he had a right to know, dammit! 'Exactly what was William Portreath to you?'

'If you'd read my papers you would know what he was,' she returned. 'William was my great-uncle on my mother's side. He made his fortune travelling the world as a diamond merchant before coming back to England to retire.'

Her left hand appeared from behind her back and she glanced down at the diamond ring circling her finger. So did Rafiq, and he felt his skin prickle when he remembered the safety deposit box listed in her assets; it was packed full of diamonds that could probably kill the sparkle in the ones she wore on her finger.

'You were his only beneficiary,' he said, as if that had anything to do with all this. It didn't. He was just linking one thought with another.

'I didn't know that until he'd died,' Melanie made clear. 'In fact I did not even know of William's existence until my twenty-first birthday, when a letter arrived from Randal's firm informing me that I was William's heir and he would like to meet me,' she explained. 'So I agreed to come here to see him, and found myself faced with this crabby old eccentric.' An odd little smile softened the defiance from her mouth. 'We had a fight—'

'About what?'

'William had known since the time when my parents died that I would inherit from him. He also knew that I had been sent off to live with another obscure uncle but, because he didn't want the responsibility of a child cluttering up his reclusive life, he chose to ignore my existence until I was—old enough to be sensible, as he put it.' Her mouth took on a bitter twist now. 'But he didn't get a sensible person. He got an angry one who was heavily pregnant and with no sign of a man to make her respectable.'

Rafiq flinched. 'I can do simple arithmetic.'

'William called me a few unpleasant names that you would recognise,' she said, retaliating to his bite. 'And I called him a few names in return. I went to leave. He stood up to stop me, tripped over his walking stick and would have fallen if I hadn't grabbed him. It—it was like holding frail skin and bone in my arms,' she recalled, not seeing the way Rafiq stiffened in recognition of that sentiment. 'H-he asked me to stay,' she went on. 'He was lonely. I was—in need of a roof over my head, so I stayed.'

Her accompanying shrug said, End of story. But as far as Rafiq was concerned it was only the beginning of it.

'So you allowed William Portreath to become both father to my son and a grandfather in place of my own father!'

'Am I supposed to feel guilty for allowing William to give Robbie something no one else would?'

'Yes…' He moved restlessly. 'You should be feeling as guilty as hell.'

Melanie was not impressed. 'You can say that now,' she mocked. 'But we both know you didn't feel like that eight years ago. You just walked away.'

'I did not know I was leaving a son behind.'

'You didn't want to know.'

'How can you say that? How dare you say that when you never gave me the opportunity to make that decision?'

'A decision?' she flicked back at him, and was suddenly lurching away from the door to come and stand directly in front of him. 'You think it required a *decision* as to whether you condescended to want Robbie or not? How dare you stand here and be so conceited?' she said angrily. 'How dare you be so bloody superior that you can even put up such an argument? You threw me out without a hearing!' Her golden eyes flicked the accusation at him. 'That was your decision, Rafiq. Anything at all that came after that was *my* decision! And I did not *decide* to love Robbie. I just *do* love him. Can you possibly understand the difference?'

'Jamie,' he installed into the argument. 'As a mother you love without question, no matter who is the father of your child. But a father needs to trust he *is* the father before he can dare to love! You slept with Jamie within a week of sleeping with me.' His hand flicked out to toss that claim at her. 'You cannot possibly have known, therefore, which of us was his father until the boy was born.'

'Is this leading somewhere?' she demanded coldly.

Was it? Rafiq asked himself. 'Yes,' he hissed. 'Once you knew for sure that I was Robert's father you had a moral duty to get in touch with me.'

Nothing—he received absolutely nothing back from that

final accusation. Her rebellious eyes held his steady; her mouth remained defiantly shut. She had planted her hands on hips and was taking him on as if she was easily up to his weight in a battle. Frustration attached itself to his ribs and his fingers. He wanted to reach out with those fingers and shake her into talking—and he wanted to wrap her to his aching ribs and just kiss her senseless!

He sighed, wishing he knew what it was that was actually driving him here, but he didn't. There were so many feelings trampling around inside him that he couldn't distinguish one from the other. His gaze shifted around a room that was not dissimilar to a room his father had in Rahman. He looked at the map again and saw the years he'd been robbed of by his own blind stubbornness represented on the desk, and also in the sound of his son's voice unwittingly telling him how William Portreath had attempted to give them to the child.

It hurt. This house hurt. This room, the dead man who still lingered inside it—this woman and her refusal to admit that she owed him something for what she'd taken away!

'I need to get out of here,' he decided suddenly. It was that quick, that desperate, and he just stepped around her and walked away.

As he made for the door Melanie felt the bitterness rise up and try to strangle her. 'So you still walk away from promises you make.' She slid the words deridingly after him. 'What happened to your "united we stand" speech, Rafiq?' she taunted. 'Or the promise you gave to your son that you would still be here when he comes downstairs?'

Rigid back, rigid shoulders; he went still by the door. 'I am finding it impossible to justify that for seven years my son has been deprived of his right to know a father's love,' he said harshly. 'And that William Portreath stole something from my father that did not belong to him!'

'William didn't steal anything from anyone. I did.'

He turned to look at her. Pale but still perfect, Melanie

thought painfully. Still loftily superior, but struggling with it. 'William Portreath aided and abetted you to keep my son hidden away from me!' He stated it clearly.

Melanie pulled in some air, then made herself say what she knew she didn't want to say. 'On the day Robbie was born William begged me to tell you about our son and offered me any money I might need to fight you in court,' she confessed. 'I refused.'

His eyes narrowed. 'I don't believe you.'

'I don't care what you believe,' she returned. 'I know it is the truth. This has never had anything to do with money. It was to do with a man who could walk away from his promises and never—ever—look back! Now here you are, intending to do the same thing again. Only this time you're going to break a small boy's heart instead of a stupid young woman's!'

'You never loved me,' he said, denouncing that claim. 'It was always the money! You were always only looking for a rich man to take you out of the hole you lived in!'

'And I chose you?' Melanie gasped out. 'Think back, Rafiq, and tell me who it was that did the chasing! Because I recall you virtually laying siege to me!'

'Tactics,' he said cynically. 'You played the game perfectly.'

'No.' Melanie denied that. 'If I'd been playing the tactical game I would have made you wait for sex until the ring was safely on my finger. But not me—not this gullible fool!' A shudder of self-disgust ripped through her. 'I gave you it all—just as I gave it to you again today—and if you think I am proud of myself for that, then think again, because you have a real knack for making me despise myself!'

She turned away from his stunned expression, despising herself all the more for letting fly at him. What was she trying to do here? Bury her pride completely? She lifted a hand to cover her mouth with it, caught the glitter of a diamond and with tears suddenly burning in her eyes she wrenched the ring from her finger and stepped up to hand it back to him.

The swine took it—he *took it*! 'Now you can leave,' she whispered shakily.

Footsteps suddenly sounded on the upper landing, then came clattering down the stairs. Both stopped breathing and went perfectly still. It lasted only a couple of seconds and Rafiq was the first to recover. His eyes gave a flash like lightning—the only warning Melanie received before she was being crushed in his arms. Heat drenched her body from the burn of the kiss; tension ricocheted through her muscles as she tried to fight him. In a single smooth movement he'd caught her mouth and was lifting them both out of the way from the door as their son pushed it open. Robbie just stood there, staring at the fascinating sight of his mother kissing his newly found father.

Deliberate. The whole swift, nerve-shaking move had been a deliberate one aimed to make a particular impression on their highly impressionable son. When Rafiq finally released her mouth Melanie found herself staring at the hand she had splayed out against his snow-white shirt front. Somewhere between the grab and the kiss Rafiq had also slid the ring back onto her finger. It was now sparkling at her in much the same way as her son was sparkling.

'You were kissing my mum,' Robbie accused.

'Mmm,' Rafiq agreed. 'I like kissing her, and she likes me doing it...'

Melanie's gaze jumped from the ring to his face. Those devil-black eyes were glinting down on her with lazy triumph. Deny it if you can, that mocking glint challenged. She was breathless—helpless—literally stewing in her own foolish response. And what made it all so much worse was that Rafiq knew it. He released a low, soft, throaty laugh, caught the hand wearing the ring, then swung them both to face their small witness. 'We have been talking about what to do about us,' he informed his son smoothly. 'How would you feel about us becoming a proper family, Robert?'

Robert. Melanie blinked at the *Robert* she'd only ever heard William use. Then she blinked again at her son, who was suddenly wearing a smile that lit his whole face. 'Will you come here and live with us?' Robbie demanded in breathless excitement.

Rafiq's brief moment of stillness was Melanie's only reward for the web she was allowing herself to be wrapped in. He hadn't thought as far on as *where* they were going to live. Then he said, 'Yes. Tonight, I think. What do you think?' he deferred to his star-struck son.

'Oh, yes!' Robbie exclaimed, as if he'd just had his dearest wish granted.

'Good,' Rafiq murmured. 'Then you may show me to the room in which I am to sleep…'

'Rafiq…'

Her one burst of protest was denied by a man intent on getting his own way. Lifting the hand wearing his ring to his mouth, he kissed it and murmured, 'Hush,' then gently let her go so he could turn his full attention on Robbie. His hand was offered to his son. Watching through a daze, she saw Robbie's smaller hand disappear inside it. As the long fingers closed she felt something clutch at her heart. The pair began to move out of the room, man and boy linked by their hands and a genetic influence that was so strong it hurt.

Maybe she even groaned at the recognition, she wasn't sure, but something made Robbie stop and turn his head to look at her. 'Is something the matter?' he asked frowningly.

'No, of course not.' She smiled. 'I am just trying to decide whether to eat in the kitchen or go all posh and use the dining room.'

The diversion was an inspiration. Robbie's eyes widened in dismay. 'Not the dining room, Mum!' he protested.

'It's all big and cold in there.' His hand gave a tug at his father's hand. 'We can eat in the kitchen, can't we?'

There's your choice, big man, Melanie thought cynically. The boy, the trusting hand, the kitchen and the house. The arc of his silky black lashes curled against his high cheekbones as he looked down at his son.

'The kitchen sounds perfect,' Rafiq agreed.

'Good.' Robbie beamed. 'I knew you'd want to. William liked the kitchen the very best—and this room, of course. Come on, let's go upstairs to my room. You'll like it...'

Robbie didn't see his mother wince at his mention of William. He didn't see Rafiq's fleeting glance her way before he allowed himself to be pulled towards the stairs.

Later they sat at the scrubbed kitchen table, eating pasta turned to rubber, pretending to enjoy it. Rafiq had probably never eaten in a kitchen in his life before, Melanie mused. He had probably never eaten from anything but the best bone china, nor been forced to sleep in a draughty old bedroom.

Then she took that last thought back with an inner snatch when she recalled her bedroom at the farmhouse. It had been cold and draughty. The bed had been an ancient metal-sprung affair with a deep feather mattress and a propensity to creak when they...

She got up from the table in an agitated flurry, bringing two pairs of matching eyes shooting questions her way. She ignored them, moved to the sink with her plate, then just stood there driven into remembering the man and the bed and the way he had drawn her down upon it, his dark face wearing the intensity of what had taken him over. He had touched and tutored her, had slowly brought her to a yearning pitch at which she would rather have died than drawn back from accepting him.

But the bed—the bed had creaked and groaned like a guilty accomplice. The room had been so cold he had pulled the heavy eiderdown over them, cocooning them in warmth and the soft, heaving rush of their own sensual breathing. Flesh moving against flesh, scents stirring the senses. They'd remained there throughout a whole afternoon while her uncle and Jamie had been out in the barn, and the old farmhouse had rattled against an icy storm hitting its outer walls—while another storm beneath the eiderdown had been hot and sultry.

Someone touched her shoulder. She almost jumped in the air. It was Rafiq. She jerked away. He released a small sigh and turned her to face him.

Big; his chest was big, wide and deep and beautifully masculine. Her breasts sprang to life, tightening and tingling and sending messages down to other parts of her that droned with an ache she did not want to feel.

'Where's Robbie?' she murmured, vaguely aware that they were alone in the kitchen.

'Gone to find a video I am to watch,' her son's father replied, with just a hint of huskiness that told her he was touched by his son's desire to share everything with him. 'But I wanted to take this moment to apologise for my remarks earlier. You were right: William Portreath is not to be blamed. He was a good man. He loved my son. I can only thank him for taking care of Robert as wisely as he did. It is no wonder Robert misses him.'

She nodded, unable to speak. He believed she had been standing here thinking of their argument when in reality her thoughts had been lost in a different kind of place entirely. She ought to be ashamed of herself, but oddly she wasn't. She was hot and hungry struggling not to close the two-inch gap between his chest and the tingling tips of her eager breasts.

'Y-you can't stay here. It wouldn't be right.' She managed the sensible sentence.

'The decision has been made. I do not back down on my promises.'

'To your son.' It was bitter. 'You are cynically using him to get your own way where I am concerned.'

'To both of you,' he insisted. 'And cynical I may be, but the sooner we place this relationship on a permanent footing, the sooner we can give Robert what he needs.'

'Stop calling him Robert,' she snapped out impulsively.

'It is his name,' he insisted. 'And why are you trembling?'

Melanie almost laughed out loud at the question. 'Because I think I am going to fall into a flood of tears,' she lied, instead of telling the truth—that she was longing to fall on him like a ravenous fool!

Though the tears weren't that far away, she realised. Tears and desire. What a combination. Both ate away at self-control. She tried to move away; his hands pressed her closer. Two inches became a half an inch. Her trembling became a fine shimmer. Could he feel it? Yes he could feel it; his fingertips were moving lightly against her spine, as if to encourage it.

'Please let me go now,' she said a little desperately.

'When you look at me.'

'No.' She didn't want to look at him so she turned her face and looked at the kitchen, with its old-fashioned familiarity, and wondered why he didn't look utterly out of place in here.

'Why not?' he challenged, and his voice was like a quiet rumble, vibrating all around her, husky, sexy.

Don't give in to it, she told herself, then tipped her head back, made contact with eyes like the darkest brown velvet set between ebony lashes. They drew her in as she'd known they would. They sent messages she'd already read via a body language that was threatening to pull her apart inside.

'I didn't betray you with Jamie,' she whispered.

On a growl of anger he swooped with his mouth and captured her throbbing declaration, captured and returned it to her with the furious flick of his tongue. He didn't

believe her. He didn't *want* to believe her. Because to believe meant he would have to place himself so much in
the wrong that his ego wouldn't cope with what that would
brand him.

Bitterness welled again, scouring out the desire that had
held her in his arms so long. She broke away from the
kiss, moved away from his body, and turned away from
the whole tempting package being sold to her.

A man with no mercy. Sex without respect. It hurt. She
was never going to repeat that denial, she promised herself
grimly as she began picking up plates from the table.

'Which bedroom did you choose? I need to go and make
up the bed.'

There was a silence behind her; it trickled down her
spinal cord like the scrape of a fingernail warning her that
danger lurked behind.

It took the form of silk-like satire. 'Our son assures me
that all his friends' parents sleep in the same bed.'

She spun back to find him leaning casually against the
sink with his hands resting in his pockets. He was enjoying
this, she realised. 'You're joking!' she insisted.

A single eyebrow mocked her horrified look. 'I was very
impressed with his forward thinking,' Rafiq answered
lightly. 'He gave me a choice. His room or your room.
And since his room has only one small single bed in it and
yours has a very large divan, I took the advice I was being
offered and agreed to share—as parents do.'

'Well, I *don't* share!' She itched to swipe that mocking
smile from his face. '*Never*. Do you understand?'

'Not even when we are man and wife?'

'I've changed my mind; I don't want to marry you!' she
said. 'We—we will have to come to some other arrangement about sharing Robbie.'

'Now, that is one area in which *I* don't share,' he
warned.

'And I won't marry a man who feels as bitter about me
as I feel about him!'

'Then we are both on a learning curve.'

'Don't talk business-speak to me!' she snapped out angrily.

He leapt on her like a cat, picked her up and sat her down on the kitchen table, braced his hands beside her legs then pushed his dark face up close. 'Would you rather I woo you into accepting me?' he purred.

She stiffened like a cardboard cut-out; if he'd said it to insult her then he had certainly achieved his aim. 'I've been wooed by you before and I would rather have a snake do it.'

'Remove that ring one more time and you will regret it,' he warned very, very succinctly.

Melanie looked down and was surprised to find her fingers trying to work the ring loose. The threatened tears came back. 'I don't want you here,' she choked.

He saw the tears, touched a finger to the corner of her eye to capture one. 'Too late,' he announced, then stepped back.

He had heard what she had been too busy to hear—their son coming towards the kitchen. She leapt from the table just as Robbie appeared to take Rafiq off to watch his video. Melanie forced herself to tidy the kitchen, then went upstairs to make up the bed in the spare bedroom. It was a cold, dark little room with a cold little bed, and she had to grit her teeth as she made it so she would not let her conscience accept that a man of Rafiq's size would never be able to sleep in it—or at least he'd freeze trying, she added as she snubbed her nose at the room and walked out.

Robbie kept the atmosphere buoyant right up until she eventually coaxed him into bed. He fell asleep blissful in the knowledge that when he awoke his daddy would still be there.

By the time Melanie trudged back down the stairs she had developed a throbbing headache and was intending to go straight to the kitchen to find some painkillers when she caught sight of Rafiq through the half-open door that led into the living room. He was standing by the fire with a hand thrust into his trouser pocket while the other held a mobile phone to his ear. He was speaking in fluent French. For a few seconds he even looked French, a smooth, sleek and dauntingly sophisticated Frenchman with the language for lovers falling from his lips.

It was not the cleverest of thoughts to have, she realised as her senses rose to the invitation to remember the lover once again. She made herself move on to the kitchen before he caught sight of her standing there looking at him like some sex-obsessed idiot. It had been that kind of day! A day packed full of old obsessions and new raging impulses. Sexual impulses; angry impulses. Her impulse to go and seek him out; his impulse to lay siege and seduce. The shocks, the grip of an old obsessive desire, the excitement in knowing they were both running out of control.

The headache got worse. She took two painkillers and set about preparing a pot of coffee. He was standing in more or less the same place when she carried the coffee tray into the room. He was still on the telephone, speaking in Spanish now, a language she recognised easily because Sophia was half-Spanish and could tumble into the language when she was angry enough to need its extra fire.

He turned his dark head as he heard the tray rattle. Their gazes clashed, and Melanie broke hers away. Five seconds later the mobile was back in his pocket.

'Coffee?' she offered politely.

'Thank you, yes,' he replied. 'Black, no sugar.'

Black with no sugar, she repeated. Like the man himself: dark and unsweetened. She poured the coffee, then handed him his cup. He accepted it with a murmured, 'Thank you.'

She looked pale and tired, Rafiq noticed, and had to smother the urge to sigh as he turned to look at the fire, taking with him the image of Melanie sitting there on faded velvet looking down at her coffee mug curled inside fingers that looked bloodless and cold. Hell, he thought in frustration, to him this whole house was cold. Even with the fire burning in the grate, the ancient central heating system only managed to take the edge of a subfreezing temperature! Despite his millions, and the loving attention he had poured into Rafiq's son, William Portreath had not poured much love into his home. It was virtually falling down around them. Everything in it came from a bygone century.

'Your requirements do not make any provision for the renovations this house clearly requires.'

Eyes like dark amber blinked at him. 'What are you talking about?'

'The papers you left with me,' he explained. 'They talk a lot about investments and trust funds but nothing about your annual expenditure or how much it is going to cost to bring this house into the twenty-first century.'

'I don't want to bring it into the twenty-first century. I like the house just as it is.'

She did? Was she lying just to go against him? 'It is cold in here, Melanie,' he said, stating the obvious. 'The walls are so cold that the wallpaper is peeling.' Not that its demise was much of a loss, he added with silent disdain. 'I, for one, see no reason why we should live like this.'

She bristled. 'Nobody is asking you to!'

He ignored that. 'I will employ someone to draw up some plans for renovation,' he announced.

Tired golden eyes began to sparkle. The mug was replaced on the tray. 'William has been gone only two months and you come in here wanting to obliterate thirty years of his life?' She rose stiffly. 'You will touch nothing,' she told him. 'It isn't yours to touch. And if you don't find that acceptable then you know what you can do!'

She was hurt; he could see it. Rafiq wanted to kick himself. Ridding himself of his cup, he offered her a deep bow. 'I have offended you,' he acknowledged. 'I apologise. It was not my intention to—'

'Y-you think I can't compare this—*home* to that super-expensive luxuriously blank space you like to live in?' she said, interrupting his apology. 'That I haven't noticed the way you've been looking on everything here with disdain? Does it offend your ego to know that your son loves this house?'

'No.' He denied that. 'I just think that it needs—'

'Well, forget it,' she said, cutting right across him a second time, and turned her stiff back towards him and walked to the door. 'You can use the room at the end of the landing. Be sure to make the fire safe before you go up. Now, goodnight.'

She'd left the room before he could speak another syllable, leaving him standing there feeling as if he'd just struck a woman for the first time in his life.

'Damn,' he muttered, and took the first step to go after her. Then on a heavy sigh changed his mind. She'd had enough for one day. He had had enough! 'Damn,' he cursed again, and turned back to the fire. It was dying fast, like the whole blasted day.

A car drew up outside the house. He listened to the sound of its door slamming shut. Another sigh and he was striding for the front door before Kadir could ring the doorbell and awaken Robert. I learn very quickly, he mused grimly as he reached out to take the suitcase from his aide.

'Thank you,' he grunted. 'I do not need to tell you that this situation is no one else's business.'

'No, sir. Of course, sir.'

He nodded, said goodnight and closed the door.

Upstairs Melanie listened to the car from the comfort of her duvet. She'd curled up beneath it after taking a shower in her *en-suite*, very ancient bathroom. Her teeth still chattered from the chills she'd given herself drying her body. She'd pulled on a knitted-cotton nightdress and was now only waiting for the duvet to infuse some warmth into her body.

Okay, she reasoned, so she knew the house needed a complete face-lift. She'd been wanting to do it for years, but William hadn't liked change. He'd been an old man who'd had a right to feel like that. And he did not deserve that some complete stranger should walk in here and start tearing his life down!

How dared he? Her throat caught on a muffled sob. How dared Rafiq believe he could just take over everything— even her bed if she let him get away with it!

The front door closed; she felt it reverberate through the floor beneath her bed. She'd heard Rafiq telling Robbie that someone was going to bring his suitcase here. Well, she hoped he'd changed his mind and had left with the delivery person! And on that final, wholly satisfying thought she closed her eyes and willed her icy feet to get warm so that she could just go to sleep. She had almost— almost—achieved both impossible feats when a curse in the darkness brought her swimmingly awake.

Suddenly the duvet was being lifted, to let the cold night air come into her warm cocoon. A short second later a body followed—a very cold, very naked body with an arm that clamped her to him and powerful limbs that curled snugly into hers.

'Oh, my God,' she gasped on a shocked little shiver. 'What do you think you are doing?'

'Getting warm,' Rafiq informed her grimly. Furious, she wriggled to get free. 'Stay still,' he gritted, close to her ear lobe.

He had to be joking! 'You could have had the decency to put some clothes on!'

'If my nakedness offends you then consider it punishment for that bed you prepared for me.'

He'd actually tried it? In a mulish kind of way Melanie was rather pleased that he had at least attempted to do the honourable thing. 'I don't want you here,' she protested nonetheless.

'The choice does not belong to you. Our son expects me to be in this bed when he wakes in the morning, and the other bed was an insult.' A hand on her shoulder turned her to face him; dark eyes glittered down into hers. 'You are a ruthless woman, Melanie Portreath,' he told her. 'Now it is my turn to be ruthless.'

And he was, in the way he wrapped himself around her, punishing her by stealing all her warmth, then punishing her again by falling fast asleep.

CHAPTER EIGHT

IT WAS a horrible weekend. There was not one single part of it that Melanie would have wanted to live through again. Daylight became an agony of hours watching her son sink himself into total hero-worship, and the nights an agony of too much intimacy with a man who clearly did not want more than to share her bed.

In his new role of father Rafiq dedicated himself to learning everything he could about his son. They talked, and they commandeered William's study, where Robbie hit Rafiq with a million questions, all of which his father answered with a considered seriousness that made Melanie's heart ache. Rafiq could do no wrong. She tried not to resent the way Robbie was turning to his father for everything. She tried to tell herself that this was what she had wanted, what she had hoped and aimed for when she had brought Rafiq into Robbie's life.

But it hurt to witness their growing closeness while she was required to contribute very little other than the odd smile or nod, or food when necessary. By the end of each day she was so exhausted playing the smiling little woman in the background that the moment Robbie was safely in bed she took herself off to bed too, leaving Rafiq to do what men like him did—use his evenings to work from the laptop computer that had arrived with his suitcase— before he came to slide into her bed, draw her in, sigh, then fall asleep.

She didn't understand him—didn't think she wanted to understand a man who could ravish her with a blind compulsion one minute then spend whole nights lying beside her and not offer one measly pass!

Their son loved the whole family scenario. In fact it made Robbie's day to run into their bedroom each morning and find both his parents wrapped snugly around each other. He couldn't be happier if he tried.

But for Melanie resentment sizzled across her senses; frustration throbbed in her loins. Had she sunk so low that she could become hooked on passion after a couple of quick sips?

Monday morning could not come quickly enough. She waved Rafiq off to work in his sharp dark business suit, and only did that because her son's hand was firmly attached to his father's. Rafiq was delivering Robbie to school, along with other children, as part of the morning school run!

I've been made redundant, she thought peevishly as she closed the front door. Daddy is the new rising star in the street and I am the fading one.

The jaded one, she corrected as her shoulders sagged wearily through lack of sleep and a whole truckload of tension. Standing there in the sudden quietness of the hall-way, she actually took a moment to consider going upstairs and just crawling back beneath the duvet to sleep the rest of the day away while there was no Rafiq to spoil it for her.

But his presence was there in the bedroom, she remembered. His clothes hung with her clothes in the wardrobe; the scent of his soap permeated the adjoining bathroom.

You wanted this, she tried telling herself. You instigated the whole darn thing and, if anything, you should be pleased by how successful Robbie's introduction to his father has turned out, not standing here wilting like a wet leaf.

The light tap on the back door was a welcome diversion. Straightening her shoulders she walked into the kitchen just in time to watch Sophia step into the house.

'Hi,' Sophia murmured, and her expression could not have looked more sombre if she'd tried. In her hand she held a newspaper, which she set down on the kitchen table. 'Take a deep breath, Melanie,' she suggested, 'because you are not going to like this...'

Rafiq was sitting in his chair behind his desk in his beautifully warm centrally heated office wishing he dared close his eyes and fall asleep because for these last miserable nights he'd lain awake in that bed with Melanie and had ached.

Ached. There was no better word for it. Was he a fool? Was he going insane, playing it this coolly? Yes, he was a fool, he accepted, because all it would have taken would have been one touch and she would have been his for the taking.

But he was out to prove a point. Melanie had hit him hard with some of the things she had thrown at him. She had made him out to be selfish and fickle. She had implied he did not have it in him to stay the course. She believed he would get weary of being a father and walk away when the novelty wore off him.

She'd also told him he thought her cheap by tumbling her into bed with him at the first opportunity. Which he had done; he freely admitted it. But not for one moment had he considered her cheap! Indeed, it had cost him a very great deal because he had been so bowled over by the strength of their feelings that he wanted to do it all again and again—and again.

She had claimed he had made love to her eight years ago then had despised her afterwards. Now she was waiting for him to despise her again. So sex was out of the question until he had placed a wedding ring on her finger. If that did not show her he meant serious business, then nothing would.

So, he thought with grim impatience. He had arranged a civil wedding service. From that day on he meant to have everything: a wife, his son, and some serious passion—

preferably in a bedroom that did not send him into a par-oxysm of shivers every time he stripped off his clothes.

And he had just the right place for this serious seduction. He knew the day on which it was going to happen. Now all he had to do was ring home and speak to half-brother, Hassan.

'Where have you been hiding?' his brother demanded, the moment the connection was made. 'I have been trying to contact you all weekend.'

'It cannot have been urgent or Kadir would have found me.'

'What intrigues me is why he refused to divulge to me where you were.'

'I was busy,' he said, and could almost see Hassan's grimace at his don't-go-there-tone. 'How is Father?'

He asked the usual question and he received back the reassuring answer he was looking for. 'He is well and con-tent.'

'And Leona?'

'The same—what is this, Rafiq?' Hassan put in curi-ously. 'You sound—different.'

Different? He grimaced. Different did not come close to describing the changes in his life. 'Do you think it would be safe to leave them for a couple of days?'

'Yes, if I have to.' But Hassan sounded puzzled. 'Is there something wrong at the bank?'

'No, this is a—personal matter,' Rafiq answered coolly. 'I need you to do me a great favour. If you could be in London on Friday I would much appreciate it.'

'Rafiq needs a favour?' Leona repeated as she lay on the bed, letting her husband smooth oil into her swollen ab-domen. 'Well, that has to be a first.'

'Not quite,' Hassan murmured. 'But it is certainly un-usual for him to ask anyone for anything.'

Leona was frowning thoughtfully. 'Do you think this

business with Serena Cordero has upset him more than we thought it would?'

'Could be.' Hassan paused in his ministrations to kiss her frown away, then went back to his duties, long fingers smoothing oil over creamy white skin stretched taut across the mound that was their growing child. 'He has been acting strangely since the announcement of her marriage.' It was his turn to frown. 'I am reliably informed that he has hardly been to the bank since the newspaper article appeared and is almost impossible to track down. Nadia gets shifty if I ask questions, and so does Kadir. So I will have to go to London if only to quench my curiosity as to what it is he's up to.'

'Of course,' Leona agreed. 'But I hope you're just a bit worried about him, too.'

'Of course,' he mimicked. 'Do you want to roll over so I can rub this into your back now?'

'No, thank you.' She declined the offer. 'I am perfectly happy with what you are doing right now.'

'Witch.' He laughed, and came to lean over her, eyes like brown velvet gently mocking hers of saucy green. Late afternoon sunlight was pouring in through the grilled window, turning everything in the bedroom a burnished gold. Leona's hair shone like fire on the pillow; her porcelain skin wore a lustrous glow. She was exquisite in every way possible. 'Why did no one warn me that pregnant women were such rampant sex machines?' he murmured throatily.

'It is nature's secret weapon, aimed to keep husbands from straying to more slender delights.' She smiled.

A black eyebrow arched. 'Was that a deliberate dig at my father?'

'Like father, like son,' Leona quoted.

'Yes.' His frown returned. 'You don't think Rafiq could be planning revenge on Serena, do you?'

'I don't get the link.'

'There isn't one.' Lowering his eyes, he began gently stroking a point on her stomach where he could feel his child's heart beating steadily. Leona reached out and gently touched a fingertip to the point where his brows met across the bridge of his arrogant nose.

He glanced up, smiled, then sighed and lay back against the pillows. 'Rafiq was hit hard by a woman once before—about eight years ago,' he confided. 'She was a beautiful blonde creature with golden eyes and a mouth designed to turn a saint into a sinner. I must add that Rafiq has never been a saint. But he fell head over heels in love with this woman, then found out she was taking him for a fool.'

'Name?' Leona asked curiously.

'I cannot remember. She was as English as you are, though, and young—quite shockingly young for one filled with such calculation. She was a farmer's daughter, as I recall, and saw Rafiq as her ticket out of drudgery. He asked her to marry him then discovered she was sleeping with her step-cousin. Rafiq severed the relationship and that should have been the end of it.'

'But it wasn't?'

'No.' Hassan shook his head. 'She tried to contact him again many months later. It was the only other time that I can recall him asking me to do him a favour. She rang the London bank while I was there and Rafiq was here in Rahman, playing the nomad while still licking his wounds. She wanted to see him. When I relayed the message he asked me to meet with her to see if she was okay.'

'He still cared?'

'He was besotted.' His brother sighed out heavily. 'I have never seen him like that with a woman before or since.'

'So what did you do?'

'I had her checked out before I did anything. Discovered she was living with a man old enough to be her grandfather and, more to the point, was as heavily pregnant as you are now, my sweet.' He caught hold of her hand and kissed it. 'I arranged a meeting; she arrived expecting to see Rafiq. She tried convincing me that Rafiq was the father of her baby. So I told her what I thought Rafiq would do if she managed to convince him that this was true. She did not pursue the claim,' he concluded with grim satisfaction. 'A very nasty paternity battle through the courts was too much for her to take, apparently. She slunk off into the ether and was never heard from again.'

'But what if the child had been Rafiq's?'

'It was not,' he stated with absolute certainty. 'You know his background. If there had been the slightest possibility that he had made the woman pregnant he would have followed the prospect until he could be certain either way.'

'What did he say when you told him she was pregnant?'

'I didn't tell him,' he replied. 'I said I couldn't find her but that I'd heard she was living with some man. He never mentioned her name again.'

'Sometimes I really don't like you,' Leona informed him. 'You have a ruthless streak so wide it makes me shiver.'

'She was a woman on the make, Leona,' he said deridingly. 'People in our position meet them all the time. They see dollar signs up above our heads and latch on like limpets.'

'But still....'

'Rafiq caught her red-handed with her other lover.'

End of story. 'What a manipulating bitch,' Leona murmured, taking it personally that some woman would dare to use her beloved bother-in-law in such a way.

Rafiq had only just put the phone down when Kadir knocked at his door, then quietly let himself into the room. He was wearing the look of a man who was walking towards the gallows. Rafiq straightened in readiness, but nothing prepared him for what he was about to be hit with.

'My apologies, sir, but I think you should see this...' Carefully Kadir placed a newspaper onto the desk in front of Rafiq. With his usual efficiency his aide had folded the

English tabloid so that Rafiq needed only to glance down and see what it was Kadir was showing him.

There was Serena, smiling up at Carlos Montez. It was the same damn article, now reproduced in spiced-up English. Rafiq couldn't believe it. He shot to his feet. 'What the hell?' he muttered.

'Apparently Miss Cordero arrived in London this weekend, sir,' Kadir quietly explained. 'Her show opens at a West End theatre on Wednesday. The—er—article is by way of a promotion for this event. I thought...'

He was talking to fresh air because Rafiq was already striding across the room with the rolled-up newspaper clenched in his hand.

'H-How did you get hold of this?' Melanie asked Sophia.

'My grandmother likes to send me the Spanish newspapers to make sure I keep in touch with my roots,' Sophia explained.

Melanie nodded unhappily. 'And it says?' she prompted.

'You don't really want me to read it out to you again, Melanie,' Sophia murmured gravely. 'The point is that this paper is dated last Tuesday—which is the same day you went to see Rafiq...'

'Meaning what?' Her lips felt too cold and numb to move properly; her whole face felt very much the same.

'Meaning the guy was publicly dumped on the day you walked into his office. He was already out for someone's blood before he even saw you. Therefore I think you have to ask yourself the question whether his actions since have been motivated by this.'

'Saving face?'

'Yes.' Sophia sighed. 'To suddenly pull a wife and son out of the hat will turn the tables on Miss Cordero. It will appear as if she is the one who married on the rebound while he walked away from their relationship of over a year unscathed.'

Over a year... Melanie lowered her gaze to the two photographs printed side by side on the page. One was of the beautiful Serena Cordero standing with her handsome new husband. The other was of Rafiq standing with Serena. Her heart crashed against her ribcage, turning her insides to jelly, because the photograph was just as Robbie had described it: Rafiq wearing Arab clothes while the lady wore a red frilly dress. William had shown this photograph to her son but hadn't shown it to her. Everyone but her—including her son—seemed to know about Rafiq's beautiful long-standing Spanish mistress!

Did Rafiq love this woman? Was the luscious dark beauty what he really wanted, and now that he couldn't have her was he prepared to take anyone?

No, not just anyone, she grimly amended, but a woman who happened to come packaged with his son.

She thought about the phone call he had taken in his office when he hadn't spoken a single word. She thought about the look in his eyes as he'd listened to whoever had been on the other end of that phone, followed by the kiss before he'd coldly thrown her out.

Then she thought about the way he had found out about Robbie and had been forced to rethink his stance. Days later had come his sudden explosion of hot passion followed by nothing since.

Nothing.

She swallowed down a lump of nausea. Clearly he had tried to burn Miss Cordero out of his system and failed. She had been nothing but a substitute, and a disappointing one at that. I must have been, she thought painfully—because look at her! Black hair, black eyes and a lush-red passionate mouth looked back at her. Miss Cordero possessed the kind of sumptuous hourglass figure that most women would kill to own.

Which makes me the consolation prize.

She caught the sound of a key in the front door then. Only one person beside herself had a key to this house. Her insides became a mess of misery as she listened to

Rafiq call out her name. Sophia straightened in her chair, her eyes growing wide and dark and curious. Footsteps sounded on the polished wood floor as he strode towards the kitchen, then arrived to fill its doorway. Melanie tried focusing on his face, but all she saw was the shadowy outline of his whole dark bulk. Weakness feathered its way through the misery, because he did not fill the doorway with just his size, but with—everything. The darkness of his hair, his skin and his clothes said so much about him, and the stillness of every perfectly formed feature warned of the inner strength that so matched the outer shell.

His gaze flicked from her face to Sophia's face, then remained there. Melanie glanced at Sophia too, and was suddenly struck very hard by her friend's likeness to Serena Cordero. Another wave of nausea lodged in her throat, because he couldn't seem to take his eyes off her.

Rafiq had not expected to find Melanie with a visitor. For a moment he was struck numb by the thought that it was Serena herself, come to cause yet more trouble. Then the likeness faded and he glanced back at Melanie to find that she was looking down at the table. He saw the newspaper, felt his fingers clench around his own, and knew what Melanie was going to say before she even spoke.

'You have a mistress.'

'I *had* a mistress,' he corrected, coming further into the room as Sophia rose from her seat.

'I think I'll leave you both to it,' she murmured, and went to pick up the newspaper.

It was a gesture that did not pass by Rafiq. 'If the newspaper is yours, then I must assume you enjoy playing devil's advocate,' he drawled icily.

Sophia being Sophia, she took up the challenge in his tone. 'I don't like whatever it is you are trying to do here,' she informed him coolly.

Sparks began to fly. 'You believe I care one way or another what you like or dislike?'

The dark beauty's chin lifted, sending ripples of raven

hair flying over her shoulders. 'I don't think you care about anyone's feelings so long as you get your own way.'

'Well, I did not get my own way here,' he said, stabbing a long finger at the damning newspaper article.

It was then that he realised what it was he was stabbing at, and began to frown in confusion. While he was doing that Melanie got up and on a soft choke, rushed from the room. The urge to stop her was halted by his curiosity about this other woman.

His eyes narrowed. 'How did you get hold of this?' he demanded.

She shrugged. 'I am Spanish on my mother's side,' she explained. 'My grandmother sends me her newspapers once a week.'

'Industrious lady.'

'Very.'

'You have a point in hurting Melanie with this?'

'You are the one playing hurtful games with her feelings,' Sophia responded. 'I didn't like it from the beginning.' She let her glance fall to the newspaper. 'This tells me why I don't like it.'

And I do not like you, Rafiq thought as he looked into her face and saw a different face once again. She was so like Serena it could be the dancer standing there.

'You are on a face-saving exercise,' she dared to accuse him.

'What is your name?' he demanded.

'Sophia Elliot,' she announced, making his gaze narrow even further, because he had heard that name before. 'I am the next-door-neighbour from hell, Mr Al-Qadim,' she informed him, with a cool humour that confirmed the impression he had gained from his son that this woman was as tough as she was beautiful. 'I am also a pretty good lawyer,' she added. 'So if you are thinking of trying to bully Melanie into accepting a situation she doesn't really want, then try thinking again,' she advised. 'Because it is my belief you don't give a fig for her feelings, and Melanie and Robbie have taken enough over this last year without you using them as a method of deflecting your little embarrassment with the—'

'Name of the law firm you work for?' he cut in coolly. She told him.

With a curt nod he stepped up to open the back door. 'You come and go via this route, I believe?'

'How did you know that?'

Because his son had been as admiringly vocal about his aunt Sophia as he was about William Portreath. 'Trouble rarely enters by conventional means, Miss Elliot,' he replied, knowing that she would work out his source later. But for now she was simply too busy bristling.

'I don't think you have the right to—'

'May I suggest that you mention my name to your employer before you begin informing me of my rights?' Rafiq drawled coolly.

'Is that a threat?' she demanded.

Rafiq's answer was a polite bow of his head meant to leave the question open to interpretation. 'Good day to you, Miss Elliot,' was all he said.

But the woman had sense, Rafiq allowed, as he watched her self-confidence begin to waver. She wasn't sure about him and therefore took the wiser route: lifting her chin and stepping through the door.

He closed it behind her, took a moment to grit his teeth. Then he was moving across the kitchen on his way to find Melanie. He located her in the bedroom, where she stood in the window gazing out on yet another cold grey frost-grained day. The room was no warmer, the woman in it was as cold as ice. Anger roared. A bloody anger aimed at Serena, at the press, Miss Elliot and anyone else who thought they could meddle in his life!

'Your cynical friend stole my thunder,' he announced very grimly.

'Don't try telling me you came back here to confess your sins.'

'It is not a sin for a single man to maintain a mistress,' he countered. 'And I was referring to…this.'

'This' arrived on the tallboy beside her left shoulder. Melanie turned to see what it was he was talking about. It might have been Sophia's Spanish newspaper, only the glaring headline shouted at her in English and the date printed on it was today's. It was one of the more down-market British tabloids.

'Now you may read the whole article for yourself,' Rafiq said cynically. 'It has been spiced up since the original Spanish version was written. But—please…' he flicked a long hand in invitation '…enjoy—if you are into this kind of trash.'

'I never read newspapers.'

He had noticed their lack of evidence about the house. 'Well, read this one,' he advised, shot back a shirt-cuff, then strode towards the door.

'Where are you going?'

'I have things to do.'

'Aren't you even going to explain about this?'

'What is there to explain?' he countered. 'Serena Cordero and I were lovers until recently. But that, and the fact that she decided to use this very public source to announce the end of that relationship, has nothing to do with you, quite frankly.'

'It does when that announcement also came on the same day that I went to see you.'

'You see this coincidence as significant?'

She folded her arms across her body again. 'You changed,' she told him. 'After you took a call on your mobile. It was her on the phone, wasn't it? That call gave you the idea of using me to save your face.'

'It crossed my mind,' he admitted. 'But if you recall, Melanie, I still threw you out.' She flinched at the reminder. He nodded in acceptance of what that flinch represented. 'And if you believe that anything I have done since then has been due to a need to *save my face*, then there is really nothing left for me to say here.' With that he turned back to the door.

'Then why did you bother to come back here now?'

'Courtesy,' he said icily. 'I believed I owed you the courtesy of an explanation for why this article appeared in the newspaper today. But since you and your—friend have already dissected the week-old version, I see I wasted my time.'

'Wasted nearly a whole week of your time,' she murmured bitterly.

He paused. 'What is that supposed to imply?'

'I am not going to marry you.'

'Why not?'

She lowered her eyes. 'You're in love with her. She's what you really want.'

He laughed; it was harsh. 'If I'd wanted to marry Serena I could have done so at any time over the last year,' he announced. 'But what interests me here is that you seem to be thinking that loving someone is a prerequisite for marriage.'

'I don't think that.' She stiffened. 'I just don't want to marry a man who is pining for someone else.'

'Pining?' he repeated.

'It's obvious.' She shrugged, then made the big mistake of glancing at the bed.

His dark gaze followed suit. One of those awful tense silences they were so good at developing began to sing in the room. Hot colour flooded her complexion; she spun back to the window, wishing the man wasn't so good at reading her like an open book!

Did she have to be so obvious? she railed at herself. Did it always—always—have to be this man who made her feel like a lovesick fool?

Sex-sick, she then corrected. God, she hated herself sometimes. 'Go, if you're going,' she snapped. Make it quick and don't come back!

'I have changed my mind.'

'Not on my account.' She tried to recover lost ground.

But she should have known by now that this man gave nothing back once he had gained it. She heard a rustle, felt a shot of alarm shoot down her backbone, spun, then just stood there staring in open dismay as the jacket to his suit hit the floor.

'Come any closer and I'll start screaming,' she warned, backing herself into the window as he began walking towards her with fingers smoothly loosening his tie.

'Scream,' he invited. 'Who will come? Your cynical friend from next door?' Reaching over her shoulder, he tugged the cord that closed the heavy curtains. The room was suddenly shrouded in darkness. A dangerous glitter burned in his eyes. 'Think of the embarrassment, Melanie, if Miss Elliot was foolish enough to come running in here only to find you begging in my arms.'

'I will never beg!' She gave an angry push at his body.

He laughed, low and deep and tauntingly. 'One kiss and you will not be able to stop yourself,' he derided. 'Do you think I have not been aware that you have hardly slept a wink in that bed because you want me so badly?'

'That's a lie.'

He kissed her. It was no lie. She dived, she fell, she almost—almost begged him. Her breathing went haywire, her senses caught alight, and she whimpered into his urgent mouth. His arms imprisoned her, but they didn't need to. She was clinging tightly.

'I hate you for doing this.'

'But, as you see, I am not pining for a lost love,' he murmured, and to punctuate his meaning he caught hold of one of her hands and placed it down his front, then caught her protesting little gasp in his mouth.

Desire pulsed with every hammering heartbeat; it bounced off the walls and back at her in wave after wave of blistering passion, battering her every sense into submission. They kissed; they lost their clothes with an urgent lack of finesse. Somehow they managed to make it to the bed; his hand grabbed the duvet and stripped it back from the mattress before he tumbled her down on it. They kissed some more; they rolled; he stretched her out and ravished her breasts, then placed a line of hot wet kisses down her front; he buried his mouth between her thighs. She almost leapt into the air in shock, then went wild, utterly wanton. Bright hot lights were propelling themselves at her eyelids; she couldn't keep still and his hands had to clamp her hips so he could sustain the torment until she lost herself completely, lost him, lost everything.

When she opened heavy eyelids she found black eyes glittering down at her, his face a smouldering cast of raw sensuality made all the more potent by triumph. 'You shouldn't have done that,' she whispered.

'Why not?' The hand he used to push the damp hair away from her face was trembling.

'Because...' she breathed. He hadn't leapt with her, and she wanted him to leap with her. It was essential that he lose touch with himself as she had, or what had he proved here except that he was the expert and she was just somebody, nobody—anybody?

So she pushed him onto his back and came to lean over him, calling upon instincts she had never used before to take him where she had just been. He lay in the darkness and let her do whatever she wanted. She kissed his shoulders, his chest, sucked deeply on the hard points of his male nipples, stroked her hands down his body when he groaned hoarsely, took her mouth on a journey that stopped at nothing. His fingers coiled into her hair and his laboured breathing drove her on. When he shifted to grasp her beneath her arms then drag her upwards for a kiss that devoured she was ready for him to finish what she had started with the deep, urgent thrust of his pelvis.

They shuddered together into a drumming ecstasy; he seduced her mouth until the very last whisper of pleasure had faded, and eventually she lay heavily upon him, limp and useless. She couldn't even draw enough energy to care that once again she had given him more of herself than she had ever wanted to.

She belonged here. It was that simple—and that sad.

'We marry as soon as possible,' he announced suddenly. Then, before she could raise so much as a gasp in protest, he switched their position and began the whole wild adventure all over again.

CHAPTER NINE

MELANIE sat in a chair beside Sophia and carefully rotated her aching shoulders. 'Can't I just wear that one?' she said hopefully.

'If you want to look like a fairy on a Christmas tree, of course you can wear that dress,' Sophia replied.

'Don't be cruel.'

'Do you want to knock his eyes out?'

'No—yes.' Melanie sighed and fiddled with a drink-starved wilting rosebud. 'I wish he wasn't so determined to make all of this fuss about a silly civil wedding.'

'I still can't understand why you are going through with it,' Sophia said with a disapproving snap.

'You've seen him with Robbie, Sophia,' Melanie reminded her. In an effort to get Sophia and Rafiq to stop sniping at her about each other she had invited Sophia round for drinks. Rafiq had been about to take Robbie to bed when she'd arrived. She had caught him holding his son in his arms, accepting the kind of love-shining hugs Melanie had witnessed many times. 'They adore each other. I couldn't stop this now even if I wanted to,' she concluded heavily.

'Do you want to?'

She hesitated a bit too long without answering.

'So you're the sacrificial lamb.' Sophia sighed.

Oh, yes, Melanie thought. I sacrifice myself every night in his arms.

Getting up, she walked back to the rail filled with frothy white dresses and began flicking restless fingers along the selection. Why did she let him get away with it? she was asking herself crossly. Had she no pride left at all?

138

She knew the trigger that set him off each time. It was called Serena Cordero. Plant the beautiful Spaniard's name into his head and he responded by diving into sex like a man in search of blind escape!

But you dive right in there with him, she admitted. In fact you only have to start thinking about diving in and you break out in a hot sweat.

'I'll try this one,' she said, choosing a gown at random which she passed to the hovering assistant who carried it off to the dressing room.

Sophia waited until the woman had gone out of earshot before she said tentatively, 'Melanie...have you thought about when you're married to him and things become... intimate?'

'Are you joking?' she gasped.

But, no, Sophia wasn't joking, she realised. She was actually looking like a rather anxious mother hen trying to prepare her innocent chick for what the big bad rooster did.

'I'm sorry to disillusion you about me, Sophia,' she responded. 'But what do you think we have been doing in my home all this time?'

For the first time ever she saw shock then embarrassment flood her tough friend's face. 'You mean you—'

The words dried up. Melanie laughed; it sounded strangled. She spun back to face the rail. The silence between them sizzled with the kind of images that just did not belong in this pretty shop adorned with chaste and virginal white.

'But I thought—'

'Well, don't think,' Melanie cut in on a tight little mutter. Her cheeks were hot. Sophia's cheeks were hot. What was it about people that they believed they could make assumptions about her? Rafiq believed she was a sex-hungry wanton; Sophia believed she was about as naive and dumb as a woman with a seven-year-old child could possibly be!

Maybe this was a good time for the assistant to reappear, because she helped to carry them over a very uncomfortable moment. Melanie scowled at the dresses on display and wondered what Rafiq would do if she turned up to their wedding in her best black suit?

A beautifully manicured hand appeared to one side of her. 'You are your own worst enemy, aren't you?' Sophia murmured sombrely. 'Here,' she said, 'try this...'

Sophia had pulled a misty-blue silk suit out from amongst the swathes of white. Her whole attitude altered from that moment on. She's given up on me, Melanie realised as she wriggled into the fitted blue suit. I've put myself beyond redemption.

But then I placed myself beyond that when I let him make love to me knowing he was using me to block out another woman, she acknowledged helplessly.

She bought the misty-blue suit. It looked right somehow—made her legs seem longer and her hair more golden, made her eyes glow a deeper shade.

'What do you think?'

Rafiq was standing in the hallway of Melanie's house while Ethan Hayes was still looking about him with an interested eye. 'You must already know that it has tremendous potential,' Ethan told him. 'But I don't know how you expect to modernise the whole house while still maintaining every worn-out feature.'

'There is an old man's life etched into those features,' Rafiq explained. 'Can we not give the shell an uplift, then simply put everything else back the way it is now?'

'I am an architect, not a miracle-worker,' Ethan said dryly 'The heating is useless, the fires belch smoke, the floorboards creak worryingly and the walls seem to be warning anyone that dares go near them not to remove a single picture unless you want them to fall down. All of that can be put right,' he stated. 'But the wallpaper will have to be hand-reproduced, the furniture will need to be sent away for some careful renovation, and nothing we replace will have the patina of age it wears now. I have a worrying suspicion that the deeper we look, we will find wet rot and dry rot, not to mention woodworm. You need Leona on this, not me, Rafiq,' he concluded.

'Leona is busy with other things,' Rafiq reminded him. 'I just wanted your opinion before I decided whether to go ahead.'

'It would be simpler to gut it and start from scratch,' Ethan advised. 'You only have to look at the other houses on this street to see what it can look like, given the chance.'

'I have no wish to make it look like the others.' This was his son's home, the place where Robert and Melanie had found love and security. Aesthetically it must not change. Structurally, he feared it had no choice.

'If Leona is out of action, then what if I hand the project over to my wife?' Ethan suddenly suggested.

'To your *wife*?' Rafiq couldn't hide his surprise.

Ethan turned a rueful grin on him. 'Yes, I do mean the flighty piece who spent the evening flirting with you a couple of months ago,' he confirmed lazily. 'She has hidden talents,' he confided. 'One of those talents being a very impressive track record in house renovation.'

Rafiq was momentarily diverted. In the space of just a few short weeks, earlier this year, Ethan Hayes had gone from being a serious enemy of the Al-Qadim family to being a good close friend due to falling into love with Eve, the provocative granddaughter of the Greek tycoon Theron Herakleides.

'The lovely Eve renovates old property for a living?' Rafiq could not withhold his disbelief.

'She shocked me with it too,' Ethan confessed. 'On the morning after we returned from our honeymoon, in fact, when she came to breakfast wearing overalls and put a builder's hat down on the table. She's been buying, renovating and selling on houses in London for years—as a hobby, apparently. Loves to get her fingernails chipped, has an affinity with dirt and grime. Give her a lump hammer and she will have that wall down in half an hour.'

His eyes were glowing with amusement. But beneath the amusement was a love and pride that made Rafiq want to sigh. At home in Rahman his brother was no doubt relaxing with the woman he adored with every breath that he took. And here stood Ethan Hayes so in love with his lovely, if highly provoking, wife, that he could not keep his feelings from showing on his face.

And here I stand, planning to marry a mere obsession, he mused heavily. A past obsession, a present obsession, but most importantly of all a sexual obsession. Upstairs their bedroom had become a place for hot and tumultuous orgies. Melanie had revealed a capacity to take eagerly whatever he chose to offer in that bed upstairs. But what really ravaged him was not knowing if she responded to any man in the same mind-blowing way.

He swung away so that Ethan Hayes could not see his expression. Sometimes he wished he had never come here, had never given in to the temptation that was Melanie Portreath. She turned him inside out, made him behave as he had never behaved in his life before. Which made him—what?

A man in love with his obsession? The words filtered like poison into his brain tissue, sending him on yet another restless swing that concluded with him frowning at his watch. Melanie was due back soon from the hours she donated to Robbie's school several mornings a week, helping out wherever she was required to do so. He did not want her to find him here with Ethan Hayes.

'Have you no ambition to do anything with your life?' he had asked her one evening.

'Should I be ashamed of wanting to be a full-time mother to my son?' she'd bristled indignantly by return.

'No, of course not. I just thought—'

'Well, don't think,' she'd snapped. 'I am comfortable

with who I am, but if you're not then you know what you can do.'

Leave. She never failed to let him know that the option was there for him to use if he wished to do so. He usually answered by kissing her breath away. But would she care if he did leave? Or would she heave a sigh of relief as she watched him walk away from this idea that marriage between them could work?

'I would like work to begin while the owners are away,' he said to Ethan with a calmness that belied what was going on inside his head. 'It will be less painful for those concerned if they do not have to witness the initial destruction of everything they love.'

'Who owns the house?' Ethan questioned.

'A—friend of mine.' He couldn't even say the words, My wife, as of the day after tomorrow, which angered him all the more. Was he ashamed? Was he afraid it might never happen? She was still having second thoughts despite the torrid sex; he was aware of that. Recently she had even withdrawn the sex. She had turned a cold shoulder upon him and said she had a headache.

A headache. The oldest excuse in a woman's vocabulary. He frowned, glanced at the time again but did not register it because he was remembering that she had spent yesterday out with her cynical friend, choosing something to wear for her wedding day. Ten minutes alone with Miss Elliot would have been long enough for Melanie to begin piling on the doubts.

'Then this house cannot be touched without her permission.' Ethan's voice intruded on his own dark thoughts.

The very walls seemed to move, as if William Portreath's ghost was stirring himself to warn Rafiq to be careful how much he took for granted. I take nothing for granted, he grimly told the old ghost.

'You said it is in danger of falling down,' he responded.

'Yes,' Ethan confirmed. 'But you will still need written permission from the owner to touch it, Rafiq,' he advised.

'Even my flighty wife would not dare come near it without written consent from the owner.'

'I will obtain it.' He nodded. By fair means or foul, he added silently, thinking of the trust with which Melanie signed any papers either he or Randal Soames placed in front of her.

Which was just another thing about Melanie that irritated him. The money she now possessed meant nothing. Her son and this house meant everything.

Where did he fit in?

The telephone in William's study began ringing. Since he had commandeered the room for himself, Rafiq assumed the call must be for him, and excused himself, leaving Ethan to wander the house some more while he went to lean against William's old desk and lifted the receiver to his ear.

'Yes?' he said brusquely.

There was a small silence, then a tentative-sounding voice. 'Is Melanie there?'

Rafiq froze on instant recognition of that deep country burr. 'No,' was all he could manage to utter.

'Oh...' Jamie Sangster sounded momentarily nonplussed. 'Who are you?' he then asked curiously.

'A—friend,' Rafiq gritted.

Another 'Oh' raked his eardrum, followed by, 'Will you give her a message for me, then? Tell her that Jamie will be in town on Saturday and could she give me a ring so we can arrange dinner or something to talk about her proposition?'

Rafiq replaced the receiver without replying. He then carefully removed it from its rest. Beyond the study door he could hear Ethan Hayes moving about the hallway. In William Portreath's study the only sound was the buzzing taking place inside his own head.

*   *   *

Melanie signed all the papers Rafiq set in front of her without bothering to look at them. She was so tired she knew she couldn't see straight to read them anyway.

'Randal tells me you have decided to set a separate fund aside,' Rafiq murmured levelly. 'Is it for anything special?'

'Is Randal supposed to pass on to you every decision I make?' She frowned.

'Taking care of your money is what you signed me up to do for you.'

Shame this relationship hadn't stayed that simple, Melanie thought heavily and got up from the desk with the grim intention of taking herself off to bed. She was exhausted beyond anything—stress and tension—tension and stress...

'So, what is the money set aside for?' Rafiq prompted an answer.

'Personal stuff,' she said.

'A million pounds of it?'

His sarcasm showed. Melanie turned to look at him. There was something different about him tonight. He'd been quiet and withdrawn, even with Robbie. And he looked paler than he usually did. Was the stress of it all getting to him also?

'I might want to go on a spending binge.' She attempted to make light of a tricky subject. 'Your know, retail therapy and all that.'

He didn't even try to smile. 'You believe you may require such therapy once married to me?'

She glanced at him, standing there in so-called casual clothes that had clearly cost the earth. 'Well, my one good suit doesn't look much next to the dozen or so suits you have hanging in my wardrobe,' she pointed out wryly.

'It will not cost a million to replenish your wardrobe.'

'I might decide I want to by loads of things—like a new car or two,' she suggested. 'Why, is there a ceiling on how much I am allowed to stash on one side?'

'No,' he answered quietly. 'But I think you have over-done it a little. Why not allow me to place, say—one hundred thousand in your account to be going on with?' he suggested. 'You need only say when you require more.'

Melanie shifted tensely; she did not want to talk about this. 'Don't talk down to me just because you know more about money than I do, Rafiq,' she told him crossly. 'If I'd wanted only one hundred thousand I would have made it only one hundred thousand.'

With that she went to leave the room.

'Where are you going?' His dark voice came after her.

'I'm tired. It's been a—long day. I want a nice soak in a warm bath, then just to fall asleep as soon as my head hits the pillow.'

'What—again?' he drawled lazily.

It was like a red rag to a bull. She whipped around to look at him. It was a terrible—terrible mistake. He was leaning against the edge of William's desk with his arms loosely folded and eyes slightly hooded by long black lashes, as usual.

Why? Because he was trying to impose another woman's image over her image. He wanted that other woman so badly that sometimes she could actually feel him ache.

'We aren't even married yet and you sound like a husband,' she lashed out. 'There has to be more to this relationship than just sex, or we are about to make a big mistake.'

The light from the desk lamp was playing across his bold dark features. She thought she saw a different kind of light glint in his eyes and stiffened her shoulders in readiness for him to throw something really nasty back at her like, Be grateful we have sex!

But he didn't say that. In fact he didn't saying or do anything but study her, and she felt herself begin to tremor, felt her inner self wanting to reach out for him with a desperation that made her want to cry. Simple eye contact and she was falling into that terrible pit. Her senses came alive, slinking terrible temptations down her quivering spine.

Then the heavy eyelids lowered even further. He began to straighten and her senses went haywire. If he starts walking, I start running, she told herself agitatedly. I don't want him to touch me—I don't! But what he did was unfold his arms and drop them to his sides before offering her one of those cold, curt formal bows he could demonstrate with such devastating effect.

'Of course,' he said. 'My apologies. Forgive my crass instincts,' he begged.

There was nothing crass about his instincts. Nothing crass about the way he could turn himself into this coldly polite, lofty giant of a stranger who contrarily made her want to be very gentle with him.

Her stomach muscles quivered; her heart began to ache. 'Rafiq…'

He turned away from the husky little murmur of his name, and picked up the papers she had just signed for him. 'I will be leaving early in the morning and will not be returning here tomorrow night. Robert knows this, but please reassure him that I will ring before his bedtime.'

All of a sudden she didn't know if she was standing on her head or her heels. Her emotions were flipping over from one thing to another; now she was experiencing stark fear.

'Y-you mean you're not coming back at all?' she managed to stammer.

He sent her a glance, a fleeting glance. 'A car will collect you on Friday morning. Please attempt not to be late.'

A car. Friday. Don't be late. She almost sank to her knees in relief. Which said it all really, didn't it? she accepted bleakly. I'm hooked. I can't bear the thought of living without him.

'Yes,' she whispered. 'Goodnight,' she said, and got herself out of there before her knees actually did give out.

Rafiq sat in the back of his chauffeur-driven car and stared out of the window at yet another cold, wet day in London.

Beside him his aide, Kadir Al-Kadir, sat quietly. He was in shock, but then who would not be to find himself hauled out of his bed at six in the morning by a man who was not happy that his plans were already beginning to fall apart?

Hassan had not made it to London. Something had come up involving important matters of state. If he had not been so stubborn and had told Hassan exactly why he wanted him here then his half-brother would have left no stone unturned in his quest to be at his side on this day. But that had not been the way he wanted to play it. Hassan had met Melanie eight years ago, during the weekend they'd spent on the Maitland estate. He knew the history of their relationship and had no kind thoughts for Melanie. Given enough time and the opportunity, he would have tried to stop the marriage today.

But he had still wanted his brother at his side on this important day for him, so he had planned Hassan's arrival to give him neither time nor space to voice his objections. As the old ones liked to say about meticulous planning, it simply begged to fall apart on you, he mused heavily.

He glanced at his watch. Thirty minutes to go. Melanie should be leaving home with their son and her cynical friend about now. 'Check what is happening with the other car,' he instructed Kadir.

The younger man located his mobile telephone. A few murmured questions later and he was putting it away again. 'The car is still awaiting its passengers, sir,' he informed him.

Rafiq nodded, slid a long finger across the tense line of his mouth and wished he hadn't asked the question. He would not do so again, he determined. Which meant he now had to endure a very tense half-hour.

'Ready?' Sophia asked.

No, Melanie thought. 'Yes,' she answered quietly.

'You look so pretty, Mummy,' Robbie told her. 'Doesn't she look pretty, Aunt Sophia?'

'Stunning,' Sophia agreed with a touch of dry cynicism. 'Now all she needs to do is smile to show she's happy about this.'

'Of course she's happy.' Robbie was jumping up and down with excitement. 'She's getting married to my daddy today.'

'Go and check if the car is still there, Robbie,' Sophia instructed. 'The innocence of youth.' She sighed as Robbie bounced out of the room and went clattering down the stairs. 'One good look at your face and he would know you are about to fall into a maidenly swoon.'

'Don't be so Gothic,' Melanie said. 'I'm fine. I just didn't sleep much last night.'

'Missed your man?'

Missed him dreadfully, she thought hollowly. Which only made the ache she was carrying around inside worse.

A telephone began ringing downstairs. 'I'll get it!' Robbie shouted.

'The big man is checking up on you,' Sophia wagered. 'He can't be certain that you are going to turn up.'

'Yes, he can. He only has to think about his son to know that I am going to be there— You look fantastic,' she put in when Sophia opened her mouth to say something Melanie knew she did not want to hear.

Her friend was wearing a dark purple suit that followed her hourglass figure to perfection. With her exotically dark colouring she made Melanie feel washed out and ordinary in her misty-blue outfit with its short straight skirt and nipped-in jacket edged with soft blue fake fur at the round neck and cuffs.

A rush of nerves suddenly washed through her, sending her heart down to her neat blue shoes. 'I don't think—'

Robbie came running down the landing 'Can we can go now—please?' he begged.

'You're not wearing something old,' Sophia murmured as they moved down the landing.

Melanie wriggled her diamond ring at her.

'Something borrowed?'

The hesitation was only slight before Melanie wriggled the self-same ring. Which said a lot as to how long she expected this marriage to last.

'Who was on the phone, Robbie?' she asked her son as they hit the downstairs hallway.

'Uncle Jamie,' he replied. 'I told him you were getting married to my daddy today and he rang off without saying goodbye.'

Melanie's footsteps stilled on the polished wood floor. But Robbie's moved him onwards to pull open the front door. Ice-cold air rushed into the house and she shivered. A man wearing a dark overcoat stood just outside, holding up a huge black umbrella. He saw Robbie and Sophia into the car and out of the pouring rain first. As Melanie stood there on the doorstep, waiting for him to return for her, she experienced the only real moment where she actually thought she was going to change her mind. Then the driver came back to offer her shelter; his smile was warm. She stepped out of the house, closing the door behind her.

Rafiq was standing with Kadir in the elegant foyer belonging to one of London's local government town halls when the entrance doors suddenly opened and his son, Melanie and her friend appeared. His son ran straight towards him. Miss Elliot became busy brushing away the few raindrops that had caught her clothes; Melanie looked at him and went perfectly still.

His heart began to pound against his ribcage; his legs suddenly felt heavy and weak. His son was talking away to him but he did not hear a single word. She was so lovely she tore at his senses, enchanting, shy and uncertain, like the younger woman he'd used to know.

'Stay here, Robert,' he instructed, and made himself

walk towards Melanie. As he came to a halt in front of her he saw her eyelashes flicker just before she looked up at him. 'So this is it,' he said with a smile that did not quite make it.

'Yes.' The single word whispered nervously from her. Her gaze drifted away. Her cheeks were pale and her fingers were trembling.

'I'm sorry we're a few minutes late,' she said in a little rush. 'The rain...'

The words became muffled by a smothering breathlessness as she picked up the aroma of his scent. He was wearing another midnight-blue suit made of a crease-free touch-temptingly smooth fabric. His shirt was so white it made his skin look darker and temptingly smooth like the suit. Her fingers twitched nervously against the little blue purse she was holding, and she kept her eyes averted in case she did something stupid like come jolting to her senses.

Was she really about to marry this tall dark beautiful man? 'W-where do we go?'

It was all she could think to say in the circumstances.

'Up the stairs.' He offered his hand to her. 'Shall we go?' he said.

There was another moment of complete stillness while Melanie stared at his hand. They never touched, unless compelled to do so by that awful sexual force. Did he know that? Was he aware that his outstretched hand was breaking new ground here? Her mouth ran dry; she tried to swallow. From the sidelines she caught sight of Sophia, watching them. Her friend too had noticed her hesitation and was probably making her own deductions as to what it meant.

The fact that Rafiq had noticed Sophia studying him showed when he turned his head to flash her a look. Sophia dared to cock a mocking eyebrow. Hostility sparked into life. Melanie responded by lifting up a hand and placing it in his. The gesture brought his gaze flashing back her way, and his fingers closed gently round hers. Warm strength enclosed icy frailty; something very dramatic began to build in the air. As he turned them towards the elegant stairway that led to an upper foyer she noticed Kadir Al-Kadir standing quietly to one side, with his dark gaze fixed on Robbie as if he could not quite believe what his eyes were telling him.

By necessity Rafiq made the polite introduction, though Melanie suspected he did not want to speak at all. He was tense; she was tense. They moved up the stairs together, with Robbie dancing behind them, his hand tucked into Sophia's, blissfully unaware of the stress-load weighing down everyone else's shoulders.

Not twenty minutes later they were walking down those same stairs again. It had all been so quick, so efficient—so impersonal. But in those few minutes she had changed her name to Al-Qadim and was now wearing a wedding band on her finger. Even more disturbing was the ring Rafiq had given her to slide on his long brown finger.

That hand now rested at the base of her spine, and remained there until they stepped outside. The rain was still bouncing off the pavements. Three cars now stood in a row at the kerb, with three black-coated men standing beside them holding black umbrellas over their heads.

With a click of his fingers Rafiq brought one man running. With a brief word of thanks he sent Kadir on his way. Next came Melanie's first shock, when the second man was brought running and she found herself being hugged by Sophia, who murmured, 'Surprise, surprise. I am taking your son off your hands until tomorrow.'

'But I don't want—'

'Not your choice any more, little sacrificial lamb,' Sophia informed her dryly, only to be replaced by Robbie, who was demanding a hug from his mother and excitedly explaining all the things he and Sophia had planned for the day, before he was ushered beneath the umbrella and hurried away.

Standing there, shell-shocked beyond speech, Melanie found herself left alone with the man she had just married, watching another car move off, which left only one—a long, low-squatting animal thing with darkened glass and a distinct air of menace about it.

The snap of Rafiq's fingers set her blinking; the return of his hand to the base of her spine had her tensing jerkily. The last black-coated man came running with an umbrella. She was directed beneath it and into the warm soft depths of black-leather car seats. Rafiq followed, the car door closed with a smooth soft thud and they were alone— really alone—encased in dark glass and hidden, even from the driver.

Silence arrived. It hummed between them. The car began moving away from the kerb. She turned to look at Rafiq and found him looking back at her. His wide shoulders hugged the upholstered corner of the car and one ankle rested easily across the other knee with a set of long fingers lightly clasping the ankle. He looked relaxed, at ease, like a lazy cat contentedly at peace. Indeed, slumberous lashes barely flickered as he studied her face. But there was nothing relaxed about those devil-dark eyes hiding behind the lashes. They glinted in a way that sent tiny hot frissons chasing down her spine.

'I can't believe you planned all of this without my knowledge,' she said, jumping nervously into speech.

'It is tradition for a newly married couple to spend this time alone.'

'This isn't a traditional marriage.' That short ceremony they had just performed mocked the very word. 'We did this for Robbie, so why shouldn't he be here with us now?'

'Robbie is perfectly happy doing what he is doing.'

Well, I'm not, Melanie thought, and with a pressing together of her lips she turned her face away. Beyond the darkened glass she could see London moving past at speed. They were crossing one of the bridges that spanned the river, she realised, and she felt those frissons chase through her again, because they didn't need to cross the river to get to her house or even his apartment.

'Where are we going?' she asked sharply.

'To a place where my sacrificial lamb can perform in complete privacy,' he murmured silkily.

CHAPTER TEN

His reply tugged her face around to him again. He was smiling, but it wasn't a nice smile. Obviously he had overheard Sophia and, despite appearances to the contrary, he was actually as angry as hell.

'I am nobody's sacrifice,' she objected.

'Shame,' he drawled. 'I was looking forward to watching you lay yourself out on some softly sprung, silk-covered altar, then offer yourself to me.'

His description conjured up exactly the image it had aimed to. Heat stole into her cheeks; she bristled in annoyance with it. 'Back to sex again,' she derided.

'Would you prefer it if we discussed other things?'

'Like what?' she asked warily.

'Jamie,' he inserted with velvet precision. 'Our son tells me he spoke to his *uncle* Jamie on the telephone this morning, but he rang off before he could invite him to come to our wedding.'

At last she understood where the anger was coming from. 'I never said that—'

'Our son has a very generous nature,' he cut in. 'He seems to hold a great affection for his uncle Jamie. Do you think this affection has anything to do with how close he came to having Jamie as his father instead of me?'

Melanie released a sharp gasp. 'That is a terrible thing to say!'

'But the truth.'

'You don't *know* the truth!'

'He is still in your life. That is a clear truth.'

'I don't—'

155

'Do not begin this marriage by lying to me,' he gritted warningly.

Melanie took a deep breath to stop herself from exploding. 'I was about to say that I don't think that is any of your business,' she said coldly.

'From now on everything that you do is my business.'

'Does that mean everything that you do is my business too?' she tossed back. 'In this country we believe in equality. So why don't you tell me all about Serena Cordero.'

'You are trying to divert me from the main issue here.'

'That is because I have nothing to say on the subject,' she declared stubbornly.

'Then let me assist,' he offered. 'I took a call from your step-cousin Jamie last week in William's study. This morning my son took another call from him. To me your step-cousin mentioned a—proposition. With Robert, he simply rang off when he discovered that you were marrying me today. Maybe if you are wise you will explain the proposition, and why this man is still so much a part of your life that my son calls him *uncle*!'

The sleeping cat had awoken. Melanie watched with increasing wariness as the long fingers slid away from his ankle and his shoulders began to tense. She lost every scrap of colour and spoke without thinking. 'Anyone would think you were jealous—'

He moved like lightning, catching hold of her nearest wrist and pulling her across the gap separating them. She landed with a thud against his shirt front; her silk skirt slithered up her thighs as he hauled her onto his lap. Her fingers clawed at his shoulders; her breath panted into his face. His eyes had turned silver; she had never seen them do that before.

'Start talking,' he gritted.

She trembled all over, but held onto this one promise she had made to herself. 'Jamie is not up for discussion between you and me.'

'He was your lover eight years ago. I will not be betrayed by you twice!'

She struggled against him. 'Let go of me. You're hurting!'

To her absolute surprise he set her free. She slithered onto the seat beside him, too shaken to notice the new expression in his eyes. 'I apologise,' he said curtly. 'I don't usually forget my own strength. Where did I hurt you?'

'My wrist.' She was rubbing it, though it didn't really hurt. It had been the fear that he was close to hurting her that had made her tell the white lie.

Careful fingers took the wrist from her; very gently he began stroking the pink area with the smooth pad of his thumb. It was a stupid thing to react so badly to, but her pulse suddenly went crazy. He felt it happen and the thumb-pad stilled; she released a strangled little sigh. The mood flipped from anger to electrified awareness so quickly that it threw her into a state of confusion.

But not him—not him. He simply accepted the change with a shrug and a grimace, then lifted the wrist to his mouth and stroked the pink area with his tongue.

'So we're back to the sex again.' It was a supposed to be a withering condemnation, but it didn't quite come out like that.

'Blame yourself,' Rafiq murmured, and in the next moment she was pulled back into his lap.

'Don't!' she protested.

'Scared?' he drawled. 'Because you know your defences will not hold through one small kiss? Or is your pulse beating so fast because you are afraid that I *won't* kiss you?'

'No.'

He tested that denial with devastating consequences: the moment her lips clung he removed his own and watched her stare at his mouth like a hungry woman. One of his hands began to stroke her silk-covered thigh, left provokingly exposed by her slippery skirt. She moved against him, breasts searching for contact with his chest, her hips pressing into the cradle of his pelvis where the thrust of his erection was making itself known.

'You don't play fair,' she groaned helplessly.

He just laughed low in his throat, then gave her back his mouth. It stayed this time, seducing with lazy dips of his tongue, while he undid the jacket buttons and removed it altogether. Beneath she wore a creamy white body. One light touch and he knew she was wearing no bra. 'Interesting,' he murmured as the hand began to follow the clinging outline of Lycra. When the waistband of her skirt stopped his progress he merely switched attention to the other hand and finished the journey via her thigh.

A single smooth slide between her thighs and he had released the tiny poppers that held the body in place.

'Oh,' she whimpered, when he discovered for himself how warm and moist she was. For the next few dizzying minutes she just hung on and let him work his seductive magic. She moved, she stretched, she curled herself around him, she moaned into his hungry mouth. He broke the kiss on a hiss of tension, caught her chin between his teeth and bit, then her throat, then her breasts, first one then the other, sucking at them through the Lycra. She clutched at his neck, his hair, the hair-roughened wrist attached to the tormenting hand. She begged, she pleaded, he growled something and came back to pester her mouth again at the precise moment she was threatening to topple headlong into the kind of orgasm that didn't belong in this situation.

'We can't do this here,' she whispered anxiously.

With a growl of impatience he pressed his body forward, taking hers with him as he reached for the in-car phone. A few husky words in Arabic and the car was sliding to a standstill. Ten seconds later, Melanie heard the thud of a car door and realised that the driver had left them alone.

Embarrassed heat flooded her cheeks. 'He will know what we're doing!'

He was way beyond the point of giving a care. His

mouth claimed hers again; his hands claimed her hips. 'Release me,' he commanded in a throat-hoarse murmur.

'I can't.'

'You can.' Capturing one of her hands, he pressed it against himself. He was trembling as badly as she was, and maybe it was those tremors that stopped any more protest. A minute later she was straddling him, her mouth devouring his hot mouth while her body slowly took him in. She had never felt so wickedly wanton, had never thought she could behave like this. She moved while he held her slender hips steady; she copied the movement with her tongue. His breathing was ragged; the car filled with the scent of heat from their bodies. As she began to rise towards the edge, her inner muscles closed so tightly around him that he had to stop kissing her to throw back his dark head and close his eyes.

Pleasure like this could never be repeated, she found herself thinking as his hands reached up to frame her face and black eyelashes lifted to capture her eyes. She drove; he let her. It was a powerful, powerful aphrodisiac. When she leapt she cried out. When he followed he pulled her face into his shoulder and held her there throughout the ragged, pulsing finish until the weakness of exhaustion made her feel boneless.

They did not speak. Not then—not later, when eventually he gently eased himself from her and set her down on the seat at his side. Clothes rustled as shaking fingers replaced them into some semblance of dignity. Melanie kept her head lowered so her hair hid her hot face. She could sense the gravity shrouding Rafiq.

Cool air hit the interior as he let down the window. A minute later the car was moving again. The window remained open, though, circulating the hot air of seduction out of the car.

They turned in through a pair of high gates and began driving down a lane between a tunnel of trees with gnarled naked branches reaching out to tangle across the gap.

The car stopped. Rafiq climbed out and came around to open her door for her. Still without daring to look at him, she arrived at his side like a cracked piece of porcelain, in danger of shattering if anyone so much as spoke.

She found herself standing in front of huge sandstone monolith with tall sash windows and an oak front door. Beyond caring what this place was, she followed Rafiq to the door, which he unlocked with a key then stepped to one side, as if to invite her to precede him. She took a single step—that was all—before he was lifting her up in his big arms.

'More tradition?' she mocked shrilly.

'For once in your life keep your mouth shut,' he grimly advised her, and stepped over the threshold with his bride. He kicked the door shut again.

She gained a vague impression of oak panelling and iron fretwork, but most of her attention was honed on his taut profile as he proceeded to carry her up a stairway that curved around a panelled wall. They walked through an archway and down a dark red-carpeted corridor, passing more oak doors on their way. When they arrived at the one he was aiming for he opened it, then walked inside.

The room was so dramatically Gothic in design that she half expected to find a headless ghost standing in one of the shadowy corners. A fire burned in the grate of a big fireplace and a tray laid for coffee waited on a low table set between two richly upholstered wine-coloured velvet chairs. But what dominated the room was the huge and heavy oak four-poster bed hung with more wine-red velvet and, of all things, a dark purple throw made of silk.

The scene for a bridal seduction was set right down to the last detail—right down to the two matching black silk robes that lay draped across the foot of the bed. Shame, she thought cynically that they had pre-empted the moment; it had certainly spoiled all of this.

Allowing her feet to slip to a thick purple carpet, Rafiq

then turned to close the door. 'Sit down—pour yourself a drink,' he invited.

She almost jumped when he spoke to her. She spun on her heel then wished she hadn't done it when she found herself looking at a man at war with himself. He was yanking his tie loose with impatient fingers; the frown on his face was a definite scowl. Heat bloomed in her cheeks; shame choked her lungs. Turning away, she felt the sting of tears in her eyes.

'I don't like what you do to me,' she breathed out painfully.

'You surprise me. I had not noticed,' he drawled.

It was derision of the crushing kind and the worst insult he could have offered her. Moving on legs that did not want to support her, Melanie went to the nearest chair and sank down.

He disappeared through a door near the bed and came back a few minutes later wearing only a long black robe. She glanced at the bed, saw that one robe was now missing. It was so glaringly obvious what he was intending to do next that she wished she had never been born.

But what made it worse was the low soft pulsing taking place between her thighs. She could still feel him there, hard and silken. She could still taste his kisses on her tongue. He took the other chair, saw she hadn't touched the coffee pot and leant forward to pour it himself.

Silently, he handed a cup to her. With lowered eyes she took it. 'Thank you,' she breathed.

He huffed out a laugh. It brought her wary gaze up to clash head-on with his harshly mocking expression. 'How can you manage to sound so prim when we both know that prim is the last thing that you are?' he threw at her.

It was like being kicked when she was already down on the floor. 'I don't know how you can sit there and speak to me like this when you only married me an hour ago,' she responded shakily.

'And was seduced by you half an hour later.'

'You started it!'

'You finished it!' he raked back. 'In the name of *Allah* I cannot believe I am even sitting here with you! You are poison to a man like me.'

'Oh.' She stood up. 'How dare you say that?'

'Your step-cousin says I can say what the hell I like to you.'

He looked hard and dark and dangerously foreign. His anger and contempt washed over her in waves. Senses that just should *not* respond to this man she was seeing stung her with their awful message.

'I n-need to use the bathroom.' She turned away dizzily.

'You need an escape.'

'I *hate* you!' she cried.

He launched to his feet. She dropped her cup and ran towards the door he had used a few minutes ago as a dark coffee stain seeped into her skirt. Slamming the door shut behind her, she expected to find herself standing in a bathroom and instead found her eyes flickering round a room full of clothes. Men's clothes, women's clothes—rails and rails of them. It took only a glance at a couple of dresses for her to realise that every female item in here was so new it still wore its label.

Bought for her? She couldn't be sure. Didn't even think she wanted to know. They were her size and that was all that she cared about, since she didn't have anything else to wear and she needed to get out of this stupid wedding outfit that made such a mockery of the word marriage— and which was impregnated with the scent of him!

With trembling fingers she stripped the suit from her body and had just removed the wretched Lycra body when the door opened. She spun, clutching that silly scrap of material to her. 'Get out!' she shrieked at him.

With his usual arrogance he ignored the instruction. Instead he tossed something at her. She had to drop the body to catch it. It was the black wrap that matched the one he was wearing. It felt like the final humiliation to have him stand there viewing her through cold opal eyes as she fumbled on the robe over her near nakedness and dragged the two pieces of black silk across her body, tightly knotted the belt.

'Tell me about Jamie,' he demanded remorselessly.

He just was not going to give up!

'Which version would you really like to hear, Rafiq?' she flashed at him. 'The one where I admit to going from your arms to his arms with no conscience? Or the one where I tell you just how fickle you were—how easy you were to dupe and how badly you let me down when you dared to believe I could play such calculating games?'

His dark face tightened, big shoulders flexing at her bitterly deriding tone. 'The truth,' he gritted. 'Just tell me the truth!'

The truth? She almost laughed, though she'd never felt less like laughing. She wasn't that sure that he could take the truth! Did she actually care any more whether his pride was up to weathering the blow she could deliver it?

No, she didn't, she realised. He had called her poison. Well, maybe it was time he discovered just how poisonous she could be. So she lifted her face and looked at him squarely.

'The truth is that you were set up,' she said. 'Uncle Thomas and Jamie always knew I would inherit from William. William actually paid my uncle money for my keep. Uncle Thomas was greedy; he wanted to get his hands on *all* of William's money. But the only way he could do that was if he kept it in the family. He encouraged a romance between Jamie and me. I refused to play. They didn't like it. Tensions in the house became pretty grim. I decided I needed to get away and started hiring myself out to the local gentry to earn some extra money so I could leave the farm. Which was how I came to meet you.' She released a short laugh which stung with mockery, for never in a hundred years would a woman like her normally have come into contact with a man like Rafiq. 'You swept me off my feet and into bed, even asked me to marry you.'

'And you saw your quick escape from drudgery?'

Her eyes widened on this darkly handsome, beautifully put together man who could harbour such a huge inferiority complex. 'If I'd known about William's money it would not have changed anything. Haven't you noticed yet that I don't have much use for the stuff?'

'Unless you want to give it away to your step-cousin.'

He was mixing the past up with the present. 'Do you want to hear the rest of this or not?' she demanded.

A muscle in his jaw clenched tightly. He gave a grim nod of his head. 'I said yes to your proposal,' she continued tightly. 'And was then left with the unhappy task of breaking the news to Uncle Thomas and Jamie. They saw their chance of getting their hands on William's money slipping away, so they decided to do something about it.'

'I saw you with him in your bedroom.' His dark eyes were glinting as if he could still see them there. 'You were standing in your bedroom window, locked in each other arms.'

'I was locked in *his* arms!' Melanie flashed out the distinction.

He didn't believe her. 'Brazen,' he gritted. 'You were kissing as if you couldn't get enough of each other!'

He was right; the kiss had been fevered. Jamie had been feverishly trying to seduce her while she had been trying to get away! 'I was young and a complete fool,' she admitted cynically. 'I actually believed that Jamie truly loved me. I was attempting to let him down gently because I believed I was hurting him!'

'In your bathrobe. It was gaping.' His eyes were black with accusation.

'It was not!' she denied, paused to think about that, then had to offer a small shrug. 'Maybe a little,' she conceded. 'Things were getting a little out of hand, and I—'

'A little?' he cut in. 'Do you believe *a little* should mean something here?'

The jeering tone of his voice straightened her backbone. She looked into his hard, condemning face and wanted to hit him! 'Well, you tell me what *you* think it means, Rafiq,' she challenged. 'Or don't I need to ask?' It was written on his face! 'Because you saw me locked in that embrace with Jamie you just had to believe that I must be enjoying it! Didn't it occur to you for one small second that I might not have had much choice in the matter?'

'So you were the victim?' His tone derided her.

'As much as you were,' she replied.

'I know your passions,' he countered gruffly.

Melanie released a hard laugh. 'I suppose I should have expected a man from your culture to think like that,' she murmured bitterly.

'Meaning?'

'Primitive!' she flashed at him. 'I let you make love to me so, in your primitive view, it therefore goes without saying that I would let any man do that same!'

'I never said that.'

'You don't need to say it when I see it written on your face every time you look at me,' she denounced. 'The day I let you into my bed I lost your respect.'

Her shrug said she no longer cared that she had. As she began to walk towards him, Rafiq stiffened in the doorway. He had never seen her look upon him with such open dislike. 'I was twenty years old,' she said as she reached him. 'I let you take something very special from me. It should have meant something to you, but it didn't or you could not have walked away.'

'Your own uncle stood beside me as I watched you with Jamie. He told me things I would have been a fool to—'

'He lied,' she stated with a cool, quiet simplicity, then brushed past him to go back into the bedroom. Rafiq turned to watch her walk across the room with her shoulders straight and her slender shape shimmering with contempt for him.

The coffee cup still lay on its side on the carpet, a dark stain seeping outwards from its rim. He stood watching as she stooped to pick up the cup then reach for a napkin to mop up the stain. The soft fall of her hair curled around her slender nape and caressed the edges of the black silk robe. He could see her profile, delicate and pure in its smooth lines, even while her lovely mouth still pursed with dislike. Something shifted inside him—not sexual this time, but more a shifting of other desires—a desire to drop his guard and let himself believe what he knew deep down inside was the damning truth.

Because if what she had told him was the truth then it damned him and not Melanie. Because she was right and he had been fickle, easy to dupe. Most damning of all, he had let her down in the worst way a man could let down the woman he professed to love.

Primitive. He almost laughed. For primitive hardly covered the way he had behaved—if she was telling him the truth. At home in Rahman women might not enjoy the same equal rights as their western counterparts, but they did have the right to defend themselves when accused of a crime. He had denied Melanie even this basic right.

And in so doing he had forfeited the love she'd used to feel for him—and seven years of his son's life. Which left him with what? he had to ask himself. A marriage filled with bitterness and resentment? A wife who would never be a real wife to him unless he could accept her truth and put the past behind him?

Patiently pressing the napkin into the coffee stain, Melanie could feel his silence with every pulse of her heartbeat. She could sense his battle with every frail breath that she took. He had a choice; they both knew it. He must believe her or not believe her. She had no proof she could pull like a rabbit from a magic hat.

There were words, of course—lots more words. Were they worth uttering?

'They knew what time you were coming to collect me that evening.' She gave the words a chance. 'By the time you pulled into the farmyard the whole scene had been set so perfectly that I didn't really stand a chance. When I was allowed to turn and see you standing there, you were already turning away. I caught the next train to London...'

She paused in what she was doing and let the next ugly scene play inside the privacy of her own head. By the way he moved over, to stand frowning out of the window, so did Rafiq, she suspected.

'When I arrived back at the farm Uncle Thomas and Jamie were having this big row and I heard enough to know how neatly we had been set up. Jamie admitted his part in it before I walked out of there for good. He felt guilt...' Because I was so distraught. She did not say it out loud.

'Where did you go?' He sounded husky.

'To stay with friends in Winchester,' she answered, her fingers pressing at the wet patch again. 'I managed to get a job there, working in a factory. But they laid me off when it became obvious that I was pregnant. So I came up to London to try you again...'

'Hassan told me you had been trying to contact me,' he inserted. 'I was at home in Rahman. I asked Hassan to meet with you but you had not left a contact number. He did attempt to find you but was unsuccessful...'

Sitting back on her heels, Melanie looked up at his tall dark shape standing by the deep purple curtains, and felt something painful slice across her chest. So his brother hadn't even told him he'd spoken to her.

Neat, she thought ruefully. Tidy and slick.

'He merely said that he had heard you were living with another man.'

Pressing her trembling lips together, she refused to say

anything. There was enough bitterness flying around this room without her adding his brother into the mix.

He moved, shifting his tense frame to look at her. 'What happened to Jamie?'

'He left home too, went up north. I didn't hear from him again until his father died.' She stood up; her fingers were sticky and covered in fine fibres from the carpet. 'He's married now, has two beautiful children and a lovely wife he adores. He works with her father on a farm in Cumbria and would have been perfectly content to live the rest of his life milking cows for a living if the recent foot-and-mouth epidemic hadn't devastated the herd.'

'So he came to you for help?'

'Financial help.' Melanie nodded. 'They want to go organic, but it takes time to clear the land of chemicals, disease and...whatever else.' She shrugged. 'They still have to live while they are achieving all this. Then they have to restock their herd. They want to specialise, so I am investing half a million pounds into their project.'

'With no real hope of any return,' Rafiq added, 'because you still care for him.'

'Of course I still care for him!' she cried. 'He was sorry for what he'd done. What use is there in bearing grudges? He is my only living relative besides Robbie!'

'Not a blood relative.'

'Does that matter? Who are you to criticise?'

'I have a father and a half-brother.'

'Would you turn your back on your brother's wife if she came to you for help?'

No, he wouldn't. She could see that in the sudden frown on his face.

'We have wandered from the subject,' he said tensely.

'I've finished with the subject,' she replied. 'You believed what your eyes told you, and as far as you were concerned I did not warrant a single word in my defence. I gave birth to your son and with William's help brought him up. When I thought it would be safe to do it I introduced you to your son, and ended up—here.' She glanced around the Gothic bedroom. 'Married to a man who can't even look at me without seeing a slut.'

'I do not think you are a slut.'

'Poison, then.'

He released a harsh sigh. 'I was angry when I said that.'

'So was I. But do you want to know something really funny, Rafiq?' She lifted cool gold eyes to him. 'I really thought that you cared about me. Right up until you placed this ring on my finger I thought that, deep inside, beneath the rock you would call a heart, you still cared enough to want to make a success out of this marriage. But now?' She turned away. 'I think we've both made a terrible mistake.'

He didn't protest it, which more or less said the rest for her. 'Where is the bathroom?' she asked, holding up her sticky fingers.

He turned to open a door she hadn't noticed on the other side of the four-poster bed. And with her expression as closed as she could make it she walked past him into a rather startlingly decadent oak-panelled room with a huge free-standing bath tub overhung by a big brass shower head and a purple silk curtain that would circle the whole thing when closed. The rest of the fittings were antique porcelain. She walked over to the pedestal-mounted washbasin, then stood grimacing at her fingers before reaching for the taps.

Another pair of hands beat her to it. She was suddenly surrounded by Rafiq. Her body stiffened, her mouth ran dry. Water gushed into white porcelain, swirling around its curving bowl before spiralling its way down the drain. He took her hands and began to gently wash them.

Move back, she wanted to say, but found she couldn't. It just wasn't fair that after everything they'd just said he could *still* affect her like this!

'Mistakes, even terrible mistakes, can be rectified. You proved this yourself when you came to tell me about the wonderful child we had made. If I made a similar terrible mistake eight years ago then you must, in all fairness, give me the opportunity to make it up to you.'

Grave words, reasonable words, words that pulsated with the promise of a different kind. 'I can do this for myself.' She tried to defer offering an answer.

'But when I do it you know there is more to the chore than a simple washing of hands.'

Oh, dear God, he was oh, so right. She closed her eyes and tried very hard to stop a sigh of pleasure from developing. But, as with everything else about this extraordinary man, whether it be with anger or hate or sensuality, he moved her so deeply she really did not stand a chance.

His mouth found the pulse just below her ear lobe and his thumbs gently circled her wet palms. She was lost and she knew it. On a helpless groan she turned to capture his ready mouth. It was, she supposed, already written that they would drown their problems in the long deep warmth of the kiss.

A telephone started ringing somewhere. No one answered it. Was there anyone else here? Melanie tried to ignore it, wanted to stay just where she was in this man's arms, with his kiss filling her up from the inside.

The telephone went on and on until, on a rasping sigh of impatience, he broke away, muttered a curse and an apology, then went to answer it. The nearest land-line extension was downstairs in the study. As he strode into that room Rafiq made a mental note to get some extra extensions put into the house.

He knew so little about its minor details, having only taken possession of it yesterday. He had wanted somewhere special to bring them while William's town house was being attended to. He had viewed many properties, but this house he had liked on sight—had seen Melanie and his son fitting into it with ease. The master bedroom up there had seemed the perfect place to take a bride on her wedding night. Though now he had pre-empted that idea by a few hours, he mused grimly, as he stretched across the big dark antique oak desk to lift up the telephone.

'This had better be good, Kadir,' he barked at the only person who knew this telephone number.

What Kadir had to say to him set him cursing. By the time he put down the phone he was different man. He strode up the stairs and back into the bedroom to find Melanie standing by the bed—waiting for him.

For a moment, a short sweet tantalising moment, he considered forgetting everything except what this beautiful woman and the bed were offering him. Then reality hit.

'Get dressed again,' he instructed grimly. 'We must leave immediately.

CHAPTER ELEVEN

'WHY—what's happened?' Melanie demanded. He could see from her eyes that she was already thinking of their son and conjuring up some terrible accident.

'No, not Robert.' He quickly squashed that anxiety, though the one threatening to strike at him was almost as bad. 'Kadir has just received a call from my father,' he explained.

'He's taken ill again?'

He gave a shake of his head. 'It is such a rare occurrence for my father to speak to anyone outside his family that on hearing his voice Kadir went to pieces and told him about you and Robert and our marriage today.'

'You mean, he didn't know?'

'No,' he answered. 'No one in my family knows,' he added as he walked towards the bathroom. 'Now my father is shocked and angry. We have to go to him.'

There was a strangled gasp he recognised as anger. 'What were you intending to do—keep Robbie and me a dark secret for the rest of our lives?'

He paused in his stride. 'I am not quite that ruthless,' he countered grimly. 'But our marriage and the fact that we have a seven-year-old son is something I preferred to tell my father to his face. It is—complicated.' That seemed to be the word to describe the situation.

Not for Melanie, it seemed. 'Explain complicated,' she commanded, following him as he moved on into the bathroom.

His mouth flattened. He did not want to say this! 'He knew about our relationship eight years ago and is therefore against you before he even sets his eyes on you.'

She did not say a word, but simply turned and walked away. In a mood that hung somewhere between fury and frustration, Rafiq closed the door, shrugged off his robe and stepped beneath the shower.

By the time they met up again Rafiq knew hostilities were back with a vengeance. They met on the landing. Melanie had clearly used another room to dress and was now wearing a suit from the selection he had bought for her. It was long and slinky, in a shade of rich moss-green that did wonderful things for her sparking eyes.

By the way she pursed her beautiful mouth as she ran her gaze over him he did not impress, he noted heavily. 'It is expected of me.' He felt compelled to defend the long white tunic, dark red top-robe and chequered *gut rah* which was covering his head.

It was only when she walked down the stairs without saying a word that he remembered another time she had seen him dressed like this: he had been throwing her out of his life. A silent curse rattled around inside him. Once again he considered leaving his father to wait while he seduced this woman of his into a sweeter temper.

But shocks were bad for his father's health. Rafiq would never forgive himself if the old sheikh took a turn for the worse while Rafiq was lost in the act of lovemaking.

As they stepped outside the car was waiting with its engine running. As soon as they were on their way he offered his mobile phone to Melanie. 'Ring your friend,' he said, 'and warn her that we are coming to collect Robert.'

Without comment she made the connection with Sophia's mobile phone. 'We have to go to Rahman,' she explained. 'Can you have Robbie ready to travel by the time we arrive to pick him up?'

Whatever her friend said to her, Melanie's expression was rueful. 'No. But you had better prepare him for a bit of a shock. His father has turned himself into an Arab, so if he knows beforehand he might not find himself looking at a total stranger.'

With that, she gave him back his phone.

'Was that necessary?' he asked.

She turned an icy stare on him. 'Yes,' she said.

He released a sigh. 'It was not my intention for this to happen.'

'Keep your excuses,' she told him. 'And just so that you know,' she added, 'I am coming with you only because I have made that decision. Your father deserves to meet his grandson. But let one person look upon him like a leper, Rafiq, just one—!'

'And you will do what?' he questioned curiously.

'I am relying on Rahman's reputation for being a free and equal society,' she said. 'If I don't like what we meet there then Robbie and I are coming home to England.'

'With or without me?'

'Without.'

He sighed and said nothing more. For what could he say other than to offer yet another apology? But he suspected it would not be enough for a woman looking at her ruined wedding day.

The rest of the journey was achieved in silence. The meeting with his son did not take place with shock but with awe. 'Will I have to dress like that?' Robbie asked dubiously.

'Not unless you want to,' Rafiq answered smoothly, while Sophia Elliot looked on in complete silence. No mocking tilt to a sleek black eyebrow, no glowering frown of disapproval.

They made their farewells and within the hour were boarding the Al-Qadim private jet to Rahman.

Within the next hour, his son was fast asleep in one of the cabins and Melanie was curled up on a soft cream leather sofa, clearly unimpressed by her luxury surroundings.

Rafiq decided that he had taken enough of her cold

shoulder. Picking her up as she was, he sat himself down and placed her on his lap, then lifted up a hand to remove his headgear and toss it aside. 'There—is that better?' Dark eyes mockingly quizzed her. 'Can you bring yourself to look at me now?'

What he didn't expect from his bit of sarcasm were the tears that filled her lovely eyes.

'You're ashamed of me,' she said.

'No,' he denied.

'If I had let you do it you would have brought Robbie with you and left me behind in London.'

'No.' He denied that too.

'You ruined my wedding day.'

'I will make it up to you.'

'You—'

It was no use carrying this conversation any further. So he kissed her. Why not? She needed kissing. So he kissed her until the tears went away. And kissed her some more until she slowly relaxed into a quiet slumber on his lap. He waved away the attendants when they walked down the cabin, and did not bother to move her to a bed because...he liked to have her just where she was.

Which meant...what? he asked himself as the air miles flew by them.

Hell, he knew what it meant. He had known it for a long time. A week—eight years—it mattered little how long he had known it.

They came in to land at dawn, circling around the perimeter of a great modern city which glinted in the early-morning sun. From the jet they transferred to a small Cessna, drawing curious glances from dark-eyed Arabs as they moved from plane to plane.

Rafiq flew them himself, leaving Melanie and Robbie to drink in the dramatic landscape panning out beneath them, with its silver thread of a river winding through a lush valley surrounded by high, lurking dunes and miles of sand. It took only twenty minutes before they were landing again. A four-wheel drive waited to receive them. Rafiq placed himself behind the wheel of this, and began driving them over tarmac towards a sandstone fortress backed by the fertile oasis of Al-Qadim.

Melanie knew all of this because Robbie had maintained a running commentary throughout both the short flight and this short drive towards his father's home. The child's grasp of this part of his heritage was so intense that even Rafiq allowed himself a couple of grimaces as he listened to him. But other than grimaces he offered nothing; his expression was sombre, the harsh lines of his profile telling her that he was lost in grim places of his own.

A pair of thick wooden gates swung inwards as they approached them, then closed behind them as they passed through into a beautiful courtyard laid with tropical plants and sparkling fountains. They came to a stop in front of a rich blue dome suspended on sandstone pillars. Rafiq got out of the car and strode round to the other side to open the other door. In silence he offered Melanie his hand to assist her to alight. Robbie scrambled out of his own accord, then stood gazing about him with dark eyes that greedily drank in every detail they could.

Then his father was quietly calling him to heel, and the small boy came with his dark head still twisting in frowning curiosity. 'Are we going to live here now?' he asked.

'No, we will continue to live in London,' his father assured him. 'And come here to visit during the school holidays, if you like.'

Nodding his head in approval, Robbie cleared the small frown from his brow, and walked happily beside his father into a vast entrance hall with a beautiful lapis-blue and white domed ceiling and pale sand marble covering the floor.

The first person Melanie saw was Sheikh Hassan Al-Qadim, and her heart slithered to her stomach. Dressed like Rafiq, he was standing straight and still beside a beautiful creature with dark red hair and perfect porcelain skin.

She was quite heavily pregnant beneath the slender white tunic she was wearing.

Both of them fixed their eyes on Robbie. Both looked shocked, if not dismayed. Melanie's fingers twitched within Rafiq's. He glanced down at her and she glanced upwards, the anxiety in her eyes making his grim mouth flatten as he looked away again.

Sheikh Hassan was looking at her now. One glimpse at his expression and Melanie knew what he was going to say. Her heart leapt from her stomach to lodge in her throat. He took a step towards her. 'Miss Leggett,' he murmured deeply, 'I must beg—'

'Mrs Portreath,' she corrected, leaping on anything just to silence him. His dark eyes narrowed and sharpened. With a minuscule shake of her head she tried to relay a message to him.

'Al-Qadim,' Rafiq corrected both of them. 'We married yesterday as you no doubt know by now, Hassan.'

'Of course. Rafiq, if you had only explained why you wanted me to be in London I would have been there. You know that.' Sheikh Hassan begged his understanding, taking the diversion Rafiq had unwittingly offered to him.

But Melanie could see he was not happy about remaining silent over their last meeting. As the two brothers greeted with an embrace and words spoken in Arabic those dark eyes so like Rafiq's remained fixed upon her over his brother's shoulder. She looked away, found herself gazing at the other woman, who had witnessed the exchange and was now looking very concerned.

She stepped forward with a smile, though. 'Welcome to our family,' she greeted warmly, and surprised Melanie by brushing a kiss to each of her cheeks. 'My name is Leona and I am married to Rafiq's brother,' she explained. 'Our child is due in two months—just in case you did not like to ask me. And this...' she turned to smile at Robbie '...has to be the most handsome Al-Qadim of the three.'

It was all very light, very eager to please, but Melanie

could sense the other woman's tension and she could see it repeated in Sheikh Hassan. She could feel it pulsing in Rafiq. When she added her own tension into it all the vast hall almost sparked with it.

'My name is Robert Portreath,' Robbie corrected with a faintly puzzled frown. The business of names was going to take some explaining later, Melanie realised as she watched Leona Al-Qadim dip down to his level to offer Robbie her hand.

'Then, I am very pleased to meet you, Robert Portreath,' she said gravely.

'You're English?' he said.

'Like your mother.' She nodded.

'You have very pretty hair and eyes.'

'And that,' Leona murmured sagely as she straightened, 'is most definitely the Al-Qadim charm. Hello, Rafiq,' she added gently.

'My lady,' he returned with a sweeping bow that held Melanie transfixed in surprise—until she realised she was seeing some kind of in-joke being enacted here, because both pairs of eyes were warm with amusement.

Then Rafiq was introducing his son to Sheikh Hassan, who bent to shake Robbie's hand very formally. When he straightened his eyes made that fleeting contact with Melanie's again.

It was Robbie who broke this next moment of tension. 'Where is my new grandfather?' he wanted to know.

All pleasure—forced or otherwise—instantly dropped away from everyone. Rafiq looked to his brother; his brother gave a reply. 'He is in his rooms,' his said quietly. 'He knows you have arrived.'

'Is he still ill?'

'Ah,' Hassan grimaced. 'His health is just fine; it is his temper that is threatening to fail him.'

It was automatic for Melanie to reach for Robbie, protecting her son being her paramount need. Rafiq noted the

gesture and his expression hardened. 'You used to be
famed for your diplomacy, Hassan,' he drawled.

'My apologies.' Hassan offered Melanie the kind of
half-bow she was used to receiving from him. 'I was referring to our father's impatience at us keeping him waiting.'

It was a slick recovery, but a lie nonetheless. Rafiq saw
Melanie's giveaway expression, went to claim Robbie's
hand, then slipped his other hand back around her waist.
She looked up at him, eyes anxiously searching his for
reassurance.

He tried to give it with a small smile. But with his
brother and Leona watching them Melanie knew there was
little more he could do. They began to walk down a wide
corridor between pale blue walls on sand-coloured floors.
No one spoke. Even Robbie had picked up on the tension
and was quiet.

They entered a room that might have been William's
study in a lot of ways, though it was bigger and lighter
and many degrees warmer. In the middle of the room, reclining on a divan, lay an old man whose fragile state
tugged at Melanie's heart. That he was seriously ill was
obvious; that he was resigned to that illness was written
in his face. He lifted himself as they came towards him,
though, sliding his thin body up a high bank of pillows
and fixing his eyes on Robbie.

Rafiq went down on one knee to embrace his father.
The old man's fingers held Rafiq's face as they spoke in
low and husky Arabic. What bowled Melanie over most
was the wave of love she could feel coming from the two
men. It filled the room, tripped her heartbeat, while she
waited for them to remember she and Robbie were here.
Then Rafiq was turning and beckoning to Robbie. Tears
glazed her eyes as she watched her brave son step into the
curve of his father's arm.

An arm settled across her own shoulders. It belonged to
Leona Al-Qadim.

'This is your grandfather, Robert,' Rafiq was explaining.

'Does he speak English?' the boy whispered.

'Yes,' the old sheikh answered for himself. 'I speak many languages. Come…will you take my hand?'

It was an old hand, a gnarled hand. Robbie placed his own hand into it without hesitation and allowed himself to be drawn towards the divan. As he did so he slipped free from Rafiq's comforting arm and, without needing any prompting, began to talk.

It was his way. Melanie knew that; Rafiq had come to know it. 'William said that you've been sick. Are you doing to die like William? I like your room; it's nice. Can you play chess? William played chess with me. Have you read *all* of these books?'

The old sheikh answered each separate question. He fell in love as they all watched. As the questions flowed so did Robbie's small figure flow into a sitting position on the divan, then he curled until he was almost on the old sheikh's lap. He was used to old men; he had grown up with one of the very best. To her son there was no fear in age and wrinkles. Melanie had always been aware that Robbie missed William, but she had not realised just how much until she saw how naturally he had drawn close to his grandfather.

Tears blanked out the old man's image. Rafiq was standing straight and still. Leona's fingers smoothed one of her shoulders, and somewhere behind her she was aware of Sheikh Hassan's silent observation.

'You have a beautiful son, Melanie,' Leona said softly.

The sound of her voice broke the loaded atmosphere. The old sheikh lifted his eyes and looked directly at her. 'You denied us all.'

It was a quiet and level accusation, designed to make its point without alarming her son. Rafiq stiffened his body. Melanie didn't know what to say. The sheikh was right: she had denied them. The guilt of that was going to live with her for a long time.

'She did not,' a sober voice inserted. 'I am afraid it is I who must take the blame for that.'

Rafiq turned to stare at his brother. Leona's fingers pressed gently into Melanie's arm.

'I'm going to take Melanie away now,' she informed all of them. 'Robert, would you like to come?'

It was not the voice of choice; little boys recognised these things. He scrambled down from his grandfather's divan and obediently walked with the women from the room.

'Don't shake so,' Leona murmured softly. 'My father-in-law is a good man. He just doesn't know the truth.'

'Neither does Rafiq,' Melanie said. 'I didn't want him to.'

'It is the way with these Al-Qadim men that they do not live well with itchy consciences. Hassan was honour-bound to tell Rafiq what he had done eight years ago from the moment he recognised your name.'

Leona led them up a wide staircase lined with pale cedar doors set into deep stone arches. It was a beautiful suite of rooms, wide, light and airy, in the coolest shades of pale aquamarine and ivory, with fretwork doors flung open to a balcony and the soft morning breeze.

A tiny dark-haired creature appeared from an adjoining room. She smiled at Robbie and held out her hand to him. 'Would you like to come and explore?' she invited.

Robbie looked at his mother; his mother looked at Leona Al-Qadim. 'This is Nina,' she explained. 'She is a trained nanny. Robert, if you want to go with Nina, I promise you will have great fun.'

The boy went without any more encouragement. As he walked away Melanie could hear him throwing out questions again. 'Are there camels here? Will I be able to touch one? Has my daddy got one I can see?'

'His daddy must be very proud of him,' Leona said gently.

'He didn't mention him to any of you,' Melanie pointed

out, and walked over to the open windows to gaze out on the kind of view she'd only expected to see on the television screen.

'Rafiq is an—unusual man,' Leona answered. 'He is a brilliant mathematician, incredibly loyal to the few people he loves, but he is a law unto himself and always has been. And his private life is generally sacrosanct.'

'Serena Cordero didn't think so.'

'Ah, Serena Cordero should be eternally grateful to you that you came along when you did.' Leona smiled. 'From what I can glean out of Hassan, Rafiq cancelled the rolling cheque that supported her dance tour, and which she was so fond of; then a few days ago he reinstated it. Said bitterness warped the mind, or some such clever phrase. We suspect this change of heart happened because you were busy turning him inside out. Though you will have to ask the big man himself, because he won't tell us anything.'

'So you speculate.'

'Yes.' Leona admitted it. 'We feel we have to. We worry about him, you see.' She released a sigh. 'I know you might laugh at this, but beneath that big tough exterior Rafiq is vulnerable to hurt.'

But Melanie didn't laugh. She shifted restlessly.

'You would have to know about the circumstances of his birth to understand this, his childhood living here in this palace as very much the resented second son of the old sheikh,' Leona continued, unaware that she was confiding in one who already knew these things. 'He is proud—too proud sometimes—and wary about letting anyone get too close to him. But from what Hassan has told me he took one look at you eight years ago and fell in love so totally that when you—'

'Accuse me of betrayal and I will walk right out of here,' Melanie cut in.

'Take note of that,' another deeper voice advised. They turned together to find Rafiq standing in the open door. There was a smile on his lips but his eyes were narrowed, and though he was attempting to look at ease Melanie could sense the tension in him, the anger that they were standing here talking about him like this.

'You're cross,' Leona murmured. She knew him well, Melanie noted. 'I was only trying to help Melanie to understand why we—'

'Then let me help you to understand,' Rafiq smoothly cut in. 'My wife did not betray anyone. But your husband may require your help to convince him that he did not do something very similar.'

'You've upset him.' Leona sighed.

'I forgave him,' Rafiq returned.

'Well, that only makes it worse!' she cried. 'You know what he's like; he will prowl around now, seething with frustration!'

Rafiq offered her one of those bows. 'Then may I suggest to my lady that she goes and joins him as he prowls?'

He was dismissing her, even holding the door open at the ready. Melanie decided she did not understand these people as she watched Leona Al-Qadim stroll up to Rafiq, smile and kiss him on the cheek before she left the room.

'That wasn't very nice of you,' she remarked as he closed the door.

'Leona is beautiful, charming and an absolute delight to be around, but she knows I dislike people meddling with my life.' With that the red-chequered *gut rah* was dragged from his head and tossed aside. 'As for you...' He strode forward, sending her spine erect and at the ready. 'You lied to me.'

'I did not lie!' she denied.

'By omission you did.'

'If your brother had kept silent there would have been no reason for you to know!'

'That you came looking for me while heavily pregnant with my son? That you took the risk of yet more cruel rejection because you cared enough to try again? That you had to sit there listening to him scare you with the kind of scenario that would make any mother's blood go cold?'

'He loves you. He was protecting you. I understand that now.'

'You understand nothing,' he denounced. 'I asked him to check if you were all right. I trusted him to do that small thing for me!'

'I was all right.'

'Well, I wasn't!' he rasped. 'I was out there—' he flung a hand out towards the sand-dunes she could see rising above miles of lush fruit groves '—pining for you!'

Pining? Melanie blinked. He spun his back to her on a tight hiss of a sigh. 'When Hassan told me you wanted to see me I did not dare go to London in case I fell at your feet,' he went on. 'But I needed to know that you were okay. I *hoped* that by some miracle you were going to tell him some magical reason that would make everything okay. I sat out there...' the hand flicked again '...waiting like a fool for the call that would send me to London on the next plane. What I got was a call telling me he couldn't find you but he had heard that you were living with a man.'

'I'm sorry,' Melanie murmured. 'I didn't—'

'Don't touch me,' he grated.

For a moment she froze in dismay. Then with a sigh she did the opposite, and walked around in front of him so she could wrap him in her arms. His heart was pounding, the great chest trembling as he fought a battle with himself.

He had lost, she thought. He had lost the battle. His arms came around her. 'I don't know what I am supposed to say to you, Melanie,' he muttered. 'You make me realise what a fool I was eight years ago. You make me face the high price I paid for my own pompous pride. You make me see that I have been treating you without honour from the moment I met you, and have done it all from a superior stance that deserves nothing but your contempt.'

'I don't hold you in contempt,' she denied.

'Then you should.'

'Because you believed what you were carefully primed to see?'

'Your uncle said some wicked things about you that day,' he said heavily. 'He poured out his poison and I, like a fool, drank it down, when any other fool would have known you were not the person he was describing to me.'

'If it had been you in that window with another woman and your brother pouring poison into me, I would have believed,' she admitted.

'Hassan did poison you.'

'He frightened me off for your sake. And he did it out of love, not avarice. There is a difference.'

'A forgivable difference?'

'You forgave him,' she pointed out.

'I forgave *him*,' he agreed. But not himself, Melanie defined from his tone. 'Tell me what you want from this marriage, Melanie,' he demanded. 'Tell me what the hell I can do to put some of this right for you.'

Lifting her chin, she looked up at him, saw glinting black eyes and harshly etched angles burnished bronze by the morning sun. 'I would like you to make love to me without thinking that you only do it because you feel utterly compelled to,' she told him softly. 'I would like to lie in your arms afterwards and know that you really want me there. I would like to look into your eyes and see tenderness sometimes, not just anger or passion.'

'You want me to love you.' He smiled oddly.

'I want you to *care*,' she amended.

'Take the love,' he advised. 'For it has always been there.' He grimaced, then released a long sigh and framed her face with his hands. 'Eight years ago I fell in love with the scent of your skin as you leant over my shoulder. I fell in love with the heat that coloured your lovely cheeks whenever I caught you looking at me. I wanted every part of you, every minute of your time, every kiss, every smile...' He kissed her. It was so tender it brought tears to her eyes. 'If you want my heart on a platter, Melanie, you can have it,' he offered huskily. 'I could not forget you—did not want to forget you. It was a lonely—lonely state of mind.'

There was nothing she could find to say in answer to that. Instinct—only instinct could respond. Her arms lifted to his shoulders and she pressed her mouth to the warm brown skin at his throat. 'I love you, Rafiq,' she softly confided. 'But you have to believe it if this marriage is going to stand a chance.'

'I believe,' he murmured. 'How can I not believe when you are still here in my arms after everything I have put you through?'

But he didn't sound happy. On a small sigh she lifted her eyes and parted her lips to speak again—only he stopped her. 'No,' he denied. 'Don't say any more. It tears me apart when we talk about those things we cannot alter. Just answer me one last question. Can we put the past behind us and start again?'

'Of course we can.' She smiled at him.

The smile turned his heart over. The shine in her eyes warmed him right through. Lifting her up against him, he caught her mouth with his and refused to let it go as he walked with her across pale blue marble and through a door on the other side of the room. The door closed behind them; he released her mouth only long enough to lock it.

'What about Robbie?' the mother in her questioned. 'He might come looking for us.'

He was already carrying her across to a huge divan bed that stood on a raised dais. 'Not while he has my father waiting to pore over maps of Rahman with him,' Rafiq lazily replied. 'And this is the beginning of our honeymoon.'

'I quite liked the Gothic setting,' Melanie said as he laid her down on a sea of dark red satin.

'Next time,' he promised.

'Why? How many honeymoons are we going to have?'

'A lifetime of them.'

He wasn't joking. Two months later they were back in England, locked away inside their Gothic mansion. Melanie was lazing in the bath when Rafiq strode into the room and announced, 'Hassan and Leona are the proud parents of a baby boy. Both mother and child are very well.'

'Oh, do you think we should fly back?' Melanie suggested anxiously. 'It seems wrong for you and I to be enjoying ourselves here when we might be needed there.'

'No,' Rafiq replied adamantly. 'Our son is with his new best friend—my father, Hassan and Leona are in twelfth heaven with their own son, and you and I, my darling, are on our second honeymoon here while Ethan Hayes and his crazy wife make William's house fit to live in.'

'You really should have told me about that,' Melanie chided as he strode towards the tub. 'I had a right to be consulted before you dared to touch anything in my house.'

'But the house does not belong to you,' Rafiq informed her as he removed his clothes. 'William left it to our son— though you saw fit not to tell me that. So I asked Robert's permission to renovate. He was delighted to give it. Unlike you,' he mocked her, 'our son had the good sense to know the house was in danger of falling down.'

'It wasn't that bad!' Melanie protested. 'And I thought Robbie loved it exactly as it was!'

'No, he has better taste—as I do,' he added arrogantly, referring to his good taste in wives.

With that, he stepped into the tub and slid himself into the water at the opposite end from Melanie. A hand reached up to pull a cord, which drew the purple silk curtain around them.

Candlelight flickered from hidden places. Silhouettes moved and came together...